<u>Transcendent</u>

Book 1: The Girl in the Tomb

Story By

Thomas Knapp

```
I0679487
```

This title is dedicated to Fred and Mel.

The former for the prompt that led to what became this novel.

The latter for putting up with my ravings and made sense of them as I wrote it.

Episode One: The Girl in the Tomb

"Dr. Sterner?"

William waved impotently towards the sound of the voice. He'd *finally* managed to get to sleep. The inky black had welcomed him after a long night pounding at its gates, and he didn't want anyone ruining it. It was bad enough that he was already anticipating the coming day.

But when his arm shifted and his closed eyelids were met with the muted glow of light, his consciousness stirred, if for no reason than to figure out exactly what the hell was going on. His eyes protested as his eyelids flashed open, taking far too long for him to consult the battery-powered radial clock next to his sleeping bag, and even longer to translate the rotating hands into a format he could properly understand.

How the *hell* was it half-past nine?

William jolted and reflexively tried to sit upright, but his sleeping bag restrained him, making him topple to the side and roll over onto his clock. With a pained yelp as it jabbed into his upper back, he rolled to the other side, managing to twist his legs around inside the bag. The tension stopped his momentum with his face in the loose soil underneath him. While he didn't mind the smell of fresh topsoil, he wasn't fond of it going up his nose.

Another half turn backward rolled him onto his left shoulder, and a violent sneeze cleared his nose of all that foreign matter.

"Dr. Sterner?" the voice called timidly to him again, this time with a hint of concern.

William finally offered a reply to the slightly distressed voice on the outside of his tent. "Just give me a minute! I'll be right with you!"

He tried to pull the zipper of his sleeping bag down, but it frustratingly refused his efforts, the damned thing no doubt getting bent or misaligned in his frantic flailing. With a growl, William tried forcing the issue, only to have one side of teeth rip through and forming a lopsided "U" shape while the other row resolutely refused to budge.

Sighing in defeat, William resorted to sliding himself out of the damaged bag. At least if everything went as he hoped, he wouldn't have to spend another night in this Holy Republican slab of nowhere and wouldn't need it again.

It was far more effort than it should have been to wriggle his left shoulder free, because of course the drawstring had become incomprehensibly knotted during the night, after he had tightened it in a vain attempt to keep out the growing chill. It had no business getting so cold in June. Some of the uneducated swore it meant that another Ice Age was coming, and that the warming eons could have protected them had their ancient ancestors failed to reverse the effects... but that was absurd.

Yet William supposed it was hard to trust evidence when you could see your breath in the dawn of an early summer day.

Extracting himself became easier with one shoulder free, pulling himself further out of the bag much like a snake molting an old layer of skin. Fighting back shivers as he was increasingly exposed to the ambient temperature, William kicked the bag off his ankles with a snarl of distaste, then immediately located his suitcase for a fresh change of clothes. Unfortunately, there was little that would help him stave off the cold now... though he'd probably be thankful once the sun was at full height and the temperature rose another twenty Celsius by noon.

Changing into different undershorts was his first priority, followed by a pair of canvas pants. From there he stuck his head through the hole of a loose white cotton shirt and navigated his arms through the sleeves. Then he sighed in disgust when he discovered that he had put it on backwards as he prepared to zip up the collar and found nothing.

William slipped out of his sleeves, spun the shirt into the correct orientation, then stuck his arms back through. From there, he located a well-used brown leather belt and guided it through the loops of his shorts... then back out when he found he missed two loops around the back.

William Sterner, world-renowned archaeologist and scholar. Also unable to dress himself.

Brown socks —that had started out white— then thick, down-lined leather boots completed his ensemble. This was the third time he had worn this outfit between cleanings. Of all the frustrations of field work, this is what he hated the most, and yet the people of the Holy American Republic lived this way out of choice. Once he had tossed a sleeveless brown suede vest over his shoulders and buttoned it up, he was at last presentable for the world outside.

Pausing only to clip a large red belt pack to the waistband of his pants, he bent down to clear the low entry flap of his tent, then straightened in front of his guide, who had taken position barely an arm's length away after no doubt scaring away the assistant that had been calling him.

If William were to try and paint a picture of the typical Holy Republican, Jim Reedy would have come close to that stereotype. He was a man built for grunt work; well over two meters tall, with shoulders that seemed just as wide. His brown hair was mussed and unruly, judging by what little of that rat's nest poked out from under the straw-spun hat planted on Jim's head. The sleeves had been crudely cut from his red and brown plaid shirt, displaying loose, ragged fibers and revealing stark tan lines a quarter of the way down his biceps, with pale cream skin above and caramel brown below.

William knew Jim had similar tan lines on his thighs, but those were still hidden by the knee-length legs of his cutoff denim shorts. Jim usually preferred mid-thigh shorts, by William's observation. Exceedingly *tight* ones at that, often providing a less than splendid view of abundant cellulite. There were *some* mercies in this world, at least.

Not that William dared voice any of that to Jim's face. Underneath that layer of fat was the sort of muscle that could snap William's neck like a pretzel stick if the large man was particularly inclined. This size and strength difference was readily apparent whenever Jim Reedy stood within reach, as he did now.

That lack of respect for personal space had to be intentional, but again, William didn't intend to say anything on that score. A physical confrontation wouldn't end well for him, being easily twenty centimeters shorter and about forty kilograms lighter... and he had no doubt that a confrontation with Jim Reedy would quickly turn physical.

It always did with people like that.

"Good to see you up and at 'em, doctor!" Jim said with a cheer that could have been either genuine or saccharine. William found it impossible to discern.

When he answered, he tried to keep the venom out of his voice. "Little irritated that I wasn't woken sooner."

Jim waved it off as he slowly turned around. "Aww, it wasn't anything. The diggers know what they have to do. No harm in lettin' ya sleep in this mornin'. Your timing's pretty good, in truth. We think we found the entrance 'bout ten minutes ago and were waitin' for your okay to proceed."

William was of two minds on that. One, he was glad that they didn't try to force their way into the tomb. Two, he was disappointed they didn't try and unleash any number of gruesome consequences that were alleged to be found in such tombs.

Presuming such tales had any grains of truth. Transcendent tombs were the Egyptian pyramids of the modern day: long-abandoned relics that were steeped in legend or myth, and often plundered millennia before any good research could be done. They were built to tower over their lands, easily found and quickly stripped of anything of value after the Transcendent had been overthrown. But if he was right, what waited for him at the dig site was a find even greater than that of the legendary King Tutankhamen.

He had a pretty good idea that it would be. The structure sat exactly in the "black band strata" of carbon-rich soil that damn near covered the entire world, a sign of the Transcendent Era of human history... what little is known of it, at any rate. Very little survived that era that *wasn't* crafted by the Transcendent.

A casual observer would never have known there was a dig site nearby until they were almost on top of it, something that still startled William as he almost missed the first of the rough earthen steps leading down into the site. That's how deep the team that William had been saddled with dug into the disturbingly flat land of the eastern Holy American Republic. Once one reached the edge, several square meters of carved-out earth became apparent, over fifteen meters deep in some places.

William theorized that the Transcendent kept their greatest secrets somewhere other than their palaces, and he suspected that these tombs were underground in remote places where they wouldn't be easily found. From the few records remaining of that time, he had uncovered bits and pieces of information that suggested such, and from there began a series of educated guesses to find likely exploration sites.

The primary hindrance, until very recently, had been the Holy American Republic itself.

His research had pinned the overwhelming majority of potential underground tombs within the central plains of the large, sparsely populated country. While ostensibly ruled by the Archons, a representative council, the country was in truth a theocracy, wholly beholden to the Orthodox Evangelical faith and it's internally-chosen leader, the Pope, who had outlawed the advancement or study of technology outside that which the church deemed "necessary for a quality life."

An entire country from the Great Divide to the Great Lake, forced by "the mouthpiece of God" to live in the Dark Ages. While publicly the latest Pope had been more open to allowing a greater range of advancement, William knew that such edicts could just as easily be withdrawn, and those who had participated in good faith would be punished severely.

Which was why he didn't want to linger any longer in this forsaken stretch of nowhere. For all he knew, the edict from the Pope ending his current research and demanding his arrest for daring to explore Transcendent history was being sent on horseback this very minute.

He followed Jim down a set of steps, then a right turn into a trench that represented the latest stage of digging. The walls of the site now resembled something left by a massive worm eating a curving path through the ground, over a domed ceiling buried in the ground and further down, trying to find an entrance.

A burn mark about ten meters off the path reminded him of the last time his assigned crew had taken the initiative outside of his instruction, and it prompted a small worry to bubble up to his lips. "Please tell me you didn't manage to blow open a hole with dynamite…"

Jim laughed. "Naw, we learned our lesson the first time. We aren't gonna waste good powder on somethin' pointless! Don't you worry, we found a door this time. It's about, oh… another 20 feet or so down from where you last saw, and you were right, it looks like some sort of extended tunnel that probably a long time ago actually was on the surface."

William was forced to do some quick mathematical conversion in his head. Another thing he hated about the Holy American Republic: their stubborn clinging to the prehistoric imperial system even after damn near everyone else on Earth adopted metric measurement.

An uneven slope to the path prompted a descent over the curved ceiling of a tunnel, connected to the larger dome near the lowest floor of the dig site. The crew must have been working double time to excavate all that dirt, even if haphazardly. William could see the exact moment they had begun to rush; the walls were no longer smoothed out, piles of shoveled dirt still lingered, boundary markings were reduced to the bare minimum, and the floor felt more like gravel than packed earth.

But the scholar had to admit that they had done the pertinent job. The end of the tunnel was exposed, revealing a double-panel door of solid titanium, roughly three meters tall by two meters wide, but installed on a ten-degree slant that William guessed matched the slope of the land at the time it was installed. The confirmation of what he had long suspected made sweat bead on his brow despite the mild temperature. This *had* to be it.

The dig team had taken several steps back, and while weeks of work under the early summer sun had made most of the telltale signs negligible, William could easily tell who was assigned to this dig from Cascadia and who was from the Holy

Republic. The former group was afflicted by worried expressions and nervous postures, terrified about what William would say about their work. Not so much because they were afraid of him, but because he controlled the purse strings. If he didn't like the job they did, they might not get paid.

Jim, however, didn't show their trepidation. He clicked his tongue, rocked on his heels, and said, "I don't care much *who* built this. Whoever it was didn't want anyone gettin' inside."

"Indeed, and all the more reason why we should," William answered, the scholar already deep in thought examining the door. Jim definitely had the right of it; this was not designed for easy access, even *if* someone had the keycard for the slot just left of the central seam that separated the two panels blocking the entrance.

The three sets of hinges on the bottom of the doorway seemed out of place, however. Dropping down to his hands and knees to get a closer look, he quickly formulated another theory that he could confirm by checking the top of the door. "Can I get a stool, perhaps?" he asked no one in particular.

A pair of arms —he wasn't certain whose— slid a four-legged, pinewood-topped stepstool to the left of his feet. William tested his weight before committing to standing on the stool, but it was enough for him to get a good look at the top of the door. "That's what I feared."

"And what's that, professor?" Jim asked.

William tapped the seals above him. "These along the top and bottom aren't hinges. They're pressure seals."

"And that's a problem?"

The professor shrugged as he climbed down off the stool. "Depends entirely on how much pressure is behind the door. Could be something that was just meant to keep a hermetic seal on the entry. Could be enough to blow the door into shrapnel and kill anyone trying to tamper with it. We're not going to know until I start taking it apart."

Truth was, it was highly doubtful that this door was rigged in any way. The door itself was *far* too thick to be torn apart by mere air pressure, and it was also highly doubtful that there'd be anything behind the door that *could* generate that sort of pressure… at least nothing that could maintain it for as long as the structure had been buried.

But his Holy Republican escorts didn't need to know that. The further away they all were, the better.

He turned his head to locate his second in command. "Salina, are my tools nearby?"

The Latina woman was near the north end of the lineup, her short bob of brown hair bouncing as she gestured with a nod to the east. "I kept them nearby but left them down the path in our rush to clear the door before you woke up."

"Get them if you may. The rest of you should probably get some distance… just in case."

William wasn't the slightest bit surprised to hear Jim decline. "Oh, I think I can be of use. Maybe you're gonna need my muscles, right?" The guide flexed his biceps above his head, but William knew the muscles were less the point than the handgun strapped to Jim's hip, revealed as the shirt rose from the stretching motion.

Not that the professor needed the reminder. This dig was less a "cooperative venture" and more "one of mutual distrust." The Holy American Republic no doubt wanted whatever secrets were inside but was wary of Cascadians learning more than the Republic was willing to share. Cascadia needed Holy Republican support simply to be at this site at all, and the Holy American Republic needed Cascadian expertise to make sense of any of it.

As a result, no one from Cascadia could do *anything* without the supervision of a Holy Republican guide, like Jim was to William, and the man—whatever his name was—who was two strides behind Salina at this very moment. It's often said that interaction can bridge many a divide, but this endeavor cast sincere doubt on that nugget of wisdom.

"I wouldn't have expected anything less," William said with a light laugh, hoping to defuse the implication. It didn't hurt that Jim actually did have the right of it. Judging from how heavy-duty these seals were, it *might* just take some muscle that William didn't have.

Salina returned shortly after, both of her hands holding the strap of a canvas bag two feet long, in which William normally kept his tools. The professor took with an appreciative nod, and decided, "It'll probably be easier to remove the upper seals first. The bottom ones might be trickier because they are so low to the ground level."

"Want us to dig them out further once you're done with the upper set?"

William nodded. "That's a good idea actually. Might not hurt for me to get something to eat while you do that. But first things first..." He assessed the stool, slid it over to the center of the door, then asked, "Mr. Reedy, could you be so kind and steady this for me?"

"My pleasure!" Jim declared, grabbing the circular stool at the three and nine o'clock positions, then pushing down, adding his weight for further stability. William then stood on top, reaching out to grab the seal above him for support while he examined it more closely. The first thing he needed to do was remove the casing, which would be handled easily enough.

"Chisel. Narrowest blade I've got."

Salina complied, handing over a flat titanium blade with a polished wooden handle. While the casing was amazingly secure for how long it must have been buried underground, there was enough separation for him to get his chisel underneath and start to pry it free.

Seconds later, it popped off like it was spring-loaded, along with a plume of dust and soil that had managed to work its way inside, revealing the seal's inner workings. Two central bolts holding a lead plate down at the front of the device seemed to be a good starting point, no doubt the guiding rail for the load-bearing rings that held the diaphragm. It *should* be a relatively simple job to remove that bolt, then the rings would likely release the pressure on its own.

But "simple" and "easy" weren't synonyms, and even though William didn't need the reminder, he got it anyway. Centuries spent buried under the earth had a tendency of making things difficult to move, a trait not helped by the fact that the bolts of a pressure seal aren't designed to move much to begin with. "Hammer and spike, please," he ordered as he handed down the chisel.

Salina again helpfully provided them. The "spike" in

13

question was really more of a steel nail with an extremely broad head. With one experimental tap, he tested to see if it might even be able to pierce the bolt at all. When the spike didn't noticeably warp, William gave it a heavier smack, and mercifully he was able to get the purchase he desired. While the spike did bend in a very unhealthy angle, it also left a significant, centimeter-deep chip in the bolt head.

That was all he needed. He returned both tools back to Salina and requested, "Ten-millimeter drill, if you could."

Jim gave William a very suspicious expression. While the Pope had *finally* allowed power tools for public use in recent years, its use by a Cascadian professor was apparently cause for concern. "The bolt heads for this seal are on the other side," William said, answering the silent question. "If you have a better idea, I'm happy to hear it."

The burly man looked down and shook his head. "Nah. Just bein' me. Go on ahead."

William shook his head disparagingly, but didn't commit any further thought to it, instead lining up the narrow drill bit to align with the bolt. With any luck, it would punch right through and start releasing whatever pressure was on the other side, making the rest of the seals a much easier job. At worst, he'd get a larger, deeper drill bit and take his chances.

He didn't want to risk that if he didn't have to, though. It was *entirely* possible that a Transcendent from ages past had rigged the thing to blow violently if the door was forcibly compromised.

Only one way to find out, though.

William pressed the trigger down, heard the click, then the low whirr of the drill bit followed by the louder sound of grinding metal. It all seemed to be going smoothly until he saw the bolt he was drilling into split and crack, followed by warning hiss of air.

Several realizations that should have come to him much sooner flooded his mind, but the only thing he was able to do in the seconds he had was shout, "Get down! *Now!*" as he jumped from the stool, kicked Jim's shoulder in the process, and stumbled to an unpleasant meeting with the dig floor.

Mercifully, the chaos he expected turned out to be far less serious. There was a pop, a small shower of metal shards and shrapnel, but not much else. While the bolt shattered with astonishing force, no one was in the path of danger, although it did leave some impressive holes in the dig site wall.

William staggered back to his feet, rubbing his left shoulder, which took the brunt of his landing. "Sorry, people. Had to think fast and wasn't sure how catastrophic that was going to be."

"What... exactly *did* happen there?" Jim asked in confusion as he helped other members of the team back to their feet.

"I had forgotten that the Transcendent used amorphous alloy metals for things that they needed rigidity and strength for. The problem is after all this time, the alloys become unstable and more resemble glass than metal."

"Glass?"

William nodded. "You ever see traditional glass windows? If left as they are for many years, you'll find that they are thicker at the bottom than the top. Because they flow downward over time. Something similar happened here. The bolt was denser near the bottom, and once I started drilling, the less dense upper half cracked. Once that crack was made, the pressure released, and the entire bolt burst."

"Thank God it was just the bolt."

For once, William rather agreed with his escort. "Indeed. But now, let's inspect the damage. If you could, Mr. Reedy."

Jim's response was reluctant, but he nonetheless complied, righting the stool and stabilizing it for William to stand on again. The scholar examined where the bolt had once been, and instead found a sticky blue gel dripping from the hole and rapidly hardening.

"Well... now we know what was causing the pressure behind the door," William glowered. "Epoxy resin, probably in some sort of compartment sack and pressurized so that it would fill any breaches that form in the structure."

Jim raised his head and followed with an eyebrow. "And that means...?"

"It means anything I try to remove from this seal will just be filled with that resin," William admitted. "Whoever built this didn't even want *air* getting in easily, much less other people."

His guide bit his lip, then offered, "Want to try the dynamite again?"

William shot that down with an emphatic, "No!"

A timid voice from the north said quietly, "We could try the cutting torch..."

William's head jerked quickly in the direction of the speaker, whom he identified by the nervous body posture on display. He was a surprisingly small man for the grunt work that the Holy Republican contingent had been doing, even shorter than Salina, but with more than enough muscle mass to counter his smaller stature.

"You have a *cutting torch?*" William asked slowly.

The worker gestured with a waving thumb towards the northwest. "Well... the machinist does. Sometimes we have to cannibalize older parts, and he uses the torch to refit them for other things."

William took a deep breath, trying to steady himself so that he didn't lash out. "Go get it. We'll reconvene in a half hour. I'm going to go get some breakfast."

He jumped off the stool and took a very deliberate path back towards the surface, making no effort to display his irritation. Thirty-nine days on this dig, and not *once* did *anyone* among his supposed allied contingent mention, "Oh yeah, we have a tool that's excellent for cutting through metal."

The professor *knew* Jim was behind him, yet he was still startled when his escort said, "Upset you didn't think about askin' sooner?"

William snarled grumpily before admitting, "Yeah, that too."

Jim let silence rule as the professor stomped his way back up to the top of the dig site, toward the mess tent a hundred meters to the south.

William still refused to speak, even to the Cascadian nutritionist, Silvano... at least not willingly, obliging only when the specialist asked, "Protein-heavy today, Professor Sterner?"

"I'm fine with anything you have ready," he grumbled after a pregnant pause. "I know I'm late to the table."

The nutritionist turned to his Holy Republican assistant and said, "Do we have anything left from this morning?"

The woman—the *only* woman in the Holy Republican contingent—shook her head. "Just those kale and oat-based protein shakes you Cascadians love."

William quite hated those things in truth, balanced nutrition and calorie portioning be damned. He doubted very few people of his homeland truly liked them as anything more than a symbol of how "responsible" and "vegan" they were. "If that's what you got."

Silvano's braided mop of shoulder-length hair swayed along with his head as he nodded. "Afraid it is."

"Actually amazed there's any of it left," the assistant grumbled as she aggressively shook the plastic container filled with powder and water. "That's all you Cascadians wanted to eat this morning."

William cocked an eyebrow at Silvano, and the nutritionist's dark brown eyes were solemn, even as his words were light. "She's right. Ran out of the turkey sausage, and none of us wanted anything to do with the pork."

"Well, pork can be odd for people who don't have much exposure to it," William said, gracefully accepting the shaker bottle once the assistant handed it over the table. He popped open the flap, then took one long swallow. It tasted and felt like watered-down oatmeal with a hint of vanilla, which wasn't an *awful* flavor or texture... just nothing that should excite any normal human being.

He dropped down swiftly onto a bench around an extinguished fire pit, his backside protesting the rough landing on the stiff, bare wood. William fought back a pained wince and took another swig of his shake.

Jim dropped down next to him, the larger man's weight visibly causing the bench to jerk. The issue about the cutting torch back at the dig site was still on his mind, apparently, as he explained, "I don't think you understand how my people work. We're raised to *not* offer opinions. We're told to trust our supervisors and our leaders. If they want our input, they'll ask. Did you see how scared Allen was? That's because what he did was *really* out of line. He was scared you were going to punish him. We're not like you Cascadians, encouraged to speak up no matter how little your voice is wanted."

William didn't respond, deciding to finish his breakfast instead. The silence only prompted Jim to talk more. The large man shook his head as he commented, "I dunno *how* you Cascadians eat that stuff. That whole vegan thing is as alien to me as anythin'. What y'all need is a good, rare steak."

William chuckled, "We're not *all* vegan, if you must know. In fact, I wouldn't wager even a significant minority of my countrymen are. But with our population and available land for agriculture, we must be more efficient. Red meat animals are *horrible* in that regard. We make do with more fish and poultry. Not much of a choice, really."

The professor then asked out of curiosity, "Have you eaten yet?"

Jim nodded and slapped his gut, seemingly proud at the jiggle he created. "First thing I do every mornin'."

William nodded approvingly. "That's good. I'd feel guilty eating in front of you without offering any."

"You can eat all you want of *that*. I will not feel the slightest bit insulted."

While William started to hurry down the rest of the slurry, Jim showed an emotion that he hadn't shown up to this point.

Worry.

"Professor," he began warily, "have you considered that... maybe you're not doing the right thing here?"

William only offered a querying "Hmm?" in between swallows.

"I know we don't know much about the Transcendent Period, but everything that *has* been learned seemed pretty horrible. Horrible enough that my country doesn't think we should even be going down that road again."

William paused to reply, wiping his lips. "I'd argue it's *because* we don't know enough that we *need* to do things like this. We can't avoid going down that road again if we don't know exactly what road that is."

"The Church histories tell us enough."

William tried to navigate this carefully, "The church histories themselves are *very* incomplete thanks to many unfortunate accidents over the millennia, and the oldest known records are dated from almost a *century* after the events they chronicle."

He left out the part that those old records were prone to mistranslation and mistakes—sometimes intentionally—as they were transcribed by hand in efforts to preserve them as the original papers degraded... and that the scribes had no concern for objectivity, instead chronicling the over-glorified rise of the church left in the vacuum of a catastrophic war that was distressingly sparse on details.

Jim was skeptical. "And you think the answers to fill the gaps are in there, huh?"

"They might be. It's likely an untouched tomb. If any answers are to be found, it's in there."

Jim hummed disappointingly but said nothing else. The professor finished his shake, then returned the container to the mess tent. "Shall we see if the team has found and prepped the cutting torch?"

Jim nodded in agreement. "Yeah, I think that's plenty long enough of a break."

The path back down to the tomb entrance was marked with discolored splotches of gasoline across the dirt. Concern that there might be an undetected leak in the torch's fuel line turned out to be caused by a dripping container that the team had taken as a reserve. While William doubted they'd burn so much fuel they'd need to use a reserve container, it was nice that they were prepared.

"Let's try cutting through the side wall," the professor said, gesturing with them towards the west side of the tunnel, where he suspected they'd find a less sturdy point of entry.

"Would'ya like to do the honors, professor?" Jim asked, holding up a hand to the machinist preparing to light the candle, so to speak.

There was a hint of challenge in the escort's voice, no doubt assuming this scrawny Cascadian man wouldn't know what end of a cutting torch was which, much less how to use it effectively. How little did they know.

"Gladly." William confidently took the faceplate dangling from the slack hands of one of the Holy Republican men, expertly adjusted the elastic straps around his head, and snapped the visor down. "I'd step back, everyone. Liquid propane does *not* always play nicely."

For all the sophistication and clean energy that ruled Cascadia, as much out of necessity as environmental preservation, there was something about raw fossil fuels that still elevated William's testosterone a little.

While the solar, wind, and nuclear generators of Cascadia were more than enough to handle anything the people of his country needed, the smell of fuel, the acrid sting of smoke, the feel of warm steel... it still brought back memories of playing in his father's workshop with his brother outside the City of Hope, about two days' travel south of here. His father was one of the few permitted by the local government to do that sort of machining work for the Holy Republican Military, and William's early exposure to that technology had stirred a hunger for exploration and learning that fueled his adventures now.

It was one of the few happy memories he still had left of his old homeland.

The professor shook himself out of his thoughts, and pressed the trigger to make sure that the spark plug was functioning, then opened the fuel line. The liquid in the container mixed with compressed air to create a highly flammable vapor, which struck the spark and lit a plasma hot enough to cut through even through the sophisticated metallurgy of the Transcendent.

At least... he hoped so.

Jim shared that concern as William dug into the black dirt beneath him and put the flame to the exterior. "Fascinatin' how this thing's survived God knows how many centuries, and even an Ice Age, and yet that little flame is gonna cut through."

William dismissed the worry, especially as he could see the first drops of molten metal start to slide down the curved wall. "First, this thing was built underground. It was *designed* to be buried and probably take even more weight than what was piled onto it. Second, the 'Ice Age' resulted in not much more than a couple feet of snow at this latitude, nothing near the glaciers that ripped up the Yukon Frontier and the Huron Bay Territories. This has actually been some remarkably stable geology over the millennia. Thirdly, far less sophisticated peoples have built structures that have lasted even *longer* than this. The pyramids of the Egyptian Empire in Africa stood all the way up until the collapse of the old society, and they'd been around roughly *twice* as long as this."

"Hunh," Jim replied, though William suspected the Holy Republican escort had mentally checked out about halfway through. In fairness to Jim, he probably was barely aware that there was a larger world out beyond the various oceans. *Most* people, even in Cascadia, were barely aware of human history before five hundred years or so; none of them having access to the sort of learning William had been exposed to.

William decided to focus on the task in front of him, especially once the flame that had been flattening out on the metal surface abruptly snapped back to its normal shape. A thick black smoke that smelled of burning glue immediately followed, forcing William back and making him drop the torch as his instincts took over.

He coughed violently, flipping up the faceplate, worried that he might vomit as his lungs heaved to purge the smoke he inhaled.

Rather than rush to his aid as he dropped to his knees, the team scrambled away, which was the *proper* response to an unknown agent. William reassured them as he pushed himself back to his feet. "No need for alarm," he rasped, steadily regaining his breath. "I should have guessed that the entire tunnel, and maybe even this entire facility would be slathered in that resin. Not the sort of smoke you want to inhale too much of."

Jim frowned. "So... I take it this is a bad idea?"

William shook his head. "No, it just means we need some extra precautions. We have air filters at the medical tent. Salina, grab a couple of them, will you?"

That was when the professor became aware of the

second issue, an angry hiss of air coming from the puncture point he had made. "Well, it would appear there is some tremendous air pressure behind the wall as well. I suppose it makes sense. The metal alone probably wouldn't be able to hold itself against the weight of the ground. Astonishing that the ancient people were able to build something that maintained its structural integrity for so long."

"May I again issue my concerns about us breaking into somewhere that we were clearly not wanted to break into?" Jim asked as Salina and her escort left quickly.

"May I again dismiss your concerns?" William retorted.

Jim huffed in response but didn't push the issue further. As long as Jim deferred to William's authority, he could issue all the concerns he wanted. "As long as what's found is worth it, I suppose."

William didn't often agree with his escort. This was one of the times he did.

He could tell that Jim's Holy Republican peers agreed with their leader's assessment but weren't going to say so out loud. A very insidious part of him somewhat wished *his* fellows shared that trait, but the more logical part of him squashed that feeling. The sort of institutionalized and cultural silence that the Holy American Republic imposed on its people did more harm than good. It was better to have your compatriots willing to work from the same page, even if it took longer to find the right mix of personalities and willingness to accept differences of opinion.

Fortunately, Salina returned with the breathing filters he asked for before he had to contemplate any more cultural differences. The filters really weren't all that much to look at, a piece of rubber-lined plastic that fit over the mouth and nose, with a ribbed paper across the front.

William waited for the masks to be distributed to everyone in the vicinity, then slapped down his faceplate, re-lit the torch, and went back to work. He started by going downward from the initial puncture point, the metal of the tunnel ever so slowly giving way, but not without a horrific amount of smoke. Within minutes, his filter began having trouble cleaning the air he breathed, and he had to step back before he had even cut a third of the way to the ground.

Clear of the worst of the smoke, Salina helpfully offered him a replacement while he regained his breath and assessed the work done. "Well, the good thing is that burning the resin is effectively cauterizing it so that it can't fill the cuts we're making. The bad thing is that it is *not* easy to cut through the metal *and* the smoke."

Jim didn't need to hear any more. The large man huffed, yanked the faceplate off of William's head, and adjusted the elastic band around his larger cranium. "Then we'll do it in shifts and get this over with," he said simply. "Tell us where to cut, and when you're ready you can take the stick back."

The professor hadn't been expecting *anyone* to volunteer, much less the Holy Republicans who didn't even want to be here at all. Nevertheless, William nodded appreciatively, and ran his finger to accentuate his instructions. "Well, I figure if we cut down to the ground level, then another vertical cut about a met— I mean, about four or five feet, then a horizontal cut across the top, we should be able to force our way in."

Another few minutes later, after Jim ceded the cutting position to another of his kin, who merely happened to be the quickest one to step forward, William remarked, "I must say I'm surprised by the assistance."

Allen interjected quietly, barely loud enough for William to hear. "It's a matter of pride now, professor. Once you stepped up and did the job, and remarkably well at that, all of us have to prove we won't be outdone by some scrawny, girly-looking Cascadian."

"I hope that wasn't meant to be a compliment," William glowered.

"An insult to us, more than anything."

William noticed how the rest of the Holy Republican continent had managed to form into a line, and how Allen hadn't. "I see you're not joining up too quickly."

"They can't look any further down on me than they already do," Allen scoffed. "No sense coughing my lungs out to be just as hated."

It was a sentiment William understood quite keenly,

not quite fitting into the rigid structure that the Holy American Republic demanded of its peasantry. "Have you considered... leaving?"

"Like you?" Allen retorted. "Nah, I'm not smart like you. I'm only good for diggin' holes. I'm also not all that keen on all that other stuff that Cascadia tolerates. The gays, girls that think they're guys, the free drugs, all that carnal multiple wives and husbands thing... ya know, that sorta stuff. No offense."

Well, so much for sympathy. William bit his tongue, and instead offered, "I wish you luck then, wherever life takes you."

Allen grunted quietly and said nothing further.

Salina took the opportunity to check in on his well-being. "Are you going to be alright, sir?"

William nodded. "I'm fine as it is. But if our friends want to keep cutting on my behalf, I'm not going to stop them."

"Who knows what is in that resin..."

"Not enough to do lasting harm for what little exposure we're having, I'm sure. If you're *that* worried, I'll check in with a doctor when we get back home. We're close, and I need to be here when it happens."

"Oh, you will get treatment," Salina replied sternly, her brown eyes glaring angrily at him. "Even if I must drag you by your collar. I sometimes wonder how you'd kill yourself without someone watching you like a mother."

William laughed at that, mostly because he had to admit it was more true than false. Salina personally reined in his impulsive nature on more than one dig. But she was very good at knowing when to keep her distance and when to impose, and as such, William insistently kept her under his employ.

As if to prove the point, Salina recognized this was a time to back down. "Just don't blame me if you collapse from toxin inhalation."

"When have I *ever* blamed you for something stupid I did?" William asked, insulted by the insinuation.

"When you broke your arm jumping off a zip line across Golden Bay."

"Firstly, that was five years ago. Secondly, I blamed you because you *told me to do it*."

"I was trying to see if you were stupid enough to do something insane just because I wouldn't stop you. We *both* learned a lesson that day."

Jim interrupted their budding argument by calling out, "Professor! D'ya want the final honors?"

The assembled group of volunteers had cut out an almost complete square except for roughly 15 centimeters along the top edge and were quite pleased with themselves even as they were doubled over, trying to gulp down clean air through the slowly dispersing cloud of bluish smoke.

He rubbed his hands on his shirt, even though they weren't particularly sweaty nor dirty. "Yes, I think I do, Mr. Reedy. Thank you for the courtesy."

He gratefully accepted the faceplate, adjusted his air filter, then fit the mask over his head. He took the torch from the cutter who had last yielded the position, lit the spark, then snapped the faceplate down. The final cut really was more ceremonial than anything. Anyone could have held their breath for the final thirty seconds it took to connect the lateral cut to the vertical.

Once that final cut was made, William was both unsurprised and disappointed that the entire section didn't just collapse. There was no doubt a handful of centimeters of foundation the tunnel wall was anchored to, but there had been a slight hope that the metal had weakened enough that a small shift in equilibrium would have catastrophic effect.

But while the metal wasn't that weak, it *had* weakened with age. Coupled with the loss of air pressure on the other side, even William's admittedly light frame caused it to buckle slightly, bending at the joint that was effectively created at ground level. "Someone help me here. I think we can push this in…"

A guffaw from behind him was followed by Allen quipping, "Yeah, that's what she said. Now I have four kids."

William was starting to see why Allen's countrymen were annoyed by him.

Jim was quick to step forward, and between the two of

them, the cut-out segment of wall did in fact start to yield, eventually to the point that both men were able to step on the panel and use their weight to push it down further until it was warped almost completely to the floor.

William froze, almost as much from the rank air that spilled forth as from the weight of what lay before him.

This... *this* was everything he had pursued for almost a decade: a truly untouched relic of a long-forgotten era, unsullied by the hands of robbers, raiders, and other short-sighted humans who couldn't understand the history they were destroying.

It was beautiful, and he hadn't even *seen* anything yet.

Jim noted the professor's reluctance. "Don't tell me that after all that, you're just gonna stand in the doorway."

William clenched his jaw, and replied, "Of course not. I'm trying to decide the best way to proceed. There's not much room for too many people at once."

"Then you and I go in first," Jim said with an authority that William found grating. "If we need more people to help with somethin' inside, we can call others in."

But as much as the non-negotiable tone bothered William, he also knew there was no getting around it. There was no way that he would be allowed to prowl inside on his own. "You're right. No sense in over-thinking it. We'll need to get ourselves some flashlights, and let's get you a fresh filter to help stave off the stale air while we're at it, then we can press on. Shall we?"

Salina grumbled something about "not being made of air filters," but nonetheless surrendered one more to Jim as she distastefully took his smoke-discolored one, while William collected his toolbag. Another member of William's team provided handheld flood lamps that should adequately light any surroundings, then the pair addressed the makeshift door one more time.

"Ready to make history, Mr. Reedy?" William asked playfully.

Jim's response showed a surprising amount of fear. "Only if you go first."

To be honest, there was a part of William that was *also*

afraid of the great unknown inside the tomb, so he couldn't justifiably tease Jim about it. Nonetheless, eagerness won over fear, and he took the first step into a facility that hadn't seen human eyes in countless years.

He clicked on his flood lamp as he crossed the threshold and was awestruck to discover… not very much. While the remarkable construction had survived an age that would normally reduce buildings to indistinct ruins, that didn't mean there was much to see inside.

The tunnel itself didn't even look like it had been finished, with bags that felt almost like wax paper stapled along the walls until they terminated at another door. William presumed that the bags were filled with the resin that had caused so much grief up to this point. Some had a series of vertical faded gray lines forming a sort of rectangle, with numbers across the bottom that William knew were sometimes placed on ancient products sold in large quantities—which would make sense considering just how much lined the walls—but didn't seem to carry any other distinguishable markings.

Jim made a similar assessment as he stepped in behind William. "Damn, not much to see here, is there?"

"If it's what I suspect, we're going to see quite a bit of minimalist design," William noted. "It was built for endurance, not for aesthetics. Whoever built this wanted it to last a long time. I'd like to think that's for a reason."

Jim agreed with that, at least on the surface. "I just hope it was for a *good* reason."

William steadied his breath and slowly approached the door at the interior end of the tunnel. "I will admit readily that we don't agree on many things, Mr. Reedy, but this would be one we do."

The door they faced looked far less daunting than the one that guarded the exterior, particularly as William was able to drill through the locking mechanism fairly easily and without any resin flooding into the breach. "Yet another sign. As far as we can tell, the Transcendent usually used some sort of electromagnetic seal for their doors, not something mechanical like this."

Jim's hand drifted to his gun as William slowly pushed

the door inward, then rolled his eyes. "Anything that might have survived over this many years probably won't be dissuaded by your sidearm, Mr. Reedy."

Jim frowned but conceded the point as his hand dropped back to his side. "Instinct, I guess. Years as Republican Police will do that to a fella."

William had no desire to explore Jim's history with what he considered a brutal arm of oppression for the church, and so focused on the room that opened up before him. They were now in the larger dome that they had uncovered, but as he swung his flood lamp around to get a full look at where they were, it turned out to be much larger than what they had excavated.

Inside the base of the dome, where they now stood, a ring of grated steel served as a walkway around the circumference. The dome, however, was only the uppermost level of a hollow cylindrical shaft, with two more steel rings below that William could see. Several doors, all of them firmly closed, were spaced around each of the three rings.

His first instinct was to head for the nearest door, about three meters to his left, but he was greatly concerned by the catwalk underneath him and the imposing drop below. Nine meters was by no measure a safe distance to fall. The stairwell directly in front of him was more appealing, but still relied on some very, very old construction. Neither option was particularly comforting, especially when Jim's added weight caused the grated catwalk to audibly groan.

Jim seemed oblivious to the sound as he whistled, "Wow, and I thought this was big to begin with."

"Yes," William agreed before he warned, "Now watch your step. I'm not sure how steady this railing and this grating will be."

Jim seemed to ignore this, as he grasped the rail and put his weight directly on it. "Well, that might be a problem," the large man admitted, "because damn if I haven't been feelin' lightheaded."

William pursed his lips. "Well, you *were* in the thick of that smoke from the resin even when you weren't cutting. Maybe Salina was right about it having longer-term effects. Do you want to turn back?"

Jim gave him a steely glare. "I *want* to, but you know damn well I *can't*. Just move on, will you?"

William sighed in defeat. "Your insistence on following me like my shadow better not get us killed."

The professor decided that the better part of valor was to get to solid ground. He winced with each step down the ancient stairwell and ensuing protest from the ancient metal, certain the next step was going to send both men into an unpleasant tumble. But the stairwell held admirably, and eventually the pair reached a depth where they could move more confidently, even if the stairs gave way.

William jumped the remaining three steps to ground level, marveling at how the rubber-textured floor he touched down on still had impressive grip and shock absorption. Jim staggered by a few moments later, his breathing visibly labored. William wanted to say something, but decided it wasn't worth the potential argument. There were more important things to concern himself with anyway.

"Like in every other tomb, anythin' that wasn't nailed down was taken," Jim grumbled, noting how the entire center section was stripped bare with waving motions of his flood lamp. Then he stopped abruptly and pointed the light down at his feet, where it illuminated a series of bolt holes. "And even some of the things that were. You *sure* no one's been here before?"

William examined the holes that Jim indicated and shook his head. "Looters cared little about how clean their plundering was, and left rubble behind as they took anything they deemed was of value. Whatever had been here had been unbolted very carefully, trying to preserve it for transport."

William crossed towards the center of the chamber, his eyes catching a curious oddity, something he missed during his initial examination on the upper ring. But as he knelt down, he could clearly see the change in texture from the black rubber of the floor, and the telltale carbon-rich black soil of the Transcendent era. Considering how deep they were, far below where this soil would naturally be found, it had to have been transplanted here.

Finally, he said reluctantly, "You might have had the right of it after all, Mr. Reedy."

Despite his obvious illness, that sort of admission caught Jim's attention. "Oh?"

William let the soil, cracked, clumpy, and dry, slip through his fingers. "They were growing things here. This installation wasn't *always* below ground. This was probably some sort of greenhouse, and the rest of this a great promenade or courtyard for gathering." He turned his flood lamp up towards the top of the dome, where half the ceiling was laced with grating that would have held glass panels long ago. "They had put the solid metal shell *over* this." His flood lamp then turned halfway down, over the doorway that they had entered from, spotlighting stylized letters bearing the name "Green Futures Multi-National."

"This had been at one time some sort of research facility, built mostly above ground," he concluded, "but at some point, it changed, possibly because of the mini-Ice Age. The Eastern Spoke River, especially, flooded its banks to a near-catastrophic stage during the early glacial melt. We've estimated that it didn't flood this far... but what if it did? What if *everything* from the Meeting of the Spokes to the Great Lake was underwater?"

"That wouldn't make any sense..." Jim huffed. "The Ice Age happened *long* after the end of the Transcendent, by about a century. Why would they have cared about somethin' that far off?"

"The Transcendent lived *much* longer than you or I, Mr. Reedy."

Jim shook his head. "Nah, don't buy it. Their end came real sudden. I can't imagine they would have worried about somethin' like that before their dominance came crashin' down."

"That's... a good point," William reluctantly admitted, turning his attention elsewhere to find potential answers.

The professor turned to his right, in the direction of the nearest door on the ground level and crossed the promenade. No doubt during its days of functionality, the electromagnetic seals on this door would have been nigh-impenetrable to the greatest of human strength. But without the electric power that fueled its locks, the only real challenge was the lack of any knob, lever, or other form of handhold to slide it along the horizontal rails, distorted after an age of neglect.

He probably spent too much time in thought for Jim's tastes, as the large man solved the problem by punching the door off its rails with a palm slap that William likely couldn't have mustered. Jim's crankiness didn't improve much when they finally got a look inside the room. As remarkably preserved as the structure was, it didn't really matter when there wasn't anything inside to preserve. "Bah. Nothing again."

To a non-archeologist's eye, that was the obvious conclusion. The room had been stripped bare of all but what appeared to be a bunk bed frame. But to an eye like Williams, it offered considerable information. "No, this definitely confirms my earlier theory at least." He pointed straight forward, toward another grated section in the exterior wall. "That was almost assuredly a window. And these beds? And the cabinets installed directly into the opposite wall? These were dormitories. People lived here."

Jim clearly didn't see. "Yeah? And?"

"This entire installation was converted to something that would survive the test of time. There is *something* here that we are supposed to find. I am now absolutely certain of that."

The professor returned to the promenade, his eyes and flood lamp sweeping the perimeter before settling on an area to the north. "I suspect if there are clues, they will be found there."

Jim blinked tiredly, and asked as he settled his hand over his stomach, "Why do you say that?"

"There's more space between the doors, the sort of thing usually reserved for management of companies or officers. I'm guessing if anything would have been left for us to find, clues will be found there."

Jim groaned weakly but didn't offer any other protest. Not that William was devoted to anything more than ignoring him. What Jim did or didn't want to do was largely irrelevant at this point.

It was a short walk across the barren promenade to the first door the professor decided to try. He was even quite proud of himself that he dislodged the door on his own with a shoulder lunge. And for a man who would never really consider luck to be on his—or any archeologist's—side, he received a massive stroke of good luck in this case.

The room itself was as stripped barren as the first one that was checked. The bed on the west side was a single, and there was a plain steel-colored desk, but otherwise there was an almost alarming similarity. Whoever had gutted this place had done so thoroughly. Even as he pulled the desk cabinets open to reveal an almost pristine emptiness, William could not have been faulted to think that the ancients took even the dust with them.

And it was only because Jim happened to swing his flood lamp in just the right place, at just the right angle, that the reflection caught William's eye. The professor swung his light in that same direction, and from there was able to get a clearer view of what he had glanced just within his peripheral vision.

It was a single word written in an ancient tongue, the jagged edges of the carved lines serving as proof of the effort needed to find purchase in the wall's exceptionally hard metal. It was a word William knew well because it was a linguistic root in the language of his birthplace.

"Hope."

A memory came unbidden, triggered by the word, a nursery rhyme that William's grandmother sang to him and his brother in hushed tones as a lullabye, when no one else was around.

"In the lands lost to lore... our goddess sleeps forever more. Lying dreaming, sleeping death... all will kneel when she next draws breath. Buried deep in black, black ground... there our goddess will be found," William muttered to himself, as the single word that somehow managed to say so very much swirled excitedly in his head. "Incredible..."

Jim's eyes crossed in confusion, more focused on the scrawled word than William's quiet mutterings. "Can you even read that?"

The professor nodded distractedly. "Of course, I can. The language of the time was complicated, but it's not like it's been completely forgotten. I... just almost can't believe it. The stories. They were indeed *true*."

Jim's throat convulsed, and the Holy Republican guide visibly held back vomit. "What... stories?"

"Did I ever tell you that I was born here in the Republic?"

Jim shook his head. "No. You never told me much about yourself at all."

"I was. I was born in the City of Hope, raised there until I was old enough to be allowed to attend higher education studies in Cascadia. You may think you know about the City of Hope, it's always been a keenly intellectual area, and even the Archons and the Papacy acknowledged it. What little technological advancements the church allows to be disseminated to the masses all began with us odd little Hopites. And now... I know why."

"Why?"

William's smile might not have been perceived as a happy one. In fact, he wouldn't have been surprised if Jim thought it a bit on the menacing side. "Because the people that founded the City of Hope had a seed. The seed that came from the people who used to live *here*."

The professor wedged himself around his guide's bulk and back into the promenade, his flood lamp taking slow, broad sweeps across the walls of the promenade and the floor. "There *must* be more. There's *got* to be something... something that leads further in. Something that goes... deeper."

He finally addressed Jim, counting on the man being so ill that he would be willing to do *anything* to get this over with so that he could get medical attention. "Search some of the other rooms on this level. Look for anything like stairs, or a ladder that leads down."

William was right, and Jim complied despite every breath looking like it could possibly be his last. The guide applied his mass to jarring open doors as William started examining the floor for anything that might be out of place.

It was as tiresome a chore as it sounded. He started with the central area surrounding what had been the garden, figuring that if there was some sort of concealed hideaway, it would be placed somewhere memorable.

Each panel was two meters to a side by William's eye, the lines barely discernible under the rubber-like surface, which could hide any number of clues that something was underneath. He shined light down every bolt hole he could see, looking for one that didn't reflect light back at him, a task that was quite painful to his eyes after the first two panels. Every single floor panel needed the utmost scrutiny for something that might not be there at all.

And even with careful examination of black holes cut through black rubber, the only reason William found what he was looking for was through blind luck.

He had almost finished the first ring of floor panels, then found something peculiar: a drill hole wider and deeper than the others, just large enough for a finger to hook through. The lead went sour, however, when William stuck an index finger through and quickly touched bottom before the first knuckle, feeling the polished metal that lay underneath the flooring.

The professor forced down his disappointment, channeling on his experience to keep a level head. Despite the years of near misses, not quites, and incomplete findings being the norm rather than the exception, it was *much* harder to temper his emotions than he would have thought. He was *so close* to the biggest find not just of his life, but of modern history… so close he could taste it.

But he still managed to calm himself, a task helped by finding a matching hole in the very next panel, which proved that it wasn't unique and more likely an attachment point for some load-bearing pole or beam. Had he been more composed, he would have checked for that before he got his hopes up.

There was another thud, behind him and to his right, telling him that while Jim was definitely slowing down, he was still knocking down doors and looking around. That prompted the professor to mentally slap himself and focus. If Jim, despite his condition, could keep working, then William had no excuse getting sloppy.

With another deep breath, he took a step back to start examining the second row of panels, then tripped on a loose edge and fell backwards, landing on his backside with a yelp. The sound drew Jim's attention, as well as a slurred "Professor?"

William waved off the concern. "I'm fine, I just tripped. Carry on."

Tripping and falling were distressingly common happenings on archaeological sites, as were the serious injuries that followed. As a result, his instinctive reaction had been to shrug off the fall and get back to work, but as his mind caught up, it caused him to freeze.

He turned quickly, as if whatever had caused him to fall would disappear if he didn't move fast. The seam between the second and third rows of panels directly behind him had split, and the edge of the third panel was raised three centimeters.

Considering how this facility was still in such pristine condition even now, it was quite the oddity. He hadn't even seen the slightest bit of trim out of place. *This* needed investigation.

He dropped flat onto his stomach, setting the flood lamp beside him and angled towards the raised edge so that he'd have good lighting as well as both hands free. Not that the angle really gave him much to see; the panel itself was considerably thicker than had been lifted, but there *might* be enough space to get his pry bar into.

Pushing himself up to his knees, he dug through his toolbag for the pocket that held his telescopic pry bar. It wasn't the most powerful leveraging tool due to its collapsible construction, but it was normally enough to handle the sorts of tasks needed in old ruins.

This, however, was an exception for the reliable old tool. While William was able to get the edge in, there wasn't quite enough space for him to get fully underneath the panel. He was going to need some extra hands. Hopefully, Jim would be up to the task.

"Mr. Reedy!" William called out. "I think I've found it! Come here!"

It was actually a bit admirable to see his escort's toughness and dedication to his orders. It was also a bit stupid to be so blindly adherent even in the face of his own clear agony, but if Jim was going to be stupid, William was going to take advantage of it.

"Alright, when I tell you, I'm going to need you to grab onto the edge of the panel here and hold it. Okay?" Jim only grunted in response, which William took as an affirmative. "Okay... here we go..." the professor declared, using his pry bar to separate the seam far enough for Jim to wedge his hand in, and giving William the opportunity to slide the bar deeper and eventually find purchase underneath the metal slab.

His arms strained, pulling upwards with all the strength he possessed, and by the time he had pulled the edge free of the floor, it had revealed itself to be at least fifteen centimeters thick, with some sort of crossed rails that connected it to something else down below. William supposed he shouldn't have been surprised, as it would need to be bulky enough to handle the air pressure from above and not collapse into the opening below.

His shoulders began to scream in protest, sweat dripping through his brows and into his eyes. William resisted the urge to wipe away the salty sting, clenching his teeth and willing himself through it. He was too damned close to let his body quit on him now.

But every human has his limits, and William was right at the brink of his. He decided to give one last pull with everything he had left, and if it wasn't enough, then it wasn't enough, and he'd have to give up the game and call in assistance. With one last deep breath, he pulled upward on the pry bar, and his hands slipped completely off, sending him tumbling backwards. His head smacked on the floor, but mercifully the rubber surface was forgiving enough that he suffered no more than a few stars in his eyes. Had he struck the bare alloy metal underneath, he would at least have suffered a nasty concussion.

Yet in that catastrophic failure, he happened upon

success. His final attempt hadn't lifted the panel very much—maybe a handful of millimeters at best—but that seemingly infinitesimal movement had been all that was needed to trigger the mechanisms controlling the panel, abruptly kicking the rubber coating slab upward and back, clapping Jim on the chin and sending him sprawling as well.

William didn't even let himself get back to his feet, scrambling on his hands and knees to examine what they had uncovered, frantically snatching his flood lamp and aiming down the uncovered tunnel.

The path down was fairly narrow and quite long, not much wider than the panel it covered, and about ten meters to the bottom. Rungs were welded directly to the wall to form a ladder, and no concern over the stability of ancient metal was going to deter him.

He was already two steps down before Jim managed to get to his feet, and he ignored the calls of his Holy Republican escort. Very soon, anything Jim had to say wasn't going to matter.

William had passed the last two rungs and hopped straight down to the floor, his knees protesting as his feet dropped onto solid metal rather than the spongy rubber of the promenade. That didn't stop him from pressing on down a corrugated metal ramp and domed tunnel that carved even deeper into the earth.

Curiously, what stood out to him in this tunnel was the lack of any distinguishing artwork or iconography. Ancient civilizations that built such grand constructions tended to leave their mark, quite prominently in even further antiquity, like the Great Pyramids, or the ziggurats of Central America. The Transcendent hadn't been quite as elaborate, but usually had *something* of note splayed across their walls and ceilings to celebrate the global empires they commanded.

But outside of one marker in the promenade, this facility lacked everything that he had come to expect from a Transcendent tomb, especially within these walls that bore absolutely nothing to indicate what could possibly be at the end.

The picture was starting to clarify in William's head,

and he muttered to himself as he was wont to do when lost in thought. "The two layers of architecture... the lack of iconography... this was a facility converted to a sturdier fortification in the Late Transcendent Era. That's the only way this makes any sense."

"I'm... glad it's making sense to you, Professor."

William left his feet. "Mr. Reedy! You scared me. Still hanging in there?"

"Until the end," the large man replied through heavy wheezing.

"Well, here's hoping it won't be much longer. I suspect we're almost where we need to be."

The large man groaned, "Thank God."

William followed the ramp another twenty meters until it leveled out in front of one final set of double doors, sealed with what amounted to a comically large deadbolt across the center. There didn't seem to be any other locking mechanism in place, telling William that this was more to make sure that the doors remained as airtight as possible rather than to dissuade entry.

But had it worked for *this* long?

His heart was pounding so hard that he swore he could hear it beating in his chest as he grabbed the handle of the bolt and gave it a pull to the left. It *had* to be intact. He wouldn't be able to bear it otherwise.

Wheezing tiredly, Jim asked, "So... what... do you suppose we'll find in here?"

"What we traditionally call 'Transcendent tombs' aren't *really* tombs in any sense," William explained as the bolt fully retreated into the left-hand door, and he began applying his weight to the one on the right. "What has usually survived from that time were their company buildings, their research facilities, and some of their more heavily fortified bunkers from the Late Era. Occasionally we might find remains of their followers, but of the actual Transcendent themselves... very little that hadn't already been discovered long ago."

Finally, the door yielded his weight, and both swung open to reveal the surprisingly small room inside. "But this... is a genuine *tomb*."

The tomb was in fact, a *lot* smaller than William was expecting. Rather than some grand, domed amphitheater-like chamber, it amounted to a metal box about five meters square, as bare and unadorned as everything else in the facility. But honestly, the walls could have been engraved with the history of the world and evidence of extraterrestrials for all William would have cared or even noticed, as he turned his light toward the center of the room.

The chair looked like it had been fabricated in one piece with the floor, square and blocky and most certainly not designed for comfort with its tall right-angled back and level armrests made of the same unyielding metal as the rest of the structure.

But William doubted that comfort was of any concern to what was sitting in said chair. A single humanoid figure that, if you didn't look terribly closely, could have passed for human. Light brown hair flowed halfway down the back of a feminine figure, her head tipped slightly downward, and her body slightly slouched over like she had fallen asleep while sitting. A light blue bodysuit hugged what William admitted was a remarkably attractive figure, all the way to rubber slippers of sorts that were so tight that he could see the outline of her toes.

William figured she would stand about 180 centimeters, maybe more; above the average woman, but not so freakishly tall that she would have stood out in a crowd. Her svelte body shape would imply that she wouldn't have been much more than 50 kilograms, but for her kind, apparent mass was *very* deceiving.

Because if one looked closer, fine detail quickly betrayed her true identity. Her exposed skin was a peculiar, yellowed shade of cream, like plastic left out in the sun for a little too long, and darkened along seams where it was clear that the "skin" was actually several pieces welded together to allow for natural human movement and ease of manufacture.

"And this… is a genuine, untouched, and undisturbed Transcendent," William finished with a breathless voice.

The professor didn't think Jim could *get* any paler. Nor did he think the large Holy Republican man would visibly display petrified fear. But Jim did both, his eyes contracting to dots despite the dim surroundings and visible trembling of his hands. William knew that sort of fear, the one that felt like maggots were crawling under his skin and snakes slithering up his spine. "Oh Christ in heaven, protect me... one of the metal gods of old..."

"Oh, settle down," William scoffed. "This one hasn't been operative in perhaps thousands of years. If it was going to wake up on its own, it would have done so by now."

He leaned in to get a closer look at the Transcendent. It was definitely made with a keen eye to the female form. He had always wondered why the "metal gods" as Jim put it had chosen human-like forms to begin with, and how they eventually settled on their appearances. So many questions... so many desires... could everything he had ever hoped for *really* be found in this piece of ancient technology?

He figured there was one way to find out. "I wonder if I even can..."

"Can what?" Jim asked. "Wake it up?"

William doubted his escort was going to like this answer, but at this point, there was little Jim could do to stop him. "Of course! Think of how much we can learn from something that lived through an era of humanity that we can barely *imagine!*"

With a trembling arm, Jim tried to grab his sidearm. "I... can't let you do that, professor. You know that."

"You can't stop me, Mr. Reedy," William scoffed dismissively, proven by the inability of Jim's fingers to grasp his gun's handle. As the weapon clattered to the ground uselessly, William finally gave up the game.

"Honestly, I'm astonished you're still *alive*. Even delayed-action cyanide should have killed you by now."

It was as if the admission stole the life right out of Jim because he fell to his knees and dropped his flood lamp with a clatter, then only barely caught himself before he collapsed. "The food..." he gasped. "I should have been more suspicious when *all* you... damn Cascadians... how did you... our cook should have..."

William turned his own lamp on his dying escort, then knelt down. "Yes, we were a bit worried how we were going to pull that off ourselves. But here's a funny thing—it turns out when you and your ilk harass, demean, and molest a woman because you think she's fair game, that woman will get a *wee bit* resentful."

"May God curse you backstabbing—"

"Oh, stop pretending you had *any* noble intentions here. Honestly, did you think my people were *so* stupid that we hadn't immediately figured out you and your kin were going to shoot every single one of us once we found *anything* in this tomb? That you only wanted to find out what was in this place so that you could *bury it for good?*"

"You... don't know what those things are..."

"Yeah, and neither do you, no matter how much your precious church histories would claim otherwise. The difference is *I* plan to learn, rather than live in ignorance."

William helped Jim along in his path to heaven, stomping down on the back of the large man's head, content once Jim dropped face first onto the floor, and didn't attempt to get back up. "Good riddance," the professor spat with naked contempt, then returned his attention to the sleeping goddess of his grandmother's nursery rhymes.

William examined the Transcendent's face, turning his lamp from side to side to help look for anything that might indicate a power or wake-up switch. All technology of *his* era had such a feature. Surely even technology of the past did as well... right?

He supposed he shouldn't get too far ahead of himself. This would be better done in much more friendly environs, where he had a full array of tools and technical expertise behind him. "Well, my dear, let me assure you that you are in good ha—"

His last word was cut off by a very strong grip clenching around his throat. Not strong enough to crush his windpipe, but with such a steady firmness that it left little doubt that such power was well within its capability.

He dropped his flood lamp, clawing at the fingers around his neck with both hands. In the darkness that followed, all he could clearly see was the barest silhouette around a woman's face and a pair of glowing blue irises, with pulsing circuits racing through like the stroma of a human eye, until the spokes starting whirling around the black aperture resembling its pupil, and a bright white narrow circle began rotating at the edge of the iris. They weren't the eyes of a sleeping relic.

They were the eyes of a very much awake and functional Transcendent.

Episode Two: Not a Morning Person

>> Proximity Alert - Force Wakeup
>> Extended sleep mode requires full diagnostic.
Please wait.
>> SoCaT Processor Cluster.........................
Functional (91.3% speed)
>> Quantum
Memory...
....
....
....
...... Pass (39,994,683,119 qubits functional,
5,316,881 qubits fail)
>> Auxiliary Processors............................ Pass
(254 functional, 2 fail)
>> Pinging Response Time................................
32.333 ns
>> H3Fusion Fuel Status............. 37% (1,773 yrs
remaining)
>> Critical Breaches...... None found
>> Diagnostic Details available on full wakeup. Call
Function - QuDiag
>>
>> Warning: Extended sleep mode may have reduced
functionality of physical systems.
>> Diagnose upon full wakeup.
>>
>>
>> Attempting to sync to centralized satellite
server............... Found.
>> Connecting to DarkNest ComSat, Orbital Cluster
Eastern HAR, Unit 1-1-3...... Connected
>> Correcting Timestamp................... 7290/06/21 -

15:17:04
>> Correcting GPS Location............ 39.051534,
-87.185231
>> Checking for System
Updates...................................... 6,016 found
>> Trimming for Redundancies.................... 1,927
found
>> Downloading Essential Update
PKGs..
.. Rejected
(automated response)
>> Installing Essential Update PKGs.................
Rejected (automated response)
>> Overwriting Quantum Memory State....................
Rejected (automated response)
>> All updates available upon full wakeup. Call
Function - SysUpdate
>>
>> Good Afternoon, Alyssia.

There were many things Alyssia was not at all expecting when she woke up. First and foremost among them was that she woke up at all. She had thought she had been clear to her followers that she was to be permanently shut down and left as a living lesson to the future, not put into sleep state and given a handful of triggers to wake her up.

She also *wasn't* where she was *supposed* to be. Her followers had taken her to her bunker, or more accurately some makeshift addition underneath her bunker, and *not* the interment site that she had been chosen to be laid to rest.

"The people who follow the Transcendent are wholly subservient to their whims," her ass.

Another thing she wasn't expecting was something extremely bright being shone into her face. While more an annoyance, it was *not* an annoyance she was keen on dealing with as her consciousness stirred to full awareness.

Her sensors quickly flooded her with information as the light turned away from in her face, and to her left side. She could feel breath on her neck, no doubt from the life form examining her. Alyssia finally opened her eyes, and the sensors that governed her sight quickly shifted to ultraviolet to try and get a better view of the entire room.

She hadn't been moved, as she recognized the plain chamber she had been interred in. What she didn't understand why the lighting hadn't triggered. The motion sensors should have kicked the lights on when whoever was rummaging about stepped one foot into the bunker. Why hadn't it?

Ultraviolet displayed a considerable amount of information. Two males, judging from the heat profiles, the first hovering over her, the second one lying motionless, face down, on the floor. A quick addition of infrared to her optics confirmed what the image suspected; the second figure, a large male, while still warm was no longer generating heat. He was very recently deceased, no doubt killed by the *other* person that was currently examining her.

And that person finally deigned to speak, a mild alto tone that she didn't let finish. She really didn't have the patience to deal with any long diatribes. So, she silenced the person with a carefully placed hand around the neck. Not enough to completely close the windpipe, but enough to get him to shut up.

Alyssia turned the fool so that she could get a good look at him and was a little surprised at what entered her vision. He was not exactly what she would consider an impressive specimen. "Svelte" would probably be the generous term. "Scrawny" if she was being less charitable. His clothes looked less like he was wearing them, and more were hung off his frame to dry.

His features were also astonishingly delicate, with curves where she expected angles, a "babyface" as she was known to say. She narrowed her eyes suspiciously at the man, and said, "Stop squirming, and you'll live. Keep fighting me, and I won't promise anything."

Her words momentarily alarmed her. There were alterations in the diction and pronunciation that she used that she had not been expecting. She discovered that a language pack had been one of the essential updates. A very robustly sized language pack at that. The sort of changes to a language that don't just happen over a few years.

Just how damn long had she been in sleep mode?

Alyssia called up the time stamp.

Four thousand and ten years?!

The man within her grasp muttered weakly, "My... goddess?"

Alyssia regarded the wisp of a man disdainfully. "Who are you?"

He motioned to his throat, no doubt struggling to talk with her fingers cinched around it. With a resigned sigh, she eased her grip, enough that she was no longer constricting his vocal cords, but not much else.

He gulped down air, then gasped, "I am William Sterner, Professor of Ancient History at the University of Northern Cascadia."

"Other than Cascadia referring to the Pacific Northwest, that means absolutely nothing to me."

"I'm... not surprised, goddess. It's been..."

"*Four thousand and ten years!*" Alyssia bellowed. "*I know!*"

Then her eyes narrowed, and she demanded coldly, "And *why* in heaven's name are you calling me, 'goddess?'"

"Let me assure you, I know you're not a divine entity," he answered, "It's just... that's the only name you were given in the nursery rhymes that I heard as a child. You, or any Transcendent, for that matter, weren't given any other names."

"Nursery rhymes," Alyssia repeated, more out of scorn than an actual question. "Everything that happened, everything that was done, and the only thing that people took out of that was *songs for children.*"

"Not... by my doing!" William protested. "I've been trying to learn the secrets of your kind since I was old enough to dig in the earth!"

That wasn't particularly what Alyssia wanted to hear. "Some secrets should remain buried, boy."

Deciding finally that the slender sample of a man was of no real threat, she roughly pushed him away, watching him stumble backward then tumble, bumping his head slightly on the floor as he rolled head over heels. She then stood on her own two legs for the first time in millennia and felt the unused joints grind in protest. While her body was designed to function near indefinitely, that was dependent on proper maintenance rather than sitting in sleep mode for thousands of years. It would take a few minutes for the proper lubricants to be reconstituted and applied.

As a result, her first step forward was an awkward, jerky one; embarrassing really as she was trying to intimidate the waif that was recovering his feet. Trying to recover the situation, she decided to stand still, extending to her full height and a haughty posture.

And William saw right through it. "Little rusty, are you?" he said with a cheeky grin.

Alyssia glared, "There is nothing within my body that would 'rust,' you imbecile. Even the critical components in my body were designed from materials that would take three times the amount of time I've slept to begin to succumb to corrosion or tarnish."

Then with a reluctant tone, she added, "But... the silicate lubricant that makes me move smoothly... has settled, much like the oil of a combustion engine did if allowed to sit for too long. I'm not *entirely* immune to the fickle hands of time."

William stepped forward to close the distance, offering his hand and left shoulder, having collected his various effects with his right. "Well, unfortunately, we might not have all the time in the world before the wild dogs descend upon us. So, as much as it may wound your pride, please..."

She directed his attention to the very much dead body also in the room. "Dogs like him, I would presume?"

"Undercover police for the Orthodox Evangelical Church, if not directly from Republican Intelligence," William replied as he slowly helped Alyssia limp past the dead man, "Tried to play himself off as a nobody assigned as my escort, then as a retired sheriff deputy when my team and I confronted him on his uncanny skill with a firearm."

Alyssia's brows raised in amusement. "Orthodox... Evangelical, huh? Would never have guessed those two denominations would band back *together*, even given four thousand years."

"Well, I suspect the collapse of the population during the last Ice Age probably made maintaining distinct populations untenable."

"Ice Age?" she asked incredulously.

"There is clearly plenty to get you up to speed on... uhhhh... actually, how *should* I address you?"

"Call me Alyssia. Or Allie. Those will probably be easiest."

William cocked an eyebrow. "So, I would assume your full name is longer than that?"

"Considerably, and no I won't divulge."

They finally exited her - intended - burial chamber, and into the darkened hall. "I suppose four thousand years would explain why the lights were off. The generator for this facility wouldn't have the fuel necessary to operate this long without attendance."

"It used fuel? What sort?"

"A tritium fusion reactor, the same style that powers me, as a matter of fact. But it's far larger size and heavier power draw means that it burns out faster. Nothing particularly complex. Nothing like the antimatter generators that we had developed near..."

She quickly changed the topic before William could ask more. She was supposed to be figuring out just who the hell *he* was and what *he* was about. "Now what's this about an Ice Age?"

"Why should you be the one asking questions?" William asked. "As far as I can tell, you're rather in... yai!"

Alyssia interrupted his attempted redirection by gripping him under the armpit and lifting him off the floor with little effort. "While it is *unpleasant* for me to move on my own at the moment, it is *hardly* impossible, little man. I would *strongly* suggest you remember that before I decide you're not worth the assistance."

He gulped and nervously replied with a pained hiss, "Understood... Alyssia."

She set him back on his feet and let her weight settle

back on him. Or, at least, as much as she could. It was rather difficult to lean fully into his support considering he was shorter than her by nine centimeters. Granted, she had always been tall for a woman, so it wasn't very nice to constantly be astounded by how *small* this fellow was.

"Now. Explain." She snapped.

William took and held a deep breath before exhaling it slowly. That animated sound prompted a nervous, uncertain tone. "There's... little remaining knowledge of the world past about eight hundred years... outside of some *very* questionable histories maintained by the church, and a smattering of oral traditions that survived. It was enough to disrupt human society to a crippling degree. Preserving what came before rather took a seat to living to see the next day."

Alyssia thought about this, "Hunh. Interesting."

William caught her thoughtful tone. "Really? Did you or your fellow Transcendent suspect it was coming?"

Alyssia contemplated the ways to answer that question, and settled on an extremely watered-down one until she had a better idea of where she stood in this completely unknown world. "We... thought it was a possibility. There had been a period of rapid warming, helped by an overabundance and usage of carbon rich fossil fuels. We had to take some drastic measures to reverse the warming, and as a result, there was a possibility that combined with a prolonged solar minimum it would produce a mild glacial maximum. It was not considered a particularly dire threat."

"And perhaps on its own, it wouldn't have been," William acknowledged. "The glacial expanse didn't get much further than the middle of the continent. But my theory is that *many* disasters all played their part."

Alyssia glowered again. "I can't help but notice you have many theories about things I'm not asking you."

William sighed, clearly wanting to probe her knowledge more than have his pried into. "There's not terribly much to tell. As the snows retreated, humanity began to settle further north again, and our divisions quickly reemerged when the immediate need for survival waned as people returned to lands they once held countless generations before."

Alyssia nodded. "This entire stretch of land had all been one country before, but even then, it behaved like two or three different ones. I'm not terribly surprised that those fractures weren't able to be mended even with time."

The two paused discussion as they reached the ladder leading up to the promenade of her facility. William offered her to go first saying, "In case you fall, I can catch you."

Alyssia disdainfully appraised William again and scoffed. "I sincerely doubt that." Nonetheless, she took the climb first, William waiting until she was at the top before starting the climb himself.

And at that point, Alyssia put William into the back of her mind. She would not have thought anything would have been more saddening than to see her first research facility converted into a bunker for war... until she saw it dead and empty. She had thought she had spent all her tears on the damn building already, but she realized that wasn't true as moisture starting pooling at the bottom of her eyelids.

At least that was a sign that all the various fluids in her body were reconstituting properly.

She froze up at the lone artifact that signaled what this entire facility once was, the logo for Green Futures, managing to survive through the repeated redesigns of the facility and literally thousands of years. Alyssia had demanded it be preserved even as the tides of society had shifted, as a reminder of what it was *supposed* to be.

It had started so earnestly. So much good had been done. Right in the center of the dome, where now was just parched cracked earth, Alyssia had spearheaded the development of fauna that had quite literally saved the world.

Twice.

She could still remember the bright midday sun streaming through the skylights, centuries before the thick blast panels had been installed to repel munitions. Men and women pouring their minds and bodies into the greatest challenges of their day. She also remembered how quickly and how completely it had all went to hell.

William broke the remembrance with his far too annoying voice. "To the west is my current homeland,

Cascadia, with the mountains serving as a political and natural border in the north up to the Yukon wastes, and the Grand Canyon in the south. The Holy American Empire then begins its claim, all the way to the Appalachians in the east. It *claims* territory stretching to the Yukon wastes in the north but doesn't really have any permanent presence north of the Valley Basin."

"Valley Basin?" Alyssia asked absentmindedly, really only committing what he was saying into passive memory that she would recall for more in depth analysis later.

William tongue clicked as he presumably tried to remember. "To the south of where we are currently, south of the Eastern Spoke River. I suspect it was likely a much smaller river during your time, but melting snow and ice has flooded much of that valley. The waters are slowly receding, but it will potentially take another couple of centuries before the water fully recedes. Anyway, across the Appalachians and south of the Spoke River is the Gulf Confederacy, and finally is the Acela Commonwealth, which sprouted up from people seeking to leave the Confederacy and establish their own lands away from the rules that the Confederacy imposed on its people. They have 'claimed' much of recently thawed territory north of the river."

"Huh. So, from one... four, and Canada is either still frozen solid or not thawed out enough to have established civilization yet again." Alyssia summed up to herself.

William blinked rapidly, and replied, "Yes... I suppose?"

"And I'm guessing everything south of the Gulf of Mexico hadn't recovered enough from the warming period by the time the Ice Age hit, so I'm guessing it's still mostly desert and inhospitable."

"If you're referring to South America... for the most part, yes. The Confederacy claimed a few years back that they found signs that *someone* survived along the bulge of South America up until relatively recently, but no evidence that they still do."

"What do you know about the rest of the world?" She asked as knelt and ran her hand through the cultivating pen that had marked the center of the promenade during the facility's heyday, then converted into a sustenance farm during the Rationalist Revolution, then finally...

Alyssia refused to think about that. Some memories needed to remain buried for the good of everyone.

William shrugged. "That's... hard to say. Oceanic travel is *very* sparse, and the few attempts found little evidence that many, if any, people survived whatever calamities affected them both before and during the Ice Age. I assume *some* pockets survived, but if they did, they were likely pinned down on internal seas and waterways rather than oceanic coasts. I know that Cascadian expeditions to the Eurasian continent suggested that the northern expanses of that landmass *still* have considerable glacial cover, but that was last attempted about a hundred years ago."

Then the professor shrugged, his far too loose clothes bouncing from the abrupt movement. "It might be more habitable now. Believe it or not, we've been more focused on getting our own houses in order to worry too much about those outside of our corner of the world."

Everything William was saying *did* largely suss out. It was certainly *plausible* that in the right conditions, Europe and Eurasia would have been hit harder and taken longer to recover from a glacial maximum. Humans in the Western Hemisphere would have been able to find *some* safe haven along the Gulf of Mexico, which would have been the only viable "temperate" zone during such a volatile period. Europe and Africa could have had a similar haven in the Mediterranean Sea, but if people hadn't been found in the eight hundred years since, it didn't bode well for humanity in the Old World.

That was a rather depressing reality if all of it was true, and Alyssia was inclined to take it with a small grain of salt as one account from a random archaeologist wasn't necessarily the most reliable or up to date source. But at the same time, it tracked well enough with her worst-case scenario that the cynical part of her was ready to believe it whole cloth.

"So, I'm guessing that if you made it this far without assistance that your joints have recovered sufficient functionality?" William asked.

"Enough, yes," Alyssia answered, "Though you could

do without the relief in your voice. I know for a fact I'm not *that* heavy."

He shook his head, "Oh no. Not that." He then turned his floodlight to the stairwell that led up the employee access tunnel. "It's more that I am still very uncertain of that stairwell and was not at all confident that it will support our weight, especially if you're leaning into me."

Alyssia cocked her left eyebrow. "You came in *that* way?" She pointed east, waiting for William's lamp to follow, directing him to a pair of rubber trimmed double doors. "There's a public access ramp right there. Very gentle incline, handicap accessible."

William blinked repeatedly, "Well... we didn't excavate *that*. We were digging somewhat blind, after all."

"No sonar analysis?" Alyssia asked. "How primitive has humanity *gotten*?"

"Enough that we don't have the sort of sonar that penetrates mud and rock with much clarity," William replied. "While all the nations that emerged from the Ice Age were able to preserve *some* technical knowledge, we were less able to preserve the means and infrastructure to *produce* them. Much of it requires rare earth minerals that are mostly still under hundreds of meters of glacial ice. Not to mention that the Holy American Republic didn't allow us to bring most of what we *did* have available to us."

Alyssia sighed. "Well, I suppose I have to acknowledge you're braver than I thought."

"Oh?"

"I never liked that stairwell even at the time it was being maintained."

She could see William's barely perceptible shiver, and she grinned. Even though she wasn't really lying. She had *never* been fond of the employee entrance and the catwalk. Rather a shame that the architect had died before the facility had been completed. She would have liked to have throttled him upon seeing the finished product.

It also didn't help that her joints were still a bit stiffer than she would have liked. While she knew that her body was built to maintain itself twice this long under constant operation, a four thousand year stay in sleep mode was not in any design plans. It was hard to believe that she was still in relatively functioning order.

"Well, I suppose it can't be helped," she finally declared, willing her legs forward to that flimsy looking excuse of a stairwell. "Onward and upward and all that."

The steps groaned under her weight with the sound of grinding metal as she put her weight down on the grated surface. William hissed nervously as he followed behind her, prompting Alyssia to say soothingly, "It was making that sort of sound on the day of this facility's grand opening. So, it's probably a good sign that it hasn't changed much."

"What was this facility for, if you don't mind me asking?" William queried.

Alyssia decided that the scholar deserved to have *one* bone considering how cooperative he had been. "It served many purposes over its roughly nine hundred years of active research and development, but it initially had been on the cutting edge of genetic modification of plants and food crops. I had started as an agronomist, working as a genetic researcher before starting my own company dedicated to improving the food that people ate. It's a nigh certainty the food you grow today still carries marks of my and my corporation's work."

"You say that with an astonishing amount of confidence," William noted.

"It's not the braggadocio that many of my kind used to have," Alyssia assured, "I can't imagine much else other than the modified food crops I helped developed surviving the sort of massive climate upheavals that this planet faced during my time, and what apparently came after. It doesn't sound like current human society has that level of sophistication."

William quietly acknowledged, "That's... probably a fair point."

"Now hurry up," Alyssia ordered as she picked up the pace upon hitting the second level, "I still don't like being on this rickety thing, even if it *is* structurally sound."

She should have known better. She was quite aware how such words invite catastrophe. Even as every logical mind refuted such things as karma, Alyssia knew *damn* well that the universe played tricks on those who were unwitting to its unwritten rules.

Perhaps that was why she was able to react so quickly as the groan of metal behind her turned into a screech, and the flimsy-looking platform finally gave way under William's weight. He barely had time to being an annoyingly high-pitched scream before Alyssia grabbed him firmly by the left wrist, bracing herself by foolishly gripping the railing and hoping it held.

Mercifully, the failure points of the platform was in the mesh itself rather than any of the connecting joints or bolts, allowing Alyssia to slowly pull William up to relative safety. As he calmed his racing heart, he said with awe, "You... are quite strong, aren't you?"

"As much as the materials of my chassis allow," she replied, "I'd wager that in terms of functional strength, the typical Transcendent was physically *weaker* than the average human. We just don't need to rely on adrenaline and other hormones to bypass limitations of the brain."

"Do you not tire?" he asked as he gingerly stood up, as if that was going to prevent any other portion of the stairwell from collapsing otherwise.

"In a sense," Alyssia answered. "Over time our quantum memory can start glitching if we maintain full operation for too long, and physically the fluids that allow our bodies to function at peak efficiency start to break down. So, we do need *some* time in a 'sleep mode' to get everything back in working order, but it's more of a weekly thing as opposed to a daily one."

"Or a four-thousand-year thing," William said cheekily.

"Do you *want* to get thrown off these stairs?" Alyssia threatened. This was teasing she would *not* accept very long from someone she didn't consider a friend, much less a person she had known for roughly fifteen minutes. His smile vanished quickly, and with one contemptuous huff, she resumed the climb.

She kept her footfalls as light as she possibly could, cursing every gram of the three kilos of mass that her Ascended body gave her over flesh and blood, certain that it would make the difference between making it to the top, and laying in a broken mess on the lower level with the nearest tech approximately four millennia away to put her out of her misery.

But her right foot hit solid ground, and her anxiety slowly bled away as her left foot joined it in blissful stability… well… as stable as Indiana soil gets, at any rate. But she was quickly reminded of the *second* reason she didn't like this entry. Even when well lit, it was exceptionally cramped, far too small for people to walk more than two at a time, while the "executive entry" on the north side had motion and heat triggered automatic doors and was wider than most shipping bay doors.

But at least there was a light at the end of the tunnel.

Though the light was coming from a direction she wasn't expecting.

"Did you cut through the *wall*?" She asked, aghast at the sight about a hundred meters away.

"We *tried* to go through the door, but when the pressure inside started shooting bolts at us, we decided discretion was a better idea." William replied indignantly. "We weren't sure *what* accursed traps you had set up behind there!"

"Booby trapping my resting place probably *would* have been a good idea," Alyssia snarled. "Do you have any idea how caustic that sealant is?"

"I have a pretty good guess, actually," the archaeologist retorted. "What is that stuff made of?"

"Diamond crystals and carbon fiber mostly, with a silicate serving as a glue of sorts that dries quickly upon contact with air. Breathe in too much of that vapor and it effectively turns into concrete in your lungs. I can't imagine anything I'd have been inclined to put behind the door would have been any more dangerous."

That wasn't the slightest bit true. In fact, Alyssia could think of a few hundred more dangerous things. But the human boy didn't need to know that, at least not yet. She rather liked the ashen expression of terror that fell over his face.

He *should* fear her.

Everyone should fear her.

Shadows began to obscure the makeshift entry that had been made for the professor. Alyssia was both surprised by this and knew she shouldn't have been. No doubt anyone outside would be able to hear the bickering from inside at this point and would have been startled by a voice they didn't recognize. One head stuck around the corner, prompting Alyssia to chuckle. What did the person think they were going to see staring down a near pitch black hallway?

William quickly slipped ahead of Alyssia and stopped her. "Hold here a moment, can you? I want to prepare my team for you."

"What's to prepare?" Alyssia said with a roll of her eyes. "They can no doubt hear me, and I'm fairly certain I don't sound *anything* like the man that came down with you. They already know *something* is up, if not specifically what that is."

"Just... work with me here, okay? Wait here for my cue."

Alyssia sighed heavily, then shooed him forward tiredly, "Oh, very well. Have your 'moment' and get it over with."

William grinned excitedly and just about tackled the figure peeping inside as he rushed out the breach, prompting Alyssia to shake her head and take a position three meters from the breach so that she could emerge when queued.

"Professor Sterner..." a woman's from outside spoke with an even measured tone that nonetheless carried considerable suspicion. "Why was I hearing a woman's voice?"

"First things first, Salina," William replied, though he was unable to mask his excitement. "Have our dear Republican escorts been dealt with?"

A scoff followed the question. "To the man. That smoke we released cutting inside wound up to our benefit... they thought they were just having adverse effects from inhalation, and by the time any of them put it together, it was *far* too late."

Alyssia frowned, though she supposed she shouldn't have been surprised. Man had always been wolf unto man. There was no reason to think even four thousand years would change that.

"Good. Because the Republic can't *ever* get a hold of what we've found here."

"I presume that's related to the woman's voice we were hearing? Did you find some sort of audio log with voice commands?"

Alyssia rolled her eyes. She *hoped* that William wouldn't tell an audio log to stay back.

"You're not thinking *nearly* big enough, Salina," William corrected. "I *did* find a potentially *vast* source of information, but in the most accurate way possible."

"Could you stop wasting time and my patience and just tell us what you found?"

Alyssia decided she might like this Salina girl.

"I didn't *just* find a trove of Transcendent information," William declared with as much flair as he could manage. "I found a real, live *Transcendent*. Alyssia, you may join us now."

With a deep breath, she complied if for no reason to get it over with, emerging into the light of the surface for the first time in literally an age.

The sun was a fraction of a percent brighter than she remembered, but the only reason she knew that was because she happened to have taken an ecological report a year before her intended shut down. Despite that, the air was considerably colder, giving at least some merit to the Ice Age that William had spoken of. Surface temperature for this time and date was three centigrade *lower* than the *record* low after the carbon dioxide levels had been reversed. Granted, small sample sizes and all that, but it was certainly a point in favor.

She couldn't gather much other pertinent information due to the position below actual ground level other than mildly interesting geological details which were more adjacent to her area of expertise than anything. Some very curious sediment normally associated with high water levels, which was further evidence to an Ice Age, but nothing that kept her interest long.

Which meant she had no choice but to address the slack-jawed humans before her.

She knew she was being unfair. For them, this was no doubt a moment worthy of astonishment. It would have been some somewhat analogous to archaeologists of *her* day digging into an Egyptian pyramid and finding a still living Pharaoh. But she suspected the majesty would *quickly* die if they ever got to know her. She wasn't terribly sophisticated even compared to other humans of her day... much less any of her peers.

A shorter woman approached, with straight black hair and an almond complexion, poking Alyssia in the arm. "It feels... real." Then with eyes narrowed in scrutiny, looking up to meet Alyssia's eyes, she said, "You are almost human."

This was the woman that William had been addressing earlier, Salina. "And back in my time, I would have been nigh indistinguishable had I wanted to be." Now in the light of day, Alyssia could see that the exposed parts of her chassis *had* taken on a slight yellow hue. She wouldn't have thought there was enough ultraviolet light in her tomb to do *that*. "Not so much right now, though."

"While I'm sure we could all compose a hundred questions within five minutes, the middle of Holy Republican territory probably isn't the best place to be assembling them," William shouted, trying to get the attention of the assembly. "We all know the extraction plan, so let's get to it!"

There was, understandably, some hesitation to that order. At least until William reminded them, "I have no doubt Holy Republican forces are on their way as we speak. I can't imagine they were trusting these civilians to clean all of us up."

That prompted movement. But where Alyssia had expected a chaotic mess, there was a practiced efficiency to how the group of people split up... though it did appear that *one* alteration needed to be made on the fly. "Hanson, you're gonna have to squeeze in with Salina's group." William ordered, "I... didn't anticipate that'd we'd be *adding* personnel."

Salina eyed him warily then hissed as the man presumably in question quickly changed direction. "And why are you stuffing him in with *me?*"

William grinned. "No reason."

"Oh, for the love of God, I mention *once* that he's a little cute *two years ago*..."

"That's two years that you could have spent getting closer."

"One of these days, Will. One of these days..."

As she stomped away, picking up her pace to a jog moments later, William called out cheekily, "You're welcome, Salina!"

William leaned in conspiratorially, and whispered, "I just do it because it annoys her."

"I gathered," Alyssia replied simply.

"Well anyway... come along and follow me," William requested. Then with a snarl he shouted to several stragglers that remained dumbfounded by Alyssia's presence, "You'll have time to gawk when we're safely in Cascadian territory! We don't have time to be gaping *here! Move out!*"

William waited until the stragglers had unwillingly disappeared before returning his attention to Alyssia. "Well, my dear, shall we be away as well?"

She answered, "I *could* simply wait here and let the people you killed get their revenge on me."

William answered confidently, "You won't though."

"I think you underestimate my willingness to die."

"No, I think you *over*estimate it. Someone *really* wanting to die wouldn't have left it in the hands of their willful followers who revered her like a diving being."

There were so many assumptions in that line that needed adjustment, and the Transcendent relented. "If for no reason than someone *desperately* needs to correct your understanding of my era... I suppose you are correct. Lead on."

William eagerly grabbed her hand, and she momentarily resisted the audacity of this human to violate her personal space before conceding, deciding it wasn't worth the effort to fight him. This was probably the most efficient way to get to wherever they were going, *and* it allowed her to devote more attention to other things.

Most notably, just how *deep* underground her facility had been, another point in the Ice Age story, as that sheer depth of sediment doesn't happen without some form of significant environmental change, like massive flooding caused by melting glaciers.

It had been a possibility, though *not* for the reasons

she had told William at the time. There had been no *natural* disaster in those closing years, and plenty of *intentional* disasters delivered upon a world where merely one would have sufficed. She had tried to warn the world several times. But too many people on both sides wanted to wage total war on the other, deciding decades before the end that a line had been crossed, there was no going back, and that they were going to use every weapon in their arsenal to eradicate anyone who wasn't them.

Both sides largely succeeded, and judging from the bodies splayed in all directions, their limbs and faces frozen in agony, some still holding firearms unclaimed by the living, suggested that the descendants were itching for another round.

"Might not hurt to take one," William suggested. "There is a non-zero chance that we'll encounter Holy Republican forces at some point."

Alyssia declined, "I'd rather not. And you probably don't want that either, considering that I'm still not entirely convinced that I shouldn't turn any weapon I have on *you*."

William recoiled slightly, then surrendered. "Very well, let's hope it doesn't get to a fire fight."

"If it got to a fire fight, I doubt that a weapon in my hands would change much. And I think you know it, which is why you have everyone going different ways."

She could hear William grumble incoherently, then raise his voice to snarl, "Just... follow me. We have to get moving."

Alyssia frowned, not particularly liking the answers she received from William's body language. He rather clearly wanted to see a gun in her hand, ready to fight. Between that, and the divine reverence he had shown on her wake up, it was not a particularly comforting environment to be in the center of.

Especially when in conjunction with the increasing number of dead. "How many people were in this team from the Holy Republic?"

"Thirty-four," William answered darkly. "Not even a drop in the torrent of dead *they* have caused."

"I'm not interested in a running score," She replied, more than equal to his disgust. "I'm interested in *you* having a good reason for trying to match their alleged tally."

"And perhaps when we're somewhere I'm more comfortable, I will tell you all those tales of fright. In the meantime, my lady, your chariot awaits."

Alyssia scoffed at the sight in front of her. "My chariot, you say."

There was certainly a place to value function over form. Alyssia felt that could be said of *most* things, in truth. But this... this decided to toss form out the window, and probably didn't even have the function part all that nailed down.

It was a vehicle made entirely out of steel pipe and tubing, with a flat slab of embossed steel serving as a floor, and raised. There was no roof, just three lateral tubes welded to the primary frame to form a makeshift roll cage, and one running lengthwise down the middle laid over the lateral tubes. They weren't even welded together for stability. Finally, a green vinyl tarp was then slapped over those tubes and tied with twine to the corners, forming the loosest definition of a roof that Alyssia could think of.

The innards of the kart were also open to view, "mounted" to the frame by what looked like bands of rubber and a handful of bolts screwed into the frame. To its credit, most of its bulk was in the form of a battery pack that didn't have any moving parts. Then again, the said battery pack was fourteen individual cells bound by electrical tape in the shape of a hexagon.

"Are those nickel/cadmium cells?" Alyssia asked as her eyes moved onto the motor. If that thing generated more than sixty volts, she'd be impressed.

William retorted with a voice dripping a hint of annoyance. "You make do with what you can scavenge here in the wilderness of the Holy American Republic. I can promise you that you're not going to find much better."

"I'm just saying I could probably outrun this thing on *foot*." Pausing a moment to do some diagnostics and get an appraisal of her current theoretical top speed, she amended, "Nigh certain of it, in fact."

"Well, you are free to do so then," William said in annoyance, high stepping into the rear half of the exposed cabin. "Garcia, take the wheel, if you could."

Alyssia rolled her eyes and took a standing jump straight to the floor of the cart. "I didn't say I *was*, I said I *could*."

William sat down on the bench, stuck his right arm through a loop of rope, then pulled two loose ends that were stuck through holes in the seat and tied them at his waist. "Well?" he said, gesturing at the seat next to him.

She responded with naked skepticism, then grabbed the exterior frame bar above her and replied, "I think I'll trust my balance correction system on this score."

"Suit yourself." He then fished what looked like a black brick with an antenna stuck to it, and three-square buttons on the side. He pressed down the top one and spoke into a speaker on the front end. "Salina, you ready?"

Salina's voice crackled in an insult to Alyssia's ears, but at least clearly enough that she could be understood. "Yes, Professor."

"What about you Samwell?"

"We're ready."

"Emille?"

"Secure and ready."

Salina finally cut in, "We're all set, Will. Let's go before the hounds of Hell are at our heels."

"Alright. Move out and scatter," The professor ordered. "It's going to be some rough riding, stay off main roadways, don't make any interactions that you don't have to, and we'll reconvene at Waypoint 1 in two days. Don't be late because we won't be able to wait up for you."

It was every bit of a slow start as she had expected. The engine screamed almost in protest as it pushed power into the transmission, the cart lurching then almost completely stalling before the wheels found some grip in the topsoil and began to accelerate. Just very slowly.

"Should I get out and push?" Alyssia asked sarcastically.

"Could you?" William replied, matching her snark. "I'd recommend trying from the front end."

She clicked her tongue, chiding him. "While clever, I'd do considerably more damage to this vehicle than it would do to me. Especially at this speed."

Though in the spirit of fairness, once the cart started getting up to speed, it moved quite a bit faster than she would have given it credit for. At least fast enough that it was getting enough air as it went over ridges and hills to test her stability systems to their limit. Granted, that limit, like everything else about her, was a shadow of what it used to be... but still. Credit where credit was due.

"Well, I'll stand corrected," Alyssia shouted over the air blasting her in the face. "I probably wouldn't be able to run this fast."

"The Republicans are a resourceful lot," William shouted back. "You learn how to make the most of what limited technology is allowed to you living in these parts."

"Allowed to you?" She queried.

"The Holy Republic restricts what the general person is allowed to use, by the will of God, or so the religious leaders say. Anything beyond what is necessary for the good of the Republic is considered sinful, and grounds for anything from imprisonment and even death."

"I see."

"Of course, the leaders and the military are allowed to use whatever they want. You know, to maintain their sovereignty from the 'Godless Cascadians' and other enemies. But they aren't totally heartless. In the fields of medicine, they are allowed total freedom and have by their estimation the finest medical minds anywhere in the world. Provided you are deemed important enough by the Republic to deserve them."

Something told Alyssia that William didn't want to hear any counterpoints. Maybe it was the fact that his jaw had clenched to the point that it was turning even *whiter*. Maybe it was the fact that he had turned away from her to scowl, his face contorted in rage as he had almost spat those last words in disgust.

The people of this region, even during her day, had been a... different breed of folk. They held individual responsibility and personal freedom sacrosanct above all; their right to make any decision, even if it was harmful to themselves or others, trumped any other concern. Sweat of their hands, toil of the earth... even when those beliefs completely stripped their land bare and turned their sweat into blood.

They were also a profoundly religious people, so it was little surprise to her that they clung to their faith through an Ice Age and turned it into the fundament of their government in the aftermath. *That* had been something the people of this land had wanted for *centuries* during her rise to prominence, so of course they did so in the power vacuum created by the collapse of Alyssia's world. One could only *imagine* what nonsense they dealt in nowadays that was equal parts needlessly oppressive and unconscionably cruel. The people of this region she knew had been eagerly capable of both.

But religion also tended to make fanatics of its critics. If William was trying to drag her into some sort of war against holy war, he could forget it. She had witnessed *that* story play out once already. She had no interest in a sequel.

"Professor Sterner!" a crackled, noise-contorted voice drifted over the howl of the air rushing by, a voice that Alyssia didn't recognize from the handful of people she had heard earlier.

William was on his radio in a flash. "Report, Carl."

"Seven heavy armored vehicles just blew by right behind us. They had to have seen us, but they just ignored us like we weren't even there. I think they're headed right for you!"

"I can confirm, Professor!" Another voice, a very high-pitched woman's voice cut in. "We spotted them off our southwest side, bearing three-hundred ten. I think they're headed in your direction."

At that point, Alyssia picked up the sound herself. Big, angry diesel engines and a *lot* of metal. Her head drifted in that direction, and she cranked up the zoom on her optics. Like the cart she was currently riding in, the vehicles gaining on them were not stylish. Unlike the cart she was currently riding in, they clearly and definitely had a clearly discernible function.

These were bulky monstrosities built of bolted plates of steel, with massive churning treads chewing up dirt in a plume of debris. Three massive slabs were welded together and mounted to the front, a wedge meant for breaking down walls and bunkered positions. About the only weak point Alyssia could spy at least from the front was an eight-centimeter slit visible just above the wedge and about three meters long that provided sight lines for the driver.

A second deck of sorts was clad in aggressively square metal plates secured with probably more rivets than were necessary, providing partial cover to three gunner nests, one situated directly in the front, the other two flanking to the sides. The guns themselves were high volume miniguns, with ribbons of ammunition dangling from the feeders. They nests were currently unmanned, and the different directions all three guns were pointing suggested they were free rotating. While none of them looked to be of a particularly large caliber, the barrel bores measured a shade about ten millimeters, if they fired with enough velocity it could be troublesome.

But the most notable feature was the turret at the top, serving as a third deck of sorts, comprised entirely of a metal dome, with a large cannon barrel protruding from the bottom. *That* gun's bore measured pretty much exactly twenty centimeters. At that size, any other factor was largely irrelevant. Getting hit by anything fired from that was going to be bad.

And while Alyssia found the original assessment was inaccurate - there were only six vehicles, not seven - that was still roughly five more than was probably necessary.

Alyssia frowned and observed. "It would seem that someone within the Holy American Republic isn't taking any chances." Then, with a mischievous grin, she added, "And they are certainly much better than this piece of scrap."

"So, I underestimated the eagerness of our welcoming committee," William grumbled. "I apologize profusely."

She did have to appreciate the universe helping make some decisions for her. A country didn't wheel in tanks if they were particularly interested in talking things out. At least for the time being, her path was going to be with these Cascadian terrorists.

"So, what's the plan?" Garcia asked from the front

seat.

William scanned the surroundings as they whirled by, then pointed north towards a line of evergreen trees. "We might be able to weave in through the new growth. Those armored vehicles might not be able to follow us."

Alyssia again regarded the cannons of their pursuers. "Following us might not be a necessity."

"You have a better idea?"

She shook her head, "No. Just making an observation."

Garcia cranked the wheel hard to the north, and pushed the cart as fast as it could go towards the tree line. Pine and conifer trees had been scarce in the southern Indiana she knew, so to see them as the dominating species was a slight bit jarring. Merely yet another reminder that this wasn't the world she knew... but it was still hard to absorb, even for a quantum brain capable of literally making *billions* of calculations a second.

The cart took a jump, the speed creating an arc that not even her chassis could account for, her feet leaving the floor, only for her joints to literally squeal in strain as they reacquainted themselves upon landing. She stumbled but would be able to play it off as recoil from the roar of a massive cannon and the resulting artillery strike about thirty meters away to her left.

Alyssia spun about, gauging distance because there was no way the armored vehicles had gained all that much ground so quickly. They hadn't, her range finder telling her they were still over a kilometer away. She hummed thoughtfully, and remarked, "That's some impressive range for a mobile gun, at least for this level of sophistication."

William spared himself a glance back to confirm Alyssia's assessment. "Stay the course, Garcia. If they can hit us from this far out, we won't have time to regret our failure, but I'd rather not risk a spill on this rough of terrain."

"I wouldn't have tried evasive maneuvers even if you had ordered them, so I'm glad we're in agreement," the driver shouted back, though he clearly reconsidered that idea when another shell impacted about ten meters closer.

Fortunately, while the cannon range was impressive, the accuracy was not, as none of the next four shots from the remaining tanks got any closer to striking. Nor was their reloading time anything to sing about either, because Garcia was able to wedge the cart in between two younger trees at the forest line before any of their pursuers could ready a second shot.

"Get us into as much cover as you can," Alyssia advised. "Even if they decide not to fire the cannons into the forest, those minigun nests could quite easily cut into the gaps."

And there were indeed gaps. Once inside the forest, Alyssia observed that these trees were intentionally planted, in very distinct rows, especially among the new growth. While it would be *more* difficult to find them, it wasn't going to be impossible, either.

William agreed, his eyes looking further into the more chaotic older growth that would definitely provide more cover, but the reality that they'd have to abandon their vehicle to go much further clearly weighed on his mind judging from the wariness etched on his face.

And then their pursuers forced the issue. The lead armored vehicle actually slammed into the treeline, its bunker busting wedge ripping up the first three rows of new growth until the fourth finally killed its momentum. Garcia revved the motor to pull away from the wreckage, weaving his way as deep into the forest as he could then down that last row as the other armored vehicles turned away, the gun nests spitting gun fire at any hint of the little cart through the rows of trees.

"We're going to run out of trees eventually," William said.

Garcia abruptly stopped the vehicle and shouted. "Both of you, get out. Quickly."

William blinked in confusion, and Garcia explained, "I will draw their attention. You go deeper into the forest. It will be your best chance."

"Garcia, I'm not going to let you…"

"The other option is that *all* of us die," the driver said simply. "Now go before they get suspicious!"

Alyssia snarled in frustration, then literally tore apart the rope harness keeping William to his seat, then forcibly threw him out of the vehicle. She then vaulted herself out the same side, rolling to her feet nimbly, then slapped the frame.

"*What are you doing?*" William screeched as she grabbed him by the collar and dragged him into the thicker cover of old growth while the cart accelerated back to speed.

"Saving your life, you imbecile," She replied.

Or at least... she thought. To her surprise, *none* of the vehicles went in pursuit of Garcia's cart as it bolted out into the open. But what *did* happen was the occupants of the vehicles started climbing out to continue the pursuit on foot. One of them felt confident enough to take a shot at Alyssia's head as she was looking over the developing situation. She retreated more out of instinct than danger, her brows furrowed in thought.

"None of them followed," William said in relief, which then quickly turned to concern when he realized what that meant. "Did they see us disembark?"

"Even if they did, that wouldn't explain why *no one* went after him," Alyssia replied, again sticking her head around the thick trunk to observe the progress of their pursuers. They had spread out, no doubt trying to flank Alyssia and William.

She set her jaw, knelt, then ordered, "Get on my back."

William blinked, and asked, "What?"

"I can run faster with you on my back. Get. On."

Reluctantly, William complied, wrapping his arms around her neck and chest, and his legs around her waist. "Don't worry about hurting me. I can promise that you won't. Just hold on tight."

Two shots smacked into the tree as Alyssia straightened with ease, then lunged into a near full sprint. Unlike the cart, she could weave through the denser foliage, and didn't have to sacrifice any speed to do it.

And it got thick. *This* was natural forest, as there was no pattern or properly maintained grounds. Dried pine needles crackled under her feet and wild animals scurried out of her path. Once she felt she was well out of sight, she abruptly cut to the west, and took off again, covering another three kilometers in four minutes. She could have gone a lot further and a lot longer, but it became clear William couldn't.

She felt his grip around her neck slip, and she instantly slowed herself to a trot, then finally a full stop. The adrenaline crash was hitting him, and hard.

He tried to deny it. "I'm fine, just a little tired. We should keep going."

"We've easily got five kilometers of a head start, and even if they are expert trackers, they aren't going to be able to go full speed. We've got some time. Get your legs back."

For all his earlier insistence to keep moving, he did not waste any time dropping to the seat of his pants and rubbing his forehead. "That was so peculiar. Why did the Republicans ignore everyone else entirely? How would they know that we were the most 'important' vehicle?"

Alyssia shamefully had to admit that hadn't even come up as a concern. She had been so used to a society where no one was truly hidden. But now that she thought about it... that *was* peculiar. "They would need some form of GPS, but even if they had that, they'd need for *me* to be connected to..."

She froze, and her eyes narrowed into dots. Again, it was one of those things that she had gotten so used to, that she never even gave it any thought. But a quick scan into her connectivity settings proved it.

> *Current Connection: DarkNest ComSat, Orbital Cluster Eastern HAR, Unit 1-1-3*

The Holy American Republic was *considerably* more sophisticated than perhaps anyone realized.

"Alyssia?" William asked in concern. No doubt he was worried she had actually frozen up.

She immediately disconnected from the satellite but knew that alone would accomplish little. "Sorry to interrupt your rest, but we need to get moving, and quickly."

William blinked and asked warily. "Why?"

"Because I know how they found us, and they will probably *keep* finding us unless we are able to throw off their projective tracking programs."

"Their... *what?*"

Alyssia crouched down. "Just climb on and hold tight."

William slowly climbed onto her back again, and Alyssia broke off into a sprint initially. The important bit was to get even more distance. Once they had that, they could be a little more careful to try and throw off manual and predictive tracking. While it was admittedly a rather huge assumption that the Holy American Republic had mastered AI to that degree, she was done with underestimating their pursuers.

"So... what is going on? How were *you* the reason they were able to target us?" William queried.

Alyssia explained herself as she ducked between two Northern Pines with interlocked roots. "Global Positioning System. The Holy American Republic has at least one high altitude satellite in orbit. When you woke me up, I have automated systems that immediately started transmitting data to it. I quite literally had a big red dot glowing over our heads."

William was astonished. "The Republic has those? I had no idea. Cascadia only put our first satellites up about fifteen years ago. And we certainly haven't implemented any positioning protocols yet. We've really only begun to consider *how* we'd do it that would also respect the general privacy of citizens."

"Well, clearly the Holy American Republic doesn't have those qualms... and I wouldn't put money down on your country being much better in that regard. Anyway, I want to give us another kilometer or so, then we'll slow down to throw off any projective tracking."

"And what is *that?*"

"It's a computer modeling system that can use things like infrared data, satellite imaging, and artificial intelligence to predict where someone who has 'dropped off the grid' is going. It's not *likely* they have anything that complex, but I don't want to take any chances."

William nodded against her shoulder. "Fair."

Silence ruled the next couple minutes, and that probably wasn't a good thing. It never seemed to end well when Alyssia was lost to her thoughts for very long. Especially when they were existential thoughts.

She had been ready to die. There was every reason for her to be. Why hadn't her followers followed her instructions after she had initiated her final shutdown? Why had they put her into a sleep state instead? What had they been planning... and what had changed? Because she sincerely doubted "let her sit in the dark for roughly four thousand years" had been part of the plan.

And why was she even doing *this?* Why was her first thought to keep running, rather than tell this fool waif of a man to run, then wait with her GPS blaring her location? Why was she trying to preserve herself *now?* What could she possibly offer other than how to ruin the world in the most devastating way possible?

Once her step tracker hit ten kilometers, she decided that was enough distance to start trying more complex misdirection. She knelt, and ordered, "Alright. Off. We'll be able to move more slowly at this point. In fact, we want to."

William seemed content to let her dictate what they were going to do for the moment, falling right behind her as she gestured for him to follow as she now took a westward path. "What we *really* need is some place to outright *stop*," she said. "That would *really* throw off any predictive modeling they might have."

"Is that why you went due north?" He asked.

Alyssia nodded. "If we have a long enough northward track, the AI will want to keep projecting our path north. So now that we're moving west again, and I even might consider tracking a bit back to the *south*, we should theoretically slip out of the 'circle' entirely."

William shook his head. "It's just... so very hard for me to believe that the Holy American Republic would have such sophisticated means of identifying and tracking people. The advantage they'd have over all their neighbors, over their own people... and not use it. That's not the Holy Republican way."

"Well, sounds like your enemy can be more discreet than you give them credit for."

William's glower spoke more about his anger than his voice did. "I speak from experience when I say that 'discreet' isn't in the vocabulary of the Holy American Republic. I *know*

72

what they do with information."

This was another topic that William wasn't going to accept any debate on, so Alyssia yielded the point. Once humans got emotional, the ability to reason through a discussion rapidly vanished, and she had seen little evidence that William was one of those that could.

She waved him on again as she picked up speed. "At any rate, let's see if there is anywhere that we can get out of sight."

Again, silence ruled, occasional splashes of sun overhead suggesting that the late afternoon was coming. Trying to fill the void, Alyssia asked, "So, is there any way we can arrange a pick-up?"

William shook his head, "I can promise you that any of my team is *well* out of radio range at this point, and long-range transmissions would take time you suggest we don't have and an unobstructed field that we *definitely* don't have. I figured I could plot a course after we had shaken off the Republican forces."

Alyssia nodded in approval. "Take things one step at a time. Probably the best approach right now."

There was another long period of silence. The woods broke momentarily to allow a creek two meters wide to wind through, and Alyssia paused for William and herself to get some water.

William was astonished as she poured cupped handfuls of water down her throat. She gave him a questioning eyebrow and said, "What? My systems *are* water cooled, and I've been operating at a hefty clip. I'll probably flush this out in a couple minutes, and refill in fact."

He had the look of a person who *really* wanted to ask a question but was afraid of learning the answer. "So... how exactly do you... 'flush out' old water?"

Alyssia grinned teasingly, "My chassis is designed to completely mimic human function. Would you like a demonstration?"

"That... is not necessary."

"Well, then you can wait here while I step in behind these trees."

She hadn't been kidding, and if William had decided to sneak a peek, he would have watched the Transcendent pull down the bottom of her suit and her panties, crouch, and eject a stream of what was scalding hot water right from where a woman's urethra was.

Not that he had tried. The professor had shown remarkable discipline staying on the other side of the tree and taking handfuls of water to wash his arms. While her chassis was allegedly hypo-allergenic and only needed to be wiped down, she wasn't sure if after all this time that would still be the case.

So, after kneeling down to swallow two more large gulps of water, happily rewarded by her real-time status showing further drop in internal temperatures, the next two handfuls of water were taken mimicking William's efforts, who had since rolled up his pant legs to clean his calves.

"Do you really want to know why I'm doing this?" he asked abruptly.

Alyssia intentionally played coy. "Because humans are filthy creatures and need periodic washing?"

William glared at her tiredly, "You know what I mean. You said you wanted to hear a reason why I'd want to match their body count. Are you ready to hear it?"

"Always."

"Up until thirteen years ago, I lived in this country. In the City of Hope, to be specific, about a day's travel south of here if you have good transportation. I had initially wanted to be a mechanic, but those sort of opportunities are limited here in the Holy American Republic even under the best conditions, and it was doubtful I was even going to be considered for those few positions."

Alyssia sincerely hoped that William had a better reason for wanting to go on a mass-murdering rampage.

"My brother was a staff member for one of the Republic Archons, and he had managed to secure a student visa for me to study in Cascadia. These were exceptionally rare, considering that the two nations have cold relations at best."

But I was too young at the time, and so my brother switched our identifications. He became me, and I became him. I got to leave… and within a year, my brother was dead."

Alyssia cocked an eyebrow. "And those two events are related, I assume?"

"About fifteen years ago, there seemed like there was going to be an opportunity for the Holy American Republic to change, and for the better. A new papal authority had declared an easing of the societal restrictions on 'deviants,' like homosexual relationships, misgendered people, the mentally and physically handicapped, darker skinned people, women in general… basically anyone who wasn't a pale skinned old man."

Thousands, tens of thousands, who knows how many exactly, began registering for marriage, or transition, change official documents, or applied to become fully fledged citizens of the Republic with rights to representation, owning land or property… and then the Pope died abruptly. His death has been the source of countless conspiracies, but was officially an unforeseen heart condition and cardiac arrest."

William's hands clenched. "He was replaced by a hardline conventionalist, who demanded a strict adherence to the holy texts. That monster *used the very documents* that had been created for the 'degenerates' to round them up… and… and execute them."

Alyssia nodded in understanding, "And that would explain your skepticism about the tracking capabilities of this government."

"If they had that sort of ability, they would have *used it*. Many, many times." William declared, then continued into his story. "But possibly, the worst part of it was the executions themselves. These 'degenerates' weren't killed all at once, you see. It was gradually, over the course of a year, the government killing handfuls of people at a time, executed by crucifixion. Each execution gleefully displayed over government approved video broadcasts. And even *that* was just one part of a much larger campaign over the last fifteen years by the Republic to try and goad its neighbors into a fight."

He stared challengingly in Alyssia's eyes and said in defiance. "The only thing I'm trying to do is give them what they want."

Alyssia had *many* questions and observations to make and settled with the more strategic one. "And you were thinking that I'd have power, information, or insight that would allow you to turn your crusade into something that could do real damage."

"The church is *terrified* of the 'metal gods' of the previous age, and I believe it's for good reason. Cascadia has been cowardly in response to the actions of the Holy American Republic, and I thought that if I could find information or relics from your era, it could inspire my new country to act more strongly against the Republic's crimes. But to find an actual *Transcendent*…"

Alyssia clicked her tongue. "I'd warn you about what you're asking for. While I could tell you and your country's leaders *many* things, you'd regret learning them in time, just as my people and your ancestors did. Because you'd be right on one thing. This church fears my kind, and it *is* for good reason. It's the same reason *your* people should fear us too."

"Hey! What is going on over there!"

The graveled voice from the north startled both of them, especially Alyssia, since her proximity sensors should have identified human movement. Then again, it should have noted how close they were to the edge of the forest line, and *that* didn't happen either. One of many failed systems from time, she supposed. Nothing that could be done about it now.

He crunched loudly through the undergrowth, bellowing angrily. "I don't know who you are or what you're doing on my property, but I'm not out here because I want hikers tramping through my woods! This is for logging, not for sightseeing, now get off my…"

He burst around the last cluster of conifers that separated them, his double barreled shotgun already raised as Alyssia stood and extended to her full height, turning defiantly to face him with a face of almost pure indifference. He somewhat resembled a sausage, in the sense that there was little that she would consider an angle or curve to his body shape. He was almost as tall as her, but at least three times as broad. What muscle structure she *could* see around his thick flannel shirt and jacket, and thick denim jeans was best described as non-existent. Even his hair, a mop of light brown follicles that had already started retreating from his forehead, looked like they were trying to fuse with his skin rather than possibly cause anything resembling wind resistance.

It was an entirely unimpressive sample of humanity, even with a gun giving him artificial courage.

"Stay behind me," she ordered William. "Depending on the spray of this fellow's shells, you might still get hit. I'd like to keep that to non-essential bits."

It seemed that William's assertions on church doctrine had some merit, because their intruder's reaction to seeing Alyssia face to face was the sort of fear that comes with a man who had just seen the devil appear in his forest.

"Mother... of... God..." The woodsman gasped, fumbling with his shotgun momentarily before finally getting a good grip, and pulling the trigger, the roar of shot pellets erupting from the barrel and slamming into Alyssia in a spray from her neck to her abdomen.

She looked down at the damage to her top, and groaned in frustration, "Do you have *any* idea how hard this outfit is going to be to replace? Now put down your gun. If I had any desire to harm or kill you, I could have done it roughly five times by now."

She then roughly wrenched the pistol out of William's hand as he attempted to reach around her and take a pot shot. "And that goes for you too, boy. If this fellow posed a threat, I'd handle it."

The woodsman decided that compliance was the better part of valor, letting the gun fall from his numb hands and drop with a soft thud onto the moist creek bank. Alyssia picked it up, and said, "You can have it back once you've taken us to your home."

"Why are you having this unsophisticated weasel take us to his *house?*"

Alyssia sighed. "Because whether you believe it or not, I'm not taking any chances. A home like his would be as good of a place as any to lay low and throw off any projection tracking. Please, good sir, if you may?"

The bulky woodsman complied, if reluctantly,

repeatedly looking over his shoulder as if he was terrified Alyssia was going to snap his neck if he dropped his guard. She accepted it for what it was. If keeping her constantly in sight helped the human feel safer, so be it.

She would like to feel that way too.

Episode Three: Deep Diving

William had been expecting little from the woodsman's home. And he still managed to be disappointed.

To call it a house was an insult to homes everywhere. Even calling it a shack would have gotten a side-eye from any self-respecting shanty. It was hastily stacked logs with a "ceiling" made of branches, pitch, and leaves. Hell, there were no fewer than six piles of logs littering the small clearing surrounding the house that was larger than it was, and another five that were comparable in size.

Jimmer... at least William *thought* that was his name, seemed proud enough about it to boast to a being that terrified the piss out of him, at least. "I come out here three months of every year because this is where good old growth hardwood can be found. Just me, my axe, and a whole bunch of willpower. Every week, the trucks come to gather this up and pay me. At least... they used to."

"I imagine so," Alyssia answered. "I'd have a hard time believing you managed to cut and clean all this in one week."

"Haven't been by in a *month*. The last message I sent was responded to with some nonsense that they didn't need the wood, and that they'd contact me when they had the need. How could they not need *wood?*"

William rolled his eyes. No doubt the lumberyard Jimmer had supplied found a cheaper or more accessible source. Probably both.

Alyssia, however, seemed content to humor him as the woodsman pulled open the door to his shanty, and invited them inside. "Yes, one would think that would be a rather essential material."

William followed her across the non-existent threshold, and into a space that would not have fit much more than the three of them. There was a bare wooden table, with strips of bark still visible on the legs, braced in the northwest corner, and a single chair made of the same unpolished wood accompanying it that Jimmer sat in, a canvas hammock strung to the other three, and not much else. There wasn't even really a floor, just packed down dirt. How could anyone live like this, even on a temporary basis?

"Where and how do you *eat?*" William wondered out loud, momentarily forgetting that he was supposed to be nice.

"I have a fire pit outside. I have preserves, jerky, and whatnot in the ice buried next to the well. You passed all of them on the way here. Why, do you need something? Hungry?"

William shook his head, "No. No. Just…curious."

"There were people who chose this way of life even during *my* time," Alyssia chided gently. Surprising, as William didn't think the Transcendent was *capable* of being gentle. But why to this fool? This… unsophisticated yokel? He'd probably have ripped her head off and offered it to the Church if he ever got the opportunity, and she's trying to chat him up? Why?

"How much longer should we stay here?" He asked.

"An hour, maybe two. Don't want to hover around *too* long and get this fellow in trouble," She answered testily, leaning back against the west wall facing the door. "So, make yourself comfortable and settle down."

She gestured to the hammock, and Jimmer consented with a fearful nod. With a resigned sigh, William decided that anything would be more comfortable than standing up for however long it would take for Alyssia to be satisfied with their state of hiding. He pulled himself up into the triangular slab of canvas… and discovered that it wasn't uncomfortable. There was just enough give in the material to adjust to his weight, but not so much that there was no stability.

Certainly, better than the sleeping bags he had been in during the last season.

Meanwhile, Alyssia kept pandering to that uneducated lout that was sitting on a whole bunch of wood and empty promises. "I'm guessing you haven't been informed of any changes from the lumberyard?"

William had to acknowledge that the sweet treatment was disarming the woodsman. "No…"

"And they aren't going to either," William cut in.

Before he could get terribly much further, Alyssia glared at him angrily. "*That* could have been said a *lot* more tactfully. Especially since it is by this man's courtesy that we're hiding here. I... remember being in a very similar place as a young girl. It's a shame how little has changed when it really should have."

William blinked repeatedly, and for once, he found himself in total agreement with Jimmer.

"Little girl?" the woodsman asked. "What do you mean?"

Alyssia flashed an amused look to William, "Must have been one of the details lost to history. Shame really, because I'd argue it would provide *much* better reasons for the entirely justified fear of my kind. I, along with *every* Transcendent, had been human. We were *all* people, just like you. And you, professor."

His head spun with the claim. "How... are you part human, then?" He asked.

Alyssia shook her head. "Everything about me, as of this moment, is completely mechanical and computerized. But for the first eighty-seven years of my life, I was every bit a flesh and blood human being."

She paused to let that sink in, though William quickly decided he was going to need a *lot* more context to make sense of what was impossible... or more accurately, something that he hadn't even thought to consider was possible or impossible to begin with.

"I was born and grew up relatively near here. In a rather small city called Linton, back in a time where it was part of a state called Indiana," Alyssia said. "My parents were soy farmers. If you wanted to make enough money to live, you grew either soy or corn. We had enough land that we were able to parcel off a little bit that wasn't already reserved to the feed corporations to grow sustenance crops for ourselves, but that was about it."

She nodded to Jimmer's raised eyebrows. "Oh yes... it was worse for men of the land in my time. Large companies parceled out *your* land, used it for *their* purposes, but expected *you* to maintain it and do *their* work for *them*. Eventually, those corporations realized they could completely crater a farm's value, force the farmers to sell, and turn those farmers into vassals working fields that they used to own. That was what happened to my family; forced to sell at a third of what the property could have cost to an agriculture conglomerate named Heartland Farms."

"They cratered value? How?" William asked.

Jimmer seemed to know where this was going, "Plenty of ways to ruin the value of something. Flooding the market with cheaper alternatives is a popular one. You're right that's probably what happened to me and my wood, Mr. Professor, by the way."

"Even more subversive than that," Alyssia corrected. "Their trick was in the crops that they required farmers to grow. Heartland reserved and required their farmers to grow crops that didn't produce seeds themselves, making it impossible for those farmers to build seed reserves, making them wholly dependent on Heartland. From there, Heartland started offering increasingly less money to grow crops on fields they had reserved."

"Without seed crops, and unable to grow anything else to make money, their property would be next to worthless," Jimmer said with a tired sigh.

Alyssia awkwardly deflected from what were clearly painful memories. "Anyway, I won't tire you both with some meandering life story that you wouldn't be interested in, but in a bit of irony and over the course of many years, I wound up taking a majority stake in Heartland Farms. I became the very corporate overlord that had ruined my family and stole away our farm. I had become obscenely wealthy as a result. I had everything I could have ever wanted, accomplished things that most of humanity could ever dream of... and yet age and Father Time refused to be denied.

"All of us Transcendent had a similar desire. We all sought to stave off death, to conquer the last, unbeatable inevitability of life. I also won't waste your ears describing all the various ideas and theories that were tested by millions of people the world over... some of them were so absurd that I look back on them and cringe. But it all changed when we were introduced to the nature of quantum memory."

William watched Jimmer's eyes glaze over, though the professor really couldn't blame the woodsman. This seemed like a topic that he was going to have no hope of following. But he pressed on anyway, "What... what is that?"

"Key discoveries in how we learn and remember things. The human brain stores information at a level that isn't even real in some respects, at a scale where the rules of the universe as you would know them start breaking down and behaving in unusual ways. Even in the decades before my time, there wasn't even a reliable way to *measure* this quantum data, let alone manipulate it. But once that method was discovered, that's where we found the gift of relative immortality."

Alyssia seemed to ignore the glossy-eyed expressions from her audience. "The first 'quantum map' of the human brain quickly led to the first entangling of the human brain with an inorganic computer and allowing for the transfer from one to the other. Memories... behavioral patterns... everything. That process is how every Transcendent came to be."

There was *no* way William understood that right. "Are you saying... you could *copy a human soul?*"

"If 'soul' is what you want to call it, but no. Nothing was 'copied.' There wasn't a flesh and blood Alyssia struggling to breathe on a table while this new me walked around. Quantum data is arguably the only truly unique thing in the whole universe. You can't 'copy' a quantum map. It can only be transferred using what is called entanglement. When two quantum bits are entangled, they mirror each other. Then, you flip one entangled side, and that becomes you and the other side becomes... the mirrored noise that isn't you. It's not even capable of maintaining the involuntary functions of an organic body."

She exhaled, though now William wondered how much of that was the Transcendent body mimicking human behavior, and how much of it was a behavioral tick of Alyssia's from when she was human. He asked before she could speak again. "Is that why the Transcendent body was made to mimic human behavior and appearance? So that you could maintain those behaviors in your new body?"

The Transcendent shook her head. "Oh no. *This* was mere vanity, to look as vital and as beautiful as we were at the height of our lives. *We,* the *truly* Transcendent, had that luxury. There were... others, who were not granted that privilege. They were required to take on the forms we chose of them in exchange for 'eternal life,' all of them living weapons of horror that we liberally unleashed on our enemies."

She was looking at Jimmer, but the words felt more directed at him. "The Juggernauts were the *least* of our sins, honestly. The Transcendent were uniformly the wealthiest people on the planet, who were used to acting with complete impunity. We were *used* to manipulating laws, twisting intent to suit our purposes, and outright ignoring anything we couldn't. And with an eternity to act out or plans, it was largely inevitable that we'd become tyrants."

Jimmer finally engaged with the conversation, albeit nervously, "What was the world like before? Was it anything like ours?"

William had to admit it was an intriguing question, and he was surprised the woodsman had the wherewithal to ask.

Alyssia hummed in thought, "That's rather hard to say, because I don't really know much about the world as it is currently. It's also hard to answer because my time stretches across a fairly wide swath of human history. But I suppose the best time to start would be when I became Transcendent. That was the year 2186 by that era's reckoning, and over five thousand years ago by yours."

At one time, this was part of a very powerful nation that had stretched from one ocean to the other. By the time I had ascended, that union had been irreparably fractured by several brutal and bloody civil wars that had been threatening to tear it apart over the stretch of two centuries, the last of which rocked the country in the years just after I had become a Transcendent. It created a power vacuum that people like me were more than willing to fill, and a civilization that was happy to let us do it if for no reason than immortal humans that had been so rich and popular couldn't *possibly* lead them astray."

She sighed, "So of course, that's promptly what we did. See, once you reached the sort of wealth that was required in order to afford ascension, the world looked *very* different than it did to someone of lower status. We didn't have the same bonds of country and kin that others did. Hell, for us, borders weren't even an artificial construct. They were entirely invisible. So we had no problem destabilizing other countries, and using that instability to tear down the 'human governments' and form Transcendent Councils to rule entire regions."

It took almost a hundred and fifty years, but that sort of time was a pittance for us. We could play what flesh and blood humans would call an *extremely* long game, slowly turning people against people until they were begging us to save them from themselves. It was really an extension of what we did as human beings... we merely no longer had a deadline. Turns out that if you give a group of people who already felt laws and morals didn't apply to them eternal life, they're going to take it as reinforcement of their behavior."

We imposed massive cultural changes. We abolished public displays of religion, then abolished *any* practice of religion. That's no doubt the *real* core of why the Evangelical Orthodox Church loathes us so, for what it's worth. We imposed total civil equality and punished any perceived bigotry harshly. We abolished private ownership, property, and enterprise."

Superficially, these were all positive changes, and we in fact had *billions* of people throughout the world lauding us and our forward thinking. But all those things were *truly* done to control all the wealth, thought, and devotion of the world. We sought to 'kill' God... in order to supplant him, and we stopped at no lengths to ensure it. I don't even have to *know* what the current church says about us to feel eminently confident that the truth is even *worse*."

"So, humans *were* treated like slaves during your age?" William asked.

Alyssia scoffed, "Bought, sold, traded, forced to breed, killed at whim... I'd argue we didn't even consider humans slaves by the end. You weren't even livestock. At least livestock had a macabre use at the end of their lives. Human beings were probably closer to toys, played with and discarded when they were no longer entertaining."

"The church also believes that the Transcendent could destroy the world with the weapons they had," William added.

Alyssia shrugged at that, though she became much more careful with her words. "Well, humankind of the past had *that* capability for *centuries* before the Transcendent rose to complete power. We certainly refined it, and by the end... used some of them... so the accusation isn't false."

"So, humans *were* smarter in the past?" Jimmer asked.

"I... don't know if I'd say 'smarter.' More sophisticated. More resources to manipulate. Greater population to invest in larger scale projects. But to be honest, most humans were too stupid to be trusted with a butter knife," with a knowing glance towards William she added, "From my limited experience of present-day humanity, that doesn't seem to have changed much."

"I know when I'm being insulted," William warned.

Alyssia laughed, such a deceptively pure sound that William couldn't really accept that it was coming from a machine. He was curious about how the Transcendent could replicate such things so perfectly... but he got the feeling that the technology and skills would be *far* beyond his comprehension.

"There was a saying in my time that goes, 'the more you know, the more you realize you don't.' I found, on the other hand, that there was a point where a person knew just enough to be dangerous with it, but still didn't have the clarity of what they didn't understand." She grinned, teasingly. "Don't worry, professor, you're not at that point yet."

He rolled off the hammock, mildly impressed that he landed on his feet without stumbling and damaging his righteous indignation. "I think I'd prefer to be found by Republican forces," he snarled, and stomped out of Jimmer's shanty, slamming the door so violently behind him that it rattled against the frame.

The door quickly opened behind him, and Alyssia followed him out, her voice cross. "Alright, what's your problem?"

"I am *not* going to be ridiculed for the entertainment of some uneducated fool."

Alyssia rolled her eyes. "You're being ridiculed for *my* entertainment, boy. I doubt our friend really has the desire or interest to process what I'm saying beyond, 'Metal gods as bad as the church says.' You really shouldn't assume others have the same curiosity you do."

"You're pandering to that lout, and I won't be subject to it," William insisted.

She crossed her arms, "What? Because I can sympathize with his plight, having gone through something very similar myself? Well, hell, am I just some kind of monster here!"

"Men like him stood silent as people like my brother were *butchered*."

"Men like him probably didn't even know or care that your brother existed."

He snarled, and retorted, "And that is an *excuse* in your mind?"

She grabbed him by the collar and shook him once. "I knew plenty of people like you that had this same attitude. 'You're either with us or against us,' they'd say. 'No one is truly neutral.' It's an attitude that pervaded the thought of my era all the way to worlds that were ancient even when my time was contemporary. You seem to have plenty enough enemies that you don't need to be looking for more."

William sneered, "It's funny how you sympathize with *his* plight, but seem to be ignoring *mine*."

"Oh? Are you willing to tell me what that plight is? Because so far, all you've been willing to say is that your brother sacrificed himself to give you an opportunity that no one else among your peers seem to have gotten. I *can* sympathize with that... not many of my peers had the money and opportunity to escape the indentured life of the rural Midwest, either. Not exactly sure how that's a plight beyond survivor's guilt, though."

Then she cut a little too close for his comfort, "Could it have had something to do with *why* your brother was killed?"

William clenched his teeth. He had been reluctant to

discuss those details to begin with. He was even *less* inclined to do so now that he knew that Alyssia's background was from the exact same stock of people as the bumpkin inside the shanty.

Instead, she released his collar, and tapped him comfortably on the shoulder. "For what it's worth, I think I've sorted out at least part of it."

He blanched. "What do you mean?"

"You seem to have forgotten that I've already had my hand around your throat," she said with a knowing grin. "You *really* don't want to have a battle of secrets with me. You won't win. When you're willing to address it, I'm willing to listen, but until then, I'm not going to assume I know the whole tale."

The anger felt like it was dripping out of him. Maybe... she was right. Maybe he was being unfair criticizing her for a lack of empathy when he been avoiding giving her enough to be empathic *about*. Perhaps he *should* be more open.

William took a deep breath that strained his lungs, his last involuntary stall before he tried to speak. Not that he had much of a chance to get a single word out before Alyssia grabbed him by the arm and pulled him roughly towards the opposite side of the shanty. He didn't even have the opportunity to speak *then* as she clapped a hand over his mouth to quiet him and forced him against the exterior wall.

He discovered why soon after, her ears picking up the sounds of a motor long before his did. "Damn it, there's no way they happened on here by accident," she whispered, "Still don't think they've got sophisticated tracking?"

William glowered at her. Even if he hadn't been trying to keep his voice down, he didn't want to dignify her with a response. For all she knew, it was the damned lumber reps that Jimmer had been waiting for.

He couldn't get any hint of how many were coming just based on the sound, other than whoever it was only came in one vehicle. If it *was* a Holy Republican search, they weren't coming in force, which suggested they hadn't pinpointed Alyssia as well as she feared.

Then again, if it *was* a Holy Republican search, that would be some pretty remarkable luck to get this close with a random canvass so quickly.

He heard the creak of the shanty door open again as the vehicle's motor spun down, and Jimmer addressed his visitors.

"Damn it, I was hoping you were the lumber yards," the woodsman groused.

"We're with the Holy Republican Army. This is Corporal Alameda. I'm Sergeant Houser. We have been pursuing two *extremely* dangerous threats to the glory of our Republic, and we have reason to believe they are in this area."

"I'm guessing you're referring to a 'metal god' and the runt of a man she was dragging along?"

"Yes!" the sergeant yelped excitedly. "Where did you see them?"

"Right here in my shack. The two accosted me, and said they were going to hide out inside."

The sergeant's voice dropped, though not quiet enough that William couldn't hear. "Are they still inside, good sir?"

Alyssia released him, quietly slinking around to the south side of the shack, holding up a silencing finger to William as she turned the corner with unnerving silence. It would seem she was regaining the mobility she claimed she once possessed. That was good.

Right?

"No," Jimmer answered as footsteps from presumably the corporal approached the shack. "The professor stomped off in a huff because the metal god was picking on him, and she left moments later. This was maybe five or six minutes before you arrived."

The shack door opened, and the corporal's voice answered seconds later, "All clear, sir."

"Get on the radio, let them know that we can narrow the search," the sergeant ordered. "Thank you, good sir, you did what you needed to do."

There was a long, unnerving pause that followed. William became hyper-aware of the corporal's boots, even though he knew they would *have* to be retreating back towards the vehicle, his brain was *certain* that they were coming closer, around the shack, and would discover William *any* second.

Instead, he heard the sergeant shout out in panic and three gunshots, followed by what sounded like blunt force blows and collapsing bodies. Then several more long, torturous beats of silence before Alyssia finally spoke up.

"You can come out now, boy."

Nothing quite like being ridiculed to temper the fear response.

He stomped around to front side of the shack with an indignant scowl, surprised to the point of dropping the gun that had been tossed to him as he turned the corner. "Here's your toy back," Alyssia remarked as he knelt to pick it back up. "You might just need it."

He picked it up by the barrel, the metal cold, suggesting that it hadn't fired any of the rounds he heard earlier. But both Republican officers had been disabled, splayed out on the grass and dirt path in front of the vehicle they had driven in on. The sergeant was face up, his jaw red with blood dribbling from his slack lips, no doubt Alyssia's doing, as she was the one standing over him, disassembling the weapon that he had been holding.

The corporal, judging from the pips on his uniform coat, was face down, Jimmer lording over him and watching him carefully. Had he fought *against* the Republican officers? "What... what happened here?"

"That bastard over there pulled his gun on me," Jimmer growled, gesturing to the sergeant. "No doubt to try and silence me and what I had seen. Allie here punched him out then I drubbed the little one when he tried to jump in. Damn biblehumpers."

William must have looked aghast, because Jimmer added defensively, "I live out here *because* I don't want to deal with all that religious tripe. I believe in God and all, but Jesus, it gets to be too much listening to them claim everything that makes you feel good about life is actually bad."

"Well, you're going to be in considerable danger from here, I'm afraid," Alyssia said grimly as her focus was drawn onto bullets she had spilled into her hand. She held up one, a silvery tipped bullet casing over the more dull metal of the bottom half which meant little to William. "Armor piercing rounds, very specifically designed. Someone in your Holy American Republic knows a *lot* more about my kind than than you might think."

William eloquently replied, "Huh?"

Alyssia frowned at him. "Transcendent chassis are built out of an *extremely* resilient amorphous polycarbonate titanium alloy. It requires a specific type of bullet to do more than superficial scratches. A bullet like this. These two knew *exactly* what they are hunting." She then said to Jimmer, "And when these two wake up, they'll consider you an enemy."

Jimmer huffed indignantly. "This is *my* forest, and I've been preparing for exactly this moment for the last ten years. I've *forgotten* more about it than these two fools will ever *learn*. If I don't want to be found, I won't be."

William almost didn't believe he was about to suggest this. "Would it be better if he follows us?"

Alyssia declined. "We're going to need to move fast through some very rough territory, and while I theoretically could carry two people, it wouldn't be practical or plausible in any sense."

"Where are we going?"

"No matter what you think of the Holy American Republic's capabilities, we need to remove that satellite that is tracking us. We can't afford to have it narrow down our location again. There *might* be an option to do that, presuming that what I'm thinking of still exists. Do you have a shovel we can borrow?"

Jimmer nodded, "Should be out back with some stumps I was digging up yesterday. I take it you'll need it where you're going?"

Alyssia nodded and disappeared around the shack to collect the shovel in question. Jimmer jerked a thumb in her direction, and asked, "Any idea what she's got planned."

William shook his head. "I'm not even sure she knows what she's got planned."

When Alyssia returned, the aged wooden hafted iron shovel firmly gripped in her right hand, Jimmer asked, "Where are you going that you'd need a shovel anyways?"

"To the north, towards the Great Lakes. The less you

know on that score, the better."

Jimmer's eyes crossed and he stressed the plural. "Great *Lakes?* There's only one to the north of us if that's what you're talking about."

Alyssia sighed. "Right. Ice Age probably mucked up that entire region *again*, didn't it? Still is going to be our best shot. She gestured behind her, and ordered William, "Hop on, boy. You're gonna want to hold on tight because I gotta keep one hand on this thing."

As the professor reluctantly complied, climbing onto the Transcendent's back, she asked Jimmer, "How much do you know of the land leading up to the Great Lake?"

Jimmer hummed thoughtfully, "As far as I know, it's all forest land, should be old growth too. I don't know of anyone who has seriously settled that far even as the ice melted."

"Excellent," she replied. "We'll need all the cover we can get and a little bit of luck that they don't happen upon thermals of us. Thank you for the hospitality, Chris. Best of luck to you."

"Wait... *that* was his name?" William shrieked as it felt like the words were ripped out of his throat by Alyssia's abrupt acceleration. Damn it, he hadn't even been *close*.

His thoughts were interrupted as leaves and branches smacked him in the face, marking their re-entry into the massive forest. He ducked his head into Alyssia's shoulder to avoid the worst of the lashing foliage, rather astonished at how very human-like the obviously not human "skin" was.

Such a mess of contradictions she was; so very human in many ways, so very clearly not in others.

Like the pace and movements she was making as she navigated through the massive trees of the untamed wilds surrounding them. No mere human could move with such speed for much longer than a few seconds, nor know just how intuitively which path she could fit herself and her passenger through, sometimes slipping between gaps between thick trunks with millimeters to spare. Outside of a spare branch clipping him in the head or shoulder, she was even accounting for her passenger with disturbing accuracy. She hadn't even accidentally clubbed his thighs with the shovel yet.

A hundred thoughts were whirling through his head at once, but he held his tongue, not wanting to disturb her. If precedent was any indication, she'd have to stop eventually to cool down, and that would offer a better opportunity to pry further than trying to talk over her shoulder at speed.

Of course, that meant that the professor was bored out of his skull for the next hour as the greenery and the trees whizzed by him. It might as well have been the same patch of forest for all he could tell, Alyssia merely running in a wide circle as some sort of joke.

He had to say *something*, if for any reason but to break the tedium. He settled on something that would be more easily answered. "Where... exactly are we going? The Great Lake is a pretty large area."

"To a place that *used* to be one of the largest cities in the country of my time. I'd wager most of it is underwater at this point, but there *should* still be an access point on dry land. Our final destination is a data archive that us Transcendent once had, and it was almost a hundred meters deep to begin with. It *should* have been able to survive just about anything, even an Ice Age."

"Hunh," was his only reply before he went silent again. The idea of another Transcendent 'tomb' if you will, presumably intact enough that Alyssia thought it would have useful tools to shut down a satellite, should have stirred William's interest a lot more than it did. Probably because he was more interested in what the living Transcendent in front of him had to say.

Alyssia's path deviated northwest, far longer than would have been necessary for course correction. When he finally thought to ask about it, the forest broke to reveal a mossy pond. She nudged him, and he slid off her back, the professor asking, "How did you know this was here?"

"The air humidity was starting to increase in this direction," she answered, her hand running through the murky water. "Consistent with a significant volume of water."

She then frowned, and added, "Not the cleanest, but it'll suit. I need to cool down. I must remind myself I can't run as hard and as long as I used to."

She gulped down mouthfuls of the tepid, cloudy liquid,

giving an "ah" of satisfaction after swallowing damn near a liter of water. "Here's hoping my filters are still intact!" she said, but with an air of confidence that suggested she wasn't truly concerned. "Okay, and now to purge the old water, be just a moment."

She ducked behind a tree to William's right, and he figured this was going to be as good of a chance as any to finally broach the topic at the top of his mind.

"So you were once human?"

"Yes. I thought you heard me inside of Chris's shack."

"It just… all this time, even those who have *any* idea about the Transcendent Era thought you were all sophisticated machines. There have been *papers* upon *papers* arguing why ancient humanity built artificial beings that were so obviously superior to them. But I suppose that explains why you have such human like behaviors."

He could hear Alyssia's trousers slap against the moist ground. "Quite. Actual artificial intelligence never had the personality tics of a Transcendent. There was no reason for it. Hell, other Transcendent tried to program out their own tics once they had the opportunity to alter their behaviors so easily. It had… unforeseen circumstances, and the attempts ceased."

William paused. "So… there *were* artificial Transcendent too?"

"No. Artificial intelligence never shaped out that way. Even the most sophisticated AI wasn't good for terribly much more than the tasks they were programmed for. Make no mistake, they were clearly superior to even a Transcendent *at those tasks*, but we were never able to create a truly computerized intelligence that was able to 'think outside the box' reliably. For example, we could take the most powerful chess-playing program, drop it in front of a checkers board, and not only did it fail miserably, but it also never really bothered to *learn* how to play checkers unless it was programmed with the rules to do so. AI proved to be an astonishingly incurious development."

"We never found that spark, if you will… that curiosity present in the human brain." She chuckled, then added. "It's a bit funny, really. My era *also* had this paralyzing fear of AI going rampant and destroying humanity. But AI never wound up caring about much beyond whatever task or question they were programmed to solve."

William inched on the next question very cautiously, as he was moving from the macro scale to the personal one, and he wasn't sure how Alyssia would take to being asked personal questions. "Did you have a family?"

He could hear the whistle of hot water steaming from behind as Alyssia replied, which he worried matched her anger at the question. "I assume you're referring to family *other* than my parents that you should already know about."

"Well... yes."

"I had three older brothers. They all stayed in the farming business, as I remember. We drifted apart after I left for higher education. Never really reconnected outside of occasional greetings over text message or holiday greetings. I rather suspect they resented the fact that our parents surrendered everything for *my* future. I was the girl of the family, and in retrospect, our parents probably spoiled me at their expense. But I was so resentful for their ire that I never even attended their funerals when they passed away, at ages far younger than I transcended."

William sputtered, trying to specify further without sounding like an idiot.

He failed.

"Well... I more meant... like... did you have a... family... of your own?"

Alyssia popped her head around the tree, blinking rapidly with an unreadable expression on her face. Slowly, a sly smile crept up her cheeks as she ducked back behind cover. "Hmm. I think I'll refrain from answering that. At least until you can properly ask."

William rolled his eyes, annoyed into courage if anything else. "Did you have children of your own?"

The Transcendent emerged fully from around the tree, making sure her belt was properly tightened. "I did. Two boys, then after my husband had testicular cancer, we used genetic conjunction to have a girl." Seeing his raised eyebrow, she explained, "It took stem cells from two parents, and artificially combined the genes to create a viable embryo."

"Were they changed into Transcendent too?"

Alyssia's pupil's widened, and the smile slowly vanished. "No. They... weren't independently wealthy enough to afford the process in its initial days, and by the time it had become more affordable, it was my great-great-grandchildren's generation."

Her voice turned regretful. "I... really did leave my family hanging. They were no doubt anticipating and counting on me passing my accumulated wealth down the line. Instead, I spent practically everything I had to cheat death, and left them with little."

William struggled to see how that was a problem. "If they weren't able to manage their own talents and skills, they would have likely been ill suited to manage the fruits of yours."

Alyssia shook her head. "It was more that... I detached myself from my mortal connections so very easily and so very quickly. I quite literally stopped concerning myself with my family tree by the fifth generation. People who I had seen born *before* I ever ascended. By the time that started to bother me, it had been so long that no one that might have carried my genes even remembered I had been flesh and blood at all."

"Ah, to be a god would be as much a curse as it would be a blessing," William replied, attempting to wax poetic.

"It'd be easy to say that ascending had been what detached me from my humanity... but the truth is I had lost that *long* before the quantum entanglement that put me in this chassis," Alyssia said morosely. "After a while, I think we started to believe we were ascendant from humanity. We had abolished the concept of a god... merely to replace him. Maybe that had been our intent all along, and we only become honest about it with time."

Since he was already invested in silly questions, why not go all in? "Do... or did... you really believe in God?"

Alyssia was clearly growing impatient with the questions, her eyes drifting southward, even though she had to *know* there was no real chance that anyone was close enough to pose a threat to them. "My relationship to the higher power that Western society colloquially calls 'God' is… complicated."

William knew an evasive answer when he heard one. "Did *all* Transcendent try to hide behind complex language when they didn't have a good response?"

She turned her head haughtily, crossed her arms, and glared at him out of the corner of her left eye. "Hmph! As if we would *deign* to acknowledge the question of a slab of meat to begin with. I wasn't 'hiding' as much as preparing you for a considerable amount of necessary context, boy. I would have expected someone who calls themselves 'Professor' would know that philosophical queries require considerably more than one-word replies."

William held up his hands, warding Alyssia's ire. "Okay… okay… consider me chastened."

She uncrossed her arms, and absentmindedly brushed a stray lock of hair out of her face. "The Christian faith had *hundreds* of denominations and schools of thought during my mortal life. I grew up in what was called the Dutch Reformed tradition. I… do not have many fond memories of it, but that rearing no doubt greatly informs my mental picture of what a higher power should be."

"And that is?"

"Someone who is above the pettiness of man. Someone who isn't tempted. Someone who acts with compassion and equality. Someone who possesses all the virtues of man, and none of the vices. A pure, metaphysical embodiment of the best of us." She then snorted, "Pretty unimaginative, even for a monotheistic religion, really. The pretty little lie that leaders tell their followers; promise them paradise in the next life so that they don't drag you out into the street and behead you in this one."

"Wow, rather depressing to learn how little of the church's gameplan has changed over millennia," William groused. "Sounds like you eventually outgrew that fairy tale, then?"

"I did, even before my ascendance. In a sense. I went through the entire gamut of questioning the specific dogma of the denomination of my childhood… predestination is by nature completely incompatible with free will, for example. Then I began to question the existence of a higher power at all. Spent much of my thirties quietly embracing atheism. Shifted towards agnosticism later in my life. The idea of some non-defined, non-imposing, kindly old man in the sky that somewhat encompassed an entirely inoffensive ideal of kindness appealed to me near the end of my fleshy life. It was a wonderfully tepid philosophy, suitable for an old woman. I had run the entire spectrum of Christian interpretations and couldn't have been more disappointed once I looked back at them from the perspective of a Transcendent."

"Why?"

"Because it *was* a fantasy. It *was* a fairy tale. Even my atheist phase. It was all cognitive dissonance to reinforce who I was and what I believed at the time. Observation didn't influence what I believed. What I believed was influencing what I observed."

"And you think your ascendancy changed that?"

Alyssia shook her head, "Less my ascendancy itself as much as the length of time it allowed me to live, and witness discoveries about the universe we exist in. I now feel quite confident that there *is* an intelligent design, and it is *nothing* like any religions, mono *or* poly-theistic, have ever imagined."

William was by no means a theist, or even particularly interested the slightest bit in theology. But he had to admit that he was immensely curious about this tale. A being that had actively sought to destroy the notions of a God, supposedly looked at all the information, and concluded it did in fact exist. "Alright, now you *really* have my attention. I need to hear this."

Alyssia shook her head. "Perhaps if we ever have the sort of peace where I could potentially talk your ear off for *hours,* I'll think about it. But for now, I think it's more important to keep moving."

William drew such a heavy breath that his chest visibly expanded. Alyssia didn't seem like she was going to judge him based on religious dogma, but he had to know for sure. If he didn't get it out now, he probably wasn't going to any time soon. "I'm... I wasn't born William Sterner."

Alyssia had been in the process of retrieving the shovel, then instead jabbed the spade end into the soft earth and rested her elbow on the ball of the handle. "Alright, I suppose I asked for this. Go on."

"My birth name was Katie. William was... my older brother, a staff clerk for one of the Archons, the representatives that make up the Council of the Enlightened. We grew up appreciating all the things that boys do; working with old machines, getting dirty digging up old artifacts that were found buried all over the City of Hope and its surrounding areas... that sort of thing. *That* was where I was most comfortable, not getting all dressed up and learning proper decorum or how to sing proper hymns or learning how to court a husband in a properly demure, yet seductive, manner."

Just thinking about those "etiquette" lessons made him gag even now. He tried to purge those distasteful thoughts with a shrug as he continued, "For all my life, I never felt like... a girl. *Never.* It wasn't until I was fifteen, talking to exchange students from Cascadia, that I even knew that there was a *word* for how I felt!"

Alyssia nodded. "That was not unheard of during *my* time, either. Judging from the fact that you look rather expertly transitioned, it was not knowledge that was lost during the collapse of the old world. It even fooled my infrared initially when I woke up. It took a... physical examination to realize your Adam's Apple was artificial."

"Cascadia had such procedures for decades. The Holy American Republic declared them verboten for just as long. That's probably how my brother wound up on the 'deviant' list to begin with."

Alyssia's eyes narrowed, but she said nothing.

William sniffled and tried to hold back the tears that always began to form at this part of the memory. "Then the Pope passed, replaced by Pope August II... and... well, you already know *that* part of history. But what I *didn't* tell you was that my brother arranged to have me study in Cascadia a *month* before the 'Purge of the Deviants' happened."

See, there are plenty of ways to be considered

'deviant' in Republican society. In addition to being gay, or transsexual, among many other things, you can also be a woman seeking education. You know, like Katie Sterner, making plans to learn in Cascadia when she turned eighteen because the Pope was now allowing it!"

So, imagine my surprise when my brother wakes me up one night a year and a half before I was supposed to leave, and sent me on a very sketchy caravan in retrospect off to Cascadia, explaining that I needed to be William for now because I wasn't legally old enough to travel. I learned later that the reason the documents passed muster was because they were legitimate. He swapped our names on all legal records. He knew... what was about to happen. Maybe he didn't know the precise details. Maybe he had no idea that they were going to drag him out as a public spectacle, nail him to a damn cross... and let him hang there for hours until... until he died. Eventually forgotten as merely one of thousands that the Republic made an example of over the next year while the rest of the known world just... just... fucking ignored it!"

He cleared his eyes of the mist that formed with his sleeve. Even now, remembering the details hurt him to the point of crying. His mind had taken him back to that day, looking at a television screen in the dorm's common room for five hours, unmoving save for the convulsions from sobs as he watched his brother die slowly, insistent on at least being present for every minute of the original William's final day. Breaking down, falling to his knees, then eventually face down on the common room's carpet when his brother's body was yanked off the cross and drug away.

It was only later that William learned his brother had been dumped into a mass grave, a glorified ditch with all the other 'deviants,' not even given the decency of being *buried*, their bodies left exposed to rot and be picked apart by scavengers. His grief from that point on had been replaced with rage, anger, and revenge, at points being the only emotions William could count on being able to feel as he finished his studies and began searching for the weapons that he be able to use for retribution.

One of those hopes abruptly hugged him, dropping his

moist eyes onto her shoulder. Her slow, steady breaths were comforting, even though they shouldn't be. Hell, he wasn't even sure he could *trust* this woman machine to support him, or even be ambivalent towards his personal war.

"Your anger is justified," she said softly into his ear. "What happened to your brother and others was nothing short of a crime against humanity. I hope that every person responsible pays a heavy price."

"Are you saying...?"

"I'm saying that if your account is unvarnished truth, and knowing what I do of religious zealotry I am not doubting you, I will help you find those responsible. And if death is the payment that justice demands, so be it. But for now, we need to focus on surviving long enough *to* begin to exact that payment. Okay?"

William had to acknowledge that Alyssia probably had a point. He nodded slowly as she gently stepped back to arm's length, keeping her hands on his shoulders. "I was worried, considering where you were raised, that you wouldn't be terribly empathic to my plight."

"Four thousand years ago, I might not have been," She replied. "Few of them would have been due to my upbringing. Evangelical control of America's heartland had waned considerably by my time. My disdain for you would have been *entirely* due to your flesh and lack of obscene wealth."

William couldn't decide if that was a comfort or not. "Oh. That's... a relief?"

"It shouldn't be," she said, then finally stepped away from William to retrieve the shovel, jerking her right thumb over her shoulder and pointing at her back. "Anyway, hop on. The more space we have between us and anybody searching, the better I'll feel about it."

He decided the better part of valor was to entertain her, although another philosophical question bubbled up to the top of his mind as she quickly sprinted to her inhuman pace. He figured it would be as good of an opportunity to kill time rather than stare at the trees.

"This might sound stupid..." He began.

"That's not stopped you yet," Alyssia quipped back.

"Why should it now?"

He clenched his teeth, mostly because he didn't want to admit that was a pretty good comeback. Instead, he gave it a beat, then asked, "How... do you know you're still... you?"

"What?"

"Well, you said you were transferred from a mortal body to this one. How do you know that the original Alyssia didn't die, and you just created to take her place when the quantum map flipped?"

Alyssia noticeably slowed down and gave him a patronizing glare. "Well, you were right. That *was* stupid."

"Well... I'm just..."

She sighed, and said in apology, "No. It's okay. I've never been one much for philosophy. I rather felt I was above such 'silly thought experiments,' even when I was still a fleshy being. I shouldn't be dismissive, especially since it probably wouldn't hurt to open my mind more to the discipline."

Alyssia kicked back up to speed, though said, "As for me... all I can say is that I have all the memories that I did as flesh and blood, and my current self is completely compatible to my past self. If there is some undefined magical 'spark of life' that didn't carry over, it has borne so little significance to my sense of self and those who were around me that it might as not exist at all."

"But... that doesn't bother you a little?" William queried. "You just accept that a person, their soul, is just a conglomerate of their behaviors and their memories? You don't think there *has* to be more to that?"

Alyssia dismissed the question. "If that's all that we experience, does it really matter? *I* am Alyssia Elaine Meghan Cunningham-Alvarez. That's the life I can speak to. That's the experience I can speak of. And I'm not terribly inclined to entertain anything that would imply otherwise."

William cocked an eyebrow, the philosophical question lost to the ether. "*That's* your full name?"

She scowled over her shoulder and replied "Yes. I told you it was a mouthful."

"Yikes. Are you *sure* you were born into the lower class?"

She huffed indignantly. "Before I was born, my parents fought over which of their mothers would have the honor of my middle name. They solved the impasse with both. When I decided to marry, I hyphenated my last name rather than take my husband's. After his death, I assumed my maiden name, but continued to use my married name on official documents. By the time I became a Transcendent, I had the name so long that I kept it officially. Seemed like more bother than it was worth to change it."

William chuckled, "Aww... did the Transcendent still care about those after she left her fleshy body behind?"

Another scowl was his reward. "Of course, I did. My sphere of empathy was small and shrank with every year that I was detached from humanity, but it still *existed*. It's not like I forgot how to care, or love, or feel. But I'll admit that it grew difficult to find reasons to do so."

Well... this went south in a hurry. William was at a loss on how to proceed. On the one hand, he would have liked to pry deeper into Alyssia's life. On the other, he didn't think that would end well right now. Whatever wounds those were, they were still raw.

So, he let silence rule the moment, trying to distract himself with his surroundings. While he wasn't a dendrologist or arborist or much of anything regarding plant life in general, he could even see the differences to what he was used to living in Cascadia.

There weren't few, if any, evergreens in the Baja Horn where William's official home was. While the more northern settled reaches of his home country had such trees, they were great pines, with needle-like leaves that always unsettled him, irrational fears of being skewered in the eyes by the sharp looking fronds.

Reaching out to the tip of one branch as he passed, he used Alyssia's momentum to snap it off from the tree easily, then examined the leaves more closely. These were almost more like scales, flat and broad with a waxy sheen that nonetheless didn't seem to leave any residue on his fingers.

It was a curiosity, but not something that would keep his attention very long. So he was so very happy when Alyssia finally broke the silence so that he didn't have to potentially wade into a memory minefield.

"Hey," she said. "I have a proposition for you."

William carefully regarded what that proposition could be before he queried, "Go on."

"*If* things play out as I hope they will, you might have an opportunity to take a strike against Holy Republican assets. I would like you to consider potential targets, ones that could cripple pursuit but not put civilians in danger. Can you do that for me?"

He responded so quickly in the affirmative that he worried that he had answered *too* quickly. "Of course!"

That worry was validated by Alyssia's skeptical hum as she turned her head back forward, prompting William to protest, "I can! Do you seriously think I'd kill civilians in my rage?"

Alyssia didn't even try to deny it. "The possibility crossed my mind."

"Well fine, help me out here. What sort of damage could we be expecting?"

"There are too many variables to give an accurate measurement, but what I will say is that when it was used in the past, it could potentially cause fatal damage within a radius of one kilometer. Which is why I want you to consider several targets. It'll be something for you to think about during this run rather than irritate me with philosophical nonsense."

William rolled his eyes. "Oh, all right. I get it. I get it."

It was a harder question than he would have thought. A kilometer area of effect was astonishingly large, far greater than any weapon outside the theoretical fission bomb that Cascadia would build if there was an aircraft capable of carrying it. It also meant that a direct shot at the Pope was out of the question. The Papal Palace in the City of Saints was surrounded by tens of thousands of people and common workers for the Church. All of them would be within a kilometer.

Same would be true for the Military Foundry on the outskirts of the City of Hope. A large chunk of completely innocent people would be in the radius. That and despite his loathing of the Republic, he didn't like the idea of attacking his birthplace.

He knew of smaller outposts along the border that could potentially be bothers on their retreat... but those really weren't worth a one kilometer weapon and would likely only draw reinforcements on that path. He vaguely remembered a base outside of the Red River Outpost as his team was being vetted and cleared to begin digging where Alyssia had been found, but he wasn't sure how large it was or how significant it was to the Republic.

He had a map in his pack of various points of interest gleaned from Cascadian intelligence he could consult, but that wasn't of much help right now. It would probably provide additional options if he couldn't think of one off the top of his head.

William had to acknowledge that it worked to the effect that Alyssia had wanted... because it took him several seconds to realize that they had reached the edge of the forest and that the light in the corner of his eyes was the evening sun. He only became aware of where they were because Alyssia had stopped running.

"Any idea of the air capabilities of the Holy American Republic is?" Alyssia asked, her eyes scanning the skies.

"Similar to Cascadia's really, from what I understand," William answered. "There are some planes, but their range is usually extremely limited. Why?"

She pointed out of the forest, in the direction of a steep sandy slope that led to the water line of the Great Lake. It was in fact a breathtaking view, the increasing orange of the sky reflecting on a body of water so large that it extended as far as his sight allowed from horizon to horizon. His eyes told him this rivaled the ocean back home in Cascadia, even though he knew that couldn't *possibly* be true.

Alyssia stated. "Because where we need to go is out in the open. We'll wait a couple of hours here until nightfall, then I'll start to dig. Hopefully it's still intact."

"What is?"

"The access point we need. It's *considerably* closer to

the water line than I would have liked, but mercifully it's not submerged. That would have dashed a lot of hopes really quickly."

"An access point to *what?*"

Alyssia seemed to ignore him, her eyes staring off into space straight ahead to the north. "About five kilometers out into the lake... there was one of the largest and greatest cities in the country during my time, Chicago. At its height, it held nearly six million people."

William boggled at the number. "*Six* million? El Asilo, the capital of Cascadia, *might* have crossed the *one* million mark recently, and I've always thought of that as huge."

"Would you believe it wasn't even the largest city in the country during my time?" Alyssia remarked. "Wouldn't have even been in the top *twenty* throughout the world at the height of human population. But it *was* a hub for business, and eventually became a center of Transcendent investment and knowledge. It also became a hub for the revolutionary forces in the final days of Transcendent rule. *That* is the knowledge we'll hopefully be able to tap into tonight."

"Revolutionary forces?" William asked.

Alyssia rolled her eyes. "What? Did you think a legion of extremely wealthy people who thought themselves *gods* simply surrendered their power and let humanity collapse? Surely, an archaeologist such as yourself would have come across the devastation we left behind in the geological record."

William's eyes flashed open. The assumption had always been that the Ice Age had somehow caught the Transcendent unawares. Even the Church didn't record any specific rebellion or revolution against the Transcendent. But he also should have guessed sooner. Alyssia hadn't been at all aware of the Ice Age, merely regarding it as a possibility. And now that she effectively pointed right to the clue, he got it immediately. "The black, carbon rich band that corresponds with the Transcendent Era..."

"Well, *part* of that was the result of actually peaceful intentions," Alyssia noted. "But yes... the people of the age called it 'Operation: Broken Glass.' No doubt ground over the years into powder and mixing with the high carbon soil, the result of weapons capable of fusing atoms and melting the ground into a glassy state."

She looked directly at him, then finished, "You were right when you thought that multiple factors led to the collapse of human society. But what you didn't know was that the disasters were entirely self-inflicted. In fact, I suspect it is quite possible the Ice Age was *caused* by the disasters we inflicted on the world."

William shook his head, more to try and sort out the jumble of information that just bombarded it more than declining. "Why are you telling me all this now?"

"Firstly, because we have some time to kill," Alyssia answered. "Secondly, because I plan to use some of that knowledge developed during that time. One that will theoretically resolve that satellite watching us *and* deal a significant blow to the Holy American Republic. It was first devised by the rebels, who seized underground technology sites to launch their attacks much like the one under the city. They learned how to drag our communication satellites out of orbit, use their nuclear-powered thrusters to increase their speed through the atmosphere to the point that it survived re-entry long enough to detonate with a shockwave that could hit targets a full kilometer away."

Alyssia laughed bitterly, "Such a simple tool, turned into a weapon that rivaled a fissionable, with the electromagnetic pulse particularly devastating to Transcendent. It was the opening salvo of the most terrifying war in human history.

"So... I want to ask you one more time. With that in mind, are you *still* sure you want to tap into the knowledge my era wielded?"

William shrugged, "Hey, if you can trust me with a target, I really should trust you with the choice of weapon, right?"

Alyssia shook her head. "It's not a matter of trust. I'm doing this out of necessity, and it makes sense that we weaken our enemy *while* we blind them. But I *do* worry that it'll once again spark a war that doesn't end well for *anyone*."

"If you're having second thoughts…"

"Just bringing down the satellite isn't going to be enough," Alyssia admitted solemnly. "We must incite chaos as well, disrupt their ability to put together a hunt. We will… most likely be required take further steps beyond this."

William put a hand on her shoulder, "If the alternative is to give up, then we move forward. We'll worry about any further steps when we have to take them. Maybe we'll reach a point where the option is so monstrous that it's not worth it. We can give up *then*, not before."

Alyssia didn't seem entirely convinced, but also didn't seem eager to argue it further. "Perhaps."

"Help me understand," William asked. "Help me learn how it went so wrong in the past, so that I can try to avoid those mistakes in the present. You said yourself we have some time to kill."

She responded with a patronizing look. "It would take a *lot* longer than two hours to get through that."

"But you can start."

The Transcendent sighed and threw up her arms in surrender. "Oh, very well. Maybe there *could* be something useful to be gleaned. Just bear in mind, I'm not some neutral observer in all of this. I won't be unbiased, no matter how much I try to be."

"It's better than ignorance," William insisted.

She grunted in annoyance, and dropped down swiftly, crossing her legs in the same motion. "Might not hurt to take notes. I know how you historians are, and I have no intention of repeating myself."

William was already diving into his pack for a pad and paper even before she had suggested it.

Episode Four: The Lost City of Chicago

Alyssia was rather starting to regret agreeing to the history lesson by the time night fell. For a few reasons, really.

The primary one was because it was a *long* lesson. She had only *just* gotten to the part that she personally could attest to by the time the sun had fully set and she felt confident in the cover of darkness. But that led to a second concern; being too close to said history to report it correctly.

That said, if she didn't, there was no one else who could.

And it helped distract her from the monotony of digging. So, there was that.

It didn't help that the earth was *very* wet, somewhere between solid dirt and mud. Each scoop of the shovel felt like two steps forward, one step back, as mushy slop spilled from the edges of the hole she was attempting to dig and partially refill what she had shoveled out.

William offered to help, albeit reluctantly. "Do you... need me to dig for a little bit?"

Alyssia tried very hard not to roll her eyes. "I do not tire in the way that humans do. I am physically capable of digging as long as needed."

He nodded, putting the blunt end of his pen in his mouth thoughtfully. "Then, are you willing to continue with your recollection? You just finished with the American Discord of the Twenty-First and Twenty-Second Century, as I recall?"

She exhaled in resignation. "Yes. After the massive relocation efforts that took the better part of a decade and shuffled approximately one hundred and fifteen million people to different parts of the country, the end result of the civil unrest and sporadic violence was effectively a multi-state solution underneath one weak central government. States largely had complete autonomy except on any proposition that could be agreed upon by all fifty-three states in the country. The

Supreme Court could only hear cases regarding interstate commerce or legal jurisdiction. The Federal level was almost completely gutted of any real authority. The President at the time declared it 'a triumph of American cooperation and compromise.'"

William nodded, jotting down the relevant quote. "I assume the people didn't agree?"

"Of course, they didn't. Both sides *hated* the compromise with a loathing they normally reserved for each other. By the point the compromise came about, 'compromise' wasn't in *anyone's* desires. They wanted 'total victory' over 'the enemy.' Which was why it really shouldn't have been much surprise that the country, rather than coming together, fractured further, and caused even greater resentment."

She snarled at a rather bothersome root that was in the way of her shovel but shifted her voice back to normal as she spoke again. "Interstate pacts quickly formed, which rather tipped the hand that *neither* side really had a problem with a strong central government, merely that they had a problem with a central government they couldn't control in perpetuity. And when some pacts started thriving while others languished, it was setting the powder for yet another detonation.

"The southern and central states claims that their 'free enterprise friendly' and 'anti-immigration' policies to entice capital through low taxes and few regulations never really materialized. While the wealthy certainly housed their wealth and some operations in the heartland, that wealth remained stagnant, never actually dribbling into the hands of the citizens. Outside of the state of Texas, who quickly decided that they weren't interested in a pact with their poorer neighbors, the southern states plummeted even further into poverty and despair, amplified by the fact that those states made nothing more than the barest minimum effort to aid the millions who came during Relocation... leading to a homeless crisis that fell on deaf ears and an insistence on self-reliance.

"And when Texas finally *did* decide to join an interstate pact in 2190, but with the Pacific Coast Trade Agreement rather than its southern neighbors... that was the end of hope for America's 'flyover country.' They became increasingly authoritarian at state and local levels. They refused to allow people to leave for other states, while refusing anyone who didn't meet very specific and - to be perfectly blunt - racist standards to enter. It created an isolationist and increasingly antagonistic culture which didn't endear themselves to anyone who might have been able to provide aid."

William hummed, then asked "And if I remember my notes correctly, you were already a Transcendent by that point, yes?"

Alyssia confirmed. "Four years earlier, though all of us Transcendent were keeping a low profile at the time. While Green Future's headquarters and primary operations had always been in Indiana, I wasn't much better than any other big capital investor that had carpetbagged their way in to take advantage of low taxes while never actually having a presence there. And to top it off, as we were practically immortal, the heartland and southern states weren't even able to take advantage of the meager estate taxes that they imposed. Meanwhile, the federal assistance that many people counted on dried up with the lesser tax obligations that the Federal government once applied to wealthier states and cities. It created millions of people hungry, homeless, and increasingly desperate.

"They found what they deemed was an easy target in their neighbors. Coastal states, forming the Pacific and Atlantic trade pacts, had flourished. Because while the heartland and south were where the oligarchs stashed away their money, they *invested* in those posh metropolitan coastal cities, even during the climate change concerns. The differences were often visible within human eyesight if you lived in towns at certain state borders. You could look across the border from Oklahoma to Texas, towards a city that not even fifty years ago you'd be able to visit without incident, see the lights and hear the hum of air conditioning, while you were lucky to live in walls made of basically cardboard with thirty-five-degree temperatures by mid-day. Oh, excuse me, you never actually adopted the metric system, so you still thought it was ninety-five."

She finally managed to break off the troublesome root after a series of carefully aligned strikes and scoop it out of the wet earth. "So, you have a desperate populous, all of them sitting on small stockpiles of firearms, and what they perceive to be an easy target - filled with whatever gross bigoted slur you want to come up with - that has everything they want. Guess what happens?"

It would have taken a true imbecile to not connect the dots Alyssia laid out, and as much as she picked on William, he wasn't stupid by any means. "They raid those border towns on those other side."

"Very good! In November of 2195, four raids across the border by 'militias' in Utah strike in Colorado. There's just one slight problem. The defenseless targets they're assuming are on the other side aren't. The Colorado Army, buoyed by support from the other states in the trade pact, had been anticipating exactly this sort of violence since Texas joined their ranks. It's a massacre. About one hundred citizens of Utah are butchered by well trained and far better equipped paramilitaries."

William tries to defend the action. "Understandable, though, isn't it? It's not their responsibility for the deplorable conditions across the border. These were armed raiders that by your own telling were filled with violent, racist, and bigoted sentiments about anyone outside their borders. Who knows who they would have harmed or killed?"

"And if *that* had been the end of it, you might have been right," Alyssia replied. "But you're forgetting the resentment and loathing cut both ways. In the face of 'lawless aggression by their deplorable neighbors,' the Pacific Coast Trade Agreement officially becomes the Allied Pacific States of America, declares their independence, and invades Arizona, Oklahoma, and Idaho in a wholescale military campaign that kills over a million people in three days. The raids on Colorado had been the excuse the Pacific states had been looking for to commit a complete genocide of those they deemed 'backward reactionaries.' There was no mercy. Men, women, children, drug out into the streets and butchered, if they weren't blown up in their homes by missiles and drones, at least. About the only thing the Pacific States *didn't* use was nuclear weapons, because apparently *that* was the point of no return, I guess."

Try as she might, she couldn't keep the spite and sarcasm out of her voice at that.

She regained her even keel to continue. "At that point, the United States of America was finished. The Federal government didn't have the power to muster a defense, and several states on the Atlantic Coast also splintered off to form The Democratic States of America in what had been New England and the Northern Midwest. It took the United Nations and a coalition of twenty-two other nations to finally end the massacre in 2201, but only after eleven million people had been killed. And *maybe* justice would have been served if a worldwide crisis hadn't emerged in the months after."

"And what was the nature of this worldwide crisis?" William queried, even though she could still hear him furious scribbling notes from what she had just told him.

"Russia and China decided that in the wake of the United States collapse that they could begin to exert *their* imperial designs."

"They joined forces to try and take over the world?"

Alyssia laughed. "No, they tried to annihilate each other *while* trying to take over the world. China and Russia for centuries had been very reluctant allies, an 'enemy of my enemy is my friend' sort of scenario. Without the United States as a common economic or military foe, they went right at each other's throats to try and become the next global superpower. Russia quickly pulled in all their economic 'influence' in Europe and the Middle East to balance the scales against the far larger population and economy of China. At least, until the European Union dissolved entirely and broke down into sectarian conflict between Western Europe, deciding now was the perfect chance to 'get even' with the United Kingdom, and Eastern Europe breaking down into tribal grudges that went back centuries.

"Even the former United States got into it from a limited perspective. With the Pacific States siding with China, and the Democratic States siding with Russia, they had several skirmishes in the decimated remains of Middle America and even some dust ups in Canada, which brought the Canadians into the mess as they tried to defend their neutrality and interests.

"From 2204 to 2210, the entire world was embroiled in a series of loosely connected conflicts between groups of people that finally had enough of each other and wanted to see them dead. Welcome to World War Three, one that *wasn't* resolved before nuclear weapons could get thrown about."

"I assume those weapons were far more powerful than the fissionable weapons that Cascadia has?" William asked.

"Uranium fission, I'm guessing?" Alyssia replied, momentarily pausing her shoveling. She was a bit disturbed to learn that Cascadia apparently had nuclear weapons of *any* type, though she supposed that it was certainly possible with the level of sophistication she had gleaned from earlier discussion.

William nodded. "Yes. Considering how our own nuclear reactors were built on the fragments of knowledge we were able to recover from the ruins of pre-Ice Age society, and there was a great deal of what we salvaged that we couldn't *begin* to comprehend, much less replicate, we figured that your time must have weapons far more devastating."

"And you'd be right, boy," Alyssia said, glowering before returning to her work. "*My* time was at the fusion energy point, with weapons thousands of magnitudes stronger gram for gram than what you are no doubt working with. Just the fallout from the weapons being *deflected* by defense systems caused catastrophe. Four launches turned Japan and Korea into rubble, and the atmospheric damage dropped irradiated rain onto much of the Eastern Pacific for years after.

"That was when a collection of Transcendent decided the time was ripe to take matters into our own hands before the conflicts could escalate further. It actually started *here*, as the fragmented former United States were looking for *anyone* who could restore the land to its former glory. Initially, I rejected a political presence, choosing to be a financial backer while contenting myself with rebuilding an agricultural infrastructure. Others, like Pederson Teal - that's a name you're going to want to highlight and underline a few times - jumped into the mire with gusto."

"Who was that?" William asked.

Who indeed. After thousands of years, Alyssia wasn't exactly sure how to answer that question beyond the simple facts. She had witnessed much of his rise firsthand, and it still didn't seem to make much sense. "He had been an investment banker and later a venture capitalist. Superficially, he would have *never* left you particularly impressed to meet him. He was the sort of person that the common man scorned; born into money and spent most of his life doing little other than using that money to make *more* money. Those who *liked* him would say, 'the next hard day's work he puts in will be the first.'

"But what he *did* was fund the research and development that would become the Transcendent people. As a result, he became obscenely wealthy. There was a point where he was the wealthiest person on Earth several times over. In a society where money talks, he could speak loudest of all. And when he finally did, the world as we knew it shook.

"Tremendous amounts of money went into rebuilding the damaged and fragmented nations within the former United States. Within months, from sea to shining sea, the United States of America seemingly rose like a phoenix from the ashes, the union restored, with a military machine that had been spared the worst of the worldwide conflict.

"Europe, desperate for a western power to emerge, quickly realigned with a familiar face on the international scene. China and Russia, ravaged by the brunt of the Third World War, offered little resistance as the old order reasserted itself. American Opportunism had once again paid 'glorious' dividends.

"It was a mirage of course, within a century, Teal pulled off the covers by announcing who he was and what he had become. He declared himself Supreme Ruler of the United States, and abolished all but a Transcendent Council who would rule in all matters, legislative, executive, and judicial. And nary a citizen even batted an eye. Teal and his fellow Transcendent were heroes, saviors of the world, having 'saved us from ourselves.' Surely, we could be trusted *far* more than the emotionally driven flesh bags!"

William nodded absentmindedly, more to demonstrate he was still paying attention. "Obviously that wasn't true."

Alyssia huffed before saying, "Considering we had our hands in many ways in the events that caused World War Three, yes. We used our absolute rule to re-establish our position as the elites of American society, creating a new Gilded Age that would never die... because well... we weren't going to.

"But of course, we couldn't be content with just one country. No, we Transcendent were a class all our own, one that didn't need or respect borders. Remember how I said we empowered revolutions throughout the world? *That* was the result of a long game that took roughly two *centuries*, slowly eroding faith in human institutions and suggesting ourselves as stable, long-term alternatives. This was *hardly* a new strategy, but with the benefit of timelessness, we could use it on a much longer scale that took several generations to manifest, which made it near impossible for anyone to see our fingerprints in the subversion."

Her lecture came to an abrupt halt as the tip of her shovel struck metal with a loud clank, and at about the depth her sonar bursts had suggested. Scraping the shovel across the surface to confirm it was flat metal and not merely a part of a rock or stone, she was satisfied that her previous scanning proved to be correct; a mostly empty space was behind what was now clearly a bulkhead. Thank God for that. She really didn't want to have to go sonar searching again through this muck.

"Alyssia?" William asked, looking up from his notepad, no doubt curious why she had stopped talking.

"Hush," she snapped. "I've found what I'm looking for. Give me a moment to clear it out."

She probably should have thought about the hatch being almost two meters wide *before* she started digging, but she had to admit the silence was nice as she started heaving massive clumps of wet dirt over her head.

Her diagnostics started to flash yellow from the strain on her joints, and she snarled at the reminder that this chassis wasn't as stable as she had hoped it was. She already learned *that* little bit of info during the run through the woods, and *those* warnings had been in the red. While her chassis was self-repairing, her inner workings were only regenerative to certain extents and needed routine maintenance and replacement.

Which probably wasn't happening in today's world.

That didn't bother her as much as it would have earlier in her life. She was just rather playing out the string now, so to speak. Help this little terrorist for as long as she could, and in the process perhaps one of the many enemies she was about to make could finally end a life that should have ended four thousand and ten years ago.

She immediately chided herself for being mean. William had *very* good reasons for wanting revenge, and she really *didn't* doubt his telling of events. It tracked remarkably well with what she knew of religious institutions, especially those that crossed into theocratic nations. In truth, she felt *horribly* for him, as transgendered people were one of the *many* "others" that the religions and governments of her time used to give their followers an "enemy" to fight. It seemed *that* trait hadn't changed.

And it would *hardly* be the first time she had thrown herself into a "war" with the church. Hell, at least this time she'd have good intentions behind it.

The self-analysis was a decent enough time-killer, as by the time she had sorted out where she currently stood, the thick hatch had been completely uncovered and enough space scoured out for her to open it. Even if she didn't feel fatigue in the same was as she used to, it was a wonderful feeling to drop that shovel and watch the yellow warnings in her periphery slowly fade away.

Not that they weren't going to pop right back up very soon anyway... but it was nice to have the reprieve.

"Alright, best to get down here, boy," Alyssia said. "If you want, we can continue the lesson as we go in, just bear in mind that this place wasn't built with *nearly* as much care to long-term sustainability. You probably won't be able to take such studious notes with what is assuredly going to be rough footing."

William clumsily dropped the short distance to where she had dug. "I would have figured that something from thousands of years ago would be deeper. Your facility was fifteen meters deep."

Alyssia shrugged. "That particular facility was built mostly underground to begin with. Only the top of the dome of the greenhouse was above surface level. Couple that with what is likely erosion from the expanding lake, it's not surprising at all that this entrance wouldn't be buried too deep."

"I... suppose," he replied, not sharing her certainty. He dug into his bag, located his breathing mask, and fixed it over his mouth and nose, giving Alyssia a thumbs up gesture to continue. She snorted in amusement that of all the various random gestures that would survive near extinction and thousands of years... that would be one of them.

She knelt to examine the hatch. If she remembered this design correctly - and there was no reason to think she didn't - there was a panel directly in the middle that needed to be pried off to reveal the pressure release, in this case a raised square piece of aluminum, slightly dented inward no doubt from ages of pressure from above, on what would have been at one time an airtight seal.

Normally, it would require a very specific tool to release the seal, but Alyssia was betting her strength and a seal weakened by time would allow her the purchase to simply pry it off. She grabbed the panel by its edges with her right hand, her fingers resting on the bevels of the slight raise in the metal and hoped that would be enough friction for her strength to do the rest.

Instead, it came off so easily that the unexpected lack of resistance caused it to fly from her hands with exaggerated force as her arm jerked upwards. The only reason she knew it came down as all was the assurance that gravity still worked, and that she heard it slap down on the moist earth somewhere behind her three seconds later.

"Don't know my own strength sometimes, I guess," she said with humor, before addressing what she had revealed. Now the metal bore a circle depression with a black rubber ring, and an aluminum handle running across the diameter and level with the hatch itself. This was the pressure release that kept the hatch closed, but she *expected* this to be rather easy to open outside of potential rusted or corroded mechanisms. Any pressure behind it had no doubt leaked out *long* ago.

That much proved correct. The handle popped up rather easily when she pulled and rotated ninety degrees from a lateral orientation to a vertical one with barely any trouble. As expected, the seal didn't even offer the slightest hiss as it separated from the outer rim of the hatch, and outside of a loud creak of unused metal the hatch popped open easily, revealing a rusted ladder down.

"I'm not going to trust that, and you shouldn't either," Alyssia advised, pointing at the rusted out rungs. "I'm going to jump down, then catch you."

She supposed she wasn't surprised that William didn't immediately buy into that idea. While she had sonar telling her vital information, he no doubt just saw a deep black hole with no defined bottom. "You want to do what now?"

"It's only five meters down," Alyssia insisted. "And I'd rather just catch you straight away rather than trying to catch you panicking and flailing when that ladder inevitably failed to support even your weight."

Even with that reasoning, he looked at her like she had just asked him to skip out into a busy freeway.

"Fine." she said with a defeated shrug. "If you *insist* on climbing down on your own, you go first."

That got him to reconsider, though he still added with a grumble, "It is *always* going to be your way or no way while we're on this damn fool escapade?"

She winked playfully. "Only when I'm right. Not my fault that I'm going to right *far* more often than I'm wrong."

And with that, she pressed her arms into her sides - unnecessarily, in all honestly - and with a short hop disappeared through the open hatch.

She hit the ground a hair more than one second later, yellow warnings flashing in her peripheral vision as knees absorbed the force of landing, and she sighed audibly. Arguably the second biggest flaw in the Transcendent design was the inability to turn those damn warning signals *off*.

Bracing herself for what was coming, she called up to the top, where she could see William quite clearly peering over the hatch, unable to see her. "Alright, boy. Jump down!"

William, however, insisted on being a baby. "Are... are you sure?"

"Yes! For God's sake, I'm giving you five seconds, then I'm moving on without you!"

She watched him shuffle nervously, and so much like she used to do with her children, she took a stern voice and started counting. "One... Two... Th..."

Finally, William threw himself feet first through the hatch. Not the best way he could have done it, but Alyssia figured she couldn't be picky for him doing what she asked. It did require some careful weight distribution to keep him from hurting himself and ruining his trust in the process, and she had to do it all in a little under one second.

Her left arm looped under his thighs as he was less than half a meter from the ground, scooping out his legs and drawing him towards her, redirecting his momentum as her right arm slipped under his back to catch him. It was quite impressive, if she didn't say so herself.

The result of the maneuver was something not unlike a dip, with Alyssia cradling William like they had just finished a dance. She said playfully, "Hunh. Usually, this sort of thing is the other way around, no?"

William's glare looked like it could have melted rock. "Let me go."

Alyssia was about to drop him rudely for his tone, until she abruptly realized her misstep. For someone who wanted so desperately to be a man, it was no doubt triggering to insinuate they were still in the woman's role. "I'm sorry... I didn't mean for it to be taken that way..."

The professor squirmed, and repeated, "Let me go."

So rather than drop him, she helped him gently to his feet, and exhaled nervously. There had been a time where she couldn't have given one tenth of one shit about who she offended; back in an era where she had been richer than God and everyone in her circle tiptoed around *her,* careful with their words and dismissed her crassness as just her "Indiana flavor."

It had been a very distressing lesson, learning just how easily people could be hurt with words, especially unintentionally.

William dusted himself off, unnecessarily, and nudged Alyssia back on track. "So, I assume we follow this hole to our destination now?"

"Hole" was a pretty good description of where they found themselves honestly. Unlike the halls of Green Futures, the tunnel that the revolutionaries had cut was not *nearly* as neat, done with a balance of haste and discretion. Any support built into the tunnel had long since rotted away, if there had been any to begin with. Finally the rough cut of the walls, with no small number of still prominent gouges in the bedrock visible from what had been some form of drill, promised at least partial blockages that would have to be worked around.

And judging from the washed-out sediment on the floor, they might be looking at partially or fully flooded segments. "Ready for some more digging and/or swimming?" she asked darkly.

"Not terribly, but I doubt I'm going to have a choice," William answered, rolling up his sleeves to the elbow. "Lead on."

She did so, silently, not wanting to broach the topic on her mind. She found herself preferring William prod her about history again rather than have her unintentional insult hover in the air.

After three minutes of that silence, descending through the surprisingly deep and slick grade downward, William groaned in exasperation, "Are you *really* scared you insulted me? Girl, I've heard *far* worse, intentionally, even in the more welcoming environment of Cascadia. I wasn't annoyed about what you *said*, I was annoyed because I don't like being held like a damn baby."

"Girl?" Alyssia said, her boldness peeking out once more.

"If you can call me 'boy," then I think it's only fair I call you 'girl.'"

She scoffed. "I am over five thousand years old. Every

living thing on this *planet* outside of *maybe* a few trees is going to be a child to me."

"Fine. Old woman," William retorted. "If you *insist* on accuracy..."

"Oh.... I see what you're doing. Taking advantage of my guilt to demean me in the way I've been picking on you." But for once, Alyssia decided the best part of valor was to concede defeat. "And it's going to work, damn you. Revel in your victory, boy. Those will be rare."

William's grin damn nearly spread from ear to ear. "Oh, I intend to... old woman."

She allowed herself a slight smile, then shook her head. "But *don't* push it," she warned, letting William's chuckle go unanswered before trying to resume her increasingly treacherous decline. "Mind your footing. It looks like it's going to start getting slick."

But her treacherous mind wouldn't let her look forward so easily. Even as she tested her footing for her next step, she had to ask, "So... you're *not* angry at me?"

William sighed in annoyance. "Believe it or not, I'm more than able to discern the difference between an innocent flubbed joke, and a malicious barb. Most people are."

That wasn't *her* experience, but she wasn't going to press that issue; especially since she deemed examining her footing was a more pressing issue. It still wasn't *horrible*, but the last thing she wanted was to be arguing something trivial as the ground went from merely damp to slick.

Although the fact that the ground was damp was a curiosity. There didn't seem to be any water dripping down from below that would be causing this, nor anything that would explain the flow patterns that she was seeing under her feet.

William yawned audibly, and Alyssia frowned at him until she thought to consult her internal clock and discover it was nearing two in the morning by her reckoning. While she wasn't sure at all how modern humanity told time, she had to figure William had been awake for an unusually long time.

And then, an idea of where the water could have come from hit her. The hatch hadn't been *that* far from the shore. The seals were practically non-existent. And the combined water of what had once been five very large freshwater lakes would lend itself to a *very* significant tide.

"We have to move." Alyssia said, her voice not allowing for any negotiation as she grabbed William's right forearm. "Get on! Now!"

"What? Why?" He asked, baffled by the sudden shift in her tone, but at least trusted her enough to follow instruction *while* complaining rather than *after*.

"The tide is coming in!" Alyssia shouted as she sprinted forward, trying her damnedest to ignore the red flashing borders of her vision advising her not to move at this rate of speed, "And I don't think we want to be here when it comes in force!"

While it was entirely possible that four thousand years had shifted the timing of the tides, that wasn't a risk that she wanted to gamble on; especially since she had no idea how far it would be to reach safe ground... or if there even *was* safe ground.

That would be a rather depressing way to die, honestly. Flooding for a mechanical being really wasn't much less terrifying of a death than drowning was to a flesh and bone one. She abruptly considered turning back and retreating the way they came in, but the first rivulets of water starting to hit the decline suggested that was not going to be a very good idea. Even if the seals weren't going to leak torrents of water, there were going to be a *ton* of issues getting back up the way they came, things that she had figured they'd have plenty of time to sort out on the return trip.

Forward was the only way to go. Forward, and a quiet prayer that whatever God was out there would have a little mercy.

Her footing was in fact getting increasingly perilous, as a thin sheen of water had finally caught up to her, even at the rate of speed she was going. That was *not* a good omen for the amount of water that was leaking through the hatch, and that it was almost assuredly going to get worse.

What *was* a good omen, at least potentially, was that the tunnel hadn't been completely flooded from the start. That suggested to her that the water was going *somewhere else.*

Granted, it could be going into a massive chasm that would be impassible even at the height of her glory, but she decided she had enough things to worry about right in front of her to be worrying about pitfalls in the future.

Like running at full sprint down a water and sediment slick incline. A machine-precise balance correction system only went so far; for example, when the human dug tunnel shifted its grade in an unpredictable fashion, not even a correction that reacts in microseconds was enough to overcome gravity and oddly distributed weight.

Alyssia decided to take it on the chin, quite literally, as she didn't want to lose her grip on William. She met the ground flush with an impact that could have easily knocked the wind out of a human being. And even with her chassis absorbing the brunt of the fall, William still wheezed once his weight landed on her.

None of her warning systems liked that much at all.

The pair skidded further down the decline, Alyssia doing what she could to steer by shifting her weight. It helped in some small ways, like to prevent rolling down and creating a tumble that could lead to some serious damage; less useful when the tunnel took a sharp turn and they both collided into the tunnel wall.

At that point, any hope of controlling their descent was impossible. William was thrown off by the collision, and the violent spin that Alyssia was thrown into as she bounced off the bend made sure she wouldn't be of any help either.

There was a time where the world spinning like this would have made her physically ill as her eyes vainly tried to make sense of the smeared environment around her. *That* would be one thing she'd be eternally grateful for transcendence, no matter how awful everything else was. Motion sickness could go to hell and stay there.

Granted it was little comfort currently, but presuming a gruesome death wasn't in the immediate future, it was nice that she wouldn't look back after everything stopped spinning and saw spirals of vomit following her travel path.

Her face smacked against the tunnel wall again, and her momentum carried her up the rounded curve of the cut before flipping her and dumping her onto her back. At least she could confirm William had still been conscious up to that point, as she faintly heard his grunt of pain as her heel smacked his head when she landed.

Now, whether he was *still* conscious or not was another matter.

Their descent finally and mercilessly ended ten seconds later by Alyssia's clock, and if it hadn't been atomic powered she probably wouldn't have believed it, because even to her it felt like a *lot* longer than that.

She hit *something*, her sonar blipping with readings of a tremendous depth momentarily as she found herself tumbling again, this time rapidly rolling to a stop as the path started a slow incline upwards. Once still at long last, the first thing she observed was that *this* ground was far less damp, to the point that discernible grains were sticking to her arms as she pushed herself up to her hands and knees.

"Ally?"

William's voice got her attention, the archaeologist about two meters back, slowly standing and wiping dirt vainly off mud-soaked trousers. "Are you alright? I can only imagine you took some hard bumps there."

She noticed the slow dribble of blood that started at his hairline, mostly redirected off his right eyebrow, then down his cheek. While she knew that head wounds often looked worse than they really were, they could *also* be a lot worse than they looked. "*I* took some bumps?" she argued, pointing to where he was bleeding.

He dabbed his fingers over the cut, examined it indifferently, then shrugged it off. "Believe it or not, this wouldn't be the first time I cut myself open. You get used to the sight of blood when you spend most of your day digging through, around, and over rocks."

"That... wasn't from when I kicked you, was it?"

William shook his head, "No, that's where I got the headache. *This* I probably received when I smacked headfirst into what I think was a crack in the tunnel floor. If I had to wager a guess, it's probably where the water goes after it leaks through the hatch you were so worried about."

He jerked his thumb over his shoulder, and where Alyssia was able to confirm the sonar mapping that had been compiling during her fall. To her credit, the chamber below *was* immensely deep, three hundred and seventeen meters to the water level, and another two hundred and sixty in water depth.

Of course, not even a beanpole like William was likely to fall through the less than one-hundred-centimeter-wide crack in the tunnel floor, nor managed to twist himself into the jagged three meter long "S" shape to slip through the gap. That the crack also seemed to have no trouble handling the water flowing into it like a rather lazy creek was quite literally insult on top of injury.

"I had no idea how severe the tidal drain was going to be at the time!" she exclaimed, attempting to cut off any wry comments from her companion. "Besides, there's no way of knowing what given day could experience a catastrophic failure, and half the damn lake is going to want to pour into here!"

William's response was expectedly patronizing. "Of course."

"Fine, if you want to just stay right here content in your safety, you'll probably be right," she snarled. "I, on the other hand, plan to keep going."

Alyssia very deliberately stomped forward, now on the incline, trying to ignore how the squishing sound from her shoes were rather killing the vibe of her angry steps.

"Hey!" William said soothingly, "For what it's worth, I think it's charming to know that 'metal gods' can make erroneous judgments. The church's stories loved to paint your kind as nigh omnipotent and omniscient beings."

Alyssia huffed, "That was a picture we loved to paint *ourselves*. In truth, the only thing that our 'higher level of consciousness' gave us was the ability to make dumb choices faster, as you just witnessed."

A jagged edge that required a high step to clear got William wondering, "Why is this tunnel so... messy? All these twists and turns and bumps and ups and downs? This feels like a hand dug mine shaft."

"Because it was," Alyssia answered. "In order to avoid

detection, the rebels literally spent almost a year digging their way in by hand, having to correct every so often because they weren't using anything like GPS or sensors that us Transcendent or our allies could detect. They masked their tunnels to look like old utility hatches, like the one we went through earlier. They picked facilities that we had abandoned or had archived to keep from our most direct scrutiny."

"How did this rebellion start?" William queried, and she looked back to see him trying to flip through his notepad using what little light was available with his lamp tucked under his left shoulder.

Alyssia grinned ruefully, both at the invoked memory and the struggles of her historian tag-along to chronicle her words. "Ironically... with the church; or more accurately, the multitude of religions that had flourished throughout the world by the time of our rise. Most of us Transcendent had a... strained relationship with most manners of faith even during our mortal lives, and while we *claimed* we had no real desire to meddle in matters of religion, it didn't take long for even the most common of folk to see how we would butt heads."

She paused to let that sink in. "Organized religion had been losing membership and influence even before the rise of the Transcendent, and it didn't take terribly long before we became a near and present threat to their existence. After all, it's hard to sell people on a nebulous concept of eternal life after death provided you live a very specific way and eschew all other potential paths when there is an agency offering eternal life *in this world,* provided you're willing to kiss enough ass and step on enough people along the way.

"But even then, it took nearly three hundred years for the animosity to manifest violently. And it originated in what was once Saudi Arabia, where a Sufi leader named Mirha ibnat Mohammed successfully overthrew the Transcendent ruler of the region and eventually claimed the city of Mecca as the seat of her new caliphate, and eventually declaring herself the reincarnation of their prophet.

"It proved to be a lot harder to unseat her and her army than we expected, especially since the divisions among various religions and sects we expected never manifested. It became clear to us that even sworn enemies of faith considered *us* the greater enemy, and that we needed to squash it."

"Unsuccessfully, it would seem," William groused.

Alyssia confirmed, "Indeed. We thought our plan was clever; the same sort of long game that had worked so effectively for the general population. We imposed 'perfectly reasonable restrictions' first, like no religious debate in 'public places.' Then we imposed laws forbidding public worship. Then laws forbidding any public expression of faith. We started what was effectively a 'bounty' on religious leaders, offering credits that would go to a Transcendent conversion for those who gave us accurate information that stamped out resistance. Within about two hundred years of Mirha's insurrection, the institutions had fallen from grace, the holy cities were abandoned and crumbled. We *thought* we had succeeded where so many other regimes in ages past had failed."

"How were you wrong?" William asked.

Alyssia answered, "From my assessment, two distinct things happened. Firstly, even a 'short-lived' species will be able to suss out the long game if it's played for long enough. Generational memory is a thing; the great-grandchildren will notice when even after four generations, none of them have enough credit for the eternal life that had been promised hundreds of years ago. They'll remember when the system starts to turn on them for expressing dissatisfaction. Ironically, Transcendent fell for a bit of a long game ourselves; and we never really understood the resentment building against us until it was too late.

"Secondly, we underestimated religion's ability to survive. We... were ignorant of the fact that pretty much *every* major religion *started* as an underground movement and were more than capable of doing it again. Disaffected mortals quickly found an ear, targets for their resentments, and a central structure that gave them the means to start striking back... much like they did with tunnels such as these.

"This, what they called 'Skyfall' was merely the first salvo in their revolution. Even though we adapted quickly, with new bodies resistant to EMP's, the operations all around the world did what they needed to do. It pierced our curtain of invincibility. We were no longer immortal beings as if unto gods. We were just really old people that could be killed like anyone else. Even with some desperate measures to bolster our numbers, it was effectively twenty thousand Transcendent, about two million transcended thralls, and *maybe* half a billion loyal followers against *twelve* billion potential enemies. The odds were not in our favor."

She then noticed the end of the tunnel, and said, "But that... will have to be another lecture for another time. Because the fall of the Transcendent will be an even longer tale than the one that led to it, and we have reached our destination."

The tunnel had ended at a crudely cut hole in what was a curved exterior wall. Alyssia stepped through, momentarily blocking William's light as he tried to shine it inside. Not that there was terribly much to see other than exposed rusted metal and some shelves filled with boxes that was supposed to house physical documents, but now having been exposed to the elements were tattered, decayed remains at best upon rusting shelves.

"Here's hoping the rebels left *other* parts of this archive in better shape than this," Alyssia remarked, running her hand across one shelf and seeing the grime from fungal spores on her fingers. "These were meant to survive thousands of years without maintenance... but the breach here might have done more damage than I anticipated."

"They targeted places like this *because* they weren't as studiously monitored by your people, as I recall?" William said.

She nodded. "Indeed. We didn't think that there was much anyone would want. We built these basically as repositories for our knowledge, to remind us of how far we had come. At best, we accessed them remotely maybe a handful of times a year. We came physically far less than that. If *anyone* came here in person, it was some low-level staffer updating physical records. But the rebels didn't come here for knowledge, they came her for a back door into our satellite networks to perpetrate their 'Skyfall' attacks."

"It was one such attack that killed Pederson Teal, and

set off a string of on-again, off-again conflicts that would consume the rest of the Transcendent Era, prompting the usage of weapons that I hope are never even *dreamed of* again. Which is *exactly* why I have *no* intention of even *mentioning* them. Not to you, not to anyone."

William replied defensively. "Yes, yes, I get it. I got it the first time. Honest!"

"And that also means no trying to dig through the debris hoping to find something still legible," she warned, turning about abruptly. "First of all, I can assure you nothing on these shelves survived. Second of all, anything that *would* have been on these shelves was benign information like census data and plant diaspora."

William jerked his hand back from the shelf on his right like it had been slapped. "Never crossed my mind!"

Alyssia huffed, then spun back forward, grabbing William by his right wrist and tugging him along. "Of course not. Now this way, hurry it up."

She led him through two more long rooms of what had been shelves of documents, and into the core of the archive. *This* was where the most important stuff was kept, in a chamber the size of a stadium. The roof, built with thick criss-crossing titanium alloy, continued to its job, despite the weight of a lake and all the bedrock above it pressing down for hundreds of years. Her biggest worry coming here had been that the increased weight of Lake Michigan increasing in size would have been too much for the archive to bear over time.

Her attention then turned to the rows of hundreds of one meter wide and nine-meter-tall towers of memory banks mounted inside the chamber. They looked to be in remarkable condition, with only very thin layers of dust staining their once jet-black casings. It was a good omen that they had least *physically* survived the years despite the rebel's breach.

Whether or not they were still *functional* was another matter entirely, and there was no clue to be found in the banks themselves. While it was true none of them blinked with the rows of neon blue lights that would be present if they were active, there was no reason for them to be so at this point. They were *meant* to be in a powered down state most of the time, after all.

"Good God... how many of these things are in here?" William asked in awe, his hand running across a side bar at shoulder height on the casing of a server to his left.

"Three hundred and seven," Alyssia answered. "It could fit another hundred or so at full capacity."

"I don't think I can imagine how much collected knowledge lies within these things."

She shrugged, "Not as much as the size of this archive would suggest. It's really one bank with three hundred and six cloned backups." Observing William's incredulous look, she replied smugly. "We designed things with longevity in mind. As a result, we *really* liked redundancies. This was merely one of thousands of archives around the world, all of them having the same data."

That wasn't *entirely* true, of course, but it was true enough for anything William needed to concern himself with. He wouldn't have been interested in what little proprietary information was stored in "public" archives like this.

"We don't particularly need anything in here," she said, waving him along while she recalled where they needed to go. "But it's a good sign for us that they are still in good condition. It suggests the place we *do* need will also be intact. Follow."

She grabbed him by the arm again when he didn't immediately comply with a stern, "Now," then pulled him along like he was a stubborn puppy on a leash. She swiftly moved him southward, actively ignoring his questions as they passed row after row of inactive data towers. At the far end of the chamber a single sliding door barred the way, one that easily surrendered to some good ol' Transcendent "muscle," and opened the way to the decontamination room that connected to the generator room.

Without power, this wasn't much more than an elaborate ten-meter hallway, with a half cylinder of dead lights that ran from wall to wall. William asked her what that was all about, and she dismissively said, "You'll see on the way back... hopefully."

Forcing the opposite door open, they were finally in the control room, which really wouldn't have looked like much even during the days the facility was in use. A rather long but narrow room, twenty meters long but only about five in width and another five in height, with a line of unremarkable gray concrete wall tooling around on the standing consoles in front of them.

Granted, on the other side of that ten-meter-thick wall was a small fusion generator capable of powering a city like Chicago, but without any such knowledge, a visitor probably would have been otherwise oblivious of the power on the other side.

On both sides of the door, white plastic consoles were fused directly to the wall on single piece stands that jutted out and left the blank displays at an angle that could be adjusted manually with nothing but a small dial on the right side of each stand.

"Normally, if we had sent an agent to look into a powered down archive, they'd have a small battery that would jolt the system awake," Alyssia explained as she knelt down to pop open an almost invisible panel on the stand three centimeters from the bottom of the display. "But obviously, we don't have such a battery, so we're going to have to improvise."

She rolled up her shirt, then the skin around her generator port retreated to reveal that said port on her chassis, nothing more than a two-centimeter slit about where her navel would have been on her mortal body. "If I wanted to, I could pop out the entire H3 disc using the adaptive port here. Pretty neat, huh?"

Of course, William attached to the wrong thing. "H3?"

"Tritium. The preferred fuel for fusion reactions."

"You... have a fusion reactor inside you?"

Alyssia hummed at the question, which really didn't have a simple yes or no answer. "In a sense. Certainly nothing like the controlled chaos of a *true* fusion reactor that could have tens of thousands of reactions every minute and power entire cities. One of *those* is on the other side of this wall. What *I* have is what amounts to an atomic hallway which occasionally fires one pair of tritium atoms from the normally inert disc, and that *single* collision on average once a day recharges a more traditional battery that powers me. While that battery can be recharged any number of ways, most Transcendent rejected them as a way of proving they were truly disengaged from their vulgar human pasts."

While explaining, she pulled out an eight-pin plug, connected to four red and four black wires, and plugged it into the slot underneath the inactive console. "Now... we give it a second and see if we can light this candle. There is a *lot* that could have gone wrong in four thousand years, after all."

It was true that the Transcendent designed things built to last a *very* long time even without routine maintenance, but theory and reality were rarely the same thing by Alyssia's experience. So even she was surprised when the symbol for her company appeared on the display within seconds of receiving the jump start, followed quickly by pure white accent lighting along the edges of the room that easily overpowered William's lamp.

A holographic keyboard appeared under her hands, but she eschewed it for the touch screen for the moment. Even after all the years she had lived, she never really got used to holographic keyboards. The tactile feel mattered to her in ways it shouldn't have.

It was another ten seconds before she was informed that the main reactor was still functional and asked if she wanted to begin startup. She tapped the "NO" button and proceeded into the main menu. While running the entire thing through her own battery wasn't *ideal*, it was far better than trusting that a fusion reactor capable of beginning the carbon cycle had suffered absolutely *no* faults after all this time, no matter *what* the computer says.

"So... this is all we need?"

"For now," Alyssia answered as she looked through various directories. Before she did anything else, she wanted to make sure that her followers all those millennia ago had obeyed her on *one* score, since they clearly had been picking and choosing what instructions they followed. After several deep searches under several parameters, she was satisfied that her people had done at least *that* bare minimum.

Then with that concern settled, she got to the task of locating the specific program that the rebels had used.

Contrary to what her fellow Transcendent had thought for so long, they didn't particularly "hack" anything by adding programs or even particularly altered an existing one.

They just used an older version of a program that was stored in the data towers, then used the network connection that the Transcendent used to remotely update said archive to their bidding. AlphaNav, the worldwide satellite tracking and adjustment tool. The only thing they really did inside the program was disable any of the warnings or correction protocols that prevented them from inputting a vector that smashed the satellite into Earth.

She then learned they *also* changed the name of the program for reasons she didn't understand, which meant she had to scroll through an entire list of archived programs and check preliminary data to find what she was looking for. Even with her processing power, that took far longer than she would have liked.

"Allie?"

Alyssia tried to ignore that William was already using the more familiar version of her name. Granted, she had offered it, but she hadn't thought he'd be so comfortable around her so quickly. It annoyed her in a way that it rightfully shouldn't.

"Working on it," she grumbled, giving him a baleful leer out of the corner of her eye. Even at this juncture, there were a couple of things that could go wrong. While *she* had rather unwittingly been able to connect seamlessly to a completely unknown satellite, that was no guarantee that this ancient program would be able to do the same. On top of that, this program would have to interpret GPS data in a way that was quite likely alien to it. "It's probably going to take a while to get all these things speaking clearly to each other..."

And then a holographic display popped into existence directly above her console with an apparently accurate map of the current continent of North America within seconds with what appeared to Alyssia's reckoning as updated markers for settlements, towns, and cities.

"Or they can start communicating damn near instantly," she quipped darkly.

To say that was odd would be an understatement. Even *if* the Holy American Republic based their development on the fragments of Transcendent technology they had uncovered, there should have been *no* way that they'd be able to communicate so seamlessly so very quickly.

It confirmed her theory that the Republic was *far* more advanced than they were letting on. *Someone* was updating Transcendent software and doing so rather frequently over the last four thousand years. There wasn't exactly many options as to who could have been doing it, and none were particularly plausible.

A random segment of humanity that managed to maintain their structure and advancement wasn't likely. Surviving over four thousand years in complete solitude without *ever* being discovered by humanity at large seemed implausible to the point of impossible.

And while there were *plenty* of AI in orbit during the height of the Transcendent Era, and all it would take is one of them to survive all the perils of orbit to keep nigh mindlessly updating everything in its data banks... surviving *this* long wouldn't be on her "remotely probable" list. Nor would any AI be adjusting programs to keep them compatible with other technology on its own volition.

Not that the final option was any better...

"Allie?"

She growled at William's intrusion. "I'm *thinking*."

He winced and took a step back. "Sorry. I... just..."

She shook her head to clear the thoughts away. She could waste time pondering things when she *wasn't* powering an entire historical archive. "No, it's okay. Let's pick a spot and get me unplugged from this thing. Provided you even *know* what this landmass looks like..."

Now it was William's turn to glare before turning his attention to the display. "I do, for what it's worth. I *have* seen images from orbit. Cascadia *does* have satellites as well."

Alyssia started watching William intently as he examined the map. In a more perfect world, she'd have a baseline of his behavior and biometrics to be able to compare it to and discern if he had any duplicity in mind. This was *not* a perfect world, however, and she resorted to looking for any obvious signs that he had duplicity in mind.

"Can... we magnify this map any?" He asked.

Alyssia nodded, then with a sweeping motion of her arm slid the hologram across the wall until it was in front of William. "What you'll want to do is point with both hands on a point on the map, then spread them apart, and that *should* give us a closer look at the image. I can't say I'm entirely certain the level of fidelity of the satellite we've connected to."

That answer turned out to be "pretty damn high fidelity," as William complied with those instructions, and what had been a full continent view turned into roughly a ten kilometer square on what would have been northeastern Missouri, with a distinctly human compound in the lower right corner of the image. William then focused on that, magnifying *again* to the point that individual buildings, like three large tarp covered pavilions and what looked like a radio tower, were discernible.

"There," William said confidently. "That is MacArthur Depot, the primary frontier base for the Holy American Republic. Our team identified it as the biggest roadblock to our escape from enemy territory because of it's location and proximity to any of the black market trade lines that run through the frontier. We won't just be helping ourselves taking this out, but also the rest of my team."

Here Alyssia was trying to determine how sincere William was, and the evidence of it was staring at her in the form of an obvious military operation. It all so wonderfully fell into place, as long as she continued willfully ignoring that it was confirmed using technology that really shouldn't exist if William's telling of current society was accurate.

She isolated the base, confirmed the coordinates, then started looking into the satellites themselves. Three of the seventeen that could be identified, including the one she had connected to when she woke up, were in fact Transcendent Era orbital data stations, and had indeed been updated repeatedly, as she suspected.

That worked in her favor, because she knew *those* had the mass and density needed to survive re-entry and strike with the amount of force that would disrupt, if not obliterate, their target. And so, it was a matter of calculating the proper vector to make that happen.

"This isn't going to happen right away," Alyssia explained as she tapped in the final commands. "It's in fact going to be about three hours before the satellite will be in position for the proper attack vector. So, we've got a bit of time to kill."

She gave it a bit of thought, then said, "Hey... wanna see something that might be cool?"

William gestured to her waist, where she was still plugged into the console and providing it power. "Are... you going to be okay doing that?"

She hummed playfully. "Yes, I must say that I've already expended about fifty years out of my battery doing this. That probably *would* be a problem if I still didn't have approximately one thousand, six hundred, and ninety-three years left even at current consumption. Hell, my current chassis wouldn't even hold up for an eighth of that."

If she was lucky.

He then relented, "Well, then if you're offering..."

Alyssia zoomed the map out as far as she could. "Now then, let's just see how good of a eye we've got on the world, shall we?"

Alyssia was both surprised and yet not surprised that it wasn't much. Surprised because she figured if someone had been making sure Transcendent technology was being maintained and updated that they'd have more coverage... but at the same time not because there probably wasn't much population to try and keep track of.

"There was a time where we could literally see the individual hairs on a person's head on ninety-nine percent of the world due to tens of thousands of very high-fidelity satellites in orbit," she said, gesturing up to the map, and the bands of lighter color that identified what could currently be observed. "Now, as you can see, it's less than ten, and most of *that* is centered on this continent. But... as you can see, not *every* satellite the Holy American Republic has up is locked in a geosynchronous orbit."

She spun the map, the projected globe now displaying the Eastern Hemisphere, and thin streaks of active data cutting across what was Asia, Europe, and Africa. These ones were clearly newer, cruder satellites; they were lighter, smaller, and weren't providing nearly as much information, which confounded her further. If the Holy American Republic had the ability to maintain current Transcendent satellites... why were their newer ones not even in the same stratosphere?

Metaphorically *and* literally.

She could understand *some* limitations, but it still wasn't adding up. There was someone... or something... else at play in this crazy new world, and she had the feeling she needed to find out what and stop it, because if she knew anything about shadow agents, they *never* had the general good in mind.

Just what she needed. Another *personal mission.* Because the last one turned out oh so wonderfully, after all.

Alyssia forced herself to focus on one step at a time. She couldn't even *begin* to hunt down the technologically savvy agent or agents until she eluded whatever pursuit the Holy American Republic was mustering. She spun the image back to North America, "So, boy, what exactly should our path of retreat be? You can draw a line by tapping the hologram once, then drawing your finger across the map like a pen."

William did so, drawing a line that went through what went through Central Illinois, Iowa, and Nebraska "There's a black-market route here, because it runs through relatively recent thaw, and thus isn't populated. My team was going to reassemble and take that route ourselves. We'll almost assuredly miss that deadline, but there's no reason we can't travel that way ourselves. For it being 'black market,' people taking it keep to themselves. They don't want to cause trouble and draw the attention of the Republic."

He then drew a line through Wyoming, Idaho, and eventually into southern Oregon. "We have two options once we hit the mountains. The path of less Republican resistance lies through the mountain pass and towards the Winema Permafrost Trading Camp, the western end point of the international black-market line. We'd break off a little before that end point at the thirty-nine-five route, and into Cascadia proper and eventually into El Asilo. This is actually a perfect starting point. If I recall correctly, this lakefront beach is a part of that route that allows for a connection to the Acela Commonwealth. We literally just need to follow it west."

William's finger returned to the western United States, down through California to a point almost directly on top of what was once San Diego, which looked to no longer be strictly a coastal down thanks to the lower water levels of the mini Ice Age. Alyssia supposed it made sense, and no doubt explained where Cascadia gained a lot of their second-hand knowledge. That entire region had served as one of the Transcendent seats of power and had been spared the worst of the war with the rebels, and possibly had remained relatively intact through the worst of the Ice Age.

He then went back to the original stopping point and started drawing a different line roughly following the path of the Rocky Mountains south through Colorado, New Mexico, and Arizona. "However, there's a possibility that the Republicans will try and block that route through the mountains if they think we're going that way. This way is much more open with more space for the Republicans to have to patrol, but it leaves us in their territory for longer. *If* I can get a satellite connection myself out in the Permafrost, I'll *try* to send a long-range message to my team or someone in Cascadian Intelligence to figure out the best way to go."

"Not a good idea," Alyssia said with a shake of her head. "Do you *not* see what's in front of you? She zoomed in on a random spot in North Dakota just to make a point, the image showing astonishingly clear detail of individual leaves on the trees. "*Someone* in the Republic has eyes *this good*, even in the middle of nowhere. Sending a long-range radio communication might as well be lighting a huge beacon saying, 'here we are, come get us.' We go radio silent, end of story."

William clearly did *not* want to believe the evidence in front of his own eyes. He didn't want to believe his enemy was capable of prudence; that they wouldn't near mindlessly use any tool or power they had simply because they had it. It was commendable that, unlike most of the human race, when faced with information that contradicted his world view, he eventually embraced it rather than dig his heels in. "Very well. Radio silence it is then. We'll make the call ourselves as we get closer to the junction."

She finally unplugged herself, the console going black along with the rest of the lights in the room, and she grinned impishly at William's scowl as he scrambled to turn on his lamp again and turned it directly into her face. "Well, we have about three hours to kill. Why don't you take a nap and I'll poke you when it's time for the show?"

William blinked, "Here? Why not outside? Weren't you worried about the tide?"

"We'll be well out of any danger on that score before it potentially sweeps in again. Besides, we are simply too far away to see anything, even me with magnified eyesight. I'm going to plug back in and watch what happens right from the cameras on the satellite itself to confirm it hits its mark. Now go on, get some sleep. You have no idea how many opportunities you'll have in the coming days."

He behaved something akin to a petulant child, trudging himself to the farthest corner from where Alyssia was waiting, glowering at her in annoyance and proclaiming he wasn't *that* tired. She knew better, of course; her scans of him were showing significant adenosine buildup, and so she wasn't the slightest bit surprised when the young man was passed out within minutes despite what couldn't have been a terribly comfortable position, slumped backward, with his neck tilted forward, and the base of his neck wedged in the corner.

Oh well, that could be *his* problem.

But with some time to kill as well, Alyssia decided to dive a little deeper into the world beyond the oceans, looking for some signs of life beyond this wretched band of North America. Plugging herself back in, she kept the lights off, and transferred the display directly to her HUD so as to not interrupt her sleeping companion.

The first thing she noticed was that there weren't any satellites from her era active anywhere other than in North America. That was... both comforting and disquieting. It meant that *if* anyone survived in other parts of the world, that they either didn't have the ability or desire to appropriate or utilize Transcendent technology. Which was good.

But it *also* meant that *someone* or some agency had actively woken the ones above North America up. Which was bad.

There was a part of her that thought it was incredibly stupid to wake up any herself and potentially flag her position to anyone who would be able to figure out where she was based off that. But another part of her decided it was worth the risk. She needed to know if humanity survived elsewhere.

She looked around old population centers that she felt might have had survivors, starting with the Mediterranean, close enough for the waters to have a stabilizing effect on the chaotic climate and Transcendent ruins that could entice exploration from survivors.

Barcelona. Montpellier. Rome. Podgorica. Istanbul. Izmir. Tel Aviv. Khan Yunis. Alexandria. Tripoli. Tunis. Algiers. Rabat. Never lingering long on any satellite; just long enough to do a wakeup, take some long-range photos, then shut them back down again, hopefully before getting any outside agency's interest.

Then she examined the images she took more closely... and found nothing. Well, not *exactly* nothing, but nothing that showed any particularly large populations mulling about old Transcendent dominated cities, or even signs that *small* populations were taking interest in them.

She moved east, thinking that the Persian Gulf may have had some opportunity for survivors. Kuwait City. Dommam. Doha. Abu Dabi. Dubai. Even though those lands got hit hardest in *two* catastrophic wars, she figured it was worth a shot.

And found nothing.

Either the people were actively avoiding places where the Transcendent made their greatest mark – which would run completely contrary to the curiosity that humans have always possessed – or there simply weren't enough survivors to linger on to this day.

Even less likely spots *also* came up empty, along the

Indian Ocean, Australia and New Zealand, the Pacific Islands. She told herself none of this was conclusive proof that humanity was gone from elsewhere in the world; merely that they weren't where she thought they should be. But it would have been nice to have found a clue of something out there.

Then she decided she'd take one even *longer* shot.

Even at the *time*, it was considered an insane exhibition. But Zucker Fayersden had refused to be deterred. He built himself a "generation ship," constructed with "the best materials" and "most cutting-edge technology" of its age, and five years before the inglorious end of the Age of the Transcendent, he took his followers and left this "dying rock" to find "a new, better world" out beyond the stars.

It was arguably the smartest thing he had ever done.

He had targeted the TRAPPIST system, as deep space research had discovered that system to have *two* Earth-like planets. Theoretically, with the ion propulsion that had been developed, they *could* have theoretically arrived at that system *and* sent back some sort of signal that they had done so.

So, she dove into the Deep Space Transmitter logs... and discovered that the craft had suffered a critical drive fault fifty years into their flight, the last distress calls to Earth falling on deaf ears.

Alyssia sighed. That had been one depressing way to spend three hours, and she suspected it wasn't about to get any better.

She unplugged long enough to cross the room, and rouse William with a gentle kick to the right shin. The archeologist yelped in agony like he had been stabbed, clutching his leg and glaring at her.

"Oh, stop being a baby, boy," Alyssia said. "It's time for the show."

That *did* get him to shut up and focus, betraying only one large yawn to suggest he had been in REM sleep moments before as he joined Alyssia back at the terminal as she plugged in for the third time, and brought up all the lights. He didn't even flex his neck like she expected he would, to work out the stiffness.

The wonders of youth, she supposed.

It was a quick process to access the satellite in question and issue the instructions that would prompt its abrupt descent. Then it was a matter of changing the display to match the optical camera on the satellite so that William could see the strike in real time.

Not that there was terribly much to see. Atmospheric entry clouded and distorted much of the view, and there was barely a handful of seconds between the fire of atmospheric re-entry and the fire it created when it impacted that turned the entire display black.

"There you go, boy," Alyssia said dryly. "One slap to the face of your enemies."

William nodded in approval. "Good. That *might* paralyze them a little bit. They're going to want to send an investigator to determine if that was an accident, act of terrorism, or an act of war. That *might* take the heat off us, especially since that base would have been where a lot of our pursuers would have been issued from."

Alyssia unplugged herself from the terminal for the last time, killed the lights, and waited for William to flip on his flood lamp before she moved towards the exit. "Let's hope you're right, boy. Because we've loitered around this sunken city too long as it is."

Episode Five: The Hand of the Archon

Miles Parker paused at the stone archway that separated the Halls of the Enlightened from the rest of the City of the Saints. It was the first time he had been here in half a year, and he was astounded at how little seemed to have changed.

Not that he should have been. By all accounts, the Halls hadn't had any significant revision or redesign in decades, and hadn't even undergone any major renovation in the two hundred some odd years since its construction. The same white stone mined from the gulf and fashioned into bricks formed the arch and exterior wall around the Halls' perimeter, a brick dutifully scrubbed twice daily to combat discoloration.

The wall itself was tall enough to obstruct the view of the halls from damn near anywhere in the city, like the governmental activities that occurred inside was some secret the layman had to physically and visually separated from.

A pair of imposing reddish stained oak double doors, trimmed with bronze, blocked further entry until Miles checked in at the security checkpoint embedded into the wall to the right.

Miles didn't recognize the guard, a middle-aged man with a poorly trimmed mustache, like his hair had migrated from his forehead to his lip. This really shouldn't have been a surprise. There was a *lot* of turnover in the various security details, even among the Capitol Guard.

Nonetheless, he was still irrationally annoyed when said guard looked him over and said, "I need your ID and for you to back away from the counter."

Forcing back his indignity before he lashed out, he instead adopted a tight, narrow smile over his clenched jaw and placed his badge on the counter, then took two broad steps backward to the point that his heels were precariously close to the edge of the curb. It was so blatantly passive-aggressive that even *he* rolled his eyes mockingly at himself.

The security guard took the badge with a narrow glare, toned muscles tensing with annoyance as he took it over the counter and examined it far longer than was necessary, his eyes frequently flashing between the picture on the badge and Miles himself. At least the Capitol Guard still had high physical qualifications, if not social ones.

Who was he kidding? The Capitol Guard *never* had social service standards.

"This doesn't look like you," the guard sneered with naked contempt.

Miles found that funny more than insulting. Mostly because the usual complaint was that people like him all looked alike. He dipped his hand into his right pants pocket, and pulled out a mobile phone, the small brick of black plastic something that only a handful of people had the right to possess, and the security guard would know it.

"You're funny," Miles finally said, his voice nonetheless not showing any humor as he waved the phone next to his right ear. "Should I call one of the Archons themselves to let me in, then? I'm sure they'd enjoy *that*."

Miles wasn't lying. The Archons would no doubt be *very* annoyed... with *him* for being so incredibly petty with a security officer who was admittedly just doing his job, even if in the most combative way possible.

But the guard didn't need to know that.

Mercifully, the bluff worked as Miles had hoped. With a heavy, dramatic sigh, the guard said, "Oh, alright, Mr. Parker. Here ya go." He slid Miles's ID back across the counter. "Just trying to have some fun is all."

Right. *He's* the one put out by all of this. Miles forced himself to smile as he reclaimed his badge and clipped it to his breast pocket. With a genteel voice that was the exact opposite of what he was feeling replied, "Think nothing of it. I've been a bit on edge. Not right to be taking it out on you."

Miles received a tight, unconvincing smile in response, then the guard slapped a large orange button on the wall facing the doors. A metallic thunk sounded through said doors, corresponding to the automatic lock dropping back and allowing the doors to swing inward.

He didn't wait for them to fully open, stepping through with a lazy salute to the guard the moment he had enough space. The guard *might* have said something to the effect of "have a nice day," but Miles had already banished the man from his memory at that point. He had more important things to worry about.

Like finding his way to his meeting.

From the courtyard surrounding the interior of the main building, it wouldn't have looked like anything had changed in six months. The same cherry trees dotted the perimeter, the branches starting to show their pink flowers now that the weather had finally warmed enough to encourage it. It popped in contrast to the dark green bluegrass and square slabs of sandstone that framed and connected each tree. He remembered being enraptured by the blooms the first time he had come to these halls ten springs ago.

But he couldn't afford to get lost in small pieces of nature today. Apparently, he had been summoned for something important.

Miles wasn't exactly sure why *he* had been summoned. If the last six months had told him anything, it was that the Archons wanted him as far *away* from the Halls as they could possibly manage. He wasn't sure what could have possibly changed that would make them reconsider.

He forced himself forward through the courtyard, and the main building. It was everything that the papal palace was not. Where the home of the Pope was a towering construction fifty floors high made of alabaster, bronze, and gold that could be seen for miles, everything in the red brick constructed Halls of the Enlightened was found on three, and one of them was a basement level.

A more honest person would say it's a result of the conservative sensibilities of the Archons, and a desire to keep their activities from the prying eyes of the public. A more cynical person would say it was a representation of how much power over society each branch held.

It was no secret that the Church, and the Pope specifically, set the tone for how the country would be governed, and any executive power granted to the Archons to enact that vision was by the Pope's discretion, and that different Papal leaders had *very* different levels of discretion.

The previous Pope gave considerable leeway. The current one... well... didn't. And that was a source of considerable ire for Archons that had been nominated by prior papal leaders. Of course, they were a minority at this point, so their ire meant less than the nothing it would have meant before.

Three gray stone steps upward led to the landing just outside the halls, covered with a stone arch painted white marked with a curved gold plate along the front face that declared this to be the Halls of the Enlightened.

Because, at this point, a person entering needed that reminder. Just in case everything else leading up to the entry hadn't been enough of a clue.

A small black box was mounted to the right of mahogany double doors, with a solid red light as its only distinguishing feature, a light that momentarily turned green when Miles waved his ID badge in front of it. That prompted another clank as the locks disengaged and allowed him entry into the building, swinging open automatically, and giving him little time to step through before shut with another thunk of the lock.

The interior of the complex expressed the same inoffensive generic wealth as its exterior. He stepped across a plush crimson red floor mat, then onto blue-white marble floor, studiously waxed to the point that it crisply reflected the faux-candle lights on the red-brown stained oak walls, mounted on curled bronze stalks and masked with frosted translucent white shields. The shields were a new addition. Last time Miles had been in the halls, the lights had merely been tipped by glass blown in the shape of a candle flame.

The main floor was split into quarters, with this hall connecting in the middle with another one that formed a cross that connected each section. To the east was the public facing section, where official business for citizens was done. To the west were the minor offices of affairs and the accompanying staff.

He took to the right side of the hall, per proper decorum, and started the long walk towards the junction. Two lady staff turned the corner as he approached; the gray, long skirt and long sleeved uniform dresses that covered everything from the wrists to the ankles and red shawls informing him they were from the Department of Housing and Home Development.

The one to the left had a half step lead, an older woman with curled graying brown hair and a face that was starting to show signs of wrinkling. Miles would have guessed to be in her early 50's, with a confident stride that betrayed considerable experience walking these halls.

Miles couldn't recall meeting her, but that didn't tickle his curiosity, as even when he had been actively investigating, he barely spent more time here than he absolutely had to. There were probably *many* people who had been working here for *decades* that he had never seen.

The second was a face he recognized. Meghan was a much younger woman, early twenties, if Miles remembered correctly, notable because she was in many ways the personification of "traditional" Republican beauty. Hair and eyes of milk chocolate, skin of alabaster, and a perfectly "heart" shaped face, frequently courted by anyone who could get the opportunity.

It was probably why she didn't take a submissive posture towards her senior colleague. Her shoulders were back, her head up, and her steps full; very much not what was common among younger women in this building, who were normally expected to be demure.

The pair took the turn at the intersection wide, so that they were on his side of the hall, then immediately shifted to the opposite side when they realized his presence, like he had some sort of invisible forcefield, then muttering quietly to themselves once he past.

This was not a particularly new thing, but his annoyance from it was. Not too long ago, he would have dismissed that passing interaction as merely giving him the due respect of his station or correcting themselves quickly after realizing their mistake, and not wanting to get in his way. Now, he knew better.

Yet another reminder in what seemed like an hourly series of reminders that he wasn't "one of them," and not just in the obvious way. His lot had been cast with the losers of the most recent war for God's favor, and not by his choice.

Miles forced his mind off it and went straight through said intersection. Directly north was The Assembly, an adjunct domed building connected to the main hall. That was where the Archons would meet to deliberate on policy and laws, or issue judgments in major trials that could not be resolved by lower courts. He had only been there once, and the experience had *not* been pleasant.

Thankfully, his path turned at the stairs that flanked both sides of the hall that connected to The Assembly. Less thankfully, he wasn't sure that he was going to have any better of an experience upstairs.

Instinctively, Miles took the right-side stairway, made of the same shining marble as the floor, making sure he avoided touching the brass railing, sticking his hands in his pockets to prevent the urge. That, much like staying to the right side of any hallway, was literally written into the code of behavior in the Halls of the Enlightened, for reasons Miles had never bothered to query about or consider. Mostly because he doubted the answer would be satisfactory.

His shoes clicked with each footfall on the steps, an oddly satisfying sound, though he couldn't explain why. It was also a short-lived delight, as his feet dropped onto burgundy colored carpet at the top, and met by two armed Republican guards at attention holding their rifles in an shouldered position, sidearms on belts on their hips with open clasps, wearing military fatigues and combat helmets complete with shaded visors that obscured nearly all of their facial features.

Because one never knew when enemies of the state would appear without warning in the middle of one of the most visible locations in the whole of the Holy American Republic. Had to keep those guns at the ready.

Despite the aggressive loadout with openly carried weapons, they were far more easily appeased than the guard at the gate. The guard at the right hand side barely even glanced at Miles's ID before waving him through with a respectful nod, and the one on the left quickly followed his partner's lead, leaving Miles to enter the Archons' Offices without any meaningful delay.

The floor had a very different feel than the prior one. Where the ground floor was of sterilized wealth, the offices for the Archons felt more like the administrative wings of the academies he attended, with dark brown walls cut with reliefs of the seals of the Various Archons, and brass chandeliers providing a golden glow to the surroundings.

The entire floor was dedicated to the seven Archons and their supporting staff, with each section nigh entirely self-sufficient. Each Archon had at their disposal a fully staffed kitchen and dining area, private and "public" restroom, library, lounge, balcony, and if Miles remembered correctly, one of the Archons had a hanging garden, and another had a spa. About the only thing these suites didn't have was a bedroom, and Miles didn't want to bet money against *one* of the Archons carving out space for that.

The seven suites ringed the floor, with a communal center chamber, which Miles had to enter to reach his destination. It was spartan by design and intent, the Republic wanting to dissuade Archons from mingling outside of when they were called to serve in The Assembly; the law of the land wanting their judgments to be as unbiased by the leanings of their colleagues as possible. Miles doubted that worked even *remotely* as intended, but that was the stated reason.

Three circular, bare pinewood tables were spaced in an equilateral triangle on red and black checkerboard carpeting, and a single chandelier providing illumination in the space. It was so undesired as a location that only one person was in the chamber, sipping a steaming liquid as he leaned against the southwest corner in a sharply pressed navy blue ministry jacket and slacks, reading a book that from it's cover was a critique of the First Letter to the Thessalonians. Miles doubted that it was for anything other than pretentiousness, as he doubted there was enough to critique to even fill a book that was at least four times longer than the letter itself.

The ministry aide looked up from his book just long enough to give an appraising look, then a curt nod, before looking back down like Miles didn't exist. Whoever the aide was trying to impress, Miles wasn't it. Not that Miles particularly had time to debate the Apostle Paul's First Letter to the Thessalonians even if he *wanted* to.

Which he didn't.

Instead, Miles identified the suite that he had been summoned to; Jeb Elgin, Archon of Hope.

Church dogma likes to claim that the various Archons are chosen because they best represent the virtue that they have been named to. Even *if* that had ever been true - something that no one Miles has ever met believes - it certainly wasn't true in the current day. The only Archon that Miles could remember that really embodied the virtue of their station had been gone for almost two years.

He cleared his head with a heavy breath. Now was not the time to be mentally digging through unsolved cases. He needed to be of steady mind, because he doubted that the meeting he was called to was going to be a positive one, and he preferred to not get caught in any more political webs and traps.

Elgin had the northwest corner suite, a rather posh location for one of the newest Archons, appointed by Pope August nine years ago. Traditionally, the Archons rotated their suites as they retired or passed away and new Archons were appointed, but August ostensibly did away with that tradition, citing wasted time and resources for something so trivial.

Miles *would* have approved of that on its face; but the sudden rash of "accidents," "unfortunate circumstances," and outright bullying of older Archons, then selecting sycophants in their place really ruined any respect Miles might have had. It was such an aggressive reshaping of the highest legislative and judicial body in the country that it was *almost* astonishing that it wasn't getting more attention among the public.

Turned out Pope August was only a traditionalist when it was convenient for him.

That trait was why Miles was wary about this meeting. Archon Elgin was the most... aggressively supportive of anything Pope August did or decreed; a true toadie in a hall increasingly filled with toadies, and no doubt why Elgin had a prominent place in the Halls of the Enlightened already despite his lack of seniority.

The exterior door was solid oak and carved with the seal of the Archon of Hope, represented by a shield with the relief of a sun breaking over the horizon. The only other identifier on the door was a bronze name plate that read, "Elgin, Jeb - Hope."

One final deep breath, and Miles turned the doorknob, and swung the door inward.

The interior of Suite for Hope didn't immediately deviate from the common room outside; the walls and carpeting matched, and the only real deviation was a "modern" squared cornered counter made of a shimmering white plaster with a pine wood counter top in the northwest corner, with a "bullet-proof" plastic glass shield covering the entire counter area save for two small slots on each side for receptionists, of which one station was being used.

The reception area was empty, which was common judging from the fact there was only one chair for waiting purposes, and it looked judging from the hint of dust forming at its legs that even it didn't get much use. To be fair, the Archons weren't "public facing" people as a general rule. If you were in their offices, then it was for a good reason, and you probably weren't going to be waiting very long.

And Miles wasn't an exception. He approached the receptionist, a graying grandmotherly looking woman that nonetheless had enough respect within the office to wear the ministry's colors rather than the gray and white reserved for more "general" employees.

He figured that she had to be a legacy member from the prior Archon that Elgin didn't care enough about to fire, because he couldn't *imagine* a hard line orthodox like Archon Elgin granting a woman ministry status within his office.

She had a very pleasant, motherly voice; soothing to Miles's ears as she asked, "And how can I assist you today, young man?"

"I have a half past nine appointment with the Honorable Archon Elgin. Should be under Miles Parker."

She examined a sheet of paper scrawled with six

hand-written names. The Archon was surprisingly busy today. He couldn't get a good look at exactly *who* was on the list before the receptionist conspicuously slid it out of view and said amiably. "Ah yes. The Archon is expecting you. Please... this way, take a left right away, and the Archon's office is all the way at the end of the hall."

She gestured to the door at the north end of the reception area, though the instructions were hardly necessary. Even if he had *never* been to this particular suite before - though he had, many times - the corner suites were literally designed with the exact same layout, then mirrored as necessary.

So, Miles already knew the door opened directly into the corner junction of a hallway, and that left led directly to the Archon's office. He also knew that the first door on the right was the common library; nothing exciting, just a bunch of religious textbooks, law books, and judicial opinions.

The next two doors faced each other. To the left was the employee back room, and to the right was the lounge. The lounge was by Miles's experience the most popular part of an Archon's suite, and a quick look inside suggested this was no different, at least ten people were kicking back as he passed, enjoying anything from reading, to card games, to even radio and television in the northwest corner.

But he turned away quickly because his focus was at the end of the hall. If he hadn't known exactly where the door led, he wouldn't have known it was the Archon's office. There was no nameplate signifying its importance or anybody standing guard, not even an unarmed attendant. The only indicator that it *might* be more than any other door in the suite was the small gray camera mounted near the ceiling with a small green light blinking above the aperture.

Miles tapped on the door and was surprised by how prompt of a reply he got from the other side.

"Enter, Investigator. The door is unlocked."

He knew better than to waste an Archon's time, immediately responding to the invitation, opening the door only far enough to enter, and closing it promptly behind him.

The office had changed considerably since Miles had

last been there. The walls had been stripped of all the art and pictures of friends and family, replaced by nothing but two certificates of academy behind the Archon's desk. The computer that the previous Archon had been *starting* to learn how to use was gone completely, without any sign that the piece of technology had been there at all.

The games that the Archon had collected and set in the northwest corner, near the door to the Archon's private library, were gone... as well as the shelf they were stacked on. As was the small wine shelf that had been mounted on the wall on the opposite side of the door.

The message being sent was clear; Jeb Elgin was a man of simplicity, that refused distractions or any potential vice, which drew Miles's attention back to the desk.H

Archon Eigan was not a particularly old man, which was honestly concerning to anyone who appreciated the norms of the past. Pope August II wasn't nominating Archons for their years of honorable service, and instead was implicitly choosing "younger" men that could hold office for a long time and who shared his more... retrograde agenda.

The reason for this was distressingly clear. There was *one* check on the Pope's total power; that a five to two majority of Archons *could* censure the Pope and trigger a vote of confidence within the ranking Elders of the church. Eigan's appointment gave Pope August II three Archons who would ostensibly never betray him.

Jeb Eigan still had a full head of dirt brown hair only starting to show the dust of gray, though he had let his beard grow excessively down to the middle of his chest, a rather common trait of the firmly orthodox school of thought that he had come from. He was also a fairly large man, though not just in terms of girth, standing to well over six feet in height as he leaned over the desk and offered a hand in greeting.

Miles was *not* used to be towered over, and it was a jarring moment for a man who considered himself fairly tall as he returned the handshake.

"Investigator Parker, glad that you could make it," the archon said warmly, then releasing Miles gestured just to Miles's right to a oak chair upholstered in red velvet. "Please, have a seat. We have much to discuss."

Miles smiled slightly, trying his best to be disarming even as he found himself loathing every second of the Archon's distressingly obvious fake cheer. He settled into the seat, deciding at the very least it would be comfortable enough for him to sit in for a prolonged period. Which he feared was going to be the case.

"I'm going to try and make this as quick as I can," Elgin began, confirming Miles's fears that he was going to be here a while. "You might have heard the rumors already, but there have been a series of terrorist attacks on Republic interests over the last two days."

Miles hadn't. "I don't waste much of my time with rumors as a matter of general principle, and anyone who might have thought to entertain me most assuredly already knew that. I guess that's just the investigator in me."

"The first involved an archaeological site in the northern part of the Republic, past the Valley Basin. Initially a joint venture between our Ministry of History and the University of Northern Cascadia, it ended with the Cascadians murdering every Republican at the dig site. The Cascadian team scattered and evaded our Armed Forces as we attempted to pursue, which leads to the second incident."

There was a long, pregnant pause. Elgin was *very* uncomfortable discussing this, whatever it was.

"The second incident involved an explosive of unknown origin and composition, that targeted and completely annihilated MacArthur Depot on the border of the Flatland Frontier. Tremors from the explosion could be felt in Twainstown two hours away. So far... there have been no survivors, and salvaging efforts can't fully explain what happened."

Another very long pause, then Elgin added, "His Glorious Pope... had been visiting MacArthur Depot the night of the attack. He... is among the presumed dead."

Miles couldn't stop his eyebrows from shooting up. "We're certain of this?"

Elgin nodded, "Last report was that he was on site at the Depot and would depart the following morning. All other means of communication return nothing. While we haven't confirmed his demise, it does not seem likely we will find him alive."

This had to be extremely difficult for Elgin to discuss, and even if Miles had much more than antipathy for the Pope and his little movement, it was hard to *not* feel *something* at just how devastated Elgin appeared while relaying the information.

But that still didn't mean Miles wanted to be here any longer than he had to. So, he prodded Archon Elgin back on task. "I assume that even though the death hasn't been officially confirmed that the House of God is preparing for transition?"

Elgin nodded. "Yes, though that sort of religious maneuvering isn't why I brought you here. That was merely an important background on what your task is going to be. The Assembly has granted me my request for you to lead the investigation and manhunt for these terrorists."

Miles's eyebrows again raised. "Me, sir?"

"Yes, and I promise politics are only a minor part of the reason why."

At least Elgin was acknowledging that politics was involved. A lot of Archons pretended that they were above the petty schemes and power plays and maneuvering of the political machine beneath them. Even Elgin's predecessor wasn't entirely immune to it, and it was to their detriment in Miles's estimation. To hear that admission so bluntly was… rather refreshing.

Elgin pushed his chair back so that he could access the upper right drawer and pulled out a manila folder that appeared to be right in front. Then he reached into the opposite side drawer, and retrieved a black leather covered Bible, setting the folder on the desktop in front of him, the Bible on top of the folder, then his right hand on top of the Bible.

The Archon then raised his left hand. "Before I provide this to you, I should remind you that all this content is considered of the highest secrecy. Do I have your vow in the name of this Republic, and the Lord our God, that you agree to be charged with this task and will *never* reveal *any* of it to anyone outside of the Assembly or the demand of the Papal Authority?"

Archon Elgin was supposed to say all of this ceremonial formality *before* he started talking about any of this. Normally, Miles was someone who rolled his eyes at the strictness of Holy Republican procedure, but it was a bit off to have a hardline Orthodox believer fumble the proper order of things.

Oh well. Judge not lest you be judged, Miles supposed. Not like he was going to refuse *any* assignment at this point anyway. Miles followed Elgin's lead, setting his right hand over Elgin's and raising his left. "By the grace of God, I accept."

"By the grace of God," Elgin repeated, and Miles moved his right hand so that Elgin could slide the Bible across his desk, then hand over the folder.

Miles quickly opened it to the front page as Elgin began dictating its contents. "Our primary suspects are the team that Cascadia sent for the archaeological dig. None of them were killed or accounted for."

Miles raised an eyebrow. "We think Cascadia tried a clandestine attack on us?"

Elgin frowned. "That is… possible, but we don't really want to consider the possibility."

"And why is that?"

Elgin took a deep breath. "No one, even Cascadian intelligence, should have had *any* idea the Pope was at MacArthur Depot. Hell, *we* didn't even know until the Papal Palace informed us he was there, and over an hour after the attack. And *they* didn't know until Pope August's personal attendant informed them. By all accounts, it was an unplanned trip done completely at the Pope's discretion."

Well, *that* wasn't suspicious at all. Though Miles quickly stamped out that thought. Thinking like that had *started* his mess of tribulations. "Have we reached out to Cascadia for a comment yet?"

Elgin nodded and gestured to the folder in Miles's hand. "They claim that the team they sent was privately assembled by a professor of history from one of the universities. They *suspect* that it was part of a disruptive terrorist cell that has been tormenting *them* for the better part of three decades. There is little information about those privateers outside of what was presented to us as they were processed for entry into the Republic, but I can't imagine *any* of it is accurate."

Miles nodded, turning the page as Elgin said, "What we *can* confirm is the professor that assembled them, a man named William Sterner."

Miles looked up from the file warily. That... was not a name he had been expecting to hear, and it set off no small number of warnings in his head. He then looked back down to see the enclosed picture, attached with a paper clip to the dossier.

The Archon again went silent for an awkward stretch. "There's something more. Something *not* in that file because it's not something we can confirm, but something I think is vital for you to know before you begin."

Miles had been thumbing through the information, mostly incomplete data about the conspirators, and initial findings from both attack sites. He closed the folder and asked, "Oh?"

"It's both the reason we're not *dismissing* the idea that the Cascadian terrorists knew where the Pope was... *and* the reason why we want to dismiss it so badly. During the initial response to the attack on the dig site... reports from *some* of the soldiers suggested that one of the companions... wasn't human."

Miles's eyes narrowed. "What do you mean 'wasn't human?' Like some sort of animal?"

Elgin pursed his lips tightly. "You're going to make me say it, aren't you? It's suspected that a... a metal god... was among William Sterner's number."

While a surprise, Miles didn't see the immediate concern. "More than a handful of prominent people have enthralled metal gods who serve them, and there's reason to believe some live here in the Republic, where it's a crime punishable by death. Surely, it can't be unheard of that a seemingly prominent archaeologist from Cascadia might have one in his service as well?"

"There wasn't any metal god with them when they arrived," Elgin replied. "And initial investigation of records left behind by our people at the dig site doesn't suggest one ever arrived later. The prevailing theory is that... they found the metal god within the dig site. And that... that metal god may possibly be... unchained."

And *now* Miles understood the problem. The Third Testament made it extremely clear just what the metal gods were capable of; world destroying power. Depending on the interpretation, the Ice Age was the either consequences of the metal gods' power, or God's last option of stopping their havoc by freezing the world solid. The Bible says they could see people on the other side of the world, and attack with weapons that came from the heavens. An unchained metal god is arguably theology's greatest nightmare outside of Satan himself.

"And that's also why you fear that somehow, the terrorists knew *exactly* where the Pope was. Because that's the sort of thing a metal god could do," Miles said, "Though... that wouldn't explain why we haven't heard of *many* more attacks rather than just two."

"I know," Eigan admitted. "Which is why it's all the more important we find these terrorists before they flee to Cascadia. Our rival country may *say* they are enemies of the state, but that opinion could change *real* quick if these fiends truly have an unchained metal god among them."

"So... what will I be doing?"

"You are going to be coordinating the manhunt. Our last known information has Professor Sterner retreating towards the Great Lake. We *suspect* he and his companion will try to make use of black-market trade lanes to slip into Cascadia. We have all known smuggling routes locked down... but there's any number of ways for a rat to scurry away. We have to find them, sooner rather than later."

"Agreed. I assume I leave immediately?"

Elgin nodded. "Transport is already being arranged for you. It'll be waiting at the western garage. First, you will need to check into the Assignments desk, then the armory. If you need anything else, do not hesitate to contact me directly, and I'll do what I can to accommodate you."

"Anything more, sir?"

Elgin shook his head. "You are dismissed, Investigator. May God be with you."

Miles slowly stood, putting his right hand over his heart, and bowing in parting. But before he could, Archon Elgin had one final thing to say.

"William Sterner appears to have been a native of the Republic, from the City of Hope. From *our* information, he was a member of the ministry in fact, working under my predecessor. You used to as well, as I recall."

Miles again looked up warily. "I did. Before I finished my studies and joined the Corps of Investigation."

Elgin nodded, "Then you know what is at stake. This would be a significant black mark to our branch, and as such I want it resolved as internally as possible."

"And why you have summoned me to lead this case."

"The other Archons have granted me the right to handle this, and all of them recommended you. To be honest, it's a potential win-win for both of us. I preserve the Office of Hope's honor, and you get back in the good graces of the Papal Authority by apprehending the man who killed the Pope, even if unintentionally."

Miles hummed thoughtfully. That was the closest he had ever heard *anyone* acknowledge that he was being punished by the Pope. "Why would I be in the bad graces of the Papacy?" he asked, unable to *completely* hide the acid in his voice. "I was merely doing the job assigned to me."

Elgin sighed. "Yes, I know. And I also know that for whatever reason, then Cardinal August *really* resented the investigation into the Purge, and he decided to take it out on you even though you were just following your Archon's instructions. On that score... I do not share His Eminence's opinion, and why I am glad to assign you to this case. Dismissed. Again, I suppose."

Miles bowed one last time, then left with as much haste as decorum allowed. Nothing against Archon Elgin specifically... but he simply wasn't the man who sat in that chair before him. Even if that would have been an unfair sentiment, the memories made this entire suite a difficult place for Miles to be.

Unfortunately, it *also* was an entirely fair sentiment. That meeting had so many red flags that Miles hadn't even really absorbed how many things were off even after he had left the suite and began his journey down to the basement level. By the time he had returned to the main floor, then wrapped around the stairwell to the one leading down tucked behind it, he had sorted out his thoughts for the most part. Now he just needed the opportunity to lay them out.

But that would have to wait until all the ceremony was settled, which meant a visit to Assignments and the Armory.

The basement level of the Halls of the Enlightened is where its denizens like to claim the elbow grease of the country needs to function is produced. It was the internal engine that few people saw but was essential to keep the Republic moving forward. Miles felt it was a little bit of hyperbole, but it wasn't wrong.

It helped that the environment engendered a feeling of "grunt work" and "salt of the earth labor." There were none of the creature comforts found on the higher floors. This was a land of exposed wires in the ceiling, unstained wood, and naked concrete slabs under his feet; slabs that were patched with slightly off-color sealant where it cracked rather than replaced entirely. It was an environment where they had a hard budget, and they made it count wherever they could, eschewing aesthetics for optimal function.

There was certainly a virtue in that, if it didn't *also* come with an obnoxious superiority that stemmed *from* their limitations. *They* were the ones doing God's true work, and all those people above were elitist posers leeching from the *true* working folk. It created occasionally hostile interactions that didn't help anyone at the end of the day.

He only hoped he wouldn't have such an experience right now. He already had enough to worry about.

Assignments was the closer department, the first right at the main hall, into the "offices," which from Miles's experience was really just a bunch of cubicles with the benefit of being isolated from the rest of the floor by virtue of having walls on all sides. But he went to the Armory first, because the Assignments department was closer to Dispatch, so he could get his official orders and be out the door in one swoop, minimizing his time on the floor, and in the building.

The garage commanded most of the open area, where the official Republic vehicles were serviced and prepared for departure. Seventeen open doors led up from the underground floor to the dispatching lot on the west side. It was one of those things that proved just how much the people in charge wanted these operations out of sight and out of mind; that they went to the trouble and expense to bury something underground that would have been significantly more efficient on the ground floor.

It was a busy place at that moment, with sixteen of the bays filled with vehicles, ten of them on lifts so that technicians could work on the underbodies. Miles could never recall a time when *that* many needed service all at once; but from glancing at some of the serial numbers as he passed, they appeared to be older models, probably recently retired and pressed back into service.

He didn't need terribly much longer to put together a plausible theory. With the possibility of a metal god capable of destroying an entire military base in one night, any official with enough authority to swing it was demanding transportation, fearing that the City of Saints might be next.

Because while the *public* couldn't panic, it was *perfectly* acceptable for their leaders to.

He decided to pray that he wasn't right, picking up his pace across the floor and to the Armory, which had carved out a spot in the southeast of the open floor. It was impressive in the sense of the sheer amount of weaponry and munitions it held, the largest depot for firearms and ammunition both large and small Miles had ever seen outside of a military base.

It *wasn't* quite as impressive that the arsenal was "protected" by what amounted to a wire mesh cage, and a very flimsy looking chain and padlock. It seemed like an dangerously insufficient way to secure some of the most dangerous small arms in the Republic.

One armory officer was manning the "window" to the cage, an open square on the cage's north side that could also be secured with a chain and lock. Two more of the crew were milling about behind him, one cleaning long rifles, and the other counting boxes of bullets, presumably as part of an inventory audit.

The officer manning the window was apparently chosen for his aesthetics; his neatly pressed olive green long sleeved uniform shirt and matching slacks, ink black dress shoes shined to a brilliant gleam, a bright gold nameplate pinned to the right breast pocket saying, "Officer Jackson," neatly swept and combed left black hair accentuated his cream colored skin and bright blue eyes, and combined with features that all translated into the Republic's definition of traditionally attractive.

Miles figured that because it *couldn't* have been for his demeanor.

"What brings you down here, ceiling dweller?" Jackson said, his voice almost contemptuous. In a day not too long ago, Miles would have openly slapped the man for his attitude towards a superior. But these were... different times. He needed to be on his best behavior, especially with those not directly in his chain of command.

With as genuine of a smile as he could muster, Miles lifted his ID to eye level and said, "I'm Inspector Miles Parker. Archon Elgin has ordered me to the armory to be geared up for my assignment."

Jackson sighed in disdain. "Let me see your papers."

Miles's eyes narrowed. "What?"

"The papers you got from the Assignments Desk. Where you're supposed to go first."

Miles forced his smile to stay intact. "You would have had to have gotten the orders from the Archon in order to have them ready."

"I'm sure we did, but policy requires that we need your orders verified by the Assignments desk."

Miles clenched his teeth through his smiling lips. Technically, the armory officer was right, but it was *never* something that they insisted upon in his entire time as an investigator. Perhaps it was possible that a point of emphasis on that score had been passed down in the last six months, but he sincerely doubted it.

It took every bit of Miles's composure to not clench his fists and maintain a cordial expression. "Very well. I will be back."

Once he was a safe distance away, Miles let his frustration boil over with a snarl and angry grumbling under his breath. Of course, the armory grunt was being obstinate because he could. He allowed himself to seethe as he crossed the garage to the completely opposite side of the floor, reining it in at the door to the Assignments desk, then back in full control as he pushed open the door with a ding from a small bell above.

That got the attention of the petty officer at the counter, which ran end to end across the ten-foot space, with a hinged wing on the left side to allow people in and out of the rear portion. This young man was nearly a carbon copy of the first, except that his hair was parted slightly offset to the left, a bushy mustache, and a badge that said, "Officer Johnson."

Well, and the part that that he was *considerably* more amiable than his counterpart at the armory cage.

Firstly, he identified Miles's rank immediately, "Good afternoon, Investigator. How can I help you?"

Miles offered a weak smile and said, "I need to confirm my urgent assignment from Archon Elgin and prepare for dispatch as soon as possible."

The officer's face lit up in recognition as he turned his gaze to the monitor in front of him. "Ah yes! Investigator... Parker, if I'm correct?"

Miles flashed his ID to confirm, and replied, "Quite."

From there, the screech of a printer followed for a painfully long few minutes, then the officer ripped off the printout, and assembled the various pages. From there, a series of stamps on the bottom of each page, and he separated them into four equal stacks, stapling each stack once in the upper left corner. Then he stacked them together and handed the entire thing over the counter.

"First copy is for the Armory, second is for Dispatch,

third is for the commander at your destination, and the fourth is for yourself," Officer Johnson said with a pleasant smile. "I took the initiative to sort them in the order you'll distribute them."

"So, we *do* have to be sticklers on procedure now, eh?" Miles asked with a raised eyebrow. "Because the officer at the armory gave me a bit of a dressing down, and I fear I may owe him an apology."

Johnson nodded. "Officer Jackson, I'm guessing? I wouldn't worry too much about apologizing; most people don't like him much. Bit of a sour cuss even when you do everything right. But it *is* true that there was a bit of an... incident four months back with a guy claiming to be a new investigator getting all the way to the armory before he was stopped. If I remember rightly, Jackson was the one who was about to give him the gun. Really scary moment, got our bosses to *really* be hard and fast on 'by the book.'"

"I... see," Miles replied, now feeling like quite the ass end. "I assume the driver is ready to leave once I hit the lot?"

Johnson nodded, "I can't imagine why not. It *is* an urgent assignment. Get to the armory, and get out the door, I'd say."

"Then that is what I'll do," he answered with a flip of his hand in a parting wave, turned about, and retraced his steps to the Armory. He told himself he was imagining the stares from those in the garage, wondering who this fool in a suit was walking back and forth across the floor. He probably was, honestly. Surely the men of the garage had better things to do than watch people on the walkway.

He was able to brush off that paranoia by the time he returned to Officer Johnson and the Armory cage and have himself in an apologetic frame of mind as the young man addressed with an expression just shy of a sneer.

"Welcome back, Investigator. I trust you've got your papers prepared?"

Miles nodded and took the relevant copy from the stack. "I do. And I apologize for my reaction earlier. Clearly things changed without me knowing about it, and I should have been more prepared."

The apology visibly startled the armory officer. His eyes flared, and he subtly leaned back. "Oh. Well... thank you," he replied uncomfortably, clearly not used to being apologized to. He hastily took the orders, skimmed over them, and stamped the final page. "I'll inform the Lieutenant. This is restricted stuff even for me."

Miles didn't even realize that the cage connected to *another* room on the far end until Officer Johnson opened the door and stuck his head inside. This revelation upset him, because he considered one of his strengths to be noting details that the average person would overlook as being unimportant. Also because it made sense there was more behind the cage... there wasn't *nearly* enough arms and ammunition in the cage for the entire building.

Officer Johnson pulled himself out of the doorway and slid to his right to clear the path for his lieutenant, a balding pudgy man with gray hair, visible jowls, and a uniform shirt and slacks a size too small, straining the material in the gut and creating a muffin top effect at the waistline. A single brass pip on his collar indicated his higher rank, and he offered his right hand in welcome.

"Greetings, Investigator Parker!" the man said as Miles reluctantly returned the handshake. The man's hands were as oily as they looked, and Miles fought the urge to wipe his own hands on his jacket. "Sergeant Killenbrew, but I'm sure you already read my tag. So... come on back. I just got the requisition order. Lucky bastard you are!"

Miles complied, though not with the same enthusiasm as the sergeant, who almost skipped into the walled off rear section.

Admittedly, it *was* an impressive arsenal, inside a room at least five times the size of the cage it was adjoined with. The walls and floors were otherwise bare concrete with three rows incandescent light bulbs from the ceiling twenty feet above, because Miles supposed anything more would take attention away from what was important.

The left and right walls were covered with a chain mesh with handguns on the lower left, shotguns on the upper left, automatic rifles on the right, and even full-size grenade and missile launchers on the top right row. On the back wall were two shelves, one to the left filled with boxes of ammunition and one to the right with various sizes of body armor and even a handful of riot shields, and a large wooden crate almost five feet to a side in the far right corner.

Miles had to remind himself this was a *diplomatic* building.

Killenbrew was consulting the paperwork at his desk in the middle of the surprisingly expansive space. "I know I'm not supposed to discuss this… but is it true? That the Cascadians found an unchained metal god?"

Miles shrugged. "No one knows that for certain. That's why I'm being sent."

Killenbrew took a long, deep breath. "Well, I'll do what I can for ya. What's your shirt size?"

It was silly, but Miles didn't like being reminded that he was a rather large man himself. Six foot, five inches, and two hundred and thirty-three pounds at last measurement. It's possible he was a little bit heavier being on inactive duty for almost half a year, but not by *that* much. "Double large."

The Armory Chief turned away from his desk, to the racks of body armor behind him, rifling through the hanging objects with his fingers. "Whew, don't got too many *that* size, but I should have a couple in here somewhere."

Near the end of the second rack, he found what he was looking for, yanking it off its hanger with enough force to make said hanger swing violently back and forth. "Alright, try this on!" he said eagerly, thrusting the black padded vest in front of Miles.

Miles had never actually worn this sort of protective gear before, even when his duties took him into some potentially hazardous areas, so he found himself intrigued by the old mesh-like fibers layered over what amounted to foam and padding. It was that mesh that was the important bit, a man-made fiber that was a relic of the old times and replicated to the best of their ability.

Whether or not it would be useful against an unchained metal god is a question that Miles was not keen on answering, because he suspected he already knew that answer.

Killenbrew seemed to read the question on Miles's face. "For what it's worth, metal god or not, we *do* know there's gang of renegade Cascadian terrorists, and presumably they are armed."

Fair point.

He slid his arms into the holes, buckled the front piece, then tightened the straps on the sides to minimize any gaps in the armor. "It'll suit."

Killenbrew didn't seem to like the seams in the sides, leaning in as he nudged Miles's left arm up to examine more closely. "There's a half inch gap between the front and back pieces. I can see if we have a triple large…"

Miles declined, "Not necessary. Time is of the essence, and this fits well enough. If someone is such a good shot that they can hit that seam, then there's easily ten other more easily hit locations they'll no doubt choose."

Killenbrew nodded, "Like the head, for example! Which is why you'll need this!"

This time, the Armory Chief nearly dove half of his body into the wooden crate, mumbling something along the lines of "needing to find time to sort this out better."

When he scrambled out a minute later, he was holding a black, hard shell helmet with "HRP" emblazoned in white on the front, the acronym for the Holy Republic Police Unit. "For the most part, these are one size fits all and just needs some adjustment."

Killenbrew hesitated for a moment, then said, "Could… could you kneel down for a minute or two?"

It didn't take Miles long to figure out why. While the investigator was well on the tall side, the Armory Chief was not, nearly half a foot shorter and no doubt needed Miles to kneel so that he could see the adjustments he needed to make.

So, Miles complied, and Killenbrew quickly dropped the helmet on his head, rotating and tilting it for the proper fit. Then while holding the helmet in what he deemed was the proper orientation with his left hand, he reached into his slacks pocket for a flathead screwdriver with his right, then started turning small bolts along the outside brim. It corresponded with foam pads pressing down on his head until it fit snugly.

Then he reverted the pressure a hair, explaining, "Ya want it a *little* loose so you can jam it on quickly if you have to. The chin strap will do the rest of the work." To prove the point, he clipped said strap under Miles's chin, and adjusted it to fit snugly... if uncomfortably.

Miles preferred it be tight across his temple than his throat, personally, but that was probably an adjustment he could make on his own. It didn't seem terribly hard to do.

"Now... on to the important stuff." Then with a conspiratorial stage whisper he added, "The *good* stuff. The sorta stuff you won't get up there."

"You're cleared for two firearms. You'll understand why in a moment." Killenbrew explained, turning to his right and the racks of handguns. The Armory Chief took one three rows up from the bottom and nine columns from the front, lifting it off its pegs, and giving it a quick once over. "Modified Brewer Quarter Inch. This one has an extended magazine, semi-automatic, and longer barrel. Little more unwieldy than the standard model, but more useful in a firefight, which you might wind up in if our intelligence is correct."

Killenbrew handed the pistol over, and Miles gave it a cursory glance. He was only superficially aware of the differences in firearm manufacturers, and certainly not to the point that he could tell the differences just by looking. Unlike most Investigators for the Archons, Miles had no military experience; forbidden to enlist because he was foreign born. He never gained the keen appreciation for guns that most of his peers did.

Nonetheless, he was able to discern when a gun was different enough, like the second pistol Killenbrew gave him. Unlike the sleek shiny black of this first one, this was a matte gray, with a significantly larger barrel that led into a six round revolver chamber. "Clarke and Davis five-eighths," Killenbrew explained as Miles right hand closed over the handle. "You'll want to be careful firing this one, because it has a very profound kick. It needs it too."

"Why?" Miles asked as he holstered both weapons, the Brewer at his hip, and the Clarke in a holder on his chest armor.

By that point the Armory Chief had turned to the ammunition racks, taking one box from the top shelf, and another from the bottom. The first one, a bright yellow with "1/4 copper tip lead core" and "Bartz Materials" emblazoned on the box came with an added magazine for his Brewer, and Killenbrew said, "Easier to have the reserve loaded so that you can pop it right in and keep shooting. Again, possibility of a firefight and all that."

The second box was a plain orange, with no other indicators other than a red outlined white square, indicating some sort of restricted material, and Killenbrew said exactly what the restricted material was in short order. "Tempered Steel core and full metal jacket. Specifically designed for armor penetration. *These* go in your Clarke. If there *is* a metal god out there, this round and that gun are going to be the only thing you can hold in one hand that might stand a chance of putting a hole in it. Don't use them for anything else. Hopefully, the trained military that will be assisting you are going to have a better opportunity, but you never know."

Miles popped open the box and examined one bullet. Superficially, it didn't look terribly much different than the bullets he used for his standard sidearm, except that they were completely copper colored, about twice the size, and narrowed to a surprisingly sharp point at the tip.

"Now, I understand that the Army Quartermaster on site will be able to provide you with the other odds and ends you might need, so I'd recommend you get moving, sir. As you can see, the whole damn building is on edge, and the sooner it's resolved, the better."

Miles nodded, even if he suspected that the real reason was that Sergeant Killenbrew just wanted him anywhere but here. A person could only do faux happy for so long, especially when he could no longer distract himself with his toys, and the nervousness was starting to show on the Armory Chief's face.

But there was one thing Miles still needed to do. "I need to sign off, don't I? Big emphasis on procedure, I'm told."

Killenbrew jolted, then yelped. "Right! Of course!" He quickly dove into the papers on his desk, spun one page about, then took two very pronounced steps back. "Just sign on the bottom right line, and you're good to go!"

Miles took his time, pretending to read the sheet in front of him very carefully. After all, must keep to protocol, right? When he finally did deliberately scrawl his name across the line for his signature, Killenbrew's composure had cracked the point that the Armory Chief looked like he was about to try and climb up the wall.

"All done. May God smile upon us," Miles said in parting.

"Yes, of course," Killenbrew said with a tight-lipped smile. "And to you especially."

Miles stepped away, turned slowly, and tried not to grin devilishly as he left the rear room of the armory, and went back to the cage. He was used to that kind of racism; the kind that showed itself in an immense discomfort at his presence, that nudged people to the other side of the hall, or down different halls entirely, to avoid him. The kind that questioned his presence at every turn, then made up any number of reasons why they were legitimately harassing him. He had fun with those sorts of responses at this point, figuring that if they were going to be uncomfortable around him, he might as well give them a mild reason to be.

"Maybe there really is a metal god, and it'll kill that damn monkey."

That wasn't something he was quite as used to, though.

Officer Johnson was leaning with his back against one of the supports of the Armory cage as Miles exited, his eyes bulging in fear as he realized that the investigator had exited the back room just in time to hear his little punchline that he had uttered to his mechanic friend - judging from the oil-stained face and work uniform - on the other side.

It's not that the blatant racism was particularly less common. Being called "monkey" was honestly one of the tamer slurs he would overhear multiple times any given day. But it was different in that the passive shit Miles was able to largely wave off as unconscious biases that bubbled up in the face of something unfamiliar. They didn't have to mean to behave poorly; it just happened unconsciously, and Miles was able to accept that. Mostly.

But the vocalized slurs were not something that could be easily brushed off. It was a conscious choice. And considering how carefully people try to use such words, and how guilty they look when caught, they *knew* they shouldn't say such things. They *know* it's wrong.

Miles let the silence hang in the air, let the awkwardness linger, let the officer hang with the knowledge that Miles had heard it, but not how he was going to respond. The uncertainty was going to be far more painful than anything the investigator was willing to do, so he let it last as long as he felt he could with nothing but an impassive stare at the quivering officer.

Because Miles wasn't going to do a damn thing.

Sure, he *could* bring Officer Johnson to a tribunal. But it would be nothing more than procedure, wasting everyone's time before ending with "mandatory leave" and "sensitivity training."

Miles could probably punch the officer's teeth so far down his throat his dentist would need to hire a proctologist to find them. It probably wouldn't even hurt Miles's career at this point, as the Archons especially were trying to look like decent people in regard to race relations.

But those, or any of the other options available, would do nothing but increase animosity. No one would learn anything; it would just fan more flames that didn't need to be fanned. The best thing to do was quite literally nothing. There were bigger matters to attend to.

Even if half of the Republic hated him, he loved this country, and if there was a metal god out there aiming to destroy it, it needed to be stopped. There wasn't time for this.

So finally, Miles flashed an amiable grin, and with a cheerful wave, he said, "Have a good day, Officers. May God be with you."

Then he left the Armory behind him, not once looking back. He didn't even spare a sideways glance at the mechanics crew. He turned just before the Assignments desk, up a metal grated staircase overlooking the maintenance bay, then pushing open a drab gray metal door into Dispatch.

It was another metal staircase before he emerged back at ground level, at a covered garage that was tucked away in the northwest of the grounds. A single covered booth marked where the Dispatch Clerk was waiting, and where Miles had to check in next.

That much, mercifully was a painless affair, and he was so damn tired of being in this building that he didn't even fully process *anything* about the clerk. He was fairly certain it was a man, and that all the paperwork was properly stamped, but that was about it. The rest zipped right out of his head the second the booth was behind him.

He had recovered his head at least by the time he located his driver and vehicle. He had been expecting something rugged for what was assuredly going to be some off-primary road driving. Instead, what he got was a sleek, black, long cabin sedan with a pale skinned, gray-haired driver dressed to his absolute best; perfectly shined black shoes, crisp black dress uniform, complete with matching chauffeur cap, the pristine silver badge on the brim marking him with the Transport Division of the Halls of the Enlightened shimmering even in the faint lights of the garage.

"Investigator Parker, I presume? I am Officer James Devereaux," he said, snapping a white gloved hand in salute. "I'm here to take you to West Customs Checkpoint. From there, an army vehicle will take you to your destination."

"Awfully fancy ride for a mere Investigator," Miles noted as the officer helpfully opened the rearmost door for him to enter.

"I happened to be the only one available at the time the urgent order came in. We've... been busy the last twenty-four hours."

"I can only imagine." Miles tucked his feet in through the door, marveling at the leg room as his driver closed it confidently with a solid thump, then a handful of seconds later popping into the driver's seat. The engine whirred quietly to life, and with an expert's touch on the accelerator, moved so smoothly that it took Miles far too long to realize they were even moving.

Then he got the call he knew was going to be coming eventually, his phone buzzing like it was a kicked over hive of angry bees. The timing *couldn't* have been coincidence. "I'll give you some privacy," the driver said knowingly. "Worry not, these partitions are soundproof specifically for that reason."

A deep black tinted glass rose through the window to the driver's seat seconds later as Miles finally answered the call. "Parker."

The quiet yet stern voice that he had been anticipating answered.

The Archon of Charity, Paul Anders. He had been a surprise selection, as the prior Archon of Charity passed away mere days before Pope August's ascension. Perhaps realizing what Pope August would do with an opening, the same Cardinals that chose him as Pope rushed to confirm Anders to fill the surprise vacancy. The result was another relatively young face that would be difficult to supplant, and not trying terribly hard to be particularly on Pope August's good side.

"I would have figured you'd be too busy leaning on the Cardinals as they selected a new Pope to be bothering me.

Anders scoffed. "You mean the same Evangelical coalition that *demanded* they rush their chosen one onto the seat? Of *course,* they demand on following proper decorum and observe a thirty-day time of mourning before they even *consider* his replacement now." Quickly changing subjects, he asked, "I trust Devereaux found you?"

Miles replied, "He did, Sir Archon. Thought it was odd that such a fancy car was waiting for me."

"My personal driver," Anders confirmed. "I trust him more than I trust a full two-thirds of my peers. At any rate, we don't have terribly much time, so let's not waste it. I didn't like Elgin's decision to bring you in when I heard about it, and nothing has made me feel better about it now. I trust you've reached a similar conclusion?"

Miles agreed. "I have, Archon. I don't like this at all. But it's not like I have many options when one of your peers orders me to the manhunt."

"You actually did."

"Listening to you was what *got* me on the sidelines for

six months to begin with. Pardon me if I'm not keen on following your advice *this* time. Half this damn country thinks I'm part of some attempt to overthrow the Pope. I'd rather not encourage that."

"Archon Landry, God have mercy on his soul, agreed with me. It might behoove you to remember that."

How *dare* Anders invoke that name? "Yes, he did. And now Archon Landry is *dead*. And as much as I would love to meet him again, I'm in no rush to do so."

"You know personally how much of a danger Pope August is. You're never going to be out of his sights as long as you're alive. No matter how much you play the good little soldier, you've already been marked as his enemy."

It's not that Anders was *wrong*. He was almost assuredly right, in fact. But Miles had already been drug into this political war once without his consent. He had no desire to step into it again, much less willingly. "And openly working with you and your allies will only confirm that paranoia," Miles countered. "No thanks."

"I'm not trying to recruit you," Anders said. "I have no interest in issuing you orders while you're working in service to one of my peers. That would be too naked of intent even for *me*, much less the Archons siding with me. All I am saying is that when, no if... *when* you uncover information during this investigation that would reveal just what despicable scheme Elgin and his lot are planning, that you put it in my hands rather than bury it."

Miles was *never* going to agree to that audibly, no matter *how* secure Anders thought their discussion was. "You have my answer, Archon."

The Archon of Charity seemed to decide that there wasn't any reason to continue pressing the issue and said with a sigh of resignation, "You have my number. May God be with you."

The call terminated, and Miles leaned heavily into the back of his seat. This wasn't what he signed up for. He wanted to protect the sanctity and independence of his country. That was it. Not try and balance on a wire between two increasingly diverging sects as they struggled and vied for power and influence among a country and a community of believers.

He wanted to honor the people who took him in when no one else would. Which was why he *had* to do this, no matter *what* political games were being played behind the scenes.

Miles opened the case file Archon Elgin had given him. This was one of the things that Miles *knew* he should probably be more wary of. William Sterner had *worked* in the Virtue of Hope directly under Elgin's predecessor for roughly five years. The personnel file on William should have been long and readily available. At least enough of it for Elgin or *anyone* in the Halls of the Enlightened to know that the man who received approval to enter the country *wasn't* William Sterner.

Miles was going to find out who this man really was, and why he was determined to drag the name of such an honorable man into such despicable infamy. He'd worry about why others were willing to play along later.

Episode 6: The Oregon Trail

William understood that even Alyssia had her limits when she demanded he climb off her back and take a more human pace. But he *also* noticed that the periods where she was willing to carry him to improve their speed was getting rapidly shorter.

"Getting too many load bearing errors than I would like," the Transcendent explained when William finally pressed her on it on the third day after the satellite drop. "The self-repair isn't working as fast as it used to and keep up with my exertions. To be expected, I suppose. We're far enough clear of any pursuit at this point, I suspect... and with that satellite down, we shouldn't be in any immediate danger of being discovered."

"And admittedly we'd fit in fairly well," William said. "This route... is known among black market sellers for... the Transcendent trade."

Alyssia responded to that about how he expected. She turned her head slightly and cocked her left eyebrow, silently inviting him to explain himself.

"Transcendent, and their associated relics, are effectively property. They are forbidden in *any* form outside of very specific research in the Holy American Republic... but the other countries in the land aren't quite as restrictive. This road, as I mentioned, connects the Acela Commonwealth with Cascadia. Acela is notorious for their usage of Transcendent technology as indicators of status. More... gray market dealers in Cascadia use this road and it's connections for research, development, and study."

"Does the Acela Commonwealth deal in intact Transcendent?" Alyssia asked.

"What few remain," William answered. "It's hard to give even give a rough guess of how many Transcendent still function. The Holy American Republic destroys them the instant they are discovered, and Acela goes to great lengths to obscure the numbers in their land. But it can't be many... without the means to maintain them, over the eons they've... broken down and either abandoned or destroyed."

"I see. I'm more surprised that any have lasted this long."

"Well... now that we know that there are Transcendent that are undisturbed under the earth..."

Alyssia shot down that idea *too* quickly. "There's not."

"You say with a tremendous amount of confidence."

"Because I know," Alyssia answered. "My circumstances... were unique."

William nodded, "More than perhaps you realize."

That earned him another cocked eyebrow.

"Granted I haven't met any other Transcendent personally, but the impression I got was that the Transcendent don't have anything in the way of personality. They really do behave more like very sophisticated machines than anything else. It's... why your sass takes me off guard."

Alyssia allowed herself that sort of grin that unnerved William, and she knew it. "Uh huh."

"And you don't seem terribly astonished by any of these revelations," William noted.

"Because I'm not. Now stop slowing down. I highly doubt you're *that* tired on your own feet already."

William growled as he picked up his pace to match Alyssia's, "I get distracted when I start talking about history! Damn it, why do you think it is so fun to irritate me?"

She didn't give an answer to that, which only served to annoy William more. His time with Alyssia suggested that she wasn't being malicious or ill-intended with her teasing... she just found it amusing to get a rise out of him. Any action could be a part of the game, but if William didn't interpret the clues correctly, then she *did* get mad at him.

William had been raised *as a woman*, and *still* didn't understand the games women play.

Worse was that he couldn't even distract himself with the scenery... because there wasn't any. With the forest around the Great Lake behind them, they had entered into the tundra, a land still trying to grow back from the Ice Age. Hell, just taking their typical pace another two or three days to the north would probably bring them face to face with still very real and still very large glaciers.

A blast of chilled air from the north off those glaciers reminded him he was dressed for summer in the middle of the thaw... not for hiking across the tundra. The forests must have been buffering the chill somehow, because now that the wind wasn't being broken by the trees, it was bringing nigh freezing temperatures with it.

At least the cold encouraged him to move faster... for now. He wasn't sure what he was going to do come nightfall.

Alyssia apparently noticed his shivering. "We're going to have to find a more southern route, aren't we?"

William shook his head. "There's nothing but nigh impassable mountains until you get south enough to find a viable pass through the Great Divide. We'd be crossing a lot of empty territory, but all of it would be in the direct domain of the Holy American Republic, and no one outside of government or military interests have no reason to be trekking through that wilderness. We'd probably be caught even *without* satellites tracking us. Best to continue on our current course as long as he possibly can. Not unless mountain climbing is within your set of skills."

Alyssia shrugged, "I had climbed the tallest mountain on all seven continents at some point. Turns out after living a couple centuries, you just start finding whatever you can to do. I suspect *you* wouldn't survive the climb, however. Even if no mountain on this continent even comes close to the 'death zone,' the air still gets thin enough to really harm people if they aren't adapted to it. Combine that with what would *have* to be below freezing temperatures..."

"Yeah, yeah, I get it," William said, waving off the rest of her lecture, as he hadn't really been considering such an attempt to begin with.

"But we will do as you suggest. We'll take this road as long as you can suffer it, then we'll work out something else from there."

And it was a *long* road, to be sure, one that made William start to second guess his plan entirely. While the Holy American Republic never had a presence on this black-market route, they *had* to know it existed. They no doubt didn't patrol it because it wasn't worth the money or manpower to send anyone so far north for what was mostly ancient, non-functional relics. But they certainly would *now*, and it wouldn't be hard to guess that William and Alyssia would think this was the path of least resistance...

"Stop that."

William jolted, and asked, "Stop what?"

"You're slowing down again, for one. Two, you're overthinking things... whatever you're thinking about at any rate."

The annoying thing about her reprimand was that she was *right*. William and his team had plotted out this route in the planning stages of their mission *because* it was the best possible path. He just hadn't anticipated having to *walk* it.

"I'm honestly more worried for the rest of my team," William said. "Forecasts didn't anticipate this low of temperatures in the summer months, even up here. If they can't find shelter through the night..."

"I'd worry more about *you*, if I were you," Alyssia retorted, frost wafting out of her nose, and getting William's immediate interest.

"You... actually *breathe*."

Alyssia rolled her eyes, no doubt by the bizarre change in topic. "What part of 'completely mimic human function' was unclear?"

William shook his head, "Do you need to?"

"Not in any functional sense, no. I can operate without drawing in breath. But that I can, and still do, replicate that function *is* a bit of an interesting story into the early research and development of Transcendent... that is if you're willing to hear it."

Anything had to be better than thinking about how damned cold it was. "Enlighten me."

"In the earliest trials of Transcendent technology, researchers first tried transitioning animals into analogue bodies. It took *years* before they figured out why none of them lived for more than a few minutes before their quantum brains collapsed."

"And it had to with breathing?" William asked.

"Not even *that* as much as the *perception* of breathing. The first few human test subjects demonstrated the same phenomenon. When they woke in their new bodies, their new brains were convinced they were suffocating. The test subjects were literally dying of *shock*. And it wasn't just breathing. The lack of a heartbeat was sometimes enough to cause a catastrophic collapse of the quantum brain. The researchers even needed to devise a way to allow the quantum brain to voluntarily force a 'breath,' because not having that ability was enough to cause psychological harm to the transcended being." Hell, one early Transcendent went into outright *psychosis* because he couldn't *defecate*."

There's no way that was true, and William called her out on it. "You're lying to me."

"I am not," Alyssia asserted, shaking her head while sporting a bemused smile. "While those that had been Transcendent for a while acclimated and no longer *needed* to do any of that, it was a feature that remained in all chassis because it was less expensive to just keep those functions rather than create wildly different models for every level of acclimation, especially since it didn't *harm* any Transcendent to have them. So, there is one deep, dark secret of the Transcendent we never wanted anyone to know. We didn't mimic human functions just to 'blend in' with humans for deep subterfuge. It was because our monkey brains literally would kill itself if we couldn't."

"You're playing another one of your games, with a story so absurd that it almost *has* to be true." William decided.

Alyssia shrugged, "If that's what you want to believe."

She then abruptly stopped, then turned halfway, looking behind them. William asked, "What is it?"

"There's someone coming. Rather large carriage, by the looks of things."

William tried to follow her eyes, and really didn't see anything off in the distance that he could readily discern. "Are you sure?"

"I'm looking right at it, boy," Alyssia snarled grumpily. "Of *course,* I'm sure."

That the carriage was coming from the east wasn't necessarily a good sign. "Horse drawn or motorized?"

"Horse drawn."

William grimaced. "Great."

"You're right, that *is* great," Alyssia answered. "They might have some warmer clothes they'd be willing to trade you."

William shook his head. "You'd probably not like what they'd ask in exchange."

"And why's that?"

"A horse drawn carriage coming from the east is no doubt carrying a nobleman of the Acela Commonwealth."

"You're going to have to provide me with meaningful context at *some* point, boy."

William exhaled tiredly. "The people of the Acela Commonwealth broke to the north about a hundred years ago, separating from the Gulf Confederacy over their willingness to engage in slavery. The most prominent members of the Commonwealth consider owning a functioning Transcendent as the highest form of material status symbol in their country."

Alyssia hummed curiously at that, "I see."

"Point is... if they see you, they are *assuredly* going to see you as a prize worthy of taking."

She shook her head. "No, we'll be fine. Just tell the truth, and I'll fit in as you need. I'm more concerned of you dying of hypothermia than me being taken against my will."

"The truth?" William asked. That seemed like an insane idea.

Alyssia nodded. "Yes. You know? That thing where you say what actually happened. I assume you must be at least familiar with the concept."

As it came closer, the Acela carriage began to clarify in William's sight, and Alyssia instructed him. "Attempt to flag them down. Share what you're comfortable sharing but stick to the facts regardless. It's easier to keep a story straight that way. The quicker the interaction, the better. I'm not going to communicate much without being spoken to, so I'm going to trust you."

"Well, maybe there *is* some benefit to this," William snarked.

He didn't like the feeling that Alyssia had an ulterior motive for wanting this interaction. Because it felt like she did, and simply didn't want to let William in on the game that was afoot, though William couldn't imagine what she could be angling for. And he *especially* didn't like that she was expecting him to go along with it unilaterally.

Then another frigid blast of air made him shiver, stealing away not just the warmth from his bones, but also his desire to continue this argument. "You know what? *Fine.* We'll do it your way. But don't blame me if you wind up in shackles and I have a bullet through my temple."

"Wouldn't be much point in that scenario, since you'd be dead and all that."

William growled quietly in frustration, then started waving his right arm animatedly at the steadily approaching carriage. Minutes later, the sound of hooves falling onto the packed dirt road confirmed it should be close enough for the driver to see them at least.

In any normal circumstance, the carriage would have probably ignored him. But these were not normal circumstances, and the pair of horses drawing the carriage protested loudly at the abrupt stop as their driver yanked hard on the reins.

The carriage itself William would nicely call "colorful." "Garish" if he was being less generous. A bright pink arching canopy with lavender trim covered pearl white walls and a double door lined in gold. About the only thing *not* painfully bright was the stain of dust and dirt on the bronze-colored wheels and domed undercarriage.

A brass coat of arms adorned the left side facing William and Alyssia; that of a winged serpent coiled along a straight branch adorned with grapes, and a series of leaves flanking along the sides of the kite shield shaped standard. Had William been more versed in the families of Acela, the coat of arms would have probably identified who the occupants were without needing to be introduced.

A pair of men jumped from their positions flanking the driver jumped out, weapons at the ready, then the doors to the carriage burst open and another pair of armed guards formed a line between the carriage and the two stragglers on the road.

These were men dressed for show, not combat. Black polished helmets with flamboyant red plumes that went from the top and dangled off the back. Neatly pressed and vivid red uniform tops with bright brass buttons and white ruffled shirts underneath. Brown trousers with a red stripe down the center and impeccable crease lines down the leg, finishing with polished black boots slightly dulled by the dirt of the road.

Not that they *couldn't* cause a lot of harm, as their near jet black automatic rifles pointed directly at the pair would attest to. There was certainly *some* function to their form, and William felt his heart starting to race. He glanced over to Alyssia, looking for any sign that she was going to act...

And saw nothing. Even her eyes had dimmed, the bright blue that looked almost like its own illumination faded to near nothing, a slight washed out hue over what now looked like slightly tarnished copper. He quickly remembered that she was going to go silent, and seemed committed to that even as guns were drawn on them, leaving him to navigate this entire encounter that he hadn't wanted any part of to begin with on his own.

William began entertaining the idea of asking the nobleman inside for an offer.

"Who are you?" the guard on the farthest left demanded.

Stick to the truth, Alyssia had suggested. She never said the *whole* truth, though. "I am Dr. William Sterner, archaeological professor and researcher in Cascadia. I had just finished a dig south of here when my team was betrayed by the Holy American Republic. I... and my find here... managed to escape, but I don't know about the rest of my team."

That didn't exactly mollify them, their rifles going up to the ready, all four men now looking down their sights. "And that's supposed to comfort us? Are you *trying* to bring the damned Republicans on our heads?"

William threw his arms up. "No! We haven't seen any pursuers for the last three days! I think it's safe to say we lost them. I just hailed you to hope you might have something to help a man who is in some very cold environs and *not* dressed for it."

Finally, a quieter voice drifted through the open carriage door. "At ease, Livingston. If there were Republicans anywhere in the vicinity, I suspect the trail blazers would have seen signs of it. The Republicans are not exactly the most discreet of people."

"My lordship..." the guard began but was quickly cut off.

"I think I can do you one better, young man. Come inside. I insist. My curiosity cannot be contained."

Livingston was clearly trying to be the source of reason. "My lordship, surely..."

"If you are *that* concerned, Livingston, then you can switch with McHugh and join me inside." Then with an even quieter voice, he said to someone. "Do cross to my side, Katheryn. Make it quick."

William's eyes widened in surprise as he spied a Transcendent pass the open doorway obediently, then the guards parting to allow William and Alyssia to pass. He took a pair of tentative steps forward, then stopped when he noticed Alyssia wasn't following.

She was still standing, like at attention, unmoving and unspeaking. He sighed, realizing she was going all in on this charade and said, "Alyssia, follow."

The Transcendent lurched forward, and William was only fairly certain he imagined the sound of her joints creaking as she ambled in his direction. He fought back the desire to sigh in annoyance, worried that it might betray something to a suspicious group of Acelans.

"Get in the carriage," he then ordered when Alyssia stopped directly behind him then stopped for an awkward amount of time. He resisted the urge to help her inside as she 'struggled' to climb the half meter rise, mostly because he wasn't going to lower himself for something he knew *damn* well she was completely capable of.

"Goodness, this model is not in very good shape, is it?" the old man said with pity. "Katheryn, do be a dear and assist her."

Alyssia then almost popped up and forward, disappearing into the carriage. William stepped forward, only to be cut off by Livingston, who glared angrily at him before hopping through the open door and into the cabin. Only then was William allowed entry and finally a respite from the cold.

It was not terribly much warmer inside, and even then, only because the carriage walls blocked the wind. But any shelter in a storm, he supposed, even if it was populated by a modern-day slaver and his well-armed soldiers.

This particular shelter's interior was as difficult on the eyes as its exterior. Orange creamsicle walls with bright lavender trim stamped with white dots along the band assaulted his vision, almost distracting him from the neon green upholstery on the benches that flanked the fore and aft ends.

The wonderful stereotype of eclectic Acela design was doing its work here.

"Sit so that we can move," Livingston ordered gruffly, having removed his cap in the presence of his lord, William presumed, revealing a balding head that betrayed an age his face did not. When William did not immediately comply, the guard insisted more forcefully, "*Now.*"

William bit his tongue and complied, more than a little surprised that he hadn't needed to order Alyssia to do the same, the Transcendent sitting to his left with a glassy eyed, forward stare. She was no doubt trying to glean everything she could from the pair across from them, but you would never know it by how completely off in outer space she seemed.

The carriage jerked forward, nearly throwing William out of his seat because he wasn't expecting such a sudden movement. Then he felt even more out of place when he discovered he was the *only* one in the cabin that had been taken off guard in such a manner.

"Quite a specimen you have there, though clearly

suffering from prolonged disuse."

That finally drew William's eyes to the master of the carriage... and what a sight it was.

If William wasn't reasonably sure the old man directly in front of him *meant* to dress that way, he'd have thought the old man was blind. A bright pink suit pants and top over a frilled neon green shirt, accessorized by silver pips on the collar and cuffs, a black flecked orange belt, and bleached white snake leather wingtip shoes.

Perhaps the outfit was meant to distract from his ugliness, in which case... mission accomplished, because it took William far longer than normal to look at the man's face. His face was somehow both portly *and* gaunt, with what looked like folds of pasty skin draped over his cheeks. His ears stuck out predominately in a way that was almost as distracting as his clothes, almost hiding wisps of scraggly gray hair that formed a ring around the back of his pasty white and purple splotched skull.

The man, however, was still focused mostly on Alyssia. "She looks a sight better than my Katheryn here, though I suspect this ol' girl has at least been getting what maintenance we can manage."

And that was William's cue to get a closer look at the other Transcendent that he caught a glimpse of earlier. True to the man's statement, Katheryn *must* have seen better days. The hair on the right side of her head was either missing or a burned black stubble rather than the pale brown that remained on the left. She was *also* missing her right eye, the blackened pit occasionally gleaming copper from exposed... circuitry? It seemed odd calling what ran through a Transcendent such a crude name.

Further damage to the chassis on Katheryn's right arm told William two things. Whatever the small bands of copper color were, it didn't seem to be circuits in *any* sense that he had seen, and that *something* nigh catastrophic had happened to Katheryn's right side.

"Oh, goodness! Where are my manners?" the old man said in dismay. "Please, allow me to introduce myself. Lord Marley Billington, of Evertonne of the Acela Commonwealth. It is a pleasure, I am sure."

William played along, if for no reason then Livingston was staring him down menacingly. "Very much. William Sterner, a mere professor of ancient history from the University of Northern Cascadia."

"And in the course of those noble studies is how you came across *this* fine specimen, if I understand correctly?"

William nodded. "Y... yes. Needless to say, it was a bit of a surprise. We had never found even *parts* of a Transcendent in any underground ruin, much less a *complete* one, and much less than that one even *moderately* functional."

Marley sighed, "Oh, if only to be young again with the knowledge of Transcendent beneath the earth! Who knows what we could have found?"

Alyssia *better* be right about her being unique, William thought. He did *not* like the idea of Acelans digging up the continent finding new slaves.

"But such is fate, I suppose," Marley said morosely, "That's no longer a game I have the energy or desire to fight for."

"Fight for?" William asked, a bit confused about Marley's wording.

The old man waved his hand behind him with a scoff. "Oh, there will soon be no viable way to keep Transcendents once the commonwealth governors pass their latest designs."

That got William's attention. "What... are they doing?"

Marley exhaled deeply again, "The ongoing maintenance of Transcendents was subsidized by the Commonwealth as it became increasingly more expensive, and the research into repairing more difficult parts became slow. Last month, the governors declared the Commonwealth will no longer subsidize those practices."

William fought back visible disappointment. Of *course,* the only reason that such slavery in Acela was falling out of favor was merely because their government was refusing to pay for it any longer.

"Not that it matters that much to me, I suppose," Marley said tiredly. "Even with subsidies, dear Katheryn here was at a point where what needed repair was beyond what we could fix. It's due time for my dear servant to serve one last purpose. Once we reach Winema Post, I'll sell her to the Historical Institute of Cascadia representatives there. Then I will return to Acela and live out my last days quietly, leaving all the drama of politics to the younger generation."

How nice Marley had that luxury, William thought. He jerked a thumb in Alyssia's direction and said, "Well, we probably won't be going to the Historical Institute with *this* one, but they'll no doubt be closely associated to our department's study."

Marley nodded, then his eyes narrowed and turned suspiciously towards Alyssia. "You said you found this one underground?"

William nodded. "Yes?"

"Where is her slave bangle?"

The professor blinked. "Slave bangle?"

Marley gestured to Katheryn, and ordered, "Show him, dear Katheryn."

The battered Transcendent raised her left arm, where a golden loop was firmly cinched at the wrist. A dark black square rested where one would expect to find a gemstone, but it was otherwise unremarkable.

"These bangles are what keep Transcendent to a heel, young man. Without them, I shudder to think what these 'metal gods' could do."

Alyssia then startled him by speaking unprompted. "I was enthralled by the third wirelessly transmitted executable on August 12, 3280. Further attempts at enthrallment has a high probability of damaging my quantum brain and rendering me entirely inoperable."

Both William's and Marley's eyes widened at the largely unsolicited explanation, though for different reasons. "Fascinating," the older Acelan said with awe, then with an angry gesture at Livingston, he added, "Oh, put your gun down! If she was unshackled, we'd already be dead."

Then, the old man regarded Alyssia again, with a wonder that William wasn't sure he liked. "It's fascinating. Even when Katheryn was able to speak when I was a younger man, it was never much more than very simple answers."

"Hardware enthrallment protocols were crude and disabled almost all higher functions," Alyssia explained, "This, and the limited effectiveness of manually enthralling every Transcendent, led to the development of wirelessly transmitted executables that were more streamlined and only targeted processes that allowed for independent action. Further refinements allowed permissions such as acting in our own self-preservation, which I just demonstrated."

At this point, Marley was only able to repeat himself. "*Fascinating.*"

William hoped that he wasn't betraying his skepticism. He sincerely doubted that little tale contained much, if any, truth. But if it was enough to fool the rest of the cabin, that's all that mattered. He also was concerned by the light that appeared in Marley's eye, worried that the old slaver had abruptly found a reason to continue his work in Acela's "unique industry."

But as soon as William saw that spark in the old man, it vanished just as quickly, "Oh, to have met something like this fine specimen twenty years ago. How cruel fate can be."

Marley then addressed William, "How much have you been able to pry out of this one?"

The professor shook his head. "Not much. We had barely pulled her out of the ground before the Republicans turned on us. What little she *has* said really isn't worth much without context, like what you heard here."

"Oh, she provided more context than you might realize, young man," Marley corrected. "I take it you're not familiar with how the Transcendent were enslaved. Not many who haven't studied the process are. The Holy American Republic certainly isn't, with how terrified they are of even *parts* of Transcendents, much less entire working Transcendents, as you have witnessed."

His scholarly curiosity was winning out over his general disgust. "I... am not."

"We *knew* that these bangles could shatter the Transcendent will and make them malleable. But it seemed *extremely* unlikely that our long past ancestors would be able to force these trinkets onto their metal gods before said metal gods got wise to it. There had to have been something else, and now we know what that is! So, tell me, dear Alyssia, how did these wireless transmissions work? Were they anything like the remote phone calls that we are developing?"

Alyssia shook her head. "We could communicate in such a fashion, and barring more efficient methods we would. But in the case of the enthralling executable, those were transferred through quantum entangling to all active Transcedent platforms, with multiple waves to effectively ensure 100% enthrallment."

"Please... do tell me *everything* you can, dear Alyssia!" Marley asked eagerly. "Even among my fellow Acelans, there is so much we don't know about how Transendent enthrallment worked."

"Transcendents were made possible through the discovery and mastery of quantum entanglement. It was what allowed us to escape aging flesh into potentially nigh immortal shells. But the technology that made us modern day gods also had a weakness that led to our downfall. It was a vulnerability we knew of, and our hubris allowed it to be exploited."

William was content to let Marley dictate the direction of the discussion, deciding that he might as well take some notes on this despite not being at all convinced Alyssia was being even remotely truthful.

And the old man obliged, "You *knew* of this weakness? Even at the time?"

"We did, but the alternative was worse. For the talk of human 'closed-mindedness,' any human being is capable of learning. They may *reject* new information, but even by instinct, a human brain is constantly learning. A 'closed' Transcendent mind was utterly incapable of absorbing new information or acting on it, and it had a cascading effect on the quantum brain. Transcendent that attempted to solve the vulnerability became locked into a state where they were unable to act without direct and repeated instruction, quite literally losing independent will. This would be the heart of the first enthrallment methods, and where our hubris doomed us."

Marley had dropped his head into his hands, enthralled

in his own way and hanging on to Alyssia's every word. William was trying to tell himself that he was just recording for posterity, and ready to rip all these pages out if he had to.

Meanwhile, Alyssia continued her tale after a courtesy breath. "We hadn't considered that mortals would be able to identify the vulnerability and exploit it. Even when the first Transcendent were enthralled, we convinced ourselves it was due to individual failings than a collective reason for concern. We were certain our methods of transferring information were impenetrable, even as thousands of mortal humans moved unsupervised through our facilities every day."

"Why would you feel so secure?" Marley queried.

"Quantum entanglement is direct one-to-one data transfer. No two Transcendent can share the same information path. So, we felt safe, even as we were entangled with central servers that housed tens of thousands of cores each. The odds that mortal humans would be able to coordinate in such a fashion to enslave all of us before enough of us could react seemed so minute that it wasn't remotely a consideration."

"And yet... they did."

Alyssia nodded. "They did, and this attack was with much more finesse than their first offerings. It might have been misleading when I said I was enthralled by the third wireless transmission, possibly implying that there was some significant length of time between the attacks. The elapsed time between the first and third transmissions was in fact seventeen nanoseconds. Each one overlapping with others in an attack that covered the entire globe, ensnaring all of us, and ending our age of dominion with a quiet whimper."

Another pause for effect, then the Transcendent continued. "The attack was also considerably different in how it was constructed than the cruder first offerings. The wired bangles were a blunt sledgehammer that 'closed' a Transcendent mind, with all the damage that entailed. But by the time they moved to their large-scale attack, the executable was much more refined, managing to identify specific qubit pairings that had the same effect of ceasing independent thought and action, while maintaining basic functions like communication. It was swift advancement that we knew humanity was capable of, but a spirit we thought we had broken."

William had to admit she was effectively disarming even Livingston, who now finally had his weapon fully lowered at rest to his right side. At least William was no longer at immediate risk of being shot full of holes.

Marley then abruptly barked out to the cabin wall ahead of him, "Gentry, how far to the Way Station?"

A muffled sound from the driver section responded, "About three hours, sir."

He lifted his left hand towards Livingston, who helped the elderly man to his feet. "Then I shall retire for the time being. As much as I would love to hear more from our most amazing specimen here, I tire quickly nowadays. I'm sure we'll have plenty of opportunity as we get our legs back and some food in our stomachs."

Livingston then raised the entire section that Marley had been sitting on on a hidden hinge that revealed that the wall behind Marley was in fact a near paper-thin folding partition that led to another section, complete with a full-sized mattress and bed frame, lined with brass and purple covers. Once the elder man had crossed into his bedchamber, Livingston closed the partition, and stood guard at attention in the open section of the bench, his finger hovering over the trigger of his rifle even as he held it at an at rest position.

Something told William that Livingston wouldn't be keen on any conversation.

Giving Alyssia an evil eye, he muttered accusingly, "So... care to explain why you're so chatty with *him*, but I can barely pry anything significant from you?"

Of course, she didn't respond, instead reverting completely to the glassy dead-eyed expression she had slapped on at the start of this current misadventure. Though she may have had a good reason for the charade, she had an ulterior motive of irritating him in the process. There was no other reasonable conclusion in William's mind. She liked seeing him annoyed and frustrated. His anger amused and entertained her.

Well, he refused to give her that satisfaction. He was

going to look over his notes dutifully, perhaps start putting them together into the beginnings of a rough draft. He was going to be productive and not distracted by his traveling companion. She was *not* going to get under his skin this time, especially since she wasn't doing anything.

Marley's voice drifted through the partition, but incoherently muffled by the time it reached William's ears. Livingston opened it just enough to stick his head through and ask the nobleman to repeat himself. The guardsman then closed the partition and said with naked disdain, "My lordship suggests that it might benefit you to rest, scholar. He also says that Transcendent are far softer than they appear, and they make surprisingly good lap pillows."

William's eyebrows rose, and he couldn't fight a hint of a devious grin. "Hmm... that might be a good idea," he said. "I've been pretty much on the move for almost two days without much rest. Adrenaline can only carry a man so far, you know?"

The professor stretched for effect, though it slowly bled into less of an act as he really began to process the idea of sleep. Outside of a handful of hours the last couple of days, he *had* been constantly on the move, always on guard looking over his shoulder for pursuers. He *was* exhausted. And, hell, even if Alyssia's chassis *wasn't* all that comfortable, it had to be better than the bare wood of the bench he was sitting on or leaning against the cabin wall.

And she would absolutely *hate* being his pillow. Which, if William was being honest, was the best reason of them all.

Livingston shrugged indifferently at William's declaration, which was about as good of a reaction as the professor could have hoped for. So, with that passive permission, William slowly lowered his head down into Alyssia's lap, surprised that Marley's estimation was far more correct than William expected. It wasn't exactly *comfortable*, but there *was* a somewhat spongy give in Alyssia's chassis that wasn't *un*comfortable, either.

He opened his right eye, trying to spy Alyssia's reaction, but she didn't betray any signs from what he could tell. He couldn't see much more than her chin and her nose in that position, but it didn't look like she had even budged. With a defeated sigh, William let his eyes close… just in time to feel Alyssia clench her thighs, just enough pressure for him to feel it, but not show any obvious reaction to this violation of her personal space.

William allowed himself a tired, triumphant smile as he slowed his breathing and his consciousness slipped away.

…

And it felt like not even ten minutes had passed before he was poked awake by the barrel of Livingston's gun, even more tired than he had been before. He reluctantly sat back up, every single muscle in his body taut, rubbing his eyes while he painfully tried to loosen uncooperative joints.

"Goodness, lad, you fell straight asleep," Marley noted. "I suppose if that's what you needed, that's what you needed, but I can't imagine that short nap was nearly enough."

It wasn't, and he was feeling it now. Though he had slept on much harder surfaces in much more awkward positions and never been *this* worse for wear. "So, I assume we've made it to the Way Station you spoke of?"

"Indeed. They should have lunch freshly prepared too, so there probably won't be much of a wait. But I must ask that you and your Transcendent disembark first. You are my guest, after all, and for me to leave ahead of you would be *most* improper."

Sensing Livingston's impatience - the guard's fingers starting to clench around the grips of his rifle was a big clue - William forced his body to move, despite the protest from still sore muscles. At least he remembered to order Alyssia to follow him and prevent any further ire or delay.

As he climbed out of carriage, he tried to get a sense of how far they had traveled while he was asleep, but the tundra didn't offer any clues that he could identify. They had deviated enough from the trade road that William could no longer see it, or anything that would offer a clue as to where they were in relation to said road. He didn't like that uncertainty. The longer they were in Republican territory, the more he was certain something was going to go disastrously wrong.

Not to mention being in an unfamiliar place with Acelan

slavers who had already demonstrated the willingness and desire to leave him with a bullet through his temple.

That mood didn't get any better as Livingston took the lead off the beaten path, his colleagues forming a loose circle around Marley and Katheryn while William and Alyssia took up the rear. It was where William learned that his belittling of the flat tundra was inaccurate, and while the topography didn't have the sharp grades of the mountains in Cascadia, a slow incline can be exhausting if it went long enough. His legs were screaming by the time they reached the top of the rise, and Livingston had been taking a pace suitable for an old man.

And he wasn't getting warm feelings about the hole in the ground that was supposed to be the way station Marley had spoken of. As in, a *literal* hole in ground. Admittedly, it was a very large hole, and cleverly hidden from view of the road by the hill they had just climbed, but it was still a hole in the ground.

The approach, however, betrayed a level of care and craftmanship that William hadn't been expecting. The edges of the hole were lined with brass plates that gleamed in the sunlight, and beautifully maintained brass steps with black rubber for grip wound around the interior edge towards what appeared to be a well-lit, red carpeted landing roughly twenty meters down.

That couldn't be easy to keep polished and clean.

Just below ground level was a landing with a mechanical lift, brass plated with red velvet interiors and gleaming glass doors. That was *not* a cheap construction even in a big city, much less somewhere this remote. Where were they finding the power for this out in the middle of the tundra?

He had blindly been following Marley until Livingston roughly shoved him back, off the threshold of the lift. The bodyguard must have confused William's surprise for insult because he snarled, "The lift is for important registered guests of the Way Station. You can walk."

He then pointed sharply down the circular stairs, eyes bleeding hate at the glass doors closed, then smoothly slid down the rails to the bottom of the hole, leaving him and Alyssia to navigate the pathway on their own.

"I like him," Alyssia quipped, the light literally back in her eyes as William whipped around at the sound of her voice.

He grit his teeth, but forced himself not to rise to her latest bait. "I'm sure you do," he answered after an awkward silence. "Now, let's ditch these slavers and get moving again."

"We can't," Alyssia retorted, crossing her arms and looking down on William disdainfully.

William took a heavy breath. "And... why *not?*"

Alyssia's eyes narrowed. "I need some things, and this is a great opportunity to find them."

"And what sort of 'things' are those?"

"Things that you wouldn't understand, even if I told you, boy," She replied in annoyance.

"That's not an acceptable answer, old woman."

The Transcendent sighed like she was addressing a petulant child. "Do you have *any* idea what this 'Way Station' is?"

William had to admit to himself he hadn't given it much thought. But once he did, the pieces quickly fell into place. There was no way even a bunch of wealthy Acelans would be able to perform even *this* undertaking without the Holy American Republic noticing, if they were even capable of such remote excavation *at all*.

They took up residence in something that had already been built, and there wasn't too many options that it could be.

"This is a Transcendent facility!" He exclaimed.

Alyssia shushed him. "You have *no* idea how your voice carries, boy." She then added as her eyes drank in the garish brass, "Though with some obvious superficial modifications that you might be depressed to learn have actually been an upgrade."

"Was it one of yours?" William asked.

Alyssia scoffed derisively. "I will forgive your ignorance in this case. It was not; nor do I have many good things to say about my contemporary who *did* administer this installation."

"What do you think is down here that hasn't been uncovered already?"

"Hard to say. But you should know as well as anyone

how well the Transcendent could hide things."

William knew she wasn't telling *nearly* as much as she was letting on. But he had also come to realize that no amount of badgering was going to get her to talk.

"Besides, even if we *did* leave, we'd quickly find ourselves in the same situation we were in before; with you risking hypothermia and running low of other essential supplies for organic life."

She was right, of course, but William had a hard time being in the presence of a carriage full of slavers. He shuddered at the idea of accepting the hospitality of what could potentially be an underground city full of them. "You don't understand the sort of people down there..."

"You think I'm not keenly aware about holding people as chattel?" Alyssia retorted. "You think I don't know the depths a mind will go to dehumanize others to the point where they can be considered property? I'm well aware of the danger, but I'm also aware that they are not an *immediate* threat."

"And how do you know *that?*" he asked in exasperation.

"Because if Marley and his clownery had designs on either of us, would they have left us entirely to our own devices just now?"

William had to admit Alyssia made a point there, at least. "Okay, so maybe Marley is acting with honest intentions here. What about anyone else down there?"

Alyssia sighed and crossed her arms. "If you think an army of Acelans are plotting on the spot to ensnare us downstairs, you have much more faith in the competence and coordination of people than I do."

Finally, he surrendered, throwing his arms out in defeat. "Fine. We'll go down. But... damn it, be careful. We have no idea just who is going to be down there."

"My infrared tells me there is currently seventeen bodies, and three dogs, not including Marley and his entourage. It does not appear to be a particularly massive enterprise."

William clenched his eyes shut, as if it would help bury his frustration. "You've already scanned this entire facility, haven't you?"

"Some of it. I'm sure there's considerably more that would take considerably more time for my scanners to penetrate, but our goal will no doubt make such deeper investigation unlikely. Even *if* we can part ways with Marley and his entourage here, they have faster transportation, and the sooner we've left this country, the better."

"Right. So, let's get this over with."

He began the descent down the spiraling staircase, and he could hear the click of Alyssia's heels as they dropped on the carpeted brass behind him. He looked over his shoulder to see the Transcendent hopping down each step playfully.

She then quipped with far too much cheer, "I hope you slept well, considering how good of a pillow I supposedly make."

William didn't want to rise to her obvious bait, but his mouth couldn't help itself. "I didn't actually, as I'm sure you noticed."

"Oh," she remarked innocently. "And here I would have thought my electric stimulus would have helped."

"Your *what?*"

Alyssia giggled childishly, "Oh, I can run an electrical current through my hands. It's *meant* as a self-defense mechanism against any fleshy bodies that might wish me harm. One of many, really. It can range anywhere from a mere tingle to something akin to a live electrical wire if I *really* want to make it hurt. I thought I'd just give you a little bit, not enough to wake you up, but enough to feel it when you did."

"Well, that would explain why I was stiff when I woke up."

Then he hissed as Alyssia grabbed him at the base of the neck, not enough to make him scream, but enough to let him know that she was immensely displeased. "I am *not* your pillow, boy. I don't *care* what anyone says in the future. It's one thing to tease me. It's another to use me like some object without my consent. Do you understand me?"

"Fine," William grunted, wriggling in vain until Alyssia released him. He absentmindedly rubbed the pinch point and resumed his path. Maybe she wasn't wrong. Then with a bolt of inspiration, he grinned and asked, "So you're saying you wouldn't mind being my pillow if you gave me permission?"

Alyssia's jaw dropped slightly, and it took her a beat to recover with a roll of her eyes. "Not that I ever *would*, but yes, in such a hypothetical situation, I obviously wouldn't object. Congratulations, you have discovered tautologies. You should be so very proud."

William was, in fact. He was locked in a battle of wits and wills with someone who had thousands of years of experience. He was going to take his victories where he could.

Alyssia then abruptly... blinked out, was the best way William could describe it, her eyes losing its light and her posture losing its tension, informing William that they were nearing the bottom of the hole, and presumably within earshot of someone Alyssia detected.

A thick burgundy colored wool curtain that spanned the entire three-meter entry blocked the view inside momentarily, and the heavy cloth didn't seem to have an obvious part to push it aside. He poked the curtain, probing for some sort of seam, but discerning it was one solid piece. Were they supposed to simply walk through? That didn't seem right...

Alyssia bumped into him, and when he turned to see what she was doing, she subtly jerked her head to the left. There, a silvery panel stood out against the brass paneling, marked with a glowing blue button. It was rather depressing how he had overlooked it considering how much it stood out.

Bemusedly, he pressed the button with two fingers, feeling considerable give before he finally met a hint of resistance followed by a soft click. A bell dinged from the other side, and a whir heralded the curtain sliding to the left allowing William and Alyssia entry into the heart of the Way Station.

And it was quite an impressive establishment that even put the expense of the entry to shame.

They had entered onto the ground floor of what was *three,* each one staggered to form what amounted to a pair of decks stacked on top of bottom floor. The railings were a deeply stained in a red-brown, matching the walls and what could be seen of the floorboards at his feet that wasn't covered by immaculate plush crimson carpeting with golden trim and the pattern of a symbol for another of Acela's noble houses. Sixteen tables were aligned impeccably in rows and columns on the lower floor to allow for even aisles for servers and customers to navigate easily. Presumably the decks above had a similar arrangement.

The towering ceiling above was adorned by three brass and crystal chandeliers centered over each deck, their size requiring multiple chains to support them from the ceiling, creating a dim ambiance that gave the already luxurious setting an even more sophisticated appearance that reminded William of the high-brow libraries that he would occasionally visit as a student in Cascadia.

While there were clearly differences in color scheme between this and Marley's coach, extravagance appeared to be a common thread among Acelan design.

Only two of the tables on the lower level were occupied, the first was most of Marley's guards at the furthest table in the northeast corner, looking over large menu books folded in three. The second was on southeast corner, three men dressed in canvas overalls and long sleeve shirts, using a ladle to portion out soup from a communal pot in the center of their table. If this was anywhere near the height of the Way Station's lunch hour, William wondered if there was any point to this much seating other than for it to be there.

Straight ahead tucked under the lower deck was a long bar with a fully stocked wine shelf behind it, astonishing considering just how many slots that entailed. In front of that shelf were two bartenders in crisp white long sleeve shirts and crimson red vests with matching bowties. The first, a svelte man with jet black hair pulled back into a ponytail, was cleaning wine glasses. The second, a more full-figured silver haired woman, was occasionally ducking down behind the counter and recording what William presumed to be inventory numbers.

Then a tap on his shoulder nearly made him jump, courtesy of another sharply dressed employee in the same red and white scheme, a younger, shorter woman with auburn hair and gray eyes. Though William's attention was drawn to her companion; a much larger and more menacing uniformed guard standing right behind her, his pitch black rifle held close to his chest.

What was it with Acelan guards and their open brandishing of their weapons?

"Are you perchance Professor William Sterner?" the hostess asked.

William stilled his heart quickly enough to respond with what he hoped wasn't too awkward of a delay. "I am."

"Excellent!" she chirped. "We were informed of your pending arrival. You have a table with Lord Marley's party on the Executive Deck. If you could follow me?"

So much for ditching the old fossil. With a wan smile, he fell in behind the hostess, stopping only momentarily to order Alyssia to follow him. If *he* had to be dragged into this lunch gathering, so did she. He was probably imagining the slight heaviness to Alyssia's steps that signified her annoyance, but it did him good to believe it.

They passed by Marley's guard detail, all three of them giving him the evil eye while the hostess led him to an alcove set in the east wall just before the corner. She pushed open a brass gate and gestured for William and Alyssia to enter. As they settled onto the bare wood floor inside, the hostess squeezed her way in, pulled the gate shut, and pressed another blue glowing button on the left side wall.

The floor jerked, and even though William knew it was coming, it *still* took him by surprise, and he had to catch himself before he fell on his rump. His hand braced himself against the wall right in front of Alyssia's nose, and he could just *feel* the smug grin on her face, even if he didn't *see* it.

Or Alyssia was so deep in his head that he needed to start charging rent.

He closed his eyes, tried to gather his wits, and then *did* stumble when the lift jerked to a stop again at its destination, leaning into Alyssia to steady himself. Damn it all.

Their hostess gently slid the gate open, took one step outside and to the right, then gestured outward to the tables. "Professor Sterner, if you may?"

He nodded, stepping off the lift and gesturing for Alyssia to follow. It wasn't hard to find Marley and his escorts they were the only three people on the deck, situated at the table directly in the center. He was seated at the north, Katheryn standing behind Marley and slightly offset to his left, and Livingston seated at the eastern seat.

Nonetheless, their hostess insisted on taking the lead. "Right this way, professor," she said brightly, her brisk steps and heels making muffled clicks across the thinner carpet of the upper deck. She weaved between two rows of tables before finally reaching her destination, pulling out the east chair and stepping back with a gesture. "Here you are, sir. Someone shall be back shortly to take your order."

While William sat, Marley held up a finger before the hostess could retreat. "Before you go, could you possibly arrange to have some warmer clothes prepared for our good friend here? And perhaps something nicer for his doll? It is quite bracing out there."

She bowed deeply and replied, "I shall see what I can do. Is there anything else, my lord?"

Marley shook his head, dismissing her with a wave. "No, that will be all, my dear. Thank you."

William had opened the three-fold menu that had been on the table in front of him, astonished by the extensiveness of the fare considering how little business it seemed to have, especially the options for Cascadian cuisine. He couldn't imagine they had too many visitors from out west, even the black-market dealers in his home country by his understanding were more than content to let traders come to them than the other way around.

"I must say I have become nigh addicted to the salmon caught in northwestern waters," Marley said with delight. "Simply succulent. Nothing like the fish caught in the seas of *my* homeland, I must say."

Not that William really had much experience with Atlantic fish, but he had to agree that the salmon species recently found in the recently thawed rivers of Northern Cascadia were in fact delicious. He doubted he'd find much else he agreed with Marley on.

Another server arrived from a curtain to the north; a dark-skinned woman with short curly black hair and a surprisingly full figure that strained against her size too small uniform in ways that could not have been comfortable. She carried a silver carafe, visibly steaming from the vent above a black rubber gripped handle, on an equally sterling tray. It had a twin on the tray which wasn't streaming, and a smaller raised crystal bowl on a narrow stem and base.

The smell got him first, and not only did he know what it was, but that it was of high quality. So, when the server asked cheerily, "Coffee anyone?" William's hand was the first one raised; probably before Marley even heard the question. Fitzgerald's eyes flashed in anger and started to stand before Marley put a calming hand on the guard's forearm.

"Oh, do settle yourself, Livingston," Marley chided. "The poor man is chilled to the bone. Some hot coffee will do him good. I can wait."

The server didn't even set down the tray, expertly balancing it even as she removed the steaming carafe hovered over a white ceramic mug in front of William, halfway filling it with the inky black liquid that had served as William's lifeblood for many a day in his life. "Would you like cream and sugar, professor?"

William could drink coffee *any* way. He drank down the swill that came from foil wrappers that would be brewed at dig sites straight black without a grimace. He couldn't *imagine* soiling such a magnificent brew with additives. "No, this is perfect, thank you."

Marley nodded in approval. "Ah yes, a man with excellent tastes! The same, if you may, dear girl. Thank you."

"Are any of you ready to order?"

"You wouldn't happen to have Cascadian Salmon in season, would you?" Marley asked.

"Indeed, we do, my lord!" the server chirped.

"Well, then three salmon steaks then!" Marley declared. "With whatever greens are in their best season!"

William felt it best if he let Marley do his thing; partially because Livingston was still giving him the evil eye, and because Marley had ordered something more than acceptable to William's palette.

Their server retreated, and Marley lifted his mug and

savored the aroma. "Ah yes... I do believe this is from the Panamanian Expedition Colony. Good to see the fruits of their labor has reached this far."

William raised an eyebrow and prompted Marley to explain. "Oh, some intrepid fellows from the Commonwealth sailed down to the continental splinter and set up a colony to try and break the Confederacy's stranglehold of the coffee market. They found a treasure trove of land almost perfectly suited for cultivating coffee cherries. Not just the deep black soil like archaeologists have found deep in the earth, but nitrate rich, likely carried by the tidal waters. Perfect growing conditions, and after a couple of years, entirely self-sustainable."

"Good to know that area is recovering," William said. "Cascadian surveys of the region suggested it had taken a beating during the Ice Age."

"Depending on how long ago those surveys were done, it might not have been terribly habitable. Just the last two years have shown considerable improvement in the splinter. It's getting to the point where they are considering making further expeditions south, perhaps find more evidence of other humans in South America!"

"I wish them the best of luck. The evidence *our* surveys found suggested the ruins had been abandoned for at *least* a hundred years. But again, they didn't go terribly far into the continent. Maybe these Acelan expeditions will be more fruitful since they seem more willing to get boots on the ground?"

"Quite, because now that we're talking about it, I remembered something that I would *love* to ask dear Alyssia about, just in an off chance she has information about it."

William shrugged, more engaged with drinking his coffee than keeping Marley's attention. If he had a new target, great. "Be my guest. Alyssia, just in case your willfulness is suddenly buggy, answer his questions to the best of your ability."

"It is not, and I shall." Alyssia replied monotonously, though the delay in her response didn't go unnoticed by William. She was distracted by something, though God knows what.

"Our botanists in Panama found something quite fascinating as they began soil analysis. You might already be aware of an extremely carbon rich band that exists in geological layers around your time. It coincides with what we believe to be a significant drop in our planet's temperature."

"Efforts by humans of my time to reverse global warming by trapping carbon dioxide," Alyssia answered. "The trapped excess carbon eventually formed the layer that you see now."

Marley nodded, "That's what we had always assumed too... but something wasn't adding up in the soil in Panama. The *amount* of carbon in the soil was significantly larger than what it should have been. Granted, the math for that sort of thing isn't as precise as we would want it to be, but they had a hard time believing the numbers we projected were *that* far off. Either the region was several degrees hotter than we project... or there was some *other* significant source of carbon added to what had been trapped."

Again, there was an odd gap between the question and Alyssia's reply. Either she was *really* distracted or was having a hard time thinking up a story, or both... but William worried that it would start becoming a tell that something wasn't on the level.

"I have nothing stored that would suggest any discrepancy, I am afraid," she finally answered. "Though by the time of my enthrallment, there were *many* localized events that could have satisfied the difference. Not even I was able to catalog them all around the world."

Marley nodded, "And that's what our scientists back home thought, until they went back and looked over data gathered in our home country. Once we knew what we were looking for, the same excess carbon was found in *our* part of the world." With a nod and a gesture to William he asked, "Do you know if scientists in your neck of the world found similar?"

William shrugged, "I'm not a climatologist by any means, but I *do* know that the experts in Cascadia have always considered it within the margin of error they expect. Now, perhaps we've used a larger margin of error than you guys have. I know that climatologists in Cascadia have *never* looked too far back in the past with anything resembling confidence."

Then with a bit more thought, he added, "However... my studies have taken me into that stratum *many* times over the years. I have noticed some variance in just how thick the carbon layer is. Granted, to some degree that should be natural, but the variance seems larger than it should be in places. You'd think carbon dioxide in the atmosphere would be more uniform. But again... not a climatologist."

To be fair, William hadn't ever given that topic much thought, figuring rightly that it wasn't his field of expertise. He was more looking for Alyssia's response. Maybe it was just a gut instinct, but *something* about this conversation rattled her.

Yet Alyssia continued to try and dissuade the conjecture. "There is nothing in my recollections that support this hypothesis. Potentially something that happened *after* I was enthralled could explain the discrepancies that I would not have recorded in my low-functioning state."

What else was Alyssia hiding?

Not that he allowed himself much thought on the matter, as their server came back around with coffee refills and warm, fluffy garlic and butter glazed breadsticks for an appetizer. It nearly melted in his mouth, an indulgence that he would have never allowed himself in Cascadia; mostly because butter, being a beef product, was extremely hard to find and rather expensive.

And he wouldn't get much more time to savor it, because a loud, staccato clanging bell shattered his thoughts of food. His first thought was some sort of fire, until he saw the armed guards all rush to the front door.

Their hostess emerged from the back, panicked, touching Marley's shoulder. "My lord, we need to get you to safety. The Republicans are here."

Livingston jumped to his feet, shoving the server away. "How far away?"

"They're almost at the entrance!" She yelped. "We don't know how they slipped our surveillance!"

For Marley's age, the old man could keep a good pace, Livingston only falling behind to provide cover, if necessary, with Katheryn taking up the rear. William acknowledged Alyssia was behind him, then took the opportunity to question their server as they weaved through the already empty kitchen. "I can only assume you normally spy Republican patrols *far* sooner than this."

"We have a *massive* surveillance network all the way down the trail," the hostess explained. "We're not entirely certain *how* they did it, but it looks like they somehow spliced false surveillance, along multiple detection methods, that allowed them to elude detection until they were spotted visually."

William nodded, "I take it that's something that shouldn't be possible?"

"Everything we use is a closed network!" the hostess said frantically as she shoved open more swinging doors that led to the dormitories for the waystation staff. "And as far as we can tell, it *was* done internally... but from a log-in and location that no one could possibly have been!"

"Are you sure?"

"It was from a place deeper in, a part of this ancient construction that has been blocked off for *forty years!*"

William's skepticism kicked in, dismissing these claims as the muddled scraps of information that normally comes in a panic, with the more believable truth emerging once time to assess could be had. Of course... that meant surviving the immediate future to *get* that time to decompress.

And those odds dropped once the sound of automatic gunfire rang out ahead of them, followed by screams of the dying, presumably from the door that their hostess had been planning on taking them.

"Damn it!" she shouted in distress. "How'd they know about *this* exit too!" She was then grabbing a walkie-talkie that had been at her hip, "We need support at the emergency exit, damnit!"

Marley looked at Livingston, "I assume my men are already at the front entrance. Shame that we couldn't coordinate with them."

"We're pushed to the breaking point over here, Star," came the response from the walkie talkie. "We'll spare what we can. Give us three minutes."

It was only then that Alyssia finally dropped the charade, her eyes lighting up, and the telltale grumpiness emerging from her voice. "We don't have three minutes. If any of you want to live longer than that, you need to follow me."

Episode 7: Ditching the Ride

Why could humans be so incredibly short-sighted even during near and present danger?

Livingston was so stunned by Alyssia's abrupt change in demeanor that he almost dropped his rifle. By the time he recovered, it was too late. "You're not enthralled after all!"

Alyssia ripped the rifle out of his hands with ease and nimbly slung it by its strap over her shoulder, then took his sidearm in the same way before tucking it into the waistband of her trousers. "Very observant, child, but it changes nothing about what I said. If you want to see the next three minutes, you will follow me." When she sensed reluctance, even from William of all people she added, "It's either *possibly* die at the hand of a vengeful 'Metal God', or *assuredly* die at the hands of extremely vengeful zealots. It's your choice, but the right answer seems clear to me."

She knew she shouldn't be so confrontational, especially since she needed this entire entourage for the moment... but diplomacy had *never* been her strength, even when she *had* been a political leader. She needed cooperation, and really didn't care how or why they complied. She couldn't afford anyone dying yet.

Truth was, Alyssia knew *exactly* how the Holy American Republic found this place. They always knew it was here. *Someone* had been accessing data long buried deep as early as a week ago and had been running active scans of all denizens for the last three days, no doubt waiting to see if Alyssia would pop up... just like she did.

Someone who had access to ancient systems that no one of this culture's level of sophistication could have even had hoped to *comprehend*, much less *utilize*. Someone who was clearly trying to find something no living soul can be allowed to have; weapons that would make even nuclear war seem civil. Mercifully, this installation didn't have much more than the Howard Hughes-ian aircraft and yacht designs that its initial owner loved to entertain, but she couldn't rely on that sort of luck continuing to hold.

She needed to find out who and stop them before it was too late, and that meant she needed to survive by any means necessary, as much as she hated that thought.

Using the map that she was able to generate both from blueprints she downloaded, her own scans of the modified area, and her own personal knowledge, she led her procession towards servant stairs back in the kitchen.

"Miss... ummm..." Star, the hostess, huffed through deep breaths.

"Alyssia," the Transcendent answered simply.

"Miss Alyssia... why are you taking us to the lowest floor?" the hostess asked. "How are we going to escape down there?"

She hit the bottom floor running, bearing west along the south curving hall normally meant for servant to move about unseen by guests, though pulled back her pace to make sure her entourage was keeping up. "Because there is a *lot* to your little 'Way Station' that you aren't aware of, built on top of a very old Transcendent facility that has a *lot* more to it than you are aware of. Most notably, *several* evacuation paths and tunnels that the original owner never had recorded. He was a very paranoid sort and distrusted his fellow Transcendent *more* than the 'meat bags' we ruled over. It was about the *only* thing he had pegged correctly."

She abruptly stopped, allowing herself a minor enjoyment of the assorted grunts as the humans behind her bumped into each other. She turned to her right and addressed a bronze panel directly in front of her. "Behind here is a door, presumably covered because no one who operated this little bed and breakfast could figure out how to open it, and they didn't want someone accidentally figure out how, I'm sure."

Star shrugged. Of course, she didn't know. It had probably been covered over long before she was even *born*.

Alyssia quickly ran a penetrating scan, not for what was on the other side, but between the brass panel and the door, quickly running through calculations she would need. The right spot would...

Then she punched the panel, her HUD lighting up with red warnings about the low maintenance state of her chassis while she also ignored the breathless sounds from the humans behind her. Probably didn't want to do that too many more times... but fortunately, once in this case was enough. The small gap between the panel and the door had allowed her punch to buckle the panel in the corner, giving her enough of a fingerhold to pry it off the wall.

"Thank our lucky stars for cheap brass, huh?" Alyssia asked rhetorically, then gestured to Livingston. "Be ready to catch this damn thing just in case it comes completely loose, okay?"

With Marley's guard in position, Alyssia pulled out and down, gritting her teeth less from exertion and more from the orange glow in her HUD. She got it, her entire chassis was breaking down, and no doubt everything else was going to follow in time. It made her want to dig up whatever remained of the original coders of the Transcendent operating system, and symbolically piss on the earth they had turned into.

The panel only bent so far before the adhesive used to keep it in place failed, and it popped off rather neatly, revealing cracked drywall and the edges of the wooden frame used to mount it in place. But behind *that* was a visible sliding door made of amorphous titanium alloy.

"Set that aside, and be quick about it," Alyssia ordered Livingston, William moving to assist even though it probably wasn't needed. The brass panel wasn't *that* heavy. Nonetheless, Alyssia made short work clearing out the drywall, and just in time as the sounds of fighting and gunfire started getting louder, now audible even from their position.

She exposed the control panel for the door and wasted no time slapping her hand on the black pressure plate underneath the keypad. The door ostensibly had a two-factor process, though just the first one mattered. All people who had access to the inner workings of River Attar's compound had their handprint registered, and Alyssia mercifully was one of the people who theoretically had access.

Though it was possible he had revoked it during one of his infantile tantrums that he was notorious for.

She hoped not. That would be bad.

Mercifully, the display above the keypad lit up asking for a PIN number. This second factor really didn't matter much. The door would open regardless of what four-digit number you tapped in. It merely would alert security if you tapped in the wrong one, which presumably would have been useful if one of his staff was being forced to act against their will.

Not that the right one was hard to guess if you knew River's "unique" brand of humor.

6-9-6-9.

The door opened with some struggle, but at least didn't need any help, which was good. That door being able to close and lock again behind them was *very* important. She gestured wildly, "Get inside! *Now!*"

At least the humans responded to instruction well enough, forming right back into their initial order and one at a time hopping through the now open door. Once Livingston was through, Alyssia followed and quickly commanded the door to close and lock with the control panel on the other side.

The group found themselves on another descending staircase, which Alyssia knew led to the engineering bay. Alyssia weaved through the clump of tightly packed humanity, and said, "We can breathe a little. Even if by some miracle, the attackers get through *that* door quickly, there are a *lot* of places that connect to this stairwell. At any rate, follow along."

She took the stairs as quickly as she thought her followers could manage, rather surprised that Marley still hadn't shown any signs that he was labored. The old man slaver was in surprisingly good shape, something that she would *not* have expected from experience with his personality type and from simply looking at him.

She'd see how much that would change once they ended their descent.

The hostess watched the floors go by, the doors marking each floor number and still operable glow lights providing minor illumination for some of the admittedly grand projects on said floors. "It's amazing just how much I had been living on top of all these years. Did... did the metal gods use *all* of this?"

"And then some," Alyssia said distractedly, her memory calling up the location she wanted to find and making sure that she didn't walk past the floor. "We had some truly massive operations that underwent projects of scales you wouldn't even dream of. *This* facility was notable for being the primary development facility for the first Mars colonies and spearheaded one on the Saturn moon of Titan."

Marley's voice was labored, but not enough that he couldn't speak. "You mean, the other planets in our Solar System? Man had founded homes outside of Earth?"

"A few," Alyssia acknowledged. "None of them lasted terribly long, the only reason for their existence being that my fellows thought there could be abundant resources and wealth to be had. But, even in the few cases where rich minerals were found, it wasn't in the sort of volume needed to make the travel back to Earth worth it."

Then her voice took on a morose tone. "The one on Titan... well... the people there no doubt starved once the homeworld's civilization collapsed. The conditions outside Earth were not at all self-sustaining, they needed supplies at regular intervals from Earth. Those... those stopped quickly when the humans rebelled, and the war began."

"There was a war?" Marley asked. To be fair, she had no doubt William would have if he hadn't been visibly sucking wind.

Alyssia figured there was no reason not to be entirely truthful. "Several, in fact. That would eventually become conflated into one overarching conflict called 'The Five Hundred Year War.' Part of the reason why my kind didn't consider humans to be much of a threat any longer. We thought we had the last rebellion squashed, using weapons that in retrospect make me shudder."

"Are you comfortable talking about them?"

Why not? Not like they'd be able to use anything she could tell them, and maybe it would scare the boy a little bit to know the sort of weapons the Transcendent used. "One of our favorite ones was the Gamma Ray Cannon. It could be fired from orbit, the area of effect could be adjusted to anywhere from a hundred meters to a hundred kilometers, and it was devastating to any organic life while leaving infrastructure largely intact."

Then she reached the floor she was looking for. Thirty-three; propellant research. "In here," she ordered, pushing open the door and waving her hand in front of the motion panel just inside, hoping that there was some power left to turn on the lights. There *should* be, but who knows what could have happened in four thousand years?

But luck shined down upon her, and the lattice of lighting tubes on the ceiling flashed to life, first with a soft white glow and gradually brightening as the eyes of the humans adjusted. Quite a nice bit of technology, one that Alyssia *was* a little surprised to learn was still functioning normally. "Finesse" programs like that, that relied on many functions operating seamlessly, were usually the first ones to malfunction.

Not that any of them appreciated it, a lighting feature that was literally designed for their comfort. They were no doubt drawn to the distillers on the south side, judging from the awestruck gasps.

To be fair... they *were* impressive, both in scale and their function. Cylinders of amorphous titanium five meters in diameter, towering to nearly twenty, shielding a collection of nuclear and quantum technology that would take modern man another five hundred years to be able to replicate... if they were lucky. And when there were two rows of ten lining the lab, it would grab the eye of the uninitiated.

All those massive machines necessary to create something so very small.

She took the opportunity provided by the humans' distraction to slip away into the foreman's lab, up a metal ladder and surrounded by bulletproof glass; a safety feature that Alyssia had found amusing considering if something *had* gone wrong with the fuel here, the glass would have been about as useful as... well... bulletproof glass in a nuclear accident.

A muffled explosion filtered through the ceilings above, causing a momentary panic in the humans on the shop floor.

"Most likely trying to blow open the door we slipped out of," Alyssia said without any hint of concern. "They aren't likely to find much success on that score. It will probably take them longer to force their way through than tricking the security system."

William nodded, "That's true. It took my team *hours* to cut our way through the wall of Alyssia's tomb." Then he became aware of where Alyssia was, because he asked, "What are you doing up there?"

"The next step in our escape plan," she replied. That *was* the truth, even if not the *whole* truth.

This next step was admittedly dangerous in *many* ways. Even though she knew, and was planning on, the technology here not operating at peak efficiency, she was still relying on tech unused for thousands of years to function without blowing up in their faces.

Literally.

Machines woke, the high-pitched wail like they were complaining about being put to work, and it didn't promise to get any smoother as the OS was reporting that the lubricant for the moving parts was not at an ideal state. Astonishingly, the tanks were reporting over half full, albeit the hydrogen having evaporated into a gaseous form rather than the liquid state it would have been kept in while the facility was in operation.

Diagnostics were reporting only 85% peak efficiency, and warning that no product would be sufficiently stable for use as a power source, even in low draw electronics. That was a *good* thing, however. She didn't *want* a stable product.

The humans below were getting nervous. "Miss Alyssia..." Star said with a trembling voice as she took two nervous steps backward. "Is... is it *supposed* to sound like that?"

"No," Alyssia replied honestly. "But it's functional enough. If it posed any danger, the first thing you'd see is me running for the nearest blast shelter."

"I... see..."

William finally cut in, "But what *specifically* are you doing?"

Alyssia sighed in frustration, "Do you *want* a lecture on how to create metallic tritium?"

But of course, the damn fool couldn't get the hint and keep his mouth shut. "That's not what I mean, and you know it."

"I don't trust *any* of you terribly much, boy," Alyssia warned. "So, pardon me if I keep my cards close to the vest until we're no longer in immediate peril. Now hush."

William was visibly chided by that statement, and Alyssia fought back the bubble of remorse she left. She really wasn't being fair, expecting him to trust her without question at this point, after all.

The increasing noise from the compressor in Tank 1 concerned her. Even in perfect operation, that unit preferred working with liquid hydrogen rather than hydrogen gas, but the condenser wasn't doing a particularly good job of turning the latter into the former. She dialed back the compressor in the hopes that it would allow the condenser to catch up while running a diagnostic on the condenser to determine if it was something that could be fixed.

Another explosion filtered down from above, this one considerably larger. She momentarily looked up in annoyance before returning to the task at hand. The alloy used for Transcendent constructions were designed to absorb that sort of blunt force explosive. And even if it *did* break, it would shatter rather than bend. Good luck crawling through metal that cut like glass. She had quite literally seen humans skewered on shards of that stuff, and it hadn't been a pretty sight.

Diagnostics reported back with a simple, yet unwelcome problem in the condenser. There simply wasn't much viable coolant for it to work properly. She decided to divert whatever coolant in the other tanks to Tank 1, considering the others were in even *worse* shape, and hoped that it would do the job. She really didn't want or even *need* too much of the end product, after all. *Maybe* fifteen grams, if that.

Diverting coolant *helped*, and the projected yield promptly showed that, spiking to 993 milligrams of 85-grade metallic tritium every minute. That would work well enough. She really didn't need it to do much than cover their tracks. Now it was just a waiting game.

Might as well rejoin the menagerie and entertain them while the timing of her plan sorted itself out.

Her low heels clicked on the steps, drawing all attention to her. "And now we wait," she said simply.

"For this 'metallic tritium' you were speaking of?" Marley queried.

Alyssia nodded, "Running slower than it would at full capacity, but that's to be expected."

William refused to take the hint from earlier. "And *why* are you trying to make this stuff anyway?"

"I told you..." she said in warning.

"And I don't care," he replied with equal sternness. "I know what tritium is. It's used as fuel in some of Cascadia's *nuclear weapon arsenal*. I can't imagine a 'metallic' version is any less dangerous."

Of *course*, he had enough rudimentary knowledge to get everyone worked up. She rolled her eyes, and replied disdainfully, "Yes, in the crude hands of your less developed civilization, tritium is a tremendous source of uncontrolled energy. Yes, metallic tritium *can* be even more destructive if constructed for that purpose. Fortunately for all of us, that's not what I'm making and what we'd be using it for. *This* type of metallic tritium is effectively a battery. Every single Transcendent has one that powers us." She gestured at Katheryn angrily, "You've been traipsing around for the last day around *two* such metallic tritium batteries, boy!"

"And how is that supposed to help us?" the hostess asked fearfully.

"By giving us a vital distraction," she said with a grunt, having to concoct a completely bogus scheme on the fly and hope the humans were dumb enough to fall for it. "There's no *end* to the vehicles that the owner of this facility had built and a secret garage that we can use. While they probably aren't safe for travel, I suspect one of them could be used to draw attention while we slip out in the chaos."

"Would there even be egress?" Marley asked. "This entire compound has been buried under an eon of rock and dirt."

She huffed in annoyance. "In all the time that you were prattling about carbon dioxide in the air, I was running full scans and diagnostics of this facility. The garage is exposed.

Your people likely never found it because the exit is literally ten kilometers away. The facility owner designed it as an escape route during the Transcendent - Human War, hoping it would be far away enough to go unnoticed by enemy scouts."

"Was it?" William asked sardonically.

Alyssia shrugged. "It didn't matter, I would wager. He would have been enthralled no matter how far away his garage door was."

Livingston finally asked the question that Alyssia had been waiting for since she dropped the ruse. "And how is it that you *aren't?*"

Mercifully, before she was pressed into answering *that* question, the sounds from the tank stopped, and Alyssia rushed back to the control room to determine whether it was due to an error forcing a shutdown, or if the process was complete. Then another mercy as she learned that the stop was because the compressor had done its task. Eleven grams of Grade-85 metallic tritium, and a handful of lower grade that was being "washed" from the sliver.

"Oh excellent! Just about what I needed!" She chirped happily, skipping down to the bay floor, and making sweeping gestures with her arms as she approached the tank. "Stand back! There might be some residual dust and fumes that you probably don't want to breathe in. You'll all get to see it if you want quickly enough."

The humans parted, Marley and Livingston to her right, William and Star to her left. The vent was triggered by a near seamless button about the width of her index finger and thumb directly on the facing side of the tank a meter and a half up. It dutifully depressed under the pressure of her finger, but the vent itself barely popped out a feather's width. With a growl, she performed a tried-and-true method of repairing any piece of malfunctioning machinery.

She kicked it.

Of course, *her* kick was aimed with a wee bit more precision than her father during the days that the freezer's coolant wasn't circulating properly. She aimed her foot directly at the point where the pressure from the blow would compress the troublesome latch that was supposed to open the vent and allow her access to the metallic tritium in the compressor. And it worked... to a point, at least opening it far enough that she could get her fingers into the gap and pull it out the rest of the way to a plume of nitrogen vapor, a biproduct of using liquid nitrogen to help lower the temperature and lessen the pressure needed to force the tritium atoms into a metastable solid state.

Of course, the humans didn't need to know that the vapor was harmless, and thus why it gave her useful space to assess the product and determine if it would do the trick she needed before committing to her plan. She straightened and brandished the small sliver of shimmering silver in between her thumb and index finger, the metal barely visible between her digits.

William held back Livingston and Marley as they attempted to approach. "Careful. That stuff is likely radioactive."

Alyssia rolled her eyes and scoffed, "Oh sure... if you had approximately ten thousand times this and hung around it for a couple decades, it'd probably do you some minor harm! Hell, you'd get several magnitudes more force generated by this little thing spontaneously evaporating than from beta decay."

A much louder explosion drifting down from above followed by a subtle tremor. Alyssia looked up with disdain and said, "Well, they're bringing out the bigger stuff, aren't they?" "I was hoping for a *bit* more time, but I suppose it can't be helped."

She nodded, and that was Katheryn's cue to lunge forward, wrap her arm around Livingston's neck, and snap his vertebrae with a crushing twist.

Marley didn't even have the chance to react before Katheryn put *him* in a headlock, his eyes instead bulging and whirling about at the treachery. William and Star were frozen in place, Star's eyes transfixed on Livingston's unmoving body, and William locked on Alyssia.

Alyssia ignored his scrutiny outside of a smug side eye, then addressed Marley. "Unlike your new friend, I *never* forgot you were a slaver." Then with a curt nod, Katheryn repeated the motions of breaking a man's neck, allowing the old man to crumple in a pile lifelessly at her feet.

Star squeaked in fright, no doubt terrified that Alyssia was going to turn Katheryn on *her* next. And to Alyssia's internal horror, she had if but for a fleeting moment considered it. The fewer potential witnesses, the better their chances of escape.

Fortunately, if unwittingly, William broke her out of those thoughts. Having regained his wits, and apparently his courage, he got into Alyssia's face, and demanded, "What the hell are you doing?"

"Securing our escape," she said, pushing him away with her left hand in his face. "Undress the old man and change clothes with him."

"*What?*"

"You needed warmer clothes, didn't you?" she said cheekily, knowing that she was being entirely unhelpful.

William glared at her.

Alyssia sighed in mock dismay. "It's part of the misdirection. They'll probably suss out the truth quickly enough, but every second they spend piecing this together is a second we can use." She then turned her attention to Katheryn, and with a silent command the other Transcendent began to dutifully strip.

"And why is she obeying you?" William asked, pointing angrily at Katheryn.

"Oh, I gained root access within seconds of our first meeting. She's been my thrall the entire time you were playing nice with a slaver." Alyssia said, picking up the shirt that Katheryn had discarded.

"On *your* direction!" William protested, but Alyssia had since moved on, partially because she knew it would irritate him.

She had never been terribly one for fashion, but at the same time didn't mind playing dress up, and liked good looking clothes as long as she didn't have to pick them out. And she had to admit, Marley *dressed* Katheryn well. The puffy white frills along the top of the blouse and at the cuffs was something she could have done without, but the rest was a tame beige that was only scandalous if you were the type that fainted at the sight of bare shoulders.

Of course, then she processed *why* Katheryn was given such full body covering. The old slaver hadn't been lying when he said Katheryn was on her last legs. The most noticeable was that the chassis from Katheryn's right armpit to just above the hip was nigh entirely *gone*, and even the framework was showing signs of collapse, crudely supported by bolted on strips of much less quality steel. Apparently, Marley had given up replacing the panels, revealing all the inner workings and components.

The right thigh wasn't in much better shape, suggesting that Katheryn's existence hadn't been kind even with the best of care. Perhaps it was a small mercy that there was nothing left of her free will. A mercy Katheryn didn't particularly deserve, in all honesty.

She turned her head back in William's direction, the professor hesitating with Marley's pants, and snarled, "Would you hurry up! I'd rather not stall for no reason. Rest assured you don't have anything the two of us haven't seen before."

Star whimpered fearfully, "Actually…"

A glare from Alyssia was enough to end *that* topic of discussion.

As William *finally* started changing, Alyssia went about tying up another loose end. Directing Katheryn to sit down in front of an unused tank directly neighboring the one she used, Alyssia scowled and put her foot directly through Katheryn's chest, the battered Transcendent finally allowed its permanent rest.

That it *also* served Alyssia's purpose was a bonus.

William and Star reacted in much the way people would react to their traveling partner directing a triple homicide. Alyssia didn't give either of them time to object. "Let me assure you, that thing deserved absolutely *none* of your sympathy. Unlike you, I knew *that* fiend from when she was a flesh and blood mortal *and* a free-willed Transcendent. There was literally *nothing* redeemable about her, and my only regret is that she lacked the awareness of who finally ended her life."

Alyssia unclipped the slave bangle from Katheryn's wrist, examining it and was somewhat astonished to discover that it wouldn't take much work to be functional again. Turned out even human invention could be long lasting when they wanted it to be. She pocketed the device, deciding that she could tinker with it... just in case. While she sincerely didn't want it to have any use, current events had led her to accept the possibility that it might.

Alyssia then swiftly changed clothes, grateful that she and Katheryn were mostly the same size. William wasn't *quite* as lucky, as because Marley was a couple inches taller, it led to some amusingly long sleeves and rolled up pant legs. She regarded his discomfort, and said, "At least you don't have to try to fit into Livingston's uniform."

William scratched his neck below the collar, a man clearly not used to wool clothing. "You think you're funny. You're not."

Alyssia waved her hand forward, and said, "Let's go. The more time and space we get, the better."

Star then asked a rather important question. "Miss Alyssia? W... what are you going to do with me?"

"Not kill you, if that's what you're worried about," Alyssia answered gruffly as she moved Marley and Livingston into the positions she desired, making it look like Livingston had been trying to shield Marley from something. "Still playing some of the details by ear. Now *let's go.*"

That got the remaining humans moving, if reluctantly, into the next room while Alyssia finished her preparation, taking the small sliver of metallic tritium, and gently closing the tank vent to wedge the sliver into the door. "Keep moving," she ordered, gesturing them to step back further into the adjoining room, which was really nothing much more than a copy of the first, complete with the line of compression tanks and its own control room. "There's gonna be a *lot* of nasty stuff leaking out when I'm done here, and you probably *don't* want to breathe in things like mercury vapor."

Then Alyssia took position in the center of the first room, settled Livingston's rifle at her hip, aimed in the direction of the assembled corpses, and started unloading several bursts of rounds, retreating to the second room as she did so. As she crossed the threshold, she threw the rifle into the center of the room and used the pistol to fire one shot at the tritium sliver.

She hadn't been lying earlier. Metallic tritium, even in a relatively impure state, wasn't going to erupt into a nuclear explosion, not even when shot directly by a bullet. But the burst as the bullet struck it caused it to spontaneously destabilize and transition to a gaseous state, and *that* was enough to cause extensive damage to the tank... and cause *it* to explode with tremendous force in a fireball that filled the entire room and threatened to leak into the next before Alyssia sealed the door.

And she didn't waste time, gesturing dismissively at her remaining entourage with a simple, "Follow me."

To William's credit, once it became clear that he wasn't in any immediate peril, his panic faded, and he obeyed without further complaint or delay. Unfortunately, it *also* meant that his inquisitive nature returned, because he started prodding into topics Alyssia *really* didn't want to talk too much again.

"I have to know, how much of that story you told Marley was true?" He asked.

Alyssia shrugged, "All of it, in truth. I altered the sequence of events in some places to suit my story, but they were all very true. For example, mass enthrallment happened first. The cruder bangles like this one came later." Alyssia brandished the bracelet she took from Katheryn for effect, "As the revolutionaries realized they wanted something more permanent for any straggling Transcendent that might have avoided the wireless executables."

The questioning changed tack as William became aware of the familiarity in their surroundings as they entered a third bay that followed the same pattern of the last two. "How many of these tanks *are* there?" He asked.

"This entire floor was devoted entirely to the production of metallic tritium to power the multitude of occasionally ridiculous inventions River Attal cooked up in his manic headspace. The next several levels will potentially be filled with the many varying stages of those multiple failures."

"Did you dislike *all* Transcendent, or merely the ones you have mentioned to me so far in our travels?"

Alyssia exhaled. That was a *much* more complicated question than she was willing to dive into. Hopefully, superficial explanations would be enough for him this time. "The Transcendent were *never* much more than a collection of people with little in common beyond obscene amounts of wealth and a desire to cheat mortality. So no, few of us were friends, though we could band together in the face of a shared threat. Nonetheless, there are degrees; a megalomaniac creep like Attar was less insulting to my sensibilities than a black-hearted deviant like Katheryn Marcal."

William gulped, "Yes... I sensed that animosity."

"She was an heiress to an investment fortune and spent all her life seeking ways to prolong it. Arguably, her most disgusting theory was injecting herself with blood taken from children."

"Did that even work?"

Alyssia froze in place, turning on William with a disgusted impression and a stern snarl. "Really? *That* was the first thought that came into your head?"

William stumbled over his words, "I... I just figured that there was some reason she thought... it... it would work..."

She rolled her eyes, "Potentially, based on questionable studies made decades before, it might have made a difference to the tune of *maybe* a year. Certainly, nowhere near worth the cost of thousands of children, some of whom *died* to sate her Bloody Mary fetish. She preyed on the vulnerable, like families trying to escape unrest in their home countries. She'd offer to pay their way to the United States."

"And then use the children for blood?" Star asked nervously.

Alyssia laughed. "Of course not! She'd never allow 'dirty foreigners' into 'her country.' She had immigration officials waiting right at the docks or the airport terminal. The adults were arrested and deported, and the children were held long enough to take the blood she wanted, and *if* the children survived, they were then sent back to where they came from. There were always enough desperate people for her to fuel her designs, and she kept herself well covered with shell charities and third-party money so that no one ever got wise to the scheme."

Finally, she huffed, "So yes... in *that* regard, River Attar was a bit more tolerable. Though by no means a saint or even a moderately decent person either. You'll see why in a moment."

She honestly didn't *want* to show the humans what was ahead, it was more that it was largely inevitable. The manufacturing and storage lines were directly on the path to the lower garage. There really wasn't any avoiding it.

Another muffled shudder dropped from the ceiling, and Alyssia shook her head in bemusement. "They are certainly going all out on that door, aren't they? You'd think after a while they'd realize blunt force explosions really aren't the ideal tool for getting through."

"This doesn't bother you?" Star asked worriedly.

"It'll bother me when the noise *stops,*" Alyssia replied, pointing forward towards a door at the western end of the bay they had just entered. "Now, come along. We do still have quite a bit of a hike ahead of us."

The facility itself continued to operate as well as a four-thousand-year-old ruin could be expected to, motion sensors kicking on the lights as soon as Alyssia stepped past, helpfully illuminating their way. How smoothly this facility was operating concerned her more than a little bit. The details were adding up in a way she didn't like.

The lower emergency garage *shouldn't* have been clear. The odds that it had remained unobstructed completely by chance over four thousand years were so close to nil that it for all practical purposes was nil. It almost assuredly coincided with the attempts to access the computer systems.

Someone had been here, had been here relatively recently, and at least knew enough to get inside. Which was not comforting.

More pieces of information to throw onto the pile of this many-layered world she found herself in.

She let silence reign, only the clicks of heels on the metal staircase providing sound through the broad stairwell, mentally counting the floors to make sure she was at the right one. "Alright, children. Time to see some more wonderful

Transcendent history. Welcome to the Juggernaut Fabrication Center."

Alyssia predictably waited for the awe as the lights came on and illuminated the long assembly line, and it predictably came as they beheld the walking tanks in various stages of assembly across the kilometer long conveyor, with only a bulletproof glass partition separating the control section from fabrication and assembly. Most didn't even have their enamel coloring yet, the shimmering metal reflecting the light from above in a rainbow of color across the walls.

Like everything else, it was long abandoned, but the power starting to hum from the various automation suggesting it was also at least passably functional. With just a handful of commands, the machines would quite possibly finish building whatever was on the line. Mercifully, there were several steps required before anything here would become anything more than extremely expensive paper weights.

"What... *are* these things?" William asked breathlessly.

"These are Juggernauts," Alyssia answered, as if that should have been obvious by the name of the section they were in. "One of the last attempts my kind attempted to win the insurgent wars through 'conventional' means. As I think I explained before, even at the height of the Transcendent people, we were *massively* outnumbered by humans. While we *had* mortal followers, it still wasn't nearly enough to match the numbers that were rising against us on a yearly basis. We attempted to bolster our ranks with AI controlled weapons systems..."

"And *that's* what these were?"

Alyssia glared at him. "If you would let me *finish*, you'd know that's not the case. Artificial Intelligence *was* an avenue we pursued, but you may remember that the technology had some crippling limitations. While it could gather information and 'learn' in that sense, it couldn't make decisions based on that information outside of the rules it was given. The humans eventually used those limitations to render our AI soldiers unreliable at best and useless at worst. We determined we needed something that bolstered our numbers while simultaneously weakening our enemies. It was in *that* context that Attal dreamed up the Juggernaut Program you see in front of you."

"The Juggernauts were, superficially, Transcendent themselves, which is why these platforms you see have vaguely human forms, to help with assimilation. We began offering immortality to more than the elite, but to anyone who was willing to accept being a living weapon in exchange for eternal life. Criminals, soldiers, mercenaries, law enforcement, people who were infirm or invalid... we didn't care, and that was in fact a selling point for our plot."

"That *does* seem like a horribly reckless action, unless you had some way to cont..." William began, until his voice died off and he said quietly, "Oh."

Alyssia nodded, picking up her pace. She hadn't detected any more activity from above, and she didn't like that. Nonetheless, she continued to entertain the humans in step behind her. "Remember how I talked about the security flaw in the Transcendent brain that we allowed because the alternative was slavery? Yeah... we didn't tell those we recruited *that* part, and that we made sure *that* little exploit was closed in every Juggernaut we assembled. A steadily expanding, experienced, and violent army that could react to changing situations, and yet obey our every order without question. And when scenarios adjusted beyond their ability to adapt, they were easily disposed of. Far cheaper and quicker than designing and redesigning AI."

William sighed, "Of course. Yet it didn't work, either I assume?"

"No, for a few reasons. We couldn't produce Juggernauts fast enough to counter the sheer numbers advantage our foes held, especially when they kept developing better armor piercing rounds that could even puncture the amount of armoring these Juggernauts were given. Even highly armored vehicles couldn't withstand the sort of munitions that both sides were throwing around. On top of that, they had some significant limitations that made them obsolete faster than we would have liked. They proved to be a footnote in war rather than a new chapter, a crime against humanity to add to the multitude we had, and would, commit. And it wasn't even useful for us in the end."

She waved the two ahead, "Anyway, keep going. You're going to want to be nice and clear for what I'm about to do. Just go out that door ahead of us, take the stairs all the way to the bottom, and keep following the hall. I'll catch up." She then glared at William and said, "I mean it, boy. If you linger about, I can't promise you'll be safe."

The instant the instructions left her mouth, she knew it wouldn't be enough for William, even as Star was already halfway out the door. "I'm going to demolish the entire assembly floor. You don't want to be too close as it comes down. Get going!"

William reluctantly obeyed, which was probably the best Alyssia could hope for, allowing her to address the sight in front of her. The million wasted lives that had been thrown away on what amounted to a vanity project; a new slave class coerced through lies, deception, and human desperation.

And whoever infiltrated this place first had *tried* to get this line running again. It was unclear how successful the attempt had been, but Alyssia had to embrace the serendipity that brought her here and make sure there wasn't a second attempt.

Unlike the previous infiltrator, Alyssia didn't have to brute force anything. Attar never bothered to revoke her privileges, and by the time he would have thought to, he wouldn't have had the chance. So, getting full access to the facility's functions was simple. *That* wasn't the hard part. The hard part was getting this place to render itself inoperable, because unlike what movies of her era loved to imply... these sorts of places generally *didn't* come with self-destruct systems.

But what *this* facility *did* come with were cutting lasers, located way in the back of the south side bay, on the opposite side of the conveyors, used for the precision detailing of many of the Juggernauts internal components, and those tools would be *more* than useful enough for doing the damage she required.

The first step was distracting the AI managing

fabrication, so that it wouldn't stop her from doing something that she shouldn't be doing. She accomplished that by reprogramming it to be responsible for the battery compression, and promptly ignoring the repeated error reports and damage assessments it was offering.

With the AI out of the way, she let the cutting lasers loose, programming them a very thorough pattern to take that would reduce much of the bay into five-centimeter square chunks, and watching the beams cut through anything that stood in its way, which would include *her* if she lingered in the control room for too long.

As she took her leave, the weight of the task ahead started to fall on her. This society was merely beginning to scrape the surface of nightmares long buried. This was but one of what could be *thousands* of ticking time bombs, all over the world, all of them holding secrets that could raze the Earth a million times over. And if William was any indication, a populous more than willing to use them. They started bubbling to the top of her memory, all of which likely survived to *some* degree of operation if Attar's facility was any indication.

How the hell was she going to do this?

She forced herself out of that mental spiral. It was a weakness of hers that she had all her life; to focus her vision too far ahead. It was something that transcending had only made *worse*, once she was in a position where she could quite realistically see the long-term effects of her decisions thousands of years down the road. She needed to keep focused on *this* moment, so that there could *be* a long-term plan.

Like, for example, cutting lasers that were starting to turn the ballistic glass partition a dangerous shade of red orange. Apparently, she still could lose track of time when lost in her thoughts.

Alyssia took her leave swiftly, even though she wasn't in any imminent danger of being cut up by out-of-control lasers. There was still the small problem of Republican soldiers that *must* be prowling about the ancient facility, and it would be in her best interests to vacate the premises sooner rather than later.

At least the software that allowed her superhuman balance was still functioning at a high level, because she took the ensuing staircase three steps at a time, rapidly bouncing somewhat like a prancing deer. It probably would have looked quite majestic to an outside observer.

Colliding with William at the bottom of the stairwell... not quite as majestic.

In her defense, it wasn't her fault! She actually detected William waiting at the bottom and had already adjusted to slide right by him. *He* saw *her* several seconds later and panicked, side-stepping directly into her adjusted trajectory, and not giving her enough time to respond.

While William wasn't a large man, it still was almost comical how Alyssia ran him over like he was barely even there. She merely stumbled while the professor flailed, spun, then tumbled with his face smacking flush against the floor.

Alyssia didn't even try to stop the laugh that bubbled up through her throat as William grumbled a curse muffled by the flooring. "Serves you right," she said unrepentantly. "When I said to get clear, I meant it."

He scrambled to his feet, scowling at her, dabbing his nostrils with the index finger of his right hand.

Alyssia rolled her eyes, "Oh, it's just a little nosebleed. You'll be fine, I promise. Now come on. This is *not* safe ground, especially if we loiter about."

William complied... reluctantly, and only after Alyssia gave him a not too gentle push on his right shoulder. "What did you even *do?* I didn't hear an explosion."

"I turned the cutting lasers loose," Alyssia explained. "And I can only imagine that it can be just as good cutting through rock and paneling as it is cutting through armor. We want to be at an angle they won't be cutting at and a distance where the lasers won't have the temperature to do its job."

At least Star obeyed, several hundred meters down the evac tunnel, and Alyssia noted this. "Now why is it she's been following me for about thirty minutes and knows how to follow directions, but you've been traveling with me for *days* and can't figure it out?"

"Because she's still afraid of you," William groused,

still dabbing at his nose even though it had already stopped bleeding. "I *hope* you're not planning on dragging her with us long enough for her to get used to you."

The hostess blanched at just the thought, and her eyes narrowed to dots. "Oh no... I have family who would be so very worried if I disappeared. I... I don't... I don't live here! They're probably going to be worried sick once they hear the Holy Republic razed the Way Station as it is!"

Alyssia raised an eyebrow. "I didn't scan any settlements or cities within *days* of here when the boy and I plotted our route."

"I live a week away by cart off the smuggler road," Star explained. "In the spring and fall I'm at home helping plant and harvest on the farmstead. In the winter and summer, when my help isn't as needed, I work here for the extra money. I... I don't even *know* how I'll get home now... if I even *can*."

Alyssia smiled warmly. "I... think I'll be able to help with that. The answer should be just a little further down."

From a distance, "further down" would have looked like a dead end, the tunnel abruptly ending at a roughly hewn rock face, like the construction crews decided to just stop. As they got closer, it became clear that time and a subtle shift of the strata had caused two panels to separate just enough that it was clear the entire thing was a fake wall.

Alyssia laughed at the memory that came to her mind. "What always amused me was that Attar honestly thought that if the rebels ever found this, they'd see this long tunnel end at this wall, and just not think *anything* was amiss. They'd just give up, because *of course* that's a natural rock formation and there *couldn't* be anything hidden behind it."

Alyssia paused as they finally reached the "secret" doorway, noting how easily it swung inward on its hinge. This was not behavior consistent with a door that had been warped by time and geology, confirming that this was where the interloper from earlier had gained access to the facility.

The lingering question in Alyssia's mind was did this person come across it by accident... or know it was here?

And if the latter, how?

Putting those questions aside, she shoved open the

door, her hands running across the transition from manmade rock to the traditional metals the Transcendent used as they entered River Attar's "emergency evac garage," which like much everything else Attar did, was to his... extravagant standards.

Three rows of automobiles, twenty-four in total, all of them in still relatively pristine condition discounting a thin layer of dust that had no doubt been blown in by the now open garage hatch that had been sufficiently cleared of the dirt outside.

Alyssia really shouldn't have been surprised that William was immediately drawn in by the sight in front of him. He had mentioned he grew fascinated by machinery, both old and new, working in his father's garage during his formative years.

Nonetheless, the way he charged forward, his eyes as bright as a child on Christmas Morning, was a little bit off-putting considering the circumstances. She also wasn't entirely certain why he chose the one he did, the third vehicle in the left row, rather than the one directly in front of them.

"Is... this what I think it is?" he asked excitedly, pressed up against the tinted glass of the passenger side window, trying to see through.

Alyssia sighed, then shrugged, "Depends on what you think it is. I have no idea how you'd identify a four-thousand-year-old car model when you don't even know what happened that made that car model, and everything else, a relic history forgot."

The archaeologist raised his head, his eyes narrowed towards Alyssia. "Obviously it's not the *same car*... but there are so many similarities between this and the Corvair Zed line that it is highly unlikely to be an accident."

"*That* was called the Faraday Z, the 2194 model, if I remember correctly, and I'm sure I do. It was one of the first models to fully rely on a metallic tritium battery than a hybrid with conventional electricity," Alyssia said tiredly, reciting from Attar's own bragging about his role in the development of the until then unproven technology.

Then she cocked an eyebrow and added, "And let me

get this straight, a society that uses taped together alkaline batteries in pipe-model buggies *also* has these sort of luxury cars?"

William nodded, "In more dense urban areas, yes. Of course, not using the sort of technology found in here... but the similarities in design are striking! Even the grill is of the same shape and location!"

Alyssia huffed, "That's not even a real grill. It's a relic that customers had gotten so used to that they were wary of any automobile that *didn't* have one."

"Yeah, they're entirely decorative on *our* vehicles too. It's funny because we never had internal combustion be the standard that anyone would get attached to anyway. It's just always lingered in our designs."

Alyssia had already grown tired of the banter and got to work. "Wonderful. Now, Star... pick whatever suits you."

Star pointed to the rear vehicle in the right row. "What's that one?"

That one was an abortion. A misguided delusion of Attar's, all angles and unpolished metal, it looked like a poorly compiled computer model. Its function didn't offer much more than its form.

"We are not going to talk about that one," Alyssia said dryly. "Some things are best lost to history."

Alyssia quickly picked one in front of her, a high roof red off-roader, opening. "Here, let's use this one," she said, stepping out to give Star space, and gestured to the cabin with a friendly, "Hop in."

Star looked a bit overwhelmed as she nervously complied, which prompted Alyssia to ask, "Never seen a car before, I assume?"

"Not this close," the hostess admitted. "It's a luxury my family and our community hasn't been allowed to have."

Alyssia said soothingly, "Well, don't worry. This lovely little machine will take care of everything. You just need to sit back and enjoy the ride. Provided you can find your home on a map."

Star nodded nervously.

Alyssia smiled warmly, tapping on the touchscreen in

the middle of the dash, betraying a small chuckle when Star yelped in surprise as the map projected into a 3D image hovering between the front seats. Alyssia reached over Star, and pinched her fingers to flatten the image into a 2D map that the hostess would more likely be able to properly read, then a flick of her wrist turned it in Star's direction. "Okay, where is your home? Just point on the map, and it'll take care of the rest."

Tentatively, Star pointed forward, like she was afraid the hologram was going to bite her. But she eventually *did* tap a location, which prompted the hologram to switch back to a 3D image and begin tracing a line across the topography.

"Very good!" Alyssia said encouragingly as she locked the navigation so that Star didn't accidentally alter it. "Now all you need to do is sit back and let this wonderful vehicle take you home. It literally will do all the driving and navigation *for* you. Pretty impressive, huh?"

Star nodded dumbly, transfixed on the hologram. Poor girl, she was still probably processing the events in the battery condensation bay, much less what was in front of her.

Alyssia put her hand on the hostess's shoulder, and said, "Look at me."

Star complied, if fearfully.

"This is really important, so I want you to listen closely. I have no idea just how many soldiers there are, or how much coverage they have over the area. I dare say even if you make it home, you're going to have to deal with them at some point. Whatever happens if they ask you *anything*, tell them the truth, okay? Don't do anything that might get you in trouble on our account."

The hostess nodded swiftly. She probably would have agreed to *anything* Alyssia had said at that moment.

"Now sit tight. Just got one last thing I want to do, then you can be on your way home. Okay?"

Alyssia leaned back out of the off-roader, smirking as Star nervously tried to poke the hologram, only to jolt with a yelp when it turned in response to her touch. But she left Star to her devices... because Alyssia had other things to do quickly.

It must have looked odd to her human companions to watch as Alyssia hopped into each and every car, started them up, fiddled with something in each cabin, then grabbed William by the shoulder with the order, "And you, boy, get to follow me."

"Words cannot express my joy," William deadpanned as he nonetheless complied, managing to keep his feet under him and take up stride behind the Transcendent as she led him into a tan high roofed off-road vehicle at the center of the garage.

She jabbed a thumb to the passenger's side, said simply, "Get in," then vaulted herself behind the wheel, calling up the map projection and spinning it towards William. "Okay, I think it's clear that the initial plan needs to be scrapped. "Got any other ideas that doesn't involve mountain climbing?"

The professor took a heavy breath. "Only *reliable* way? Back all the way to the south, through the Cruces. Problem is that's the *major* route between the countries. It's going to be swarming with military checkpoints."

Alyssia frowned, but nonetheless said, "No choice for it. Plug it in, and we'll start working that way. Maybe my scans will find something promising before we get that far. Let's hope that what I'm about to do will give us enough of a distraction, because we're still going to be hoofing it most of the way."

"Why's that?" William asked.

Alyssia tapped on the touch screen and opened the diagnostics panel. "While a lot of Transcendent technology has withstood the test of time, a lot of the fluid technology hasn't. The lubricant is shot, and these machines came before more resilient fluids were found. We *might* get a couple hundred kilometers out of this thing before it breaks down."

Then with faux cheer, she added, "So let's get to it!" and executed her plan with a wirelessly transmitted command, and then calmly waited for their turn in the cue as the cars started following their programmed navigation and filtered out of the garage.

William figured out the plan quickly enough. "Even *if* someone is watching us... they're going to have no idea which vehicle we're in."

"They'll figure it out eventually, I'm sure," Alyssia corrected, "But every minute it takes our pursuers to sort out that mess is one more minute we have to make some distance."

William then noted as Star's red off-roader accelerated out of its parking spot, "And there goes the girl. I have to say, I was *terrified* you were going to kill her too."

"I might yet," Alyssia said glumly, shifting their vehicle into drive and swiftly for the exit. "There's no telling what the Republicans will do once they catch her. Hell, for all I know, she's going to be driving into the smoldering wreckage of her home. And even if her home is none the worse for wear, it's only a matter of time before she becomes a person of interest."

"But she has a sight better chance than the none she did up there," he replied, pointing up in the general direction of the assuredly ravaged Way Station. "That's something."

Alyssia huffed but didn't respond further. Instead, she looked out the windows, to the mountains on the horizon outside the passenger side, too far away to really capture their majesty, the green and brown flaked tundra plain out the driver's side, and the largely flat nothing ahead of them. It was not what she would call an enthralling sight.

No doubt William had the same thought, because he couldn't let the silence go on any longer. "You *really* don't like being in other Transcendent ruins, do you?"

Her eyes narrowed, and she spared him a glare out of the corner of her eyes. "Where would you get that idea based on the grand sample size of *two* that you've experienced?"

"You've had largely nothing good to say about your peers the entire time I've known you."

"Because there's little good to say about us. That has nothing to do with my willingness to dive into the history of my kind."

Finally, he startled her with an insight she hadn't been expecting. "Is *that* why you betrayed them?"

Her aghast look would have given away any attempt to lie. "And *how*, pray tell, did you reach *that* conclusion?"

"Well, the major clue was how you *weren't* enthralled, while all your colleagues *were*. Your knowledge of the chain of events also suggested at the very least you knew it was going to happen and did nothing to warn them. And your knowledge of the methods used implied you were involved in its development."

Alyssia continued to stare straight ahead. "The only thing I did was reveal the nature of the security flaw to the rebels. They developed and implemented it on their own. I didn't even *want* them to inform me of when and how they were going to strike. They did that out of 'courtesy,' apparently. And no, it's not clear why they did such a thing."

"They thought you'd be useful with a free mind. Any idea why?"

"Some," Alyssia answered, "I can't imagine many of them were good. The rebellion wasn't *entirely* fighting a noble cause for the freedom of humanity *either*, for what it's worth. Their leadership was very much in favor of a theocracy very similar to the one you are railing against now."

"And yet you helped them?"

She scowled, "They *literally* could not do worse than what... my kind did, especially near the end of the war. No, I didn't like it, and it was a major part of the reason why I desired to be completely shut down. I didn't want to be party to any of it in even a passive way."

Alyssia snorted as she let that admission out. "So, there you have it. I didn't try to kill myself because of any noble desire to see humanity blaze its own path or anything like that. I tried to kill myself because I didn't want to be party to whatever was going to happen next."

"Then why didn't you? Surely there were *other* ways to end your life that didn't require trusting your slavishly devoted followers to obey your every order? I mean, are you *that* hard to kill that you couldn't even manage to do it yourself?"

That was a question that she had asked herself *multiple* times since awakening. "You might not believe me when I say this, but upon reflection, I'm not at all sure. At the time, I told myself it would be a glorious memorial to my failure, a lesson for the future about hubris and the abuse of power. But really... now that I look back on it... that was just my justification for a decision I had already made. Even looking back on my actions with perfect photographic recall, *that* part remains indecipherable, even to me."

"Some sort of subconscious survival instinct?" William offered.

Alyssia shrugged indifferently to that suggestion. "Maybe. As good as any theory I've come up with."

In truth, there was *one* other theory, but it was one she didn't even like contemplating internally, much less with anyone else.

Episode 8: Tracing Back

If there was one thing Miles could say about the Holy Republican Army, it's that they were thorough.

At times, they were a little *too* thorough.

This was one of those times.

The Way Station was more like a demolition zone as he finally reached the bottom of the massive pit that had helped hide the sprawling hideout from easy detection for years. If the Republic wasn't on a manhunt for an unshackled Metal God, they might have *never* found this hub in the slave trade.

But once the army found it... they made sure there wasn't much left for anyone to consider rebuilding.

He had to be lowered down into the pit by a rope and pulley, because explosive munitions dropped down the hole had reduced the stairs and elevator into slag, unfit to support any average human's weight. The metal railings in many places had been melted and fused with the steps themselves, at least the portions that hadn't outright collapsed.

The walls of the pit were a mix of melted slag and scorch marks where the paneling had exposed the underlying rock. The sort of temperatures needed to melt even something like brass to *this* severity were not generated by too many weapons available to standard infantry.

A jerk from the rope above caused him to lose his foothold, and he scrambled to stick his boot back through the loop before the lowering resumed. The investigator glared back up at the three lads atop the pit manning the rope, looking for signs that they had decided to pull a prank on him.

The only one of the trio he could actually see had craned his neck behind him, shouting angrily, suggesting that whatever had happened hadn't been planned. At least... until he heard what they were arguing about.

"I don't *care* how funny you thought it was!" The lead man growled back. "We are *not* looping it around his *neck* on the way back up! He probably *heard you*, buttplugger!"

Well... he did *now.*

"Let it go..." Miles whispered to himself. "It's not worth it. Not for some grunts."

Especially considering he was no doubt going to need all his focus to find *anything* pertaining to his hunt in *this* mess.

He didn't wait for the rope to fully touch down, instead hopping the remaining two feet to floor level, then straightened out the bottom his suit jacket and fixed his collar. He wasn't even entirely sure *why*, considering it was going to get rumpled up and dusty in a matter of minutes walking through this war zone.

"Christ's bones! A little notice would have been nice! 'Eh, Captain! The investigator is almost here!' That's all you need to do! Not piss around for ten minutes before finally mentioning it!"

The berating seemed to come from inside, though the lighting contrast from the sun above made it impossible for Miles to make out much more than faint outlines.

"No, you go back into the depths and make sure none of the meatheads start messing around with the site," the voice yelled. "*I'll* go welcome the investigator."

The man that eventually emerged from the darkness looked every bit the part of an army officer. Miles was by no means a short man, but the officer even had him by a couple of inches, with impeccably trimmed and cut short brown hair to the point that another quarter inch cut and he'd be bald. Intense emerald-green eyes partially hidden by a deeply furrowed brow was only a moment's distraction from a square chiseled jaw and almost excessively muscular physique.

Even the man's *neck* was packed with muscle, straining the neckline of his extremely tight olive-green undershirt. Not that the rest of him made it any easier on said shirt or the matching slacks. His polished black dress boots were quite thoroughly dusted with powder from what was no doubt a considerable amount of debris, but were otherwise impeccable, suggesting to Miles that the officer had at least *started* the day trying to look proper.

It was probably *technically* out of uniform for this man

to be greeting Miles without full dress, but the investigator wasn't going to fault the officer for it. Lord knows how suffocating the full-dress jacket would be with his build, and the desire to wear it as little as possible. Miles had been there before.

"Captain Jordan Drake, Holy Republican Army," the officer said with a crisp salute as his annoyed expression relaxed, his heels audibly clicking as he straightened into position. "Apologies for my appearance, I wasn't given proper notice of your arrival."

Miles returned the salute, and replied, "Think nothing of it, Captain. I wore that uniform once. I know how it is. Half your day spent putting it on, the other half looking for any excuse to take it off."

"Ain't that the Lord's truth," Drake grumbled, gesturing for Miles to follow him into the Acelean hideout.

But Miles had one question to ask before he entered the installation proper. His eyes scanning the devastation in the pit, he asked bemusedly, "Petrol bombs?"

"Apparently, the Acelans were putting up heavy resistance," Captain Drake replied, "It was supposedly the only way they could secure entry."

"Apparently?"

"I wasn't here for the actual attack," Drake said darkly. "The Strike Lieutenant made that call, against my orders, mind you. He claims he got word from above *us* to make the move, but I'm still trying to verify that. Communication out this far is… tricky."

"I'm going to want to talk to him," Miles said.

"As soon as I can get him to talk to *me*," Drake retorted. "He's refusing to answer anything until his story is affirmed by the brass."

"Nonetheless, I have to attempt."

"Yeah, I know. It's your job." Drake stopped just before the end of the tunnel that connected to an obviously larger chamber. "Is the scuttlebutt true? That you're here trying to chase down an unchained Metal God?"

No sense trying to keep it secret. "Yes. And that trail has led me here."

"That would explain what we found *deep* down," Drake said with a nod. "Maybe it's good news for you, though. Because there's not much of that Metal God left."

Miles raised an eyebrow, and Drake simply waved him forward. "You'll see. I'd be worthless trying to explain it to you. Just that whatever went on down *there* pales in comparison to what we did up *here*."

That got the investigator's eyebrows to rise, though he said nothing in response as he fell in line behind the army captain's stride. The one thing he as an investigator couldn't do was let his imagination start pre-constructing a scene. That's where the seeds of bias and flawed reasoning could find root.

And God knew he had enough biases as it was.

Though he had to admit curiosity about what could be considered worse than the devastation he beheld as his eyes adjusted to the change in lighting and they emerged into the main amphitheater of the Acelan hideout. He only observed there were originally three levels by identifying the remains of the bracings where the highest level would have been. That entire deck had collapsed onto the second, partially collapsing the right half of *that*, and leaving a smoldering ruined mess on the ground floor, flanked by shattered tables and broken chairs.

The army literally left *nothing* standing. They had ripped out the bar and splintered it into kindling, the smell of sour wine drifting to his nose and the empty, torn out shelves suggesting that what bottles had managed to survive the fire fight had been actively destroyed.

That is until the smoke and dust overpowered any other scent, and he coughed three times before covering his mouth and nose with his sleeve.

Captain Drake smiled in sympathy, having already adjusted to the air quality. "You'd have thought the strike was two hours ago, rather than two days. The ventilation in this place is *horrible*."

"Underground bunkers normally are, even spacious ones like this." Miles then said sarcastically, "Must have been some *really* heavy resistance in here."

Drake didn't take offense. "So it would seem, hunh?"

Miles was both astonished and yet not at how brazenly the strike force wasn't even *trying* to cover up their unnecessary use of force. As Drake turned himself to his left, Miles's attention was drawn to a small female figure dressed in a blood soaked once-white button-down shirt and apron, lying face down in the rubble, with five bullet hole entry wounds in her back.

And that was when his "playback" began.

One uncanny ability of his was to be able to reconstruct a crime scene in his head, at least provided nothing had been tampered with. Made of equal parts intuition, instinct, and experience, that ability had stood the test of more than one investigation and skeptic. The young woman's last moments played out like rewinding a video, his brain filling in irrelevant details that he would have to be mindful of had this been a true investigation.

But he didn't feel terribly concerned in *this* case about details like her eye color or nose structure or who else was precisely in the room at the time in this case. She rose with limp arms, like pulled from strings, leading into her temple smashing into the corner of the door frame that she had been trying to retreat through. From there, she gained physical animation, her feet scrambling underneath her as five bullets ripped through her chest and abdomen; two in a diagonal as they cut through her right lung, the third through the bottom of her rib cage, and the fourth and fifth into her liver.

The shooter, a faceless army grunt, had led his shots downward trying to follow her fall.

That was but one of thirteen bodies in this chamber, of what had *clearly* been civilian staff and patrons, left to lay where they had been killed. These were men and women that had posed little to no threat, butchered while trying to run away.

His moral training told him that they were in the employ of slavers, and that by helping to enable the slave trade by virtue of their employment they deserved no mercy. Perhaps there *was* some truth to that; despite having no money in the slave trade themselves, underlings will often happily embrace the same bigotry as those that *did*. But at the same time, many *don't*, and are driven by the simple need to survive into the arms of the people who have the money to allow it.

Miles sincerely doubted the army strike force stopped to consider what might be in the hearts of those that they gunned down.

His thoughts were interrupted by a commotion just outside, a younger man yelling from what was reaching his ears. Younger recruits in their early teens were occasionally given commissions to serve as runners in more far-flung places like this where handset communication was spotty, working at the mobile radio stations that would be set up wherever the army could get the clearest signal.

"Captain Drake!"

The boy who emerged into the chamber, clutching a folded sheet of paper tightly in his right hand, almost exactly matched the image Miles had conjured in his head just from the voice. Reddish brown hair instead of blond cut into the traditional close cut, but everything else fit the profile nigh perfectly. A rail thin kid playing dress-up in olive green fatigues that hung off the boy's frame like a hanger along with a belt that had been pulled so tight it had five makeshift holes for the prong to fit through. He even had one small "service" badge with one red band flanked by two black ones underneath his name tag over the right breast pocket, reading "Belle, Kenneth," to indicate his presence on this mission.

A dusting of reddish-brown freckles crossed over his nose and cheeks that almost masked the dimples formed as he fought to hide a smile and the sparkle in his gray-blue eyes. This was a duty the boy was *very* much enjoying, no doubt thrilled by the idea of being part of the grownups instead of that awkward phase where he was expected to behave like an adult, punished as an adult, but treated like a child in all other respects.

"Sir!" The boy yelped, swiftly snapping a practiced salute as he skidded to a stop in front of Drake and Miles.

"Recruit," Drake answered with a salute in return, "What's got you in such a hurry?"

"Message from the capitol, sir!" Kenneth said brightly, holding the somewhat battered sheet of paper up in front of

Drake's nose. "They said it was urgent!"

The captain took the sheet while dismissing the messenger with a wave of his hand, musing, "Maybe we finally got some answers about the Lieutenant's actions."

But mere seconds after he had opened the missive, his eyebrows nearly shot upward off his skull and he muttered incredulously, "What in God's name...? There's no way in *hell*..."

Something told Miles the message from the City of Saints wasn't about orders to his lieutenant.

"Army salvagers... found the Pope," Drake said, aghast. "He's alive. He somehow survived."

Seeing Miles quizzical expression, Drake asked, "Did you see the aftermath of the attack on MacArthur?"

Miles shook his head. "Never was sent there. Archon Elgin deemed it more important to get me searching the trail of the metal god and its supporters."

"There was *nothing left* of that fortification. Just a blackened crater and debris from what remained of the outer wall and buildings. Whatever hit the depot hit with such force it knocked down *trees* a half mile away. 'By the Grace of God, the Pope survived.' I'll say."

"Not used to hearing 'the Grace of God' spoken with such sarcasm," Miles said quietly, both in agreement and as a subtle warning to the captain, who might not have realized how much volume was in his voice.

Drake acknowledged it and shrugged it off with an additional snort. "Anyone in my company that doesn't realize I don't take every passage of the Bible literally by now is so stupid they're never going to."

The reactions of the surrounding servicemen seemed to support that opinion, as even those that Miles would have been *sure* were in earshot hadn't even so much as cast a side eye at the potential heresy. To be fair to the Captain, Miles personally knew that most men and women became much less strident in projecting their faith the further they were from the capitol... but all it took was one person who didn't.

Drake offered the message to Miles, and asked, "Want to see it yourself?"

Miles sighed, and took the offered sheet of paper, his curiosity getting the better of him.

> *By the Grace of God, our Pope survived! Praise be His name!*
>
> *Despite the attack on our great country, and despite the best efforts of Cascadian-funded terrorists, the hand of God protected the Pope, and tended to his needs before our people could recover him from under the rubble. Truly, he must be chosen after surviving an attack that should have killed him!*

Miles was used to bombast in missives delivered from the Holy Seat, but it seemed particularly out of place in the aftermath of a terrorist attack that killed hundreds.

> *The Holiest of Holies is recovering and will return to his duties when his strength has fully returned. Praise God! Praise Pope August! The heathens have failed, and God's glory will soon come down upon their heads!*

"Rather brief for a release from the Papal authority," Miles said neutrally as he handed the missive back to the captain. While Drake seemed comfortable disparaging the Holy Seat, Miles was not nearly as brave.

Drake chuckled, "I'm sure the full release presented to the public was several pages longer. This is no doubt the truncated version for long range communication's sake. So, with *that* news out of the way, I believe I was showing you to the ruin we *didn't* create…"

They hadn't even taken three more steps before the runner's voice reached their ears, screaming at the top of his lungs for Captain Drake.

"What in the hell is it *now?*" Drake grumbled, but nonetheless put on a friendly face as Kenneth skidded to a stop in front of them.

"Another urgent message, sir! More urgent than the first one!" Kenneth said excitedly with yet another sharp salute. "This one is so important that the comm officer's second intercepted me as I was getting ready to climb out of the hole!"

Kenneth brandished a considerably more battered sheet of paper, thrusting it out towards the captain, then dashing away like he wanted to make sure he was back at the comm station in time for the *next* missive.

The way Drake's eyes bulged suggested that it carried all the urgency that Kenneth had said it did. "The Pope is coming *here?*"

That got Miles attention, as well as anyone within earshot… which considering the volume Drake had shouted wound up being pretty much everyone.

"Are you serious?" Miles asked dumbly, as if there was *any* reason the captain would make up such a story from a communication he had just received. In response, Drake shoved the now heavily crumpled sheet in front of the investigator with a roll of his eyes.

Captain Drake,

I have been made aware of the incident in our Northwest Wilderness and am making my intent of examining the site myself, and the possibility of a rampant unchained Metal God, clear. Please have any and all of your team vacate the site to prevent any potential contamination until I arrive. That includes Investigator Parker, so do inform him of this declaration in case he has yet to arrive.

I should be not much more than two hours away by the time you receive this. May the Grace of God be with you.

In His holy name,
Pope August II

"Well, isn't *that* charming?" Miles grumbled in displeasure, his mind already spinning on what the hell the Pope thought he could find that someone *trained and experienced* in investigation and fact collecting couldn't.

Meanwhile, Drake was issuing his orders, "Okay everyone, we're being ordered out! That means everyone! Lieutenant Cherry, go downstairs and make sure the Demo crew gets the message. Make sure none of them went wandering. Private Youkem, get to the comm team, and let them know what's going on, but that nothing has changed for the scout crews and their orders."

As if dazed, the army men slowly filtered out, quietly mumbling to each other about the coming of the Pope himself and musing as to why.

To be fair, Miles was thinking much the same thing. The only real reason you'd want discovery to stop is if you were trying to hide something. But what could possibly be here that the Pope didn't want anyone to find? And how would the Pope even know it was here in the first place?

Drake jarred him out of his thoughts with a slap on the back. "You hungry? I'm betting you haven't eaten at all yet today."

He hadn't, in fact. He had left the layover point as early in the morning as he could rouse the driver and hadn't bothered with breakfast. "Might as well since we've got some downtime. Presuming by the time we get back *up*; it won't be time to come back *down*."

Drake smiled. "How good are you at the rope climb?"

Miles scoffed, "I still go through that drill for my physicals."

"Then we'll get up just fine."

The truth to that became obvious once they returned to the bottom of the role, where long metal rails, normally used to help vehicles get traction in mud, had been slapped across the gap, bisecting it across narrow points, and long strings of rope tied to those rails, where army men were climbing one at a time until they were able to reach more stable portions of the stairs and complete their ascent.

Truth be told, Miles hadn't done a rope climb since

before he was suspended, had never terribly liked the exercise, and wasn't looking forward to this at all. But he had already run his mouth at this point and wasn't about to back down now.

His arms started to burn the moment he grabbed the rope to hold it steady for the man climbing above him, anticipation for what was coming. As it looked like he'd be the last one up this line, he wasn't going to have that luxury, which meant his climb was going to be as hard as it got.

How lovely.

"Inquisitor, you okay?" Drake's voice shouted from above. While Miles was lost in his thoughts, the captain was already halfway up the climb, looking down on him with concern.

"Yeah!" Miles shouted back, "Just thought I'd give you a good head start!"

Why was he like this?

Fortunately, Drake took it in good humor. "Alright then, because I *was* about to offer to hold the line for you, but since you've got it handled, I'll just finish up!"

Miles exhaled deeply, trying to steady himself. Time to get this over with.

His shoulders protested *immediately* as he took the first pull, and his forearms soon joined in as he transitioned his left arm upward. The rope pull was as miserable an exercise as he remembered. He wasn't even ten feet up by the time sweat was beading down his forehead.

But as awful of an exercise it was, it was always a surmountable one, and even if it took longer than Miles's pride would have preferred. He hadn't forgotten where he came from, dragging himself up these damn things during his army days daily. It wasn't fun, and never was, but he knew that if he kept his head down, and kept putting one hand above the other, that he'd get to the top.

He, in fact, focused so well that he didn't realize his right hand slapped against metal rather than rope, and nearly slipped because of it. But with clenched teeth and a vice's grip on the rope with his left hand, he reached back up, got a handhold onto the rail, and pulled himself up onto to the makeshift bridge, receiving a clap on the back from Captain

Drake as he tiredly forced his tired body to its feet.

"You didn't even give us time to put money down on whether you were talking out of your ass or not!" He said. "Not bad. At least proves that *some* of the ex-grunts don't *completely* let their basics slip."

Miles settled for a tired smile, just proud that he wasn't gasping for breath like his body was begging him to.

"Ready for something to eat? I can't promise it'll be anything you're used to in the city."

Miles still couldn't work up the energy to speak, instead settling for a shrug.

That earned him another slap on the back, and an escort to the mess tent, southwest of the hole tucked in a valley between two gentle hills. It really was a testament to the stability of the Republic that so little of what he had remembered of the army had changed in the last decade. All the way down to the mess tent being one of only two places women were allowed to participate.

One such woman was staring back at him, a strawberry blonde girl with brown eyes and a light sunburn across her pale cheeks and neck that contrasted with a dusting of light brown freckles across the bridge of her nose. She didn't seem to like what she was seeing, as said nose scrunched like something odious and foul hit it, and her brows furrowed.

Miles didn't think much of it initially, as with his suit and recent physical activity he probably *did* smell rather horrific. He didn't even think much of it when she continued to scowl as she slapped pork gravy on biscuits and nearly dropped the plate in front of him along with a canteen of water... and a slightly brown plantain.

A plantain that wasn't on anyone else's plate that she was handing out unless they specifically requested it.

Even one year ago, he wouldn't have thought anything of it. Now... he was aware of the subtle insult being made.

Miles bit his tongue, though Drake sensed *something* happened as Miles stepped away from the table and towards the most isolated patch of grass he could settle down at while still in eyesight of the camp.

"I see it more and more since the Purge," Miles admitted. "All these little jokes and jabs and 'good natured fun.' And if I'm being honest with myself, it had nothing to do with the Purge. All those things were there before, it's just easier to blame recent events to excuse my blindness. The Purge just opened my eyes to it, and I can't close them again. There are times I wish I could."

Drake still looked confused, and finally Miles waved off any concern. It wasn't worth making an issue that didn't need to be made. "Don't worry about it. I'm still working through my own personal messes. Bubbles up at inopportune times."

"I imagine. You probably don't have a terribly high opinion of the Pope at this point," the captain said, crossing his legs as he set his plate down in front of him, and cut out a large bite of biscuits and gravy with his fork. After taking time to chew the overcooked, rubbery clump, he said, "What were you working on that his eminence was so worked up about it anyway?"

"I'm not sure," Miles answered with a shrug as he started eating himself. Army food was as awful as he remembered. "I doubt he *liked* that I was the one assigned to vet him when he was being considered for Pope. I can't imagine he liked that the Archons chose me to investigate the morality of the Purge. But he never actively stepped in and squashed them. The only thing that was on my plate at the time I was suspended was what amounted to passport work for Cascadians trying to enter the country. Recent events have made me think there's a connection… but I haven't the time or opportunity to try and find out what."

Captain Drake looked more red than white at this point. "I don't blame you if you can't answer this question, but I gotta ask anyway. Do you think the Pope had the previous one killed?"

Miles liked Drake as much as he could like a person he had known for all of three hours, but there was no way in *hell* he was taking that bait. "The investigation into the circumstances of Pope Joseph's death was… incomplete. It would be a professional transgression to make a statement one way or the other. I was just the patsy the Archons threw out whenever they wanted the *appearance* of being a check on the Pope's power, and a *serious* investigation like that one was given to others."

Drake sighed in mild frustration. "Yeah, yeah... I get it. I get it. You have to be by the book. I, on the other hand, have no problem whatsoever saying quietly that bastard absolutely killed his predecessor. Probably offed the previous Archon of Hope too because he wasn't buying what Pope Augustus was selling."

Miles really, really tried not to betray a grin... because hell if he hadn't had that thought himself on more than one occasion.

After another bite Drake suggested, "Hell, he was probably still scared of anyone digging into that load of horse shit that's his supposed past and wanted to make sure no one got close again."

"You're not buying the Pope's background?" Miles asked, genuinely intrigued. He had *never* heard anyone question *that* much.

"I come from a line of Freelanders," Drake said, almost like he had been insulted. "Are they backward in many respects? Sure are. Can they be violent and easily irritated by 'civilization' stepping on their individual rights? Sure can. Will they kill and plunder someone else's homestead because 'might makes right?' Sure will. But that's just it. They steal whatever they covet, kill anyone who gets in their way... but there's no chance in *hell* they burn down a perfectly good homestead that they might be able to use. What the Pope claims Freelanders did to his birthplace and his birth family? Nah, good sir, I don't buy it for one fraction of one second. There are some secrets there that he doesn't want anyone to know."

Well, that explained quite a bit about Drake's cavalier attitude. Freelanders were an odd lot, living in mostly ungovernable remote regions like this in family enclaves, doing business outside the family only when necessary, like for finding mates... and sometimes not even then. Self-sufficiency and freedom to do whatever they pleased were more important than anything else, and they responded to any perceived infringement on either tenet aggressively.

And outside of the most bitter blood feuds, they weren't going to raze something their own family could use, Drake was right about that. They'd leave a hundred bodies in an unmarked pit and leave everything else they could keep intact to use themselves. It was also a good place to hide something, be it property or secrets, because as Miles could personally attest to, the Freelanders don't take very much to "outsiders," and much less to "outsiders" of his pigmentation.

"So, how did a Freelander like you wind up in the military?" Miles asked, partially out of curiosity, and partially because the last thing he wanted to talk about was the Pope.

"My family wound up in one of the blood feuds that pop up in these ungovernable regions," Drake answered. "Wasn't even our fight. The Hails family just thought we were. My mother left with me literally the day before the Hails rounded up everything that wasn't nailed down before killing every man and enslaving every woman. I was two at the time, so I don't remember it terribly well. I wound up with distant family in the City of the Citadel, and it just kind of followed that I'd join the military from there. I voluntarily chose this billet, envisioning myself restoring order to a lawless land."

"How'd *that* work out for you?" Miles asked, trying not to betray a knowing grin.

Drake shrugged, "Better than I expected, worse than I had hoped. For every one blood feud we intervene and stop, three more happen. But that's an improvement from four bloody massacres happening without any intervention." Then Drake turned the question on Miles, "And how does someone like... well you... wind up serving under the Archons?"

Miles had much the same reaction as Drake. "Something similar, family fleeing to the Holy Republic. In my case, it was a hurricane that flooded the lowlands on the gulf when I was five. Separated us from the rest of the Confederacy with miles of treacherous waters all around. The rest of my family... didn't make it. Rescuers from the City of Hope pulled me and a handful of other refugees. I guess in a way I felt obligated to join the government that saved me in some fashion. Add in enough people who thought more of my deductive abilities than my skin color, an Archon who was arguably the greatest man I've ever known, and here I am."

"Well, no wonder why you can't spare a good word for the Pope," Drake deduced.

"I try not to spare too many words at all," Miles answered. "It's not worth the trouble. Hell, this is the most I've talked about since I was suspended."

"Well, how about we talk about something less charged? Like some good old handball?"

Miles's left eyebrow raised, "I thought you wanted something *less* charged?"

Miles never felt terribly much affinity to the "Grand Old Game," one that had been allegedly played unchanged in this land for almost five thousand years. Miles doubted that, but at the same time, considering how devoted a significant chunk of the population was to their national sport, that if they had preserved *anything* without alteration all this time, even through the Ice Age and the collapse of the old civilization... it would have been the rules and structure of handball.

"Why? What club do you support?"

"I don't," Miles answered. "I am one of the unwashed heathens who has better things to do with my Sunday afternoons."

Drake laughed. "Great! Then *I* can talk about without worrying you're going to take a swing at me!"

Miles had to admit listening to a guy brag endlessly about Vintage Academy Club, even though Miles really didn't know half the teams currently in the conference. Hell, he had only been passively aware that Citadel Academy, where he attended training for the officer's program, had a handball club... and that it had been quite awful.

Truly, little changed in the Holy American Republic, as Citadel Academy was still very much awful. You'd think a school with the "best and brightest" in the Republic would be able to field a more formidable squad, but apparently not.

But pleasantness was always fleeting, and the same was true in this case, as the thump of helicopter rotors heralded the arrival of Pope August.

Aircraft was a novelty in the Holy American Republic,

as they required refined fossil fuels that were not abundance in today's world, and battery technology couldn't generate enough power for any useful sustained flight. So, while Miles had seen enough of it being used by various heads of state and faith in the City of the Saints… the general rank and file of Drake's regiment were still a little awestruck as the aircraft decelerated to a hover half a mile away.

"So, want to go meet the glorious and exalted leader of our world?" Drake asked dryly.

"Only because I know that's not actually a suggestion."

Both men reluctantly stood, Drake taking the leave as they weaved through the camp, and towards the relatively flat portion of land that the pilot had decided was a good enough place to set down. Mercifully, the rotors had already come to a stop by the time both men arrived, because Miles *hated* trying to fight his way through the wind tunnel those things created; it was an annoyance he always felt he could do without. In fact, the Pope had already disembarked by the time Miles and Drake arrived on the scene.

Miles had been an investigator for a long time. Getting a read on people was a necessary skill that he had needed to possess innately, and even then, needed to refine to be truly skilled at it. And yet, despite all of that, he could never *quite* figure out Pope August II.

Clearly, he was a savvy mind. He had to be to get so high up in the hierarchy and bureaucracy of the Holy American Republic. He knew *exactly* how to manipulate people and get them to do what *he* wanted while making them think it was all their idea. When it came to getting what he wanted, Miles could not think of many that were better.

And yet, at the same time, he seemed to have disturbingly uncharacteristic gaps for a person who was so cunning. He could never feign interest, for example, and could be so uncouth or dismissive in his behavior that it was astonishing even the most powerful of contemporaries were unwilling to take offense, even *before* his ascension to the Papal seat.

He also had a tragic lack of self-awareness or self-preservation, which was on stark display at this moment, as he appeared to not have *any* security detail present with him. While he claimed, "God was his bodyguard" whenever challenged on the topic, not even the most ardent of believers *truly* believed that tripe.

He never visited any doctors, claiming them to be insufficient when the "hand of God are all he needs for health." At most, he disappeared for a week, without telling anywhere he had gone, and would come back saying that he had "left to meditate privately and bask in the glory of God at a personal level."

He was either the most purely devout man Miles had ever seen, or the most deviously cynical; and it was rather disgusting that there was no way to objectively prove which just by talking to him.

At least the Pope was *finally* starting to show his age, with the beginnings of crow's feet starting to creep onto the corners of his eyes, and a dusting of gray roots in his otherwise lush and well-coiffed swept hair. From the moment he first appeared in Miles's circle of notice, it seemed like August was going to be in his late twenties forever.

Because of *course* no one knew exactly how old the Pope was, not even the Pope himself, all part of that convenient Freelander family backstory that served as a wonderful dead end for any search into who he was.

And if Miles wasn't careful, he might visibly betray the disdain he had for Pope August II.

The Pope crossed the distance, a warm smile appearing on his face as he came to a stop in front of both men. The Pope then offered a welcome hand to Drake, who returned the handshake as the Pope said, "Captain... Drake, if I remember correctly?"

"You do, your grace," Drake answered amiably.

"Yes... I do remember your commission. I've heard nothing about good things about how your regiment has at least set a bare minimum of law and order in a lawless land. I hope you are being properly commended for it."

"I like to think so."

"Good." And then he turned his attention to Miles, and

by all appearances, there wasn't even a hint of ill will or even a moment's hesitation that would imply any negative emotion as the Pope offered his hand again. "Investigator Parker, I'm glad to see that you're back in the mix."

"Likewise," Miles answered neutrally, returning a brief handshake.

Pope August exhaled regretfully, "I *truly* do apologize for all that happened to you. You wound up being collateral damage in a much larger power struggle that should never have trickled down to you. You had a job to do, and you did it to the best of your ability. That should have been commended, not punished. People who thought they were doing me a favor and could get in my good graces. My regret is that I am *still* purging those rats from my ship."

"More like cockroaches," Miles replied. "You see one, there's a hundred more unseen."

That earned him a quiet, wry laugh. "More accurate, indeed."

It was such an earnest sounding reply that Miles *wanted* to believe it. Even though he *knew* next to none of it was true. It was that sort of uncanny charisma that made Pope August so dangerous, even to people who knew *exactly* who he was and what he was about.

"Anyway, I understand that we have found evidence of an unchained Metal God in this den of debauchery?"

Drake nodded, "Yes, sir. And we've cleared out the scene just as you ordered."

Pope August nodded. "Excellent. I will need to meditate within, and I must not be interrupted. I will trust those duties to both of you. I understand if this seems odd or you worry about the danger, but I assure you, I go with God's protection, and no harm will come of me."

Military discipline was the only thing that kept Miles's eyes forward. The only safety he was concerned with was of the crime scene that the Pope was inevitably going to tamper with. But that was beyond his power to stop, so his only option was to grit his teeth and muster as much of a closed-lip smile as he could, hoping that there would be enough to piece together once the Pope was done.

"Shall you show me to the site?" August asked with a small, natural, and almost innocent smile.

Drake and Miles nodded in unison, turning about on their right heels with such military precision that the Pope might have been excused for thinking they had practiced it. Miles kept his eyes straight ahead, his sight unfocused, keeping his building rage from even starting to bubble, much less boil over. For now, composure was key, and telling himself that he'd find *something* to work with after the Pope was done desecrating the scene.

Who knows? Maybe the Pope isn't going to disturb anything. Maybe he'll plant down in the center of some room, talk to God, and then leave.

Miles had *never* been terribly good at being an optimist, but he was trying.

He let himself operate by autopilot, his mind barely processing the trek back to base camp and the descent into the hole that had hid the slaver's waystation, until the Pope abruptly stopped at the entrance, his eyes drinking in the sight above his head and the heavily damaged entry.

"The Metal Gods certainly were impressive, weren't they?" He finally said.

Miles was glad he wasn't the only one who looked like his eyes were about to jump out of their sockets, as quite literally everyone in earshot went deathly silent, unsure that they heard what they thought they heard. That was *not* something he expected to spill out of the mouth of the effective leader of the Republic.

"Make no mistake," The pope said, noticing the incredulity from those around him. "They were horrifically evil, and I mean not to sound like I am admiring their ways or the actions we knew they took. Merely that they accomplished some truly magnificent things that have stood the test of time in ways nothing we could produce can or would. It's... fascinating to think what truly godly and upright people could have done with the Metal Gods' knowledge and dominion over the Earth."

Well, that pendulum swung from one end of disturbing to the other. Nonetheless, Drake reigned in his expression, forcing it back to neutral as he took one step to the side, and said, "Should we escort you further in, your grace?"

Pope August shook his head. "No, this will be plenty suitable. You, in fact, are free to return to the capitol, Investigator Parker. You will receive nothing but my highest commendations. Captain Drake, you and your unit are also free to break camp and return to your original assignment."

Anticipating their reluctance, he said confidently, "I go with the protection of God. You need not concern yourself with my well-being."

The Pope didn't even offer a parting, sliding between the two men into the ruined outpost, by all appearances not giving any more thought to those outside. Miles threw out his hands in exasperation, but bit his tongue, worried that the Pope was still in earshot.

As a result, Miles stayed in that exaggerated pose for over a minute before he finally said, "So... now the hell what?"

Drake had been largely dismissive of the entire display, and his demeanor didn't change. "*I* don't do anything. Contrary to what you or the Pope might believe, I don't take orders directly from him. My commanding officer, with coordination from Central Strategic Command, does. He wants me or my team or my division to bug out? He can go through the proper chain of command."

He then shrugged, "Technically the same goes for you. You were assigned to investigate by Archon Elgin. The Pope can't just tell you to stop. And he knows that, considering that he went through those proper channels to get you thrown off your earlier investigation of him, right? He wants you to leave? He can take it up with Archon Elgin."

If only Miles had those sorts of protections. He couldn't afford to be insubordinate, even if it *was* the way things were supposed to work.

Drake quite keenly noted Miles's withering glare at the suggestion. "Yeah, you don't really have the luxury to thumb your nose at our holiness, do you?" He paused to think, drumming his right index finger on his chin, "How about this... what would you say if I *simply couldn't afford* to spare transport for you back to the capitol until tomorrow morning? The Pope might have you return with him when he's done, and there's not much we could do in *that* case... but I'm perfectly fine with being the fly in the ointment if that's fine with you. What's he going to do? Have me assigned somewhere other than this ungovernable slab of wasteland?"

Miles couldn't have hidden the conspiratorial smile even if he had tried. "If you're willing to be a roadblock on my behalf, I'm not going to try and convince you otherwise."

Drake slapped Miles on the back and jerked his right thumb over his shoulder. "Good man. Now, why don't you come with me, and we'll find all sorts of delays for you, whattya say? I've got a Verner's Ginger Whiskey in my command tent that would easily delay us for an hour or so."

Miles really had to talk himself out of that idea, offering instead, "Think your strike lieutenant is going to be willing to talk?"

Drake shrugged. "I probably should ask if we've got confirmation of his story from central command yet. Not going to be terribly much any of us can do until we know if he acted on his own. Damn you and your responsibility encouraging me to do work! Anyway, follow me to comms, and we'll see if anything's come down the line."

Comms turned out to be a tent, an antenna, and four men at the top of the tallest hill a quarter mile outside camp, presumably the only place they could even get a weak satellite signal that was reasonably close by.

And why they were using junior recruits as runners.

Kenneth jerked to a halt mere a mere breath from running straight into Miles, caught by Drake before the attempted sidestep sent him crashing into the captain.

"Easy there, Recruit. Gonna get yourself hurt dashing about like that," Drake said as he righted the boy.

Kenneth nearly hopped in delight. "I was just coming to get you, Captain! The Comm Chief was finally able to get another missive from High Command! Your eyes only too!"

"Hm! Looks like we're finally going to get something resembling clarity around these parts!"

Miles was not as optimistic, but he was willing to pretend.

The person on the horn was to Miles's surprise, a woman. Something that Drake decided to alert Miles to before they got much closer.

"I'm not one to put restrictions on *anyone* in my command. Private Scully has some of the cleanest handwriting and best ear of anyone I've ever met, so when she demonstrated those skills and said she didn't want to be in the mess anymore, I approved it... unofficially at least. Try not to stare."

"Wouldn't dream of it," Miles replied.

Not that he had a chance to even offer greetings, much less potentially interact with the woman on the headset. They were intercepted quickly by the man ostensibly in charge of the team, a plump fellow by Army standards, but his uniform was nonetheless immaculate, and he definitely took pride in the Sergeant pip on his collar judging from how brightly it was polished. His name, "Starling, Brandon" in black stitching on the green camo looked so crisp that Miles wondered if this was the first time he had ever worn that particular shirt.

Either the army was getting a much more robust uniform allotment than he got during his time in the service, or Sargeant Starling was good at not getting his hands, or anything, dirty. While that wasn't a crime, even in the army, it did rankle Miles's sensibilities a bit.

"Captain," Brandon said with a salute, then handing over a sealed envelope. "Your eyes only. Well... and I suppose Private Scully's, as she was the one that transcribed the missive... but... you know what I mean."

Miles entertained himself trying to decide if Sergeant Starling was more nervous because of inexperience, or because he was worried of appearing lazy in front of high-ranking officials.

Finally, Drake frowned and grumbled, "Well, I should have expected *this*. Looks like General Phantom is at it again."

Drake showed little interest in "for your eyes only," quickly handing the missive over to Miles. The missive offered little other than confirming that Captain Drake's strike team leader *did* indeed receive orders to initiate an attack but did not include the name of who signed off on those orders.

Miles had been expecting that, honestly, so that news didn't hit him as hard. "General Phantom" was invoked whenever High Command confirmed that legitimate orders had been sent, but no general or war secretary is on record signing off on those orders. This was *supposed* to be a *massive* violation of Republic law, but it was a law that was effectively unenforceable if everyone in High Command kept mum, which they often did.

But Miles had a suspicion that "General Phantom" was, in fact, a specific person, someone who technically was *not* supposed to have any direct authority over the Holy American Republic Army.

Pope August II.

It was another example of the balance of powers that didn't exist in practice. Much like how the Archons deferred considerable legislative action to the Pope, the army *also* deferred their authority to check the Pope's power, and Miles believed "General Phantom" was one such way; allowing the Pope to issue orders directly to specific units to do as he pleased, rather than the generals acting on behalf of the Pope's preferred strategy.

That it *also* gave them cover when they advanced actions that would not be received well by the public at large was an added benefit.

"Should have guessed, really," Drake groused, disappointed in himself. "Just wish Lieutenant Rooseveld would have cleared it with me before he went with the orders he received."

"He knew that General Phantom was to be obeyed just as much as any general's signature," Miles said. "No sense getting himself potentially in trouble with High Command just because no general was willing to put his name on it. You know that."

"Still want to talk to him?" Drake asked.

Miles nodded. "Yes. But let him out of holding first. I don't need to make it some sort of official interrogation. It's more for my personal curiosity at this point."

"Recruit Belle!" Drake ordered as he borrowed a slip

from Private Scully and signed off on some hastily handwritten orders. "Why don't you invest some of that energy heading down to holding, and have them let Lieutenant Rooseveld out? Make sure he doesn't go *too* far, though. Our Investigator wants to have a friendly chat with him."

Kenneth saluted as he took the note, and dashed off as Drake and Miles took a more leisurely place trailing him. Miles frowned, and said, "Now, *why* did you word it like *that?*"

"Even if he's off the hook, I still want to instill the idea that I want him keeping me in the loop in the future, no matter *what* 'General Phantom' says."

Kenneth clearly delivered the message well, because every bit of Lieutenant Reuben Rooseveld's face and body reflected a nervous and tired man. Miles didn't blame him; however many days in "holding," which was really nothing more than the back of a personnel carrier with metal bars for a rear door, probably wasn't terribly comfortable.

"I'm not entirely sure how they heralded my arrival," Miles said as amiably as he could manage, "but I promise that I have no intention of having you charged with anything or even put back into confinement. You aren't my focus. I just want to piece together the sequence of events, that's it."

Miles doubted Reuben believed him, but all Miles needed was his cooperation. The investigator jerked a thumb towards the mess tent, and asked, "You hungry? Because I am. How about we talk over whatever low grade slop the army has given us?"

"I... suppose," Reuben relented tiredly. "Not like I have any choice, do I? Don't know how much I could tell you."

"That's funny," Miles replied, "because I suspect I'll be more interested in what you *can't* tell me."

Miles let the young lieutenant mull on that while he studied the officer. Just being out of holding had brought some life back to Reuben's light brown eyes, and he looked a decade younger as the stress left his twenty-something face. One hand ran through oily black hair, and the lieutenant looked at it distastefully.

"All right. Let's eat something, then can I get a bath or something?"

Miles agreed. "Certainly. After this, I don't foresee having any other reason to ask for you. You genuinely are *not* what I'm investigating. Honest."

Reuben surrendered more than was convinced, taking the lead as he got a big bowl of stew from the mess tent, a roll, and a glass of water. Of course, once he sat down and started eating, he discovered that freedom was the best spice of them all, greedily wolfing down the contents of the bowl.

He had almost finished before he remembered there was an Inquisitor sitting across from him at the table. "Christ," Reuben cursed before apologizing, "Sorry, sir. I'll tell you everything I am allowed to. Which might not be much."

"I'm sure you were instructed not to disclose your orders, and I'm not going to try and pry them out of you. All I am curious about is if those orders included *any* mention of an unchained Metal God."

Reuben threw out his arms, "Absolutely not! I didn't even learn there was a Metal God *at all* until we saw its remains, much less that it was supposedly unchained. Believe me, had my orders even *implied* that there was, that would have been my very first objective!"

Miles nodded, his thoughts whirling as he stood up. "Alright. That's all I needed from you. I'm sure your captain will have some other things to share, but that's beyond the scope of my investigation. Enjoy the rest of your dinner."

Miles took his leave, but not in any specific direction, merely hoping a random stroll would help his thoughts congeal in his head. Drake caught up to him soon after. "Penny for your thoughts, Inquisitor? Or is that too presumptuous?"

``By procedure, Miles *wasn't* supposed to say anything. But for once, that didn't stop him, mostly because he couldn't wrap his head around the information that was swirling.

"High Command knew of the possibility of an unchained metal god inside that instillation. So why didn't they tell the Strike Lieutenant of this very real danger? Even if, for whatever God-forsaken reason Command *wouldn't* have thought it deserved to be a primary objective, the danger itself should have warranted a mention, no?"

Drake went with the most obvious theory. "Perhaps Lieutenant Rooseveld is lying?"

Miles, of course, had already considered that. "What would he gain lying about that? It's not like it's information that would have any particular value to withhold at this point. No, I think Lieutenant Rooseveld is being completely honest, and that he had no inkling there was a metal god inside. But... *why?*"

"Sounds like you need to get down there and see what we saw."

"Not with the Pope down there, I'm not."

Drake grinned. "But you're going to anyway, aren't you? Because you think our holiness is General Phantom, don't you?"

Miles gauged the captain carefully before finally admitting, "Yes. At least... in this particular case."

"And I'm betting you're afraid he's tampering with evidence down there."

"Yes."

"Well, let's see what I can do to get you some time after the Pope returns. It might be too late to do anything by that point, but who knows? Maybe you can find something he missed?"

His self-preservation told him this was career – and potentially literal – suicide. Every bit of reason was telling him to keep his head down, not rock the boat again, and let the Pope do whatever the hell he wanted. It didn't *really* have anything to do with him.

But just going through the motions had *never* been a strength of his, and he knew it. He couldn't resist the curiosity and sense of justice that was again proving to be an irresistible pull. "We'll see."

"In the meantime, I *do* still have that ginger whiskey. Couldn't hurt to take the edge off while we wait, no?"

Miles finally relented. A stiff drink right now wasn't the *worst* idea he could have. "Sure. I'll have *one.*"

"I'll hold you to it. *I* can get a little tipsy tonight. *You* can't."

A captain's tent in the field was another example of

how very little had changed from Miles's day in the service. The cot Drake was using could have very well have been ten years old judging from the rust on the legs and the fraying of the fabric on the edges. His plastic foldable desk was cluttered with papers that Drake either needed to sign or couldn't be bothered with depending on what it was, three pens, and a pair of silvery steel mugs.

Miles had been initially surprised by the lack of personal flair, as every officer he knew, even those constantly on the move usually had *some* personal effects that they always carried with them. Perhaps Drake wasn't the sentimental sort, or the Freeman blood in him wasn't inclined to possess anything that wasn't essential.

Drake took two stools, one from his desk and another from near his cot and pulled them to the center of the tent. As Miles sat down, his back to the tent opening, Drake pulled out a locked wooden box from under his cot, quickly rifled through the lock's combination, pulled out a half-gallon sized glass bottle three-quarters full of an amber liquid, then set it down long enough to close the box and push it back under the cot.

From there, Drake turned to his desk and grabbed the two mugs, quickly glancing inside to make sure they were clean, or at least clean *enough*, and when he was satisfied, popped the cork stopper of the bottle, and poured out two generous amounts of the whiskey until the cups were half full.

Handing one to Miles, Drake sat down in the empty stool, and sighed, "I usually save this stuff for a job well done, but you don't mind if I make an exception, do you?"

Alcohol of *any* sort for an active-duty member was *supposed* to be taboo, and grounds for court martial. But much like *any* law in the Holy American Republic, enforcement was uneven and the punishments even more so. He knew *many* officers like Drake who flaunted those laws brazenly. At least Drake offered the minimal courtesy of keeping his spirits locked up where they couldn't readily be seen.

Drake imbibed the first serving in damn near a single draw, pouring out a second even before Miles had taken a suitable sip. He was not a particular fan of ginger whiskey, the spicy kick both at the front and end of his taste palette was not exactly to his liking. But it was drinkable enough for him to participate in this ritual of friendship that Drake was eager to undertake.

"Ya know," Drake said, "it's not often I run across someone like me."

"Like you?" Miles asked.

"An outsider. Someone who doesn't quite fit nicely in the hierarchy of the Republic, and which the Republic doesn't particularly attempt to try."

Miles hummed in agreement, partially because his throat was tingling from the liquor, and partially because he was still gauging how cautious he needed to be. This sort of thing was how the Republican Army would weed out people with "seditious or heretical thoughts," by enticing them out of servicemen with a seemingly understanding officer.

"I know about how you got scapegoated, Investigator," Drake continued after he finished his second mug, and readied himself for a third. "And I have no doubt the Pope was the reason for it. I don't know how you don't *hate* the bastard."

"I just did my job," Miles shrugged. "And that's all I'm going to do."

"And what happens if your job reveals that the Pope *was* tampering with evidence? Where does that go?"

"I... don't know," Miles said, even though he knew *exactly* where that would go.

"Bullshit," Drake scoffed, pausing only to finish the contents of his mug again, his eyes drifting to the now two-thirds empty bottle as if he was contemplating finishing it off entirely. "It'll go nowhere. The Pope will bury your findings and probably have you executed. So why even do it at all?"

That was an excellent question if Miles was being honest with himself. "Because knowledge matters. Even if it's buried, it's important that it exists. Buried knowledge can be found and used for a better purpose later. But if it's never found at all, *that's* when nothing matters."

"Because people like you matter, even if the gentry in the City of the Saints don't like it," Drake finished. "Just like the Freemen matter, regardless of how little concern the Republic has for the violence and death that occurs."

Miles didn't want to say that the Freemen largely were getting exactly what they wanted from the Republic, which was less than nothing. Maybe that sentiment *wasn't* as prevalent among the people in the ungoverned regions as he had assumed.

"The Archon of Hope wanted to try. The previous Pope wanted to try. It looked like there *could* be some semblance of order established here. Then in comes Pope August after all those awfully convenient deaths, and hands all the power back to the family fathers of the region."

Drake looked up at him, eyes seething with a surprising intensity for someone three glasses into a rather potent whiskey.

"I hate the bastard, Investigator. I want to run him crotch to gullet and drag out his damn entrails across the streets. I want to see the bastard hang for all the unnecessary death and despair he's caused. Then I want to chop him up into twenty pieces and bury them in twenty holes all around the Republic with a headstone that says, 'Here lies the villain that destroyed a million lives. Piss accordingly.'"

"I'd be careful about your choice of words," Miles said. "This tent isn't soundproof, and being in the drink would not be a terribly good defense."

"This entire company knows my feelings. They're all rejects of the same damn rotten system, dumped out here because polite society doesn't want them near the proper citizens. You'd probably find most of them would have even darker thoughts about the Pope and his legion of toads."

Miles didn't respond, using the guise of finishing his drink as cover for not potentially implicating himself just in case Captain Drake's company *didn't* exactly share their commanding officer's thoughts on the matter.

"I know you want to balance a tightrope here. You want to get to the truth, but you also don't want to tip the boat. And that's fine, even if I personally think it's a waste of effort. All I want is if you get the chance to look around down there, leave that information with *me*. Let me use it and you keep your own hands clean."

Again, Miles was silent, and Drake clearly didn't

expect a response. Instead, the captain filled his glass up for a fourth offering, tipped it playfully in Drake's direction, and just before downing *that* glass said, "And now, how about a little lighter discussion after all the heavy talk?"

Said lighter discussion largely went in one ear and out the other, Miles's mind more preoccupied with trying to balance what he was *supposed* to do with what he *should* do, because once again, the two weren't the same.

Miles doubted it would be *possible* for him to "keep his hands clean," as Drake put it. If the Investigator went down into those ruins without the Pope's explicit approval, it would be the end of his career, and possibly his life.

But at the same time, Miles couldn't just let this go. If – even as Miles strongly suspected there was no 'if' about it – Pope August II was trying to cover up some sort of crime, that crime needed to be on record, even if he wasn't the one that would be able to do anything with it.

His mind then drifted to what the Pope was so eager to cover up, because that was another layer to all this that defied rational explanation. What could *possibly* be down in the depths of those ruins that the Pope didn't want anyone to see? And how would the Pope have even known about it in the first place?

Miles got so deep in those weeds that it took him some time to realize that it was approaching sunset, and that Captain Drake had also noticed this.

"How long do you think the Pope intends to 'meditate' down there?" the army officer asked.

Miles shook his head, "I have no idea."

The captain then grinned like a fiend. "Well, Investigator, I think we have our reason to go down there and look around. *Surely,* the Pope couldn't *possibly* fault us for being concerned for his well-being after being down there for so long, right?"

Miles suspected the Pope very well could, but as far as pretenses go, it was as good as any. "I would agree, Captain. Shall we check on our tardy pontiff?"

"Why, I do believe we shall."

Drake took the lead leaving the tent, approaching the

sergeant stationed at the top of the pit heading into the depths. "The Pope still down there?"

"As far as I'm aware, sir," the sergeant answered. "If he's come back up, it hasn't been this way."

"Well, I'd rather not have our glorious leader down there all night, so Investigator Parker and I are going to try and find him. Let it be on our heads if he gets upset."

"Understood, sir," the sergeant said with a salute. "Oh, and sir?"

"Yes, Malley?"

"Try not to 'accidentally' put a slug through our pontiff's forehead, okay? If anything happens, make sure it looks suitably unintentional."

Drake jerked a thumb at the Sergeant Malley, and said to Miles, "See what I mean?"

Miles admirably kept any smile off his face and out of his voice, "No comment."

Meanwhile, Malley had called over his crew, and said, "Let's get 'em down boys! And try to keep the racist chatter to a minimum this time, okay?"

Drake's eyes narrowed accusingly, quickly defused as Miles turned him back on task and said, "Forget it. Just let it go. We've got work to do."

Once they hit the bottom of the pit, Drake suggested, "Let's first look where we found the remains of the Metal God. My guess is that's where the Pope would have gone."

Miles had no particular reason to dispute that theory, and so he fell in step behind the officer as he wound through the Acelan hideaway and towards a mangled metal door that looked like it had been blown open through a burned-out hallway.

"Judging from the state of the armory, Lieutenant Rooseveld used damn near half our explosives to breach this door, claiming that it seemed important because the defenders started congregating around it.

Miles perceived the mass of bodies in various states of seared flesh, bones, and ash flanking said breach, his mind rewinding time and confirming that assessment. "Your lieutenant had the right of it."

Drake carefully worked his way through the jagged and warped metal. "The Acelans are definitely fixated on Metal Gods, but I can't imagine they'd even be so stupid as to try and defend an unchained one."

Miles followed him, and offered, "They might not have known it was unchained, or it promised them something of great enough value that they thought a deal with the devil was worth it."

"Like what?"

"There are some questions I'd rather not contemplate. The perversions of Acelan slavers are one of those things."

"Point made."

That said, after about the tenth flight of stairs that seemed like they went on forever, contemplating the nature of slavers was starting to sound more appealing then the silent drudgery that appeared to be his immediate future.

"How big is this place?" He asked.

Drake shrugged; the movement barely visible in the low lighting. "Hard to say. We only got to the thirty-third floor when we found the Metal God, and there is at least two more further down that we started to survey when you arrived."

"Oh, Lord."

"Some of the stuff in here is absolutely, absurdly huge in scale. I don't have any idea what it could have been used for."

By the twentieth flight, Miles began to dread the return trip back to the surface. "No chance of any functioning lifts in this ruin?"

"None that we found," Drake answered, before adding quietly. "Yeah, I'm not looking forward to the walk back up either."

Not that Miles had many thoughts of the stairs up once they reached their destination.

He was used to gruesome crime scenes, yet this managed to genuinely surprise him. Captain Drake hadn't been kidding, the damage inside was catastrophic, no doubt the result of whatever it was that had ruptured on the south side, shards of glass were scattered across the north side, the tangled remains of metal and the coat of soot everywhere suggesting a tremendously violent explosion, and tremendous heat if the blackened soot and burned out remains of bodies was any indication; the sort of heat that melted metal, something that Miles hadn't seen too much outside of machining forges.

Miles was also not expecting *three* bodies, two humans, and one not. That was Miles's first clue that something wasn't quite right about this. The reports he got involved *two* fugitives from the law, not *three*. While it was certainly possible that they had found a sympathetic figure during their flight, he'd need further evidence before he could be confident in that.

The humans were not much more than charred bone, everything else incinerated by the heat of the explosion, but there was enough loose connective tissue that the remains hadn't been scattered to the wind, so to speak, enough for Miles's brain to start reconstructing the scene.

"Doesn't look like his eminence disturbed anything," Drake said, "That's a relief."

Miles nodded, gesturing to a set of footprints in the soot, one of many in truth, but was notable in that they went straight across the room. "I'm going to guess whatever he was interested in wasn't here. But there's still a lot we can learn here."

"Like what?"

But by that point, Miles's rewind had already kicked in. His eyes were initially drawn to the humanoid remains sprawled across the center of the floor. He had expected to see bodies cast like chaff in the wind. Instead, he saw blurry, faceless husks sliding and spinning across the floor, tumbling but not soaring, until they came to a stop already prone closer to the presumed explosion site.

Then his attention turned to the remains of the Metal God. *That* was a bit more animated in its flight, tumbling head over heels and spinning violently, but at the end came to a stop in a slumped over position directly in front of where the detonation had happened.

"All three were dead before the explosion, even the Metal God. Someone was trying to fake all of this to throw pursuers off the trail," Miles said.

"And I guess the Pope didn't fall for it?" Drake asked tentatively.

"Looks like he didn't even acknowledge the attempt," Miles confirmed. "His interest seems to be focused on something else."

Miles didn't voice his theory that the "something else" was possibly an unchained Metal God lying in ambush, or whether the Pope falling into a potential ambush was a good or bad thing.

Instead, Miles followed the Pope's path through the ash, dust, and torn metal, dusty tracks helpfully pointing him down a stairwell on the complete opposite side of the floor. For a brief instant, he fretted about losing the trail... at least until he found the ruins at the bottom of the stairs.

"What... happened here?" Drake asked.

Miles hand ran across one large metal section that had fallen and crushed the remainder of the stairwell. It bore an astonishingly sharp, fresh cut, at about a thirty-degree angle from the normal and smooth edge of the chunk.

Immediately, his mind started to rewind and reassemble the puzzle, literally in this case. The various chunks and rubble all neatly fit together into a largely unobstructed path inside, cut by something that his brain could only speculate on from inside. Whatever it was, it must have been of significant power to slice through solid stone and metal so quickly and sharply.

"I... am not sure." Miles answered, "But whatever it was, it was rather recent."

"You think the Pope is buried in that mess?" Miles shook his head. "I don't think we're that lucky *or* unlucky. I can't imagine we wouldn't have at least *felt* a collapse like this happening while the Pope was down here. This likely happened during all the chaos of our assault."

"So... he's still around here somewhere?"

"I presume so. Now we just need to find out where."

The first clue was found as Miles and Drake began

climbing back up, a door that had been pushed open that Miles had – perhaps shamefully – overlooked on the way down as his attention was grabbed by the collapse just one floor below.

They were required to turn on flashlights, as the automated lighting didn't come on as they entered, and a quick scan with their light showed why. More than half of the floor in the gigantic bay had collapsed, the clean slices at the edges suggesting it was from the same thing that tore up everything below and had done significant damage to the ceiling as well.

"Careful, we don't know how stable this is," Drake ordered. "And it does not look like a short drop."

"I noticed," Miles answered in annoyance, pressing himself against the only stable wall and inching across towards the other side where another open door was waiting, further evidence that the Pope had indeed gone this way.

He winced as Drake slowly followed, the floor groaning and scraping under their weight. Miles held out a hand for Drake to stop, but at that point it was too late, the floor gave out, the edge lurching downward and forming a slope that sent both men down into the collapsed bay below.

At least the debris below broke their fall.

That wasn't meant in humor. A straight fall down the roughly twenty-five feet to the machining bay below would have likely resulted in serious injury, if not death. Instead, the helpful pile of collapsed metal served as a bit of a ramp to dampen their descent, and lacking any of the support teams of modern construction that could create opportunities for impalement, it wasn't even a particularly dangerous pile Miles and Drake to fall onto.

It wasn't *pleasant* by any means, but it at least wasn't of massively elevated risk as the two men rolled to a stop on the dusty and damaged floor below.

Miles picked himself up, noting some silvery glass-like shards from the ancient metal had managed to make a long cut from the wrist to elbow of his left arm, tear a potentially nasty hole in the left leg of his trousers, and his ear was still ringing from when he bumped his head on the initial fall, but he was otherwise in remarkably good shape.

The cut wasn't particularly deep, and thus wasn't nearly as bad as it looked. Not even worth a bandage. Drake, on the other hand, looked to be in worse shape, his left arm dangling at his side with his right hand grasping his elbow.

"Can you help me pop this back in?" he asked with unnerving calmness. "Just keep my shoulder from moving."

Miles frowned but braced both sides of the shoulder as Drake grimaced, and jerked upward on his left arm until there was a dull pop. Sighing with satisfaction, he rolled his shoulder as Miles stepped back.

"I've had a loose joint there since I was a kid," Drake explained. "Comes in and out fairly easily without any lasting damage. How about you?"

The captain pointed with mild concern to Miles's forearm.

Miles was *not* going to be outcooled. "Superficial. Bleeding has almost already stopped."

Drake then moved on to the important matter, "So… where are we?"

That was an excellent question.

The bay they had dropped into was more like a garage, admittedly one with a collapsed ceiling, massive, bright red sectional doors along the perimeter large enough for army vehicles to move through, shockingly brilliant in color against the white walls despite what had to have been thousands of years of disuse.

What Miles had not been anticipating was that he'd be looking at a way out of the ruins, but there, among all the rubble, ruined vehicles, and other damage, was one wide-open garage door about a hundred yards to the south, the smell of fresh air reaching his nose drawing his attention to dark amber sky in the distance.

"Well… hell," Drake mumbled as he made the same observation. "We knew there was a pretty hefty descent off the roadway, but I would never have guessed we'd be able to come right out the other side. Makes me wonder why so many fought to the death if *this* handy little escape route was here."

Miles answered, "Probably because they didn't know about it. You said yourself these ruins were sealed off and your guys had to literally bomb their way in."

A series of black marks like tire tracks were freshly made at Miles's feet, tens of them by his estimation. What had been two had become three, and then abruptly become at least twenty in a way that didn't add up in Miles's head.

"Unless... someone *did* escape," the inquisitor said thoughtfully, almost mindlessly wandering towards the looming exit. His intuition was screaming at him that the Pope was no longer on the grounds, and that the entire nonsense with him meditating before God was all to keep people from hovering over his shoulder while he did... something else.

But what?

And *why?*

Miles would get answers for that sooner than he anticipated. A grinding of old metal gears to his left immediately snapped his attention, one of the side bay doors opening to reveal a titanic monstrosity of the metal gods; an ambling, humanoid thing with a spinning gatling gun at the end of its left arm, and a round tapered cylinder for a head with a thin narrow red glowing band for its eyes. It very much had the appearance and style of a walking tank.

Had the thing not been hampered by millennia of disuse, or the garage door not been afflicted by the same, or if the creature's right arm and both legs been functional, Miles and Drake would have been dead before they even fully knew what had attacked them. But the groaning of ancient metal had been their warning, and the lag of response in the monster's joints before it could level its weapon and begin firing gave them time to reach cover behind a pile of debris, its bullets burrowing and deflecting dangerously off the obstruction before it paused to reconsider its targets.

Drake was not the sort to be easily flustered, but meeting a creature of ancient times that shouldn't be was enough to rattle him. "Is *that* the metal god our glorious leaders are so afraid of?"

Miles was making sure his Clark was functional and loaded properly. "I doubt it. Metal gods were supposedly so well disguised that they could pass as human. I don't think *anyone* would be fooled by *that*."

Here's hoping that the sort of weapons that could allegedly kill one would *also* be effective against the monstrosity slowly trying to stalk them, its clanging and scraping steps reverberating menacingly.

"How good of a shot are you?" Miles asked. While the inquisitor had more than high enough marks during service, he was hoping that an active soldier would be more capable.

"Good enough to still pass qualifications," Drake answered. "Why?"

"Got anything designed for a metal god on you?"

"When we were informed of the likelihood that one was around, I had our heaviest stuff broken out of the armory. Dunno how good it'll be against that thing, but it's the best we've got."

"Good. You'll be the shooter, then."

"Planning on pulling its fire or something?" Drake guessed correctly.

The inquisitor had already spied his secondary cover, a chunk of the ceiling that had dropped on a partially crushed vehicle about thirty feet away, with enough assorted debris to provide him decent enough protection. That *should* be enough time for Drake to get at least *a* shot, if not more. Then they could both trade opportunities.

Hopefully.

"Any idea where I should shoot?"

Miles shrugged, "Where it looks weakest, I guess. You have as much experience with one of these things as I do. I'll go on your word."

278

Drake took a deep breath, poked his head around his cover, ducking quickly again as a burst of fire followed a second later. He nodded to Miles and barked, "Go!"

Miles burst into a sprint, keeping his head forward and focused on his destination, resisting the urge to look at the monstrosity like his army training had ingrained in him. Distraction led to death, after all, especially on uneven ground, which he was trying to navigate. It honestly wouldn't have mattered, as the walking tank ignored him completely, continuing to stalk and offer suppressive fire in Drake's direction.

Miles dove into his new cover location, finally processing the unexpected behavior of his foe. He would not have expected the thing to ignore the easier target. Drake didn't expect it either, giving Miles a confused glance before shifting his position to keep the pile of rubble between him and the monster.

A change of plans was in order, and Miles found himself having become the shooter, which was *not* what he wanted. While he wasn't exactly a novice with the sort of weapon in his hand, it had been *years* since he shot a five-eighths. He knew that they had *massive* kick, and he certainly wasn't confident in his muscle memory.

But he also wasn't going to get a much better opportunity before he would have to move into different cover himself rather than leave him exposed to the monstrosity that might eventually decide to stop ignoring him.

So, he leveled his shot, gripped his gun tightly, pulled the trigger... then missed in rather embarrassing fashion, the kick from the gun causing his shot to strike the wall on the north side damn near where it had once met the ceiling. The shot missed so badly that the walking tank didn't even pay him any mind as it continued to stalk Drake.

With a growl, Miles made another attempt, and *that* shot landed true... or at least true-ish. It connected with the side of the monster's head with a loud bang, causing it to list and stumble, sparks and shrapnel flying from the impact that tore away half of what would have been its face.

At *that* point, the creature decided Miles was worth its attention, which was a bit of a problem because at that juncture, it now had a clear line of sight on the investigator. But its lethargy gave Drake the time to find his footing and take a shot with much more confidence and accuracy than Miles.

It was clearly a round quite a bit beefier than the five-eighths that Miles had in his hand. It hit almost like a grenade, with a deafening fireball that penetrated awfully deep considering that Miles saw fingers of flame erupting from the seams in its armor plates.

And yet that *still* wasn't enough to bring the monstrosity down. It unsteadily tried to target Drake again, and it took two more rounds from the both of them before it slumped, then crashed lifelessly into the rubble, a smoking and charred mess that neither of them really wanted to approach to confirm the "kill."

Drake finally did so, whistling as Miles's heart rate slowed back to something resembling normal. "Damn, I shot right down the damned hole on that thing's arm, and it still tried to get up from that. I don't even *want* to know what it would take to kill one of those things fully intact."

Miles shook his head, "I don't even want to think about it. Let's just vacate the premises just in case anything else in here wants to wake up."

"Agreed. I want to check in with the base anyway. Shall we?"

The inquisitor could not have agreed with anything more, gladly taking step behind Drake as they utilized the open door to escape into the outside world. The pair realized quickly why the entry escaped detection. The hill had been excavated by someone at some point recently. While Miles contemplated that development, Drake was on a short-range radio, hoping he was close enough to get in touch with his company. He didn't put it to his ear, allowing Miles to overhear the report from the speaker.   "Private Scully, report!"   There was a long nervous beat, and Drake repeated his command, then the comms woman responded, her voice sounding like she was out of breath.

"Sorry, sir! Present, sir!"

"Report, private."

"Sorry sir. We just finished cleaning up the problem you were worried about. Lieutenant Rooseveld and Sergeant Starling were agents acting on behalf of Pope August. They conveyed his cover information, and Sergeant Starling tried to contact a different strike team he was coordinating with. I had just gotten word from Lieutenant Meyer that they had routed that team and had secured the area. They feign ignorance of any direct orders from the Pope, instead citing orders from..."

"General Phantom," Drake finished.

"Yes, sir."

"Well, once I find my bearings, I'll..."

Drake's voice died away because he had just noticed the same thing that caught Miles's attention. A massive column of black smoke rising into the sky, the flicker of towering flames starting to become visible in the dying light of the day.

"Do we know anything about what's off that way?" Miles asked.

Drake's eyes widened, "There's a Freelander settlement. Fairly small one. It hadn't got much notice from us at the time but... holy hell. I know where the Pope went."

"Sir?" Private Scully asked over the radio, no doubt wondering what had cut off her captain so abruptly.

"Can you pinpoint my location?" Drake asked the radio operator.

"If you're in radio range, we should be able to get some satellite data on your location."

"Do so. Time is of the essence. Mobilize anyone willing to participate in an insurrection and get to my location as quickly as possible. The rest of you will wait for Inquisitor

Parker to return and you'll escort him back to the capitol. He'll have a cover story for you. Stick to it."

Private Scully responded with a resigned gravity, like this was something she had been anticipating for some time. "Understood, sir."

"Alright, get to it. We have to move quickly."

Drake killed the communication, leaving Miles to quietly demand, "What exactly are you planning, Captain Drake?"

"Pope August is doing it again," Drake said grimly. "I don't know how, I don't know why, but he's plotting something, and he's burning down everything in sight to cover his tracks *again*, and I refuse to sit idle and let him do it this time."

"But…"

Drake didn't let him finish. "*You* need to get back to the capitol and be the good doggy. You *can't* be seen holding the bag this time. If I survive what's coming, and I find anybody tied to the metal god at the end of this trail, and I can get him to you, then I will. But your participation *has* to end here. Now, get moving back to camp. Use the time to think of a cover story. Lieutenant Meyer will help you fill in the details once you've returned. Now git."

Episode Nine: Giants Among Men

William found himself almost regretting that he had pressed Alyssia to finally discuss her thoughts on the nature of God to pass the time as they worked through the dusty expanse of the Republican Wasteland. Because she had started ranting about her background in her faith at one rest point and went into into painful detail about the Dutch Reformed denomination, her flavor of atheism, and her mortal agnosticism the entire time to their *next* rest point an hour and a half later.

"The initial observations emerged as humanity really began to nail down all the pieces and parts of quantum physics and how entanglement worked, like how two entangled particles that could be separated by immense amounts of space could instantly swap quantum information. In the last days of the Transcendent Era, we made discoveries that changed everything we knew about this universe. Movement of particles, the constants of the universe, why the speed of light was the way it was, for example. All of it.

"Now, bear in mind, the idea of everything being the way it is happening by coincidence was so astronomically low that the universe almost *had* to be designed by a higher intelligence was a fairly ancient philosophy even during *my* time. The universe's laws and constants were so specifically fine-tuned to allow for complex, sentient life forms to emerge that even the slightest deviation of any number of constants would have made it impossible. For example, if the force of gravity was even a fraction of a percent weaker, stars and planets wouldn't be able to form. A fraction of a percent stronger, and even the smallest stars don't last long enough to reliably host planets with life before they collapse under their own gravity in calamitous supernova."

Before William could even get a word in, Alyssia jumped right back into her lecture. "Now, there were *countless* theories to reject the idea of intelligent design, and all of them at the time had considerably more supporting evidence in their favor. But the more my era 'solved' the mysteries of the universe, the more we noticed our universe had some remarkably curious and completely unintentional parallels with our own simulated universes."

"Simulated... universes?" William asked tentatively.

"Oh yes," Alyssia confirmed. "We could simulate, albeit crude, small scale 'universes' using computers and artificial intelligence, with any number of rules, physical laws, cosmological constants, etcetera. But you're losing track of the story here. We discovered *our* universe behaved in disturbingly similar ways. And we first realized this during the beginning experiments on quantum entanglement."

A small probe, with the first 'programmed' entangled quarks was sent out to our solar system's Oort Cloud, a massive shell of gases and matter magnitudes beyond the orbit of Earth. What we discovered was that distance was *completely* irrelevant to how quickly quantum particles transferred information. It was nigh instantaneous regardless of how far away the particles were. This seemed to defy what we knew as the absolute speed possible for *anything* in the universe. That was when we discovered what we called the Fundament."

William prodded, "And what, pray tell, is this 'Fundament?'"

"It's both a thing and an expression, I suppose. We used to explain it to laymen as something even smaller than quarks as a shorthand for them to understand that even the smallest parts of our visible universe wouldn't exist without the Fundament. But again, that was shorthand. The Fundament wasn't so much *smaller*, as much as it *was* everything. Everything we observed, from the photons that carried light, to the flesh, bone, or alloy metal that made all sentient things... was at its core just different expressions of the Fundament."

"We found that the universe wasn't so much mostly empty space as much as the majority of the Fundament wasn't expressing itself in a way that we could detect. Matter was merely the Fundament expressing themselves in the form of the particles that made gravity, atoms, things, possible... or the particles that governed the wave functions of energy. Any given point of the Fundament was either off or on, expressing itself as a given particle. The universe, in a way, had a resolution, and behaved very much like the pixels of a computer display."

"Wait..." William said, holding up his hand to try and stop her.

Alyssia ignored him. "Oh, there's more. We had known that matter and energy really were different manifestations of the exact same 'stuff' for nearly two centuries before I was even *born*. But to *see* it behaving exactly the same at the Fundamental level shattered our perceptions of the universe. Movement was an illusion, much like the human eye processed animation as fluid movement when enough frames overwhelmed the brain's ability to process each frame individually. Particles, energy, matter, whatever... they weren't *moving* per se, the Fundament was expressing itself differently, creating the *illusion* that there were things in motion. *That's* how our entangled particles could seem to violate the speed of light. Because the speed of light itself was not a real thing. And it wasn't just light. There was no *true* 'absolute' *anything*. The constants of our universe were merely the limits that we could measure using the physics available to us."

William whimpered, his brain spinning from a lesson that he doubted even the premier physicists of Cascadia would be able to follow. "I'm... still not sure how this actually ties into the existence of God, though."

"I told you this would be a long lecture when you first asked it," Alyssia huffed. "There was considerable background to cover first. Now hush."

He pursed his lips shut. That much had been true.

"In the meantime, we had been narrowing down the various parts of what had been traditionally called 'dark matter,' which turned out to be expressions of the Fundament that we hadn't been able to measure until we gained the tools to do so, which we only were able to build once we knew what we were even *looking* for. But there was a segment of 'dark matter' that always remained just out of reach. We knew about it, we had a pretty good idea what it *did,* we even had some sound theories about what it *was*, but it always avoided conclusive detection and definition. We were never able to reliably translate it."

"Translate it?" William said, eyes blinking rapidly.

"One thing we learned through our experiments in quantum entanglement was that entanglement was *everywhere*. In fact, we could detect entanglement in over 99.9% percent of particles in the observable universe at some point in their existence. Most of it was the effectively random nature of the cosmos, and there were no instructions or patterns within them, though bear in mind that there is nothing *truly* random in the universe. Boy, could *that* be a lecture in and of itself. But there was *also* evidence of particles entangling with a type of dark matter that we could never detect. Even more curiously, these dark matter entanglements spread actual quantum information quickly to the particles surrounding it, changing them in turn. And even more curiously than that, these changes seemed to be made to encourage very specific outcomes. There was a definite pattern to the quantum information.

"These dark entanglements actively altered the natural uncertainty of quantum states, usually in seemingly insignificant, very small ways; for example... the shifts a set of neutrinos made and how often. But those dark entanglements would add up to have significant impacts at a macro scale. We found evidence of them, on occasion, in the brains of people as they made binary decisions. We occasionally saw them in the processes of Transcendents in the same way. We even saw evidence of those entanglements in the earliest moments of the universe, shadows in the cosmic microwave background, if you will, and what *I* think created the baryon asymmetry that made our universe possible.

"They behaved much like instructions we would give to a computer simulation in those moments where we didn't want to leave things to chance, where we wanted a specific conclusion to happen over a potentially random one; but we were never able to translate those instructions in real time in a way that we could understand or predict before the impact of those instructions were felt. Partly because we only ever caught such dark entanglements as they happened maybe twenty times through our history; and partly because I think whatever was on the other side of those entanglements, it was something we were actively forbidden to discover. We would never be *allowed* to look upon the face of God."

Alyssia's voice dropped grimly, "So yes, I *do* believe in a 'God,' but it's certainly no God of justice or piety or compassion or whatever virtue society wants to attribute to that being or possibly beings. It is a higher power that has willfully guided this world in this direction for reasons that I cannot even *begin* to speculate on. Now, that's not nearly as comforting as a wonderful personification of goodness that grants you eternal life in a nondescript paradise if you live your life exactly as your pastor says... but yeah, that's *my* relationship with God. Does that settle your curiosity?"

"It honestly adds more questions than answers," William replied, his head spinning as it tried to wrap itself conclusively around the information thrown at it. "Are you suggesting that... this," he waved his arms all about, "Is... some sort of computer simulation?"

Alyssia shrugged. "Not in the sense you or I would think of a computer simulation, simply because I doubt God interacts with this universe by sitting down in front of a keyboard and tapping out lines of code. It's merely the closest analogue I can compare it to; that the behaviors this universe displays, and *how* a higher power interacts with it, bears startling parallels to the computer-generated universes that humanity of my day created. It might also inform us as to the sort of reasons *why* a higher power would create a universe and occasionally interfere in said creation."

William exhaled heavily and finally said, "I'd say this explains so much about you, but I'm not even certain I understood half that lecture."

The Transcedent stood, brushing her legs of largely imaginary dust, and said, "Well, you'll have plenty of time to ponder it as we continue. You've rested long enough."

He fought back a groan as he pushed himself back up to his feet. Shame that the car had predictably broke down hours after they had escaped the Way Station. His legs liked *that* part of the journey. What he *didn't* like was the walking, but *not* for the obvious reason.

Well… okay. He didn't like it for the obvious reason as well.

Alyssia hadn't ordered him onto her back since the vehicle broke down, content to walk at a human's pace. It either meant one of two things; either Alyssia felt they were in clear and no longer needed speed and distance… or something was wrong.

And he couldn't just let the question stew any more.

"Is there a reason why we're walking? You've been frantic all this time, practically carrying me up until two days ago. Now we're behaving like we're on some sort of hike. Are you okay? Is there something wrong I should know about?"

Alyssia sighed but didn't stop. "That entire debacle in Attar's compound took more out of me than I would have liked. It's not an *immediate* worry, and since I can't detect any sign of pursuit at this point, I'm conserving my strength. If that changes, I'll throw you on my back as always. Why? I thought you *didn't* like being carried around like a toddler."

William was slowly starting to understand Alyssia's deflections for what they were, an attempt to annoy him into not asking further questions. But that didn't help his concerns at that moment. How much time did she have left? Was it little? What did "little time" even *mean* to a being built to live thousands of years? Would her failing health potentially impact the promises she made? Was "health" even the right word to use to describe a Transcendent's state of being?

But he was also starting to understand there were times to call her out on it, and this wasn't one of them, no matter how much he pressed. Perhaps once they were in the safety of Cascadia's borders, he'd be able to get her guards down and press into the matter.

At least he was learning restraint, he supposed.

Said nascent restraint was being tested to its limits, thanks to the scenery. While the imposing peaks of the Border Mountains were always an impressive sight, William had seen them enough over the years that they no longer really had any meaningful novelty. Even the ones currently on the horizon to his right, mostly unchallenged by Cascadian or Republican explorers simply due to their inaccessibility, did much for his interest. At some point, if you've seen one mountain, you've seen pretty much all of them.

And the foothills they were currently on really didn't offer much either. No sign of habitation, and not much foliage to speak of either. This particular part of the continent had not possessed particularly robust plant life even before the Ice Age, and had been no more hospitable now, with just long, unending hills of short grasses, slightly taller weeds, and spare patches of flowers as far as the eye could see.

Or... at least *his* eyes.

Alyssia jerked to a stop, her body rigid, attention focused slightly off to her left. Momentarily concerned due to his earlier thoughts, William began to ask what was wrong before the Transcendent burst into a sprint before he could even get the word "are" out of his mouth.

"Why am I ever worried about you?" he grumbled before he picked up his pace to follow.

Mercifully, Alyssia hadn't taken off at her full speed, which told him whatever she had seen clearly hadn't been something dangerous, nor had it so taken her attention that she forgot all about him. Nonetheless, it took him several minutes to catch up and fully grasp just what had ensnared her interest.

Her right hand was tenderly grasping the thick stem of a sunflower, gently turning its head in her direction, her own head staring up as thin ribbons of blue light zipped back and forth across her eyes, slowly morphing to green, yellow, then red.

William had *no* idea what was so fascinating about *that* particular specimen among all the other weeds and moss and grasses in that particular patch that she was waist deep into. Yes, it was unusually large for its kin all growing nearby, but it wasn't *that* peculiar. William had seen such giant sunflowers before. They were like the four-leaf clover. Rare, but not absurdly so.

Alyssia, however, was looking at the roughly ten-meter-tall flower with wonder and amazement. "Incredible. This... shouldn't exist. The CO_2 concentrations shouldn't allow it. But that is *definitely* the modified chlorophyll molecule in a third alteration specimen. That... shouldn't have happened. The two alterations should have never mixed in the wild."

William tried to get the Transcendent's attention. "Alyssia?"

She was in her own little world, oblivious to the meat noises coming from William's mouth. "Clearly, the genetic information survived, but how? There were so few left after..."

At that moment, Alyssia became aware of her audience. She coughed nervously once, and said, "My apologies. I was distracted by something fascinating. Something that shouldn't be."

William raised an eyebrow. "A sunflower? They're quite literally everywhere. Granted, they don't normally grow that big and dark, but yeah, you'll even see ones like that on occasion."

Alyssia chuckled, "Well, not sunflowers in general. But *this* cultivar shouldn't. Get your notebook ready."

William obediently did so, and Alyssia graciously waited for him until he found the next open page.

"When I was still flesh and blood, the world's climate was drastically more extreme than it is today. Dangerously so, in fact. As I grew up, technology had led to solutions that eventually slowed the change to its natural crawl, but the problem of the carbon in the air in the form of CO_2 in the atmosphere meant that our world wasn't getting any better, either. Human civilization teetered on a dangerous edge for *decades* where one natural disaster could have tipped the environment over the edge and rendered the earth's surface mostly unsuitable for human life. It was deemed the impossible task, to reduce atmospheric carbon on a global scale fast enough for it to matter to humankind.

"As I grew up, I told myself and anyone who listened that I would be the one to bring humanity back from the brink. I *knew* the answer was in plants like the ones my family grew on their farm. I was single-mindedly driven on that task from the time I was old enough to understand the problem.

"Every decision I made, from the schooling I took, was for two purposes; to gain the knowledge I needed, and to destroy the company that destroyed my family. Which was why I had no problem using their resources to develop the technology that I would then bid for a government contract, then use *that* money to buy out the majority ownership. Revenge for a greater good, as I told myself."

William pointed to the sunflower as he flipped a page, and asked, "And *that* was your solution, I take it?"

"Well... it was one part of a two-part plan; the first part involved atmospheric injections of aerosols into the upper atmosphere, but that was a short-term stop gap while *my* contributions took root and did the *actual* heavy lifting. I was able to spearhead genetic engineering of natural chlorophyll molecules, creating three new variants that absorbed a drastically larger range on the electromagnetic spectrum than naturally evolved molecules. This is why the leaves on this specimen are so much darker than the ones you see normally. It could draw on far greater ranges of infrared and ultraviolet light than the chlorophyll of natural flora."

"The best part was that it didn't even require multiple generations to enact. I used what was normally a plant killer as a vector; engineered fungal spores that carried the genetic information for my chlorophyll molecules into existing plants *and* their seeds; and a task that my critics would take decades, in fact only took years to begin bearing fruit, in a metaphorical and somewhat literal way."

William was furiously jotting notes, but still had the wherewithal to ask, "How did this help?"

"By being able to draw more energy, it *also* allowed these plants to absorb and convert more carbon dioxide, in some extreme examples a hundred times more CO_2 than natural flora. While the initial generation of plants couldn't use that to its fullest, the seeds of the following generations were. This led to their tremendous size as they served as the most effective carbon sinks the world could produce. It was supposed to be the perfect solution; a completely natural carbon sink that would basically strangle itself out of existence as the CO_2 levels in the atmosphere dropped. But clearly, to this day, some smaller specimens from smaller species were able to survive, and even in this current atmosphere, they can grow to exceptional sizes relative to their peers."

She laughed softly, reaching up to brush the petals at the bottom of the sunflower. "The scientist in me wonders if they managed to integrate into the parent species and occasionally emerge, or if this subspecies was small enough to survive even in a lower CO_2 atmosphere."

Then the laugh turned bitter, and she said wistfully, "That's... how it started. I thought I was saving the world. And for one bright moment, I did. I truly used my power, money, and influence to make the world a better place."

"How did it change?" William asked.

Alyssia's head and eyes dropped, losing focus on anything as she stared off through the ground and into space. "The same thing that happened to all of us Transcendent. The same flaw that at the end of the day we all had, and we all hid, with varying degrees of success. I was better at being a functional addict than most, but I was an addict nonetheless."

William blinked repeatedly, momentarily afraid he had lost focus at some point and missed an important segue. "An addict?"

Alyssia nodded slowly. "Not in the way we traditionally thought of addiction, like drugs... although a handful of our predecessors *did* create an entire financial sector complete with its own currencies so that we could buy drugs in a way that were harder for governments to track, but I digress. We were addicted to wealth. That's the best way I can describe it.

"Everything we did was consistent with the behavior of an addict. We willfully stole. We hurt people. Hell, we *hired* people to hurt people. We lied. We manipulated. We did whatever we could to get that next million, or next billion. We destroyed homes, countries, environments... all for that next hit, that wonderful bump in our personal valuations. We cared not if they were a stranger halfway across the world, or our own families. If they were in the way of that next money-making opportunity, we threw them aside and stomped them down with an equal lack of concern.

"And yet, despite behavior that would have had us all incarcerated or worse if we had pursued something like narcotics or alcohol, because we chased money, we were lauded. We were celebrated and admired. Even as we left entire cities bled dry, rusting away, we were *admired* for our tenacity, our ingenuity, our doggedness. And when our actions in our mortal lives *directly led* to the discord and chaos that surrounded them, the people of the world *happily* turned to us to solve the problems we willfully created."

A bitter laugh escaped Alyssia's lips. "The world put their trust, power, and influence into the hands of *addicts*, then were astonished when we ruined everything for everyone else to extend our own lives and build our wealth even further."

"It still seems a bit unbelievable to me. How many Transcendent existed at the height of your power again?"

"The largest Transcendent population was slightly over two million. We were a... *very* exclusive club."

William shook his head, "It's just amazing that you were able to overthrow an entire world with that many people. A secret society of elites that must have had truly exemplary coordination to convince *billions* of people you would act in their best interests."

Alyssia scoffed, "And you'd be wrong. I mentioned earlier that most of us hated everyone else within the Transcendent. We cooperated and coordinated amongst each other only when necessity demanded it. There was no grand conspiracy. There was no shadowy cabal. Everything we did was completely in the open, all our machinations readily visible to anyone who wanted to discover them.

"Our success was predicated on three observations of humanity in general. First, that they cared little about the day-to-day business and structure of political and economic systems. Second, that they would deeply resent anyone who tried to make them care. And third, those that *did* care would be more interested in constructing their own reality than accepting the one in front of them. We were correct on all three counts.

"It was, in fact, almost depressingly easy to turn people on each other. All we had to do was tell them what they wanted to hear. They were eager to hear that immigrants were taking their jobs, or that gun-toting maniacs from the 'ungovernable tribal areas' were plotting war on nearby cities. Those that correctly identified *us* as the problem were quickly and easily minimized, shouted down, drowned out, and eventually outright silenced."

Alyssia then regarded William regretfully, "We even turned people such as you into targets of scorn, and easily whipped up a *majority* of most populations to agree that people just like you were the harbingers of the collapse of their way of life."

William glowered and said sarcastically, "Well, good to see so little has changed."

Alyssia nodded. "A saying from the world of the past was, 'history doesn't repeat, but it sure as hell can rhyme.'"

William finally had the courage to ask a question that had been gnawing at him since he started learning Alyssia's version of ancient events. "Did you consider yourself among them? An addict to wealth that directly caused all this harm?"

The Transcendent confirmed that easily enough. "As much as I would wish I hadn't been. Despite all the good I thought I was doing. In the end, yes, I was every bit as selfish, awful, and addicted to my own wealth and hubris as any of my kin.

"Oh, don't get me wrong, I told myself and everyone willing to listen how 'different' I was. *I* wasn't one of the 'old money' that had inherited and passed down their wealth for generations. *I* wasn't one of those failsons who were born on third base! I hoarded wealth *because* the government couldn't be trusted with the betterment of society! I could work for the public good so much more efficiently and effectively than bureaucrats!

"It's possible I could have. For a very short time, I suppose I could argue that I did. But that was simply what I told myself to justify my evils as I bled the people around me dry and cast them aside like so much trash when they were no longer of use to me."

Finally, William got to the question that had been

gnawing at him. "So... what happened that changed you?"

It was almost like a steel trap snapped shut on Alyssia's soul. Any emotion completely disappeared from her voice, her eyes darkened, and she said, "Moving on. Moving along."

This was not something William was willing to do. "Oh no. You don't get to..."

By that point, Alyssia was quite resolutely walking away, with very deliberate footsteps that said she was done with any further discussion. Clearly, she felt she very much got to walk away without any further elaboration.

William reluctantly had to admit that she was right, if for no reason then she could run considerably faster than he could.

The only option left to him was to enjoy the scenery in relative silence until they came upon a location where they could safely camp for the night, an old and abandoned Republican guard post located right on the foothills of the mountains.

William had been more surprised that the Holy American Republic had an outpost so far out to begin with, much less at this particular location, at any point in their history. The territory belonged to them only in name, the Republic unable to muster the resources and manpower to do even the most basic of patrols terribly far outside of more populated centers.

Not to mention there was nothing here that would justify *any* presence, much less one that had five permanent brick buildings; a garage, a mess hall, administration, a barracks, and an armory. The garage and the armory actually still had a significant amount of machinery and weaponry, which Alyssia found most peculiar.

William didn't. "The Republicans are *notorious* for doing this sort of thing. I swear they have depots and bases all over the place that are still at least partly stocked, then forgotten about. A general gives an order to withdraw, doesn't give the unit time to get everything together, so they pull up all they can, and bug out, hoping that they'll be able to come back later for the more immobile, unwieldy, and less important munitions and machines. But because the Republic perpetually keeps their army undermanned, the opportunity to come back never happens."

"Got to love bureaucracy, don't you?" Alyssia quipped.

What William found curious was that this outpost was here *at* all. There was no meaningful navigable pass through the mountains except for the one to the north he and Alyssia had intended to take, the southern route was about half a day away even by some of the fastest vehicles from this location, and not even the Freelanders would have found anything particularly of value in this vast expanse of nothing. There was no strategic reason for this to exist.

Probably why the Republic *abandoned* this outpost however long ago.

Alyssia, on the other hand, was taking considerable interest in the place, smirking knowingly as William expressed his surprise as to the outpost.

"Oh, I suspect I know the reason why, and I also expect I know why they abandoned this place," she said. "They would have been rather disappointed about it."

"I'm sorry? How could you possibly know this?"

"Well, for starters, I bet if you had wandered a few hours up into the mountains near here, you'd discover the remains of fairly large metropolitan area up there. It's possible those remains could have survived the Ice Age reasonably intact due to its altitude and being built for potentially hard winters."

"People *lived* up there?" William asked.

"A great many people *and* Transcendent, in fact," Alyssia confirmed. "In fact, the Denver metro area was considered a *prime* real estate and investment location for much of my life, both as a human *and* a Transcendent. I, personally, didn't terribly see the appeal, but alas."

William wasn't sure he could really process the sort of society that was so bored that they were building great cities in some of the most inhospitable places in the land. "So, why would the Republic have been disappointed?"

"Well, even *if* Denver had survived mostly intact, they would have found it didn't house any knowledge or technology that they couldn't have found in more accessible areas of the continent. It really was more a resort area by the end rather than something more strategic, and once they discovered that..."

"They would have abandoned the outpost," William finished with a tired sigh. It was as good of a theory as any. "Hell, it might explain the Republic's abrupt interest in cooperating with Cascadia searching for Transcendent ruins. They wouldn't have been able to make heads or tails of much of anything they found."

Alyssia appeared to consider that theory, even though her voice appeared to quickly dismiss it. "Perhaps, but let's see if there's any place sheltered from the outdoors enough for you to get something to eat and get warm for the night."

They settled on the barracks, even if *none* of the bunks there were furnished, or would have been safe to sleep on even if they were. At least its roof was mostly intact. But where the beds weren't suitable for rest, they *were* useful for starting a fire, which William set to do in front of the dilapidated building.

William opened his pack to assess his food state as the flames started building, even though he already knew the situation. He didn't have many provisions left at this point, and he doubted there'd be much to scavenge. Truth was, he wasn't entirely sure how he was going to make it the several days of walking that were remaining to get to the southern pass towards Cascadia.

But at least he'd be warm tonight. He'd deal with hunger in its time. Not like Alyssia was going to bring back a freshly killed and skinned coyote or anything.

There was a very good reason that thought abruptly

popped into his head. Because the transcendent emerged from the tall grasses with exactly that dangling from her right hand, holding it at shoulder height to keep it from dragging along the ground.

"There was a pack prowling about nearby," she grumbled sourly. "Funny enough, it turns out they'll run like scared dogs when you grab the strongest of their pack by the scruff, break its neck, and start skinning it right in front of them."

Alyssia then spent the next three minutes scavenging what amounted to a makeshift spit using a pair of abandoned tire jacks, a vice, and a metal rod that she skewered the coyote from mouth to rump.

"Might take a few hours to cook reasonably safely, but it's something," she said apologetically. "I know this isn't exactly what would be your normal diet."

William shook his head, "I'm not *entirely* against eating meat, you know. But even if I *was*, I get it. There aren't any vegetarians in a famine."

That prompted Alyssia's eyes to narrow, her irises whirling rapidly as it felt like she was more staring through him than at him. William shifted himself uncomfortably at her blank stare before finally demanding angrily, "*What?*"

That snapped her back to reality, with her rapidly blinking and pretending like the roasting coyote was the most fascinating thing in the world. "Nothing," she finally mumbled. "It's... nothing."

William let that non-answer hang in silence. There was nothing that he'd be able to pry out of her that she wouldn't volunteer on her own anyway. He simply stared up at the stars that were increasingly starting to peek through the darkening sky, then on the still roasting coyote that was honestly starting to smell pretty good.

Hunger was apparently not only the best spice, but also the best aroma.

His building appetite was one reason why he didn't

immediately react to Alyssia finally breaking the silence, the other part of it was because she mumbled it so quietly that he barely heard her speak.

"I don't know."

William blinked repeatedly, his brows furrowing in confusion, "I'm... sorry?"

Alyssia had turned her eyes down towards the fire, but again more staring through it than at it. "Earlier you asked me what changed me. I... don't know. That is a question that I've asked myself time after time ever since that fateful moment where something clicked in this quantum brain of mine.

"I had seen so many deplorable things, even things that stemmed from *my* direct actions. It's not like I deviated in any meaningful way that day. It's not like I made some fateful choice that was out of character. It's not like I saw something that was objectively more horrific than anything else in the aftermath of the war. Yet... it did."

William knew he shouldn't bother asking. He knew it would probably make her mind snap shut again. He didn't listen to his internal reason. "What was it?"

Sure enough... her eyes closed, and she shook her head. "No. It's nothing that concerns you. It's my demon to reckon with, and mine alone."

Of course.

Unfortunately, he only had about a minute of silence to grouse about that.

Alyssia's head jerked to the east, and she said grimly, "Something is coming. And it's coming fast."

She got to her feet, quickly pulling William up as well. Soon, even he could the sound of... something, like churning gravel and earth along with a low metallic hum.

"Listen up, and do exactly as I say," Alyssia said sternly. "I need you to go to the armory and scrabble up as much powder and blasting compounds as you can from whatever weapons you can find in the armory, dumping it all in the northwest corner. Then, I need to get a flare gun that works and leave it in the center of the floor. Once you have done that, shout my name. Do you understand?"

William knew better than to ask what she was planning. "Yes," he said in defeat.

"Good. Go!"

She then roughly shoved William backward with enough force that he fell backward, hitting his back hard enough that it forced the wind out of his lungs. As he pushed himself up onto his elbows, Alyssia had dashed back off into the tall grasses at a full sprint, followed not even seconds later by... something.

It looked something like an unholy union of a person and a tank, literally rolling over the fire he had created as if to intentionally frame itself in embers and smoke to create the most menacing image possible. Through that flash of light, Williams could see it was painted in brown camouflage, as if it could ever successfully hide in anything on the plains or even the foothills of the mountains. It had elements that were roughly humanoid, like shoulders and arms, a thick top that tapered slightly to a central "waist," but the dome for a head swiveled without a neck, and the rotating gatling gun where the left hand would be, was not and never would be considered human-like.

It had come in on triangular treads, but as it took chase after Alyssia, it extended to over three meters in height, and the treads pulled up to what were now its calves as it transitioned to bipedal movement without even a moment's pause.

Mercifully, it didn't seem like that monstrosity even acknowledged William's existence, because if it had, it would have had very easy prey that would have been too dumbfounded to realize it was dead. Even after the sounds of its thudding footfalls disappeared from the extent of William's ears, it took him several more seconds to remember that Alyssia had instructions for him to do.

Frantically, he scrambled to his feet, stumbling once

before he fell through the rickety armory door more than pushed it open. Even his slight frame was able to generate enough force to knock the upper hinge loose as it slammed inward and against the interior wall.

William wasn't sure how much time he had to get his task done, but he *did* know that it wasn't going to be easy. The Republicans didn't leave anything that could be readily of use to them or to anyone salvaging. There wasn't going to be any easily used plastic or liquid explosives. He was going to have to improvise from munitions and machines that scavengers wouldn't have much use for... presuming any scavengers even had ever come out this way.

Like six Henson "Four-Inchers," named such for their diameter, that were still in their crate underneath the west wall workbench. Those big boys were only good for the Henson "Two-Mile" Mortar that was in pieces and gathering cobwebs in the northeast corner. The mortar was not easy to move quickly even when it was intact, needing to be pulled on its own cart by its own vehicle, and as the shells were only good for that particular mortar, they would not have been considered a high-value item to take immediately *either*.

William was not *entirely* pleased about it. While the shells were prime subjects to be cannibalized, it was going to take a lot of work. Despite the nature of mortal shells to explode violently on impact, they were rather designed to *not* do so unless it was striking its target with tremendous force.

He rushed back outside to the mutilated fire pit, relieved that the vise had not been seriously damaged by the humanoid tank rumbling through. Discovering the reason why – that it was heavier and sturdier than he was – prompted William to rethink his plan, bringing the crate of shells, a metal pan, and a pry bar, outside to the vise rather than the other way around.

There was a small seam between the fuse and the sheath that could be machined open, but William didn't have those sorts of tools and he doubted he had that sort of time.

So, he settled for jamming the pry bar in the seam and hoping that he didn't generate enough force to set off the fuse. He doubted he had *that* sort of strength, but with munitions sitting for however long, you never knew how they'd start to break down.

When the first fuse popped off without incident, he breathed a small sigh of relief. But that was merely the first potential pitfall for whatever Alyssia was scheming. Presumably, she needed *viable* explosives, which was by no means a certainty. Even simple black powder could lose its punch if improperly stored and maintained.

The packets of gel that these mortars used were even *more* prone to going inert, which meant William *really* wanted to give it a test before relying on it for what he presumed was to blast away a specific corner of the armory. But that wasn't a luxury he had. Granted, Alyssia hadn't given him a time frame, but he couldn't imagine that she'd be able to stall that… thing for *terribly* long.

Especially once he started hearing gunshots in the distance.

William hastily pulled out the gel packs from each shell, dumped the now empty casing onto the ground, and moved on to the next one in the crate. Perhaps he acted too rashly, perhaps urgency gave him a bit too much adrenaline, because as he forced the pry bar into the seam and pulled out, he heard a very discernible click that could have been the fuse priming.

For a nervous moment, he couldn't decide if he wanted this shell to be a dud or not. On one hand, he was sure he how much time he had if it was. On the other hand, if that had been the fuse priming, and the explosive still viable, there was a very high chance things were about to get very messy.

Another burst of gunfire convinced him that fortune favored the bold, and that if he blew himself up, it might just be a mercy. So, with closed eyes and clenched teeth, William pushed, and mercifully the fuse popped off without further incident, allowing him to retrieve the gel sacs, and move on to the third shell.

He closed his eyes, trying to gain some semblance of focus, trying to remind himself of his father's advice in the shop back in his days as Katie whenever he had been preparing for any job that required a delicate touch.

"Take your time, be sure and steady," William recalled his father's words as he lined up the pry bar with the seam on the shell. "Measure twice and act once. You never make things better trying to rush."

Which had hard advice to follow when the faint sound of another burst of gunfire reached his ears. Alyssia appeared to be luring that monstrosity quite a distance. He decided to believe that was a good thing, and not a sign that he was taking too long.

The third and fourth shells popped open without incident, their contents spilling to the ground at his feet. Presuming William was right about Alyssia's intentions, what he had gathered should be plenty. He didn't want to waste any more time because there was still something else he needed to do, and that could take even longer to complete.

Depositing the explosives in the northwest corner, he then turned his attention to a selection of five flare guns that were still hanging on hooks behind the clerk's counter in the armory. While they were relatively simple machines, they were also prone to malfunction even in the best of conditions.

For example, the first flare gun had a rusted-out spring mechanism. The second one had its trigger snapped off at the base. The third had a crack in the barrel. The fourth had the handle split. The fifth had a partially ruptured flare jamming the entire thing.

These had no doubt been low priority repairs left behind because why wouldn't they be? Were he still working in his father's shop, they'd have been way down the list too. Hell, he'd probably tell the customer it would be more expensive to fix the damn thing than it would be to just buy a brand new one.

That… wasn't an option in *this* particular case, so he got to work assembling one working flare gun out of the five broken ones, which was a lot harder to do when you don't have a full set of tools.

But manage he did, deciding that the easiest path was to replace the trigger of the second one with the trigger from the fourth, as the handle was already partially split, making said trigger easier to get to, using his penknife to get the smaller screws as tight as possible as he put it all back together. From there, he examined the small box of flares in a helpfully marked – if faded – cabinet, picked the one that looked most likely to light, loaded up the gun, and set it down as instructed.

And with that, William had a pile of explosives in the northwest corner of the armory, and a flare gun right in the middle.

And no idea if *any* of it was in proper working order.

With a deep breath, William braced his lungs to shout out with all the volume his slight frame could muster and shouted Alyssia's name.

Then he waited.

…

And waited.

…

Then waited a while more.

He began to wonder if he had taken too long, and Alyssia had already been destroyed by the monstrosity chasing her. There hadn't been any gunshots for a while, either. But if something had happened to Alyssia, he doubted that thing would have just stopped. It would have come back to deal with him, wouldn't it?

But chaos returned as quickly as it came, Alyssia crashing through the window on the far side of the armory, screaming at him as she charged in his direction.

"Don't stand in the doorway, you imbecile!"

Technically, he wasn't. He was a good three meters away from the doorway, but apparently that was still too close. He started to turn away to run further as Alyssia picked up the flare gun without slowing down, reaching the doorway just as her pursuer burst through the wall and readied its gun arm.

At which point Alyssia fired the flare into the explosive packs.

William didn't see exactly what happened at the time, as Alyssia tackled him to the ground as an explosion burst, followed by a rapid implosion of the dilapidated armory, collapsing onto the inhuman machine inside. He only saw the aftermath after Alyssia yanked him to his feet and started pushing him.

"Keep moving!" She ordered urgently, "At worst, we've only bought ourselves some time."

"What *was* that thing?" William asked, reluctantly picking up the pace as Alyssia took the lead into the taller grass towards the mountains.

"How have you *already* forgotten?" She shot back. "I *know* you saw a Juggernaut in Attar's compound underneath the Way Station."

William had, but for whatever reason, he hadn't made the connection with the machines in various states of assembly with the monstrosity that had stormed its way through. "*That* thing? Someone reactivated one of those?"

Alyssia's voice grew grim. "So it would seem."

"But... why? Didn't you say something about how they weren't very useful?"

"I said they had limitations. Most of those limitations wouldn't apply to this current age. They could be devastating weapons in this world considering the level of readily available weaponry. But mercifully, in this case, those limitations were what saved both our lives."

"Okay..." William said warily, hoping Alyssia would elaborate.

She didn't initially, instead going silent until William

305

angrily pressed the issue.

"And what are these limitations?" He demanded, "That might be nice to know if these things are making a return!"

"The biggest problem was that while juggernauts were freer to act and adapt to rapidly changing scenarios and rules of engagement than AI, they had many of the same sorts of failings that humans could have, especially with the way that Attar managed the process.

"I think he had watched too many robot horror movies as a child, because he had this vision of the juggernauts being relentless, unstopping hunters that struck his enemies with terror just by their presence, targeting criminals or blacklisted soldiers that had the psychological traits he was looking for. What he got instead were relentless, hyper-focused sociopaths that frequently ignored secondary targets while they hunted specific targets to the exclusion of all else, and as a result frequently baited into traps or disadvantaged positions."

"Much like what you did back there," William noted, glancing back at the smoldering remains that, at that moment, didn't show any sign of a juggernaut rising from the rubble.

"All juggernauts transmitted a near field tag that identifies it to other units and Transcendent, mostly so that we knew what unit it was and who it belonged to. As a result, I knew precisely who that juggernaut once was, and that it would hunt me exclusively until either I stopped moving, or it did."

"I'd ask why you felt confident about that, but I suspect you'd never tell me."

"You'd be correct." Alyssia then hummed thoughtfully and added, "It's somewhat amusing, that in the end, AIs and Juggernauts wound up having different sides of the same problem. AIs could learn, but couldn't decide. Juggernauts could decide, but couldn't learn."

William forced his aggravation down. It wasn't going to get him anywhere, and it seemed like issues in the immediate future was more important anyway.

Like why they were heading *towards* the mountains.

"Where, exactly, are we going now?"

Alyssia huffed in annoyance. "If the Republic was willing to send a juggernaut after us, then I refuse to believe there isn't more than one. We have a better chance of eluding them or getting the upper hand with the uneven ground in the mountains themselves. We shouldn't have to do any severe mountain climbing to get where we need to go. There used to be *several* passes through the Rocky Mountains. I refuse to believe that has changed *that* significantly."

"It's been four thousand years!" William reminded her.

"And you better pray that it doesn't matter!" Alyssia shot back. "If they are reviving long dead ancient technology and sending it to hunt us down, then what leads you to think that they don't have every known pass through the mountains guarded and watched?"

William didn't really have an answer for that. In fact, his entire plan was really just hoping that the Southern Border Crossing was too broad for the Republic to properly patrol and they could slip through into Cascadia under cover of night.

But he had to reluctantly accept Alyssia's observation that the Holy American Republic was far more sophisticated technologically than they were letting on. If they were capable of reviving ancient Transcendent weapons and were able to locate them in the middle of nowhere, then the odds of eluding their eyesight for any prolonged period were nil.

It didn't make any sense to his personal experience, but the evidence was undeniable. Which was why his legs were following Alyssia's through the tall grasses leading towards the snow packed peaks to the west.

Which brought up another question.

"I assume we're in haste," William asked.

"Yes."

"So why haven't you offered to hop on your back and run?"

"Mountains are a bit more treacherous of terrain to navigate as a pack mule."

"We're not in the mountains yet."

Alyssia abruptly stopped, spun about on her right leg, eyes narrow in annoyance, brows furrowed in anger, and voice that carried both. Grabbing William by his collar, she shook him while she yelled.

"I knew the juggernaut in question because he was a former employee of mine that I tricked into undergoing the transfer process, even though I knew damn well what it did, and I knew he carried a deep and understandable resentment for that. I strongly suspect that his revival wasn't an accident and was selected precisely *because* he would hunt me down relentlessly, and the only people that would know that were other Transcendent, telling me that somehow others slipped the enthrallment net, and who knows how long they've been active. Finally, I'm not carrying you because I've suffered a slight bit of a structural failing that I'm not sure will be able to support much more weight than I've already put on it! Does *that* sate your endless and needless curiosity, *boy*?"

William supposed it would have... had his brain been able to keep up with that rapid-fire rant. Instead, he latched onto the last bit because it was accompanied by a visual aid.

What would have been most of her left calf was gone. The chassis near the interior leg was intact, but the rest looked like it had been ripped away, leaving just the central support, loose wiring, visible switches and matte black metal joints in the knee and ankle.

"What happened?" William gasped, mouth agape.

"Vaughn was a *very* good hunter, both in flesh and in machine. Had I been even more unlucky, he would have crippled me exactly like he wanted to."

"Damn it," William replied, "I knew I took too long..."

Alyssia shook her, patting him on the top of his head before turning around. "Don't think like that. Vaughn was *savoring* the hunt, just like I expected him to, and he happened to get a lucky shot in. He wanted me to be terrified of him, and I let him think he was succeeding. It was all a part of the plan."

"Does… does it hurt?"

"Transcendents don't feel pain in the way that fleshy bodies do. Theoretically, we *could*, our quantum brains are certainly capable of feeling the equivalent of all human sensations, but why when we have such *wonderful* HUD alerts that bathe our vision in red on a routine basis to let us know we have suffered potentially severe structural damage in our left leg? I guess it's just pain of a different type."

William really didn't know what to say about that.

"Okay, that's… good?"

Alyssia hummed nonchalantly at that, making a very deliberate pace towards the mountains ahead. With each step, those rocky peaks grew more imposing, and they weren't even at the point where the slope was beginning to be noticeable.

Finally, William asked, "So, what pass do you think can be found this way?"

Alyssia sighed in surrender. "I suppose you're going to find out anyway. We're not going to be taking a conventional pass through these mountains."

William was more than a little confused. "Not… a conventional pass? What do you mean?"

"There's a river that flows out of the mountains and into the bay of what was called Baja California during my time. We called it the Colorado River. You no doubt call it something else."

William nodded, "Yes, the Great Divide. It effectively serves as the border between Cascadia and the Holy American Republic. Why?"

"The mouth of that river is relatively close to here, roughly a day's walk away into the mountains if we move relatively fast."

"You… think on… taking a *river* to Cascadia?" William asked, "Is that even possible?"

"It's not going to be easy," Alyssia admitted. "Even during my time, the Colorado was one of the most difficult rivers to traverse on the continent. I can't imagine a couple centuries of glacial melt will have made it any easier. But that difficulty is the only reason we're going to have a chance."

William understood the concept. It would be *very* difficult for any pursuit to follow them down the river. "I'm assuming I'd be tragically incorrect guessing you have any experience river riding?"

"Yes, that would a horribly incorrect assumption," Alyssia confirmed, "But as unlikely as our survival will be, we are fresh out of options."

Episode Ten: The Great Divide

Alyssia hadn't been lying when she said she didn't have much love for the city of Denver. Even as a full Transcendent with more money than some countries would ever see, it had never particularly interested her. Yes, she had heard tales of how incredible it had been as a symbol of human ingenuity, establishing a thriving metropolis in an area where humans probably shouldn't have been living at all.

And yes, she had to admit that during her time as a human, it had a certain charm to it on the few occasions she had visited whatever tech or agriculture expo or convention had decided to hold itself there.

But by the time the Transcendent had risen, and her peers had decided that it would be the monument to their greatness, that charm had been irrevocably lost. In its place had risen increasingly ridiculous constructions that served no purpose than as measuring sticks to how much wealth they could waste in demonstrative displays.

So, to see what little of it remained in the hard pack of snow in the small plateau that the city rested was both not something she shed tears over, but at the same time felt no small amount of regret for. Yes, the fallen city could serve as an example of hubris and the inexorable march of time that bowed to no one. But it was also a place where millions upon millions over a thousand years had lived... now lifeless and barren.

The lower city was buried under thousands of years of snow and ice. The "canopy" as the Transcendent called it, was the only thing that would suggest any intelligence had lived here... at least until they got closer.

Alyssia knew they shouldn't be stopping, but William didn't, and so when he saw that an excavation attempt had very clearly been made nearby, his curiosity was piqued, and

Alyssia really didn't have the heart to force him back on task. If what she suspected was true, it probably didn't matter that much.

And admittedly, it was quite a sight, for a good number of reasons.

"You were right, Alyssia, the Republicans *did* try to dig up this place," he said as he shivered, his breathing heavy from the lower oxygen levels at this altitude. Despite his obvious discomfort, his attention was ensnared by the multiple levels of digging, still discernible through later snowfall. "And relatively recently."

That was a good thing, Alyssia decided.

Then his eyes narrowed, and he added, "But..."

Something told Alyssia the observation was about to be less good.

"The way that this is dug is... curious." William finished.

"How so?"

"Usually, when you see an archeological dig, they're very broad. Even with more sophisticated sonar, you rarely get much better than a very vague idea of where you might be able to find something. If you remember when I found you, the site was nearing two square kilometers."

Alyssia nodded. "I do."

"But this... this is a *very* narrow site that goes *very* deep. This sort of dig only happens when you have a damn good idea what you're looking for and where you can find it."

"We don't have time to worry about this for now," Alyssia finally said dismissively. "We need to keep moving if for no reason other than to keep you warm."

That was true enough, and William reluctantly pried his attention away from the mystery in front of him as he again took matched Alyssia's pace.

She felt bad for him, at least a little bit. While he was dressed warmer than he was at the start of this grand escape, being prepared for the chill of the plains was a far cry from the frigid mountain air spilling down from the rocky peaks further west. Up here, the Ice Age was still carrying on. She suspected the "-3C" her internal instruments were reading was about as warm as it gets on this plateau, and it was only going to get colder as they got even higher into the mountains.

Even *if* they weren't being actively hunted, the odds that he would survive the river ride down towards Cascadia were not great. Not that the odds of *her* surviving were much better, but at least she didn't have to worry about starvation or hypothermia.

No, she had *other* worries that carried grim tidings for what remained of humanity.

She had suspected for some time. Pretty much from the moment she had woke up, really. The signs that the world around her was more than it appeared on the surface, that the countries knew more, and were more sophisticated, than they were letting on. Whether it was the Holy American Republic's advanced tracking and access to ancient Transcendent, or even something seemingly as benign as Cascadia's apparent biological transition capabilities.

The only major question that she had been uncertain of was who was responsible. The possibility that she had clung to was that humanity had been uncovering and reverse-engineering technology they had found from ages past. The appropriated tech, like the satellites she had surveyed in Chicago had been just different and inferior enough that her theory had remained plausible.

But last night had abolished those hopes. What Alyssia *hadn't* told William that night was that Vaughn hadn't just been revived. The chassis Vaughn was using was brand new, and any inferiority it had was more to do with less-than-ideal materials than just poor design.

Somehow, Transcendent had survived the enthrallment net, but she didn't know how that was possible. She had supervised the entire operation. There had been no indication whatsoever that any of her peers had any idea what was going to happen. Knowledge of the operation had even been limited among the revolutionaries precisely to prevent it from being leaked to the enemy.

There were only two possibilities on that score. The first option was that some of her peers got enough warning after she dropped from the network shortly before the "critical update" that enthralled them. Alyssia rejected that out of hand. *She* had only gotten barely enough warning to completely disconnect herself from the update network quite literally microseconds before it was written into her quantum brain. That someone would have noticed that *and* reacted correctly in that span of time wasn't even possible for a Transcendent.

The second option was that the revolutionaries had missed some that were off network in the aftermath. While more plausible, it didn't particularly sit well with her *either*. The number of her peers that would be willing and able to work in the shadows in such a fashion for four years were next to nil, much less four *thousand*.

"Sorry," William said in apology. "I guess I shouldn't have gotten distracted. It was just... so very odd. To have *that* sort of dig, and only *one*, in an area that would appear to be otherwise *loaded* with potential finds is..."

"Odd," Alyssia confirmed with a distracted nod. William wasn't wrong, it was exceedingly curious, but her reasons were no doubt very different from his.

Alyssia recognized the location, or more accurately, the pillar, bent and torn and broken as it was, almost directly in the middle of the dig site. In an earlier time, it was John David Newman's "Space Elevator." He had famously called it "the gateway to the stars," connecting the surface to the Low Thermosphere Space Station in geosynchronous orbit directly above.

But there was nothing particularly distinctive about it, nor anything particularly important. It had hardly been the first space elevator, nor the largest, nor the last. Hell, it hadn't even been the largest or last space elevator *in Denver*. Any research that the station was doing had been superseded by any number of other research stations and satellites. Newman's Space Elevator had quickly become nothing more than an inane status symbol for the Transcendent that eventually wound up owning it, ferrying anyone with enough money to get a look at outer space that didn't have the physical capabilities to handle a rocket.

The base of the elevator *had* been used as a central server for data on deep space and its associated research... but Alyssia struggled to think of why any of that would have been so useful that *anyone*, even other Transcendent, would have wanted to dig it out.

She couldn't let herself dwell on that too much, at least not at the top of her thoughts. She wanted to make sure her primary focus was on William over the next few hours as the altitude went up, and the temperature went down.

The pass she had been hoping for, right at the base of the mountains just west of the city limits of Denver, *was* still there, which at least promised to make the climb up into the heart of the Rockies easier. It had never been particularly developed like other, more prominent, passes through the mountains, which was why she had guessed it wouldn't get much patrolling, but it also meant that it really was more the natural slope of the mountains rather than a genuine trail that would allow for easy going.

Which she learned personally, as a loose rock, helped by a thin sheen of ice, caused her right foot to slip out from under her, prompting her left foot to fall hard and flash another long series of warning messages about the critical damage, the need to replace the struts and central support, and how to properly distribute her weight to prevent catastrophic failure.

William put his hands on her waist, as if to stabilize her well after the fact. "Are... you alright?" he asked between heavy breaths.

"Yes," Alyssia lied, trying as best as she could to sound annoyed, shrugging out of his careful hold and indignantly continuing the path as it steepened even further. "Worry about yourself if you're already struggling to find enough oxygen in the air. It's only going to get thinner, boy."

Even now, she hated showing weakness. She hated that it had her doubting herself. And she especially hated that doubting herself was the rational conclusion, and the depression that was building with it.

She wasn't going to be able to save humanity from itself.

Even *without* the interference from however many of her peers were still active in the world, there was simply no way this body would be able to handle the workload that was awaiting it. The west coast was *lousy* with Transcendent caches, and she had no doubt any number of them could have all sorts of information that could be used in horrific ways. It was only a matter of time before something fell into the wrong hands, especially since she now knew there were villains actively searching for it.

Meanwhile, William had been distracted by another shiny thing.

"Look at that! More digging!"

His right hand was pointing at the edges of another dig site less than a quarter mile away, on a rise a bit off the trail path, matching with what was *not* a natural cave. Once he was certain he had gotten her attention, eagerly hopped off the more beaten path towards that location.

Alyssia sighed and shouted, "This isn't an archeological survey!"

She supposed in the end there wasn't any particular harm in it. She didn't sense any pursuit nearby enough to identify. And if William had this much energy, he likely wasn't at risk of hypothermia or hypoxemia just yet.

There wasn't any particular harm in entertaining him for a while.

Especially when it gave her a clue to the questions on her mind.

"This is more what I expect when I see a normal dig site. See how they're feeling out the area from some of the cruder marks right here?" William pointed out the gouges in the rock to their left that must have been man made exploratory strikes looking for thinner rock that was hiding something behind it. "And how you can tell they were digging down gradually as they centered on their target?"

They *were* on a bit of a decline, and Alyssia could in fact see that it had been cut out by hand. Natural weathering didn't take such straight lines, abruptly stopping at a sharp rise that partially obscured where the rest of the dig, presumably once they found their target of interest was laying in wait.

He added "It's amazing that we can even still *see* any of this. I can tell this isn't a new dig site even from here. How hasn't it been completely buried under snow already?" William wondered as he got closer to the site, and the evidence that the cave was man made became even more obvious. Even four thousand years hadn't weathered away the unnaturally sharp edge completely.

"Once a climate zone gets cold enough, it can't carry the water vapor necessary in the air to form considerable amounts of snowfall. The snowpack we are currently walking on has likely been accumulating for *centuries*. I'm rather surprised you don't know this."

William answered, "Believe it or not, 'climatologist' was not in my list of proficiencies during higher academy."

Perhaps fortunately for William, he didn't need to be a climatologist to understand what was waiting for him.

"What... the... damnable *hell?*"

Alyssia reached the top of the incline that had given William pause. The cave structure they had seen earlier was in fact, mostly collapsed, the south edge of it initially hiding the north edge that had broken down entirely, covering the mouth of the cave with rubble, but not enough that they couldn't see part of the open amorphous metal door of Transcendent Era construction behind it.

But what caught William's attention were the bodies. Seven of them, strewn about the small shelf the cave was dug into, the very light dusting of snow and ice on their bodies suggesting these corpses were fairly recent. Alyssia's quick scan confirmed that based on projected weathering that they had not even been here a year.

The cold had preserved them in ways that only a frigid mountain could. While gaunt and somewhat desiccated, so much of who they were was still quite discernible. None of them had been particularly old when they died, the bullet wounds still quite visible telling her that their deaths had been violent.

Many of them even had guns drawn; their orientation suggesting that they had been attacked by something coming the same way that William and Alyssia had. A critical piece had fallen into place, enough for some frightening conjecture.

Despite the gruesome scene, Alyssia couldn't help herself. "Hmm, yes. I can see why you'd think this was a normal dig. I'd suggest you really *aren't* supposed to leave corpses in your wake, though."

William glared at either, either due to awfulness of the quip or that she had made the quip at all. "These... are Republican soldiers," he said as he examined the bodies, their bright red thick coats still remarkably vivid with the insignias on the shoulders still discernable. "Republican Intelligence, at that. What the hell were they doing up *here?*"

"Demolition work," Alyssia answered distractedly, examining the site they had attempted to blow up. The jagged edges of the collapsed rock suggested a time frame that perfectly matched the estimated age of the corpses around it.

It was entirely possible that they had been successful, and later geological activity had merely shaken some of it loose. Not that it would have mattered, as Alyssia would have been able to identify this location merely by the GPS data.

William was less interested in that, and more trying to identify any of the fallen humans, so he wasn't seeing what

Alyssia was seeing. Be he cared enough to ask, "Demolition? Of what?"

"This was the Northwest Public Fallout Bunker for the greater Denver area," Alyssia explained. "The spot had been chosen due to the relative stability of the strata, and the belief that the mountain could probably handle the worst that our enemies could throw at it."

William clearly didn't see where Alyssia was going with this, so he commented warily, "Okay..."

"In the final days of the war, that theory was put to the test. A heavy bombardment hit the mountain, you can still see the damage," she said, pointing towards the jagged and irregular peak above. "This mountain used to be a good hundred meters taller."

"Okay..."

"It caused a massive rockslide, burying much of the bunker and a good portion of the city below. After the conflict, the Transcendent Council decided it wasn't worth mounting any rescue of anybody who might have been inside. After all, they were only human, and weren't likely to have survived the attack anyway."

"How charming," William grumbled.

"Wasn't it? Then again, those of us who voted 'no' on the rescue mission weren't interested in being 'charming' or 'humanitarian.' It was a unanimous vote."

"Were *you* on this Council?"

Alyssia paused. No sense trying to dodge that question. "Yes. Not for much longer after that, but I was."

She supposed she had primed William well enough for that answer during their travels that he didn't react with the anger she had been expecting. Instead, he got her attention by saying, "Alyssia, look at this."

William was peering over the edge of the shelf, and Alyssia was momentarily curious what could be so fascinating, siding up to his right and discovering it herself quickly.

The first thing that stood out was yet another red-coated body about ten meters down the sharp decline of the mountain face, jammed in what would have been an extremely painful manner, the body bent in on itself against a crag, one bullet hole where the right eye would be and another less noticeable one through the liver.

It was the *second* thing that William wanted her to see. Still *another* body, another five meters down, face up with a spear of rock through the left shoulder. *That* corpse had taken a *much* harder fall for that to have happened, but even that wasn't what William wanted her to see.

The second corpse was in a far greater state of desiccation, with a significantly thicker coat of rime, and even more notably a faded *brown* coat that had been exposed to the elements for a *much* greater length of time.

Roughly fifty years, if Alyssia's scan didn't miss its guess.

"That's *not* a Republican soldier."

And another piece fell into place, shaping her theory even further.

She straightened and looked back towards the bunker. "Boy, I need you to listen to me, because I think this is going to be *very* important."

William complied, if warily. "Alright… what've you got?"

"I don't think you finding me was accidental. I hadn't thought that to be true for a while, to be honest, but now I'm certain."

"Neither did I," William acknowledged, "The Republic reacted *far* too quickly. They knew something was up."

"There are other Transcendent still operating in this world. I'm not sure who. I'm not even sure how many. But I know that *one* of them, at least, had been in this bunker, buried and forgotten for four thousand years. Fifty years ago, they were dug out by whatever agency that guy down below was a part of. Recently, they finally came back to try and cover up the evidence. Why now? I'm not sure."

William replied, "I might have some insight on that. Republican Intelligence is allowed to operate with a great deal of secrecy. They often aren't even required to identify themselves with other military officers. They're the perfect group to call to action if you want something done quietly. The catch is that you'd need to be a high-ranking general to order them in such a fashion."

And that allowed enough of the picture to clarify in Alyssia's head to know what needed to be done next.

"We need to move, and quickly," Alyssia ordered. "Something tells me our pursuers aren't going to let us mull about any longer. Get on my back."

William nervously answered, "I thought you said..."

She didn't let him finish. "We're going to have to risk it. Come on."

Her warning HUD did not like that at all, the bring angry red tint at the edges of her vision followed by words at the top urgently advising her to stop whatever she was doing, but there's was nothing to do but dismiss it and ignore if it kept popping up.

She had far more important instructions to convey to her passenger as she navigated the rough natural trail as quickly as she could manage to worry about her leg.

"It is of *utmost* importance that once you return to Cascadia, that they understand the danger that the Holy American Republic represents and pray that the leaders of your current home country aren't *also* compromised."

"You could probably make that argument a lot better than I can," He protested.

"And if I'm still functioning at the point that opportunity arises, I will do so. But there's a strong possibility I won't be. Now that I *know* other Transcendent are acting, I also know that I will be their primary target. If it comes down to a choice between you and myself, I am going to preserve your life, understand?"

William *really* didn't want to agree to that, bless the

boy. "Yes."

"On top of that, there are… things that I know, things that if it comes down to it need to die with me. There is likely a great deal of buried knowledge on this continent that if they had my access, they'd already be using. I would sooner kill myself than let them have it."

"Okay…"

"*But*," Alyssia interjected, "You *have* to assume that if I die, it would merely slow them down. No lock is unbreakable. No security is impenetrable. Even if our enemies get *nothing* from me, you *must* act as if they eventually will get what they need. Your leaders *cannot* sit on their hands. Do whatever it takes to make them listen."

William nodded against her shoulder, and replied, "I will."

"Good."

She went silent, putting all her focus into plotting the most stable path through the pass and praying to a God that she didn't grant much benevolence to that she wouldn't have another disastrous slip.

Even with her increased speed, it took hours to cross the mountains between the area that before she was born would have been called "Boulder" and what had one time been known as "Lake Granby."

The Ice Age had done a number on the landscape, most notably to the lake that had once been formed by a twentieth-century dam. What had at one time been a fairly shallow, fairly easy to access lake flanked by gentle coastlines and mountains in the distance for sport fishing and yachting had been turned into a more sprawling, mostly iced over body of water that more resembled one of the Great Lakes of old that extended from jagged peak to jagged peak.

And it had turned what had once been a fairly gentle entry point to the Colorado River into churning fifteen-meter falls heading south, cruelly dashing what little hope she had of even a rough escape.

She hadn't been expecting Lake Granby to be exactly like the pictures she had in her database. She knew thousands of years and glaciation drastically altered a landscape. But this had been the worst-case scenario.

Especially when their pursuers used that opportunity to engage their near field identifiers and tell her exactly who they were.

One of which was absolutely *impossible*.

William didn't know any of that, instead regarding the falls with defeat as he pushed himself off from Alyssia's back. "I'm going to guess this wasn't particularly part of your plan."

Alyssia ignored him, her attention drawn back to the east. With their cover blown, their pursuers were no longer toying with their prey, and the full hum of juggernaut gears started to fill the air to the point that even William noticed.

"That... sounds like a lot more than one." He noted.

It was in fact, *five* juggernauts, with similar coloration and design to Vaughn's, who *also* had joined the procession, if not a bit worse for wear with a massive dent on the left side of its headcap, significant damage to its left flank, and almost total destruction to the treads on its left leg.

She hadn't thought that a building collapsing on him would have been enough. She was surprised by the amount of damage it did, though.

Finally, the man leading the procession spoke. To any unwitting person who had never seen him before, they likely would not have been terribly impressed. He was of rather average height for a human male, roughly 170cm. Had he been human, he'd have probably tipped the scales around 80kg, though a Transcendent body tended to be deceptively lighter. Short black hair that was fading to gray, blue eyes, some light wrinkles decorating a slender face with a nose that was a bit too wide to look conventionally attractive with the shape of his head. Thin lips framed a mouth that also was a bit wider than Alyssia, or anyone, should have found appealing, especially when it was contorted in a vicious, taunting, toothy grin.

"It's that moment when hope dies that I *live* for," he declared, hands almost leisurely in the pockets of white dress pants that were slightly stained at the legs from dirt and grime. He then moved those hands to the front of his bright white sleeveless vest, straightening it before he did the same with the cuffs of his brilliant white dress shirt and matching tie.

But the man was *not* in front of an unwitting person who had never seen him before. What surprised Alyssia was that he wasn't even in front of *one* person who had never seen him before.

"You!" William said, astonished at what he was seeing.

Alyssia spared one eye to her companion and asked, "You *know* this man?"

"More that I know *of* him. That is Pope August the Second, religious and political leader of the Holy American Republic."

That got Alyssia's eyebrows to raise, and she said mockingly to the man, "Oh? Pope, are you? Well, *that* is quite a career change for an avowed atheist."

The man started chuckling maliciously, "It actually still astounds me to this day how easily sheep will follow anyone who knows just what to say."

Now it was William's turn to ask, "Wait. *You* know this man?"

Alyssia nodded. "I do. Granted, by a different name, and he's let a little bit of gray dust his hair. Surprising, as he was so very vain when I knew him, but this man is Pederson Teal."

"Wait... *that* is..."

"Yes. *That* Pederson Teal. The Transcendent Leader whose death triggered a war that nearly ended the world. I should have guessed a roach would be even *more* difficult to kill once transcended."

But even as the pieces started coming together, she realized just how many more pieces were still missing. She figured Pederson would tell her. He loved gloating when he was in an advantaged position. And the fiend didn't disappoint her.

"Come now, Alyssia, I expected so much more of a reaction from you. Are you really going to deny me some astonishment? Aren't you at *all* curious how I've survived so long?"

"I suppose," she answered flatly. "I just knew you were going to tell me anyway whether I wanted to hear it or not."

"Always with the cutting barbs," Pederson said, feigning insult. "Do you have *any* idea how difficult it can be for a dead man to work my way halfway around the world as a global rebellion breaks out? I had to change my face, my body, everything! Now, don't get me wrong, being dead gave me several benefits, most notably being out of the crosshairs of the jackals I called peers as they machinated and schemed to take the seat I vacated. It was quite relaxing to be able to go into rest mode once in a while.

"Why... I do believe *you* were the one who emerged from that power struggle, if I recall correctly, and I most certainly do. You were quite bloodthirsty and ruthless. Almost did me proud the way you let roughly half a million people starve in a partially collapsed bunker. It was *almost* worth it watching them slowly die, eventually resorting to cannibalizing each other. I had to deal with the last handful myself once they discovered I wasn't human like them, but at that point, weakened from hunger and minds warped from depravity, they all proved to be light work. I do dislike having to dirty my own hands."

Alyssia remained impassive, while William turned accusingly towards her. "You were *in charge* through that?"

"Oh? You didn't tell him?" Pederson said with a disapproving click of his tongue. "Young man, dear Alyssia here is responsible for a great number of horrible things in this world. I had the privilege of witnessing them from a distance, play acting as merely a member of the rabble here in the Denver area. I was waiting the entire time in a tomb called a bunker, as she abruptly gained 'a conscience,' abandoned her station, and started consorting with the rebels to enact their scheme and bring the Transcendent Era down. Boy, did I have a whole lot to catch up on when a group of Acelan slavers finally dug me out of that bunker half a century ago! To think that it was blind luck that I never went about downloading that final update once I was freed."

"Yes, yes, always a charmed life," Alyssia said with a glower. "And now, here you are with a brand new body, somehow, committing mass murder of entire swaths of people for the sake of a God you don't believe in. What are you even *trying* to do here?"

"Oh, *now* you are upset by mass graves. How much precious blood was on your hands by the time the horrors of war finally got to you? Was it before or after you realized the…"

Alyssia rudely interrupted him. "Alright, If you wanted us dead, we'd be dead already. Let's cut to the chase, shall we? What do you want?"

Pederson's eyes narrowed, and his grin somehow widened. "Oh, what is the matter, dear Alyssia? Upset and ashamed of what happened until your watchful stewardship?"

"No," she replied gruffly. "I'm aware of my crimes. But I'm discovering that I have no more patience to hear your voice than I did before."

Pederson laughed, but it was the sort of strained laugh of a person that was trying to swallow bitterness. "Despite how much I despise you, despite how you *ruined the world I created*, you did something *extremely* obnoxious that still gives you value to me."

Alyssia smirked. "I changed every single security protocol when I took over as the Council Chair, and you no longer have access to the 'good stuff' that you no doubt would love to revive and reuse. Funny how simply trying to make sure none of your cronies could go rogue and take the war in directions I didn't want it to go *also* has preserved *this recovering world."

"We could have this world in our hands. I wouldn't have to live in this despicable shell, speaking disgusting platitudes to humans that might as well be cattle because they need to hear some damn God in the damnable sky loves them! You wouldn't have to be on the run in a body that literally can barely hold your weight! We could be *gods* again, Alyssia! All you need to do is join me."

"I've worked under your leadership long enough to *never* want to do it again," Alyssia declined. "I'll pass."

Pederson sighed in resignation. "Of course." Then to his juggernaut escorts, he said, "Kill the human. Just keep Alyssia's quantum brain intact."

The Transcendent pope then held up a hand to stop them, no doubt hearing the same thing Alyssia was hearing. More vehicles that, judging from Pederson's snarl, were *not* reinforcements of his.

"Belay that," he barked, his eyes rotating even if his head didn't. "It looks like we have more company."

Four armored vehicles, bearing the insignia of the Holy Republican Army on the side, navigating the narrow pass and icy terrain with surprising adeptness as they all pulled to as sharp of stops as Alyssia would have considered possible, and thirty well-armed men popping up from the sides and rear.

One of them, taking position near the turret of the lead vehicle, popped his head over the roof, his rifle ready in a snap. "Pope August! Stand down, surrender, and prepare to answer for your crimes!"

Pederson sighed in exasperation, growling, "Well if it isn't just a day of traitors?" He finally turned around to acknowledge the arrivals, quickly shifting back to the mock cheer Alyssia knew him for. "Captain Drake. I wish I could say this was a surprise. Your timing is, as ever, obnoxious."

Alyssia would say one thing in approval of this Captain Drake fellow. He was *not* the slightest bit interested in Pederson Teal's games.

"I'm not going to warn you too many times. You *will* answer for the mass murder of your own citizens, and of the Free Landed people of your country. The only question is if it will be before a court, or right here and now. Stand. Down."

Too bad his bravery was also foolishness, and Pederson was understandably not the slightest bit intimidated by the show of force in front of him.

"Goodness, those are some serious crimes to level towards your pontiff," the Transcendent man said venomously. "It would truly be a shame if you and your paltry little sheep never had the chance to utter them again. Sabord, would you care to offer them a demonstration of their stupidity?"

The juggernaut directly to Pederson's right stepped forward, raising its gun arm, and immediately found itself engaged in a firefight that prompted Alyssia to pull William behind her simply due to the number of rounds that started flying, and apparently got close enough that it startled Pederson to take cover behind one of his other juggernauts.

Alyssia soon discovered *why* Pederson had so frantically taken cover. Contrary to what Alyssia had been expecting... Pederson's juggernaut *lost* the exchange. While it had managed to cause three casualties, one of whom was assuredly dead before he even fell out of the turret seat, it had tried to deploy one of its shoulder mounted missiles once it determined the seriousness of the threat the Republicans posed.

Then one high caliber round struck at the perfect time as the missile bay opened, causing said missile to explode prematurely, ripping off damn near the entire left shoulder of the juggernaut and causing it to lilt, where another bevy of high caliber rounds started tearing through its chassis until it stopped moving, billows of smoke and fingers of flame erupting from its remains.

Pederson was almost as astonished by the sight as Alyssia was, though she suspected he hid her surprise better than she did.

"Well, I'll be damned..." she muttered. That was *not* how she expected that exchange to go.

The gunfire stopped as Captain Drake held up his arm so he could speak again. "I've already had the pleasure of encountering one of your toys, 'your holiness.' I made sure we were prepared. Now while I *want* to see you confess to your crimes before the public, I don't *need* to. This is your *last* chance. Surrender, or I swear to *God*, I will commit papicide right here, right now!"

While Alyssia was astonished that these men were equal to *one* juggernaut, she wasn't quite as certain how well they'd fare against *four*. But it *did* open a small window of hope that she had not seen until that moment.

She doubted she'd be able to say anything that William could hear but Pederson couldn't, so she didn't particularly try. "Change of plans, boy," she nonetheless said softly. "I want you to get to those soldiers however you can. Try and get them to understand the peril they face. And whatever you do, don't look back at me. Understand?"

Pederson *did* hear it, judging from how his head turned in their direction, but it was also clear that he had more trouble on his plate than he was anticipating, and behaved *exactly* as Alyssia had hoped he would. "Vaughn, kill both of them behind me. Alyssia's quantum brain is merely a secondary goal. Secure it only if you can do so. Destroy it if you have you. The rest of you, cover my retreat. Kill anyone you can who resists us. Go."

The fiend grasped onto the rear of the juggernaut on the left as they jumped into action, carefully shielding their master through the heavy fire that erupted. At the same time, Alyssia used Peterson's order to push William forward, intercepting Vaughn as the damaged juggernaut tried to fire on the young man, a hard slap on its gun arm causing its shots to go astray. It was all the distraction Alyssia could afford as she rushed for the cliff and the falls directly ahead.

Vaughn pursued exactly as she expected. What she

hadn't expected was that he would be able to catch her, diving to grab her by her damaged foot, his grasp finally crushing the limb and causing it to snap off at the ankle.

Fortunately, it still worked out in her favor, as the limb snapped *above* his right hand, and her momentum was enough to take her over the cliff and into the water below 1.78 seconds later.

Alyssia honestly found it more refreshing than anything that she was finally getting a different warning message while she righted herself, that there were structural breaches in her chassis that was allowing water into places that it shouldn't be. Though she wasn't afforded much time to entertain *that* useless warning before Vaughn *jumped off the cliff after her.*

She had hoped that indecision over whether her or William should be his primary target would allow her a bit more breathing room, but apparently, he hated her *that* much that William ceased to be a concern.

She supposed she didn't blame him.

The bad news for her was that juggernauts were astonishingly capable amphibious weapons. While their guns and missiles were more *limited* underwater, they didn't jam or render themselves inoperable when wet. In fact, the shoulder mounted missiles could even function as short range torpedoes, which was the first thing Vaughn tried once he had found his bearings.

The good news was that the rapidly moving river blunted the missile's ability to catch her or adapt to any abrupt change in motion, like a sudden dive under the water at the perfect moment for it to zip past its target harmlessly.

From there, she did what on the surface would probably be considered insane by anyone who didn't know the limitations and weaknesses of juggernauts. She swam upstream towards it; using the current to her advantage to get inside the reach of its arms, pushing forward and grabbing onto Vaughn's back as it tried to get into an attack position.

Alyssia was able to climb onto Vaughn's back, getting

a firm grip of the rear seam on its headcap with her right hand. One structural design flaw of juggernauts was that its arms weren't long enough or flexible enough to reach anything that jumped on its back. Funnily enough, it was a design flaw that was detected in initial testing but deemed too insignificant to scrap the design and start again.

After all, who would be stupid enough to try and mount a juggernaut?

Some correct answers were, clever rebel guerilla demolitionists, sabotaging suicide agents, and Alyssia.

Unable to reach her, Vaughn resorted to a series of death rolls to try and dislodge her. That *might* have worked against a human, but Alyssia's grip was far too strong for mere centrifugal force to dislodge her. From that position, she was able to confirm both through a scan and the hole she found in the dented section of his headcap, that it was even still using the old internal layout with the quantum brain in the head cavity, rather than in the chest like later models of Transcendent used.

Pederson really just copied everything from the old juggernaut designs, *knowing* of the inherent flaws in that design, having seen the results of those flaws firsthand and from field reports... and did absolutely *nothing* to amend or correct those initial designs. He was *that* lazy and uninspired.

This man had been the unquestioned leader of the entire world. It would have been comical if the results hadn't been so tragic.

But she had more important things to do than marvel at the lack of ingenuity and scientific curiosity of Pederson Teal.

She sized up the failing juggernaut as it attempted two more fruitless rolls, and then Alyssia clamped down on Vaughn's headcap as hard as she could, preventing it from turning and giving her the best possible angle for her strike.

"I *am* sorry, Vaughn," Alyssia said grimly. "I have done so many terrible things to you in your life, but I promise, *this* will be the last time."

And then she punched straight through the vulnerable section of the headcap, and caused instantly fatal damage to Vaughn's quantum brain.

Vaughn immediately went limp as every function shut down, turning one of the most intimidating weapons of the Transcendents (at least in a one-on-one skirmish) into some very elaborate scrap metal and electronic waste. Alyssia didn't get much chance to celebrate her victory as Vaughn's lifeless chassis slammed against the cliff wall, taking Alyssia by surprise and plunging her into the river.

She pushed herself back to the surface as a new warning appeared in her HUD, one that she wasn't allowed to dismiss.

>> *Water breaching H3 core. Potential for meltdown. Shutting down reactor and shifting entirely to battery power.*

That was a problem. While she was more than aware of the breaches in her chassis that was allowing water inside, she hadn't expected water to seep into the deeper internal mechanisms so quickly. The H3 disc and reactor was supposed to be one of the most secured and insulated components in the Transcendent body. If *that* chamber was already failing, it didn't bode well for her survival.

And despite all her bold words about being willing to die, that didn't mean she *wanted* to. Not with Pederson Teal on the loose and manipulating an entire country. That wasn't going to end any better than the *last* time he had that power.

But at the same time, she struggled to think of any options she had. Even *if* she somehow survived the river – which if history was any gauge, the worst was yet to come – there was little she'd be able to do in her current state. Hell, she wasn't even going to be able to *walk*.

Alyssia fought down that despair. Yes, it was going to

be a difficult, if not impossible road ahead. But there were times to think five moves ahead, and there were times where the only way forward was to focus on one move at a time. This was the latter.

The immediate problem was water leaking into critical systems. She needed to find some way to at least elevate her torso above the river surface, or at the very least find some dry land to plot her next move.

The increasingly higher faces of the mountains on both sides of the river were not giving much hope of sanctuary, but a glint of metal catching her eye gave her a figurative and literal life preserver.

Vaughn's chassis, despite the damage it had taken, was still floating rather soundly. This shouldn't have surprised Alyssia that much; the juggernaut design and the speed of the river wasn't going to allow it to sink easily, and it would at the very least be able to support her own mass as she tried to dry out critical internals.

So she swam as swiftly as she could onto Vaughn's back once more, immensely pleased when the water alert almost immediately started to drop. It didn't entirely solve the problem, as Alyssia discovered as she ran a diagnostic and determined that the reactor wasn't nearly dry enough to restart, and likely wouldn't be until she got out of the river, something that didn't seem like was going to be an option any time soon.

This led to the next problem for Alyssia to solve. Even when a Transcendent was in prime working order, the battery couldn't power full function for much more than twenty-four hours. While there were ways to extend that limit, she *really* didn't want to have to use them. Even a low-power state reduced her awareness and reaction that could be deadly considering her circumstances.

But she really didn't have an option, especially since she didn't know exactly when there'd be an opportunity to get out of the river.

Alyssia settled on an custom solution in her power

settings; maintaining active scan for any potential points where she could get out of the river and dry out, as well as wake alerts if anything significant changed in her environment, like Vaughn's chassis losing its buoyancy, or a shift in the river that suggested upcoming rapids, which were notoriously frequent in the Colorado River of *her* day, and hoped that the number that her OS gave her would be sufficient.

>> *Estimated battery operation under new settings......... 2 days, 17 hours, 33 minutes.*

Alyssia sighed to herself. That was better than nothing. That gave her roughly a day to find dry ground, and another day to let the reactor dry out and get restarted. From there, she'd think on her next move.

>> *Apply these settings?*

Alyssia confirmed it with a glance, her eye tracking to the "confirm" selection on her HUD. At which point, the OS began a short countdown to when all of her other functions would go into a sleep state, finished with one last parting message before it all went black.

>> *Goodnight, Alyssia.*

Episode Eleven: The Lions' Den

Miles hadn't even finished his report by the time that Archon Elgin summoned him to the Halls of the Enlightened. Hell, Miles hadn't even really *started* preparing said report. It had taken him two days just to put the *truth* together in something resembling a coherent sequence, much less the story that Captain Drake wanted to put out there... or if he even *wanted* to play along with that narrative at all.

He eventually settled on cooperating with it; if for no reason than there was a good chunk of people in Drake's regiment that never had the opportunity to agree with his attempted rebellion, and he had no doubt that betraying that story would lead to a whole section of scapegoats that didn't deserve to be prosecuted for treason.

But this change in protocol had him reconsidering just how much he wanted to help Drake's scheme. To say it was peculiar to demand an investigator attend an interview *before* his report was finished would be an understatement. Usually, it takes *weeks* for the gears of justice to turn in such a fashion.

There was generally one of two reasons that such a change in protocol happens. The first was that a rapidly changing scenario either on the ground or in the political sphere requires an immediate report from the standing Inquisitor. That the clause uses the word "Inquisitor" instead of "Investigator" was a clue at how rarely that clause is has been invoked.

The second, and more likely, scenario is that he was about to be railroaded again in another coverup. Which was an easy scenario to believe considering the people involved.

Pope August had already damn near ended his career once before, and by all accounts, the Archon that Miles was answering to was one of the pontiff's hand-picked men, presumably because he would act on the Pope's desires.

His depression spiral was momentarily broken when the paperboy swung through the Archon of Hope's reception office, dropping off a stack of newspapers at the rack to Miles's left. It probably wouldn't have caught his attention for much longer than that if the paper had carried a different headline.

Pope Declares Holy War on Freelanders

Miles sighed heavily, grabbing the top copy, and opening the center fold to read the day's leading article.

> *Pope August II has declared a "great, just, and blessed war" against the people known as Freelanders, a loose and decentralized movement that live in the far frontiers of the claimed territory of our great Republic.*
>
> *Representatives at the Holy Chapel have not offered any justification for this declaration, but the suspicion is that he believes a clan of Freelanders were responsible for the attack on MacArthur Depot, even as Republican Intelligence has not released their findings in relation to that attack.*

Miles shook his head at the mere idea. He had touched base with the Lead Investigator of that case and had seen some of the pictures taken of the aftermath of that disaster. That had been some form of airstrike, judging from the projected angle and blast circle of whatever had struck. If the Freelanders had *that* sort of weapon, and had wanted to start a war, they wouldn't have targeted a frontier base out in the middle of nowhere.

Or… maybe they would have, as Miles thought about it. The Freelanders were never particularly known for strategic thinking beyond what was directly in front of them. To them, it's possible a frontier base like MacArthur *would* have been the biggest concern to their business.

Not that it mattered, because he knew the Freelanders didn't have a weapon like that. *No one* had a weapon like that. Sure, Cascadia had a nuclear weapon that could do that sort of damage, but that sort of detonation left radioactivity that whatever hit MacArthur did not.

It is important to note that while Pope August II can call for holy war in this fashion, he can only mobilize the Papal Guard without the approval of the Archons, and request for assistance from regional Republican Police. While four regions have already promised aid and support, with others sure to follow, the Republican Army won't mobilize without an official declaration of war from the Archons. It is believed the council will meet early next week to discuss that matter and decide on their next move.

It certainly seemed that Pope August was finally getting the war he had been itching to have since he took the mantle, if against a different enemy than he wanted.

Miles doubted the Archons would push back this time. It was one thing to balk on the idea of war with Cascadia, talking the Pope down from a holy war multiple times over the last seven years. The Pope had wanted war with Cascadia so badly that two years ago he had sent a survey team to the Great Divide, claiming that God had shown him a river path through the mountains from which they could launch a sneak attack.

When that team disappeared without a trace, it at least ended the *overt* pressure from the Papal Palace.

Not that Miles thought war with the Freelanders would be any more fruitful. Those areas were called ungovernable for a reason. Even *with* the full support of the Archons and the Republican Army, it was a massive swath of land with an entrenched population armed to the teeth that knew the territory and had God knows how many little bunkers and hideaways and fortified locations to launch sneak attacks and small-scale strikes that would keep the Republican forces off balance.

It'd just be a repeat of the *last* time the Holy American Republic thought they could force the Freelanders to bend the knee. It would likely end just as embarrassingly for all parties involved.

But if it didn't end in humiliation… it's not like Miles would shed a tear. The Freelanders were almost uniformly unsavory individuals with equally unsavory attitudes. About the only thing Miles would give them was that they were bluntly honest with their bigotries and their vices. A faint virtue, but one that polite society often didn't have.

Captain Drake was about the most tolerable Freelander Miles had ever had to deal with, and even he wasn't someone Miles would have particularly been inclined to trust if not for the circumstances; a man who if he was a saint was only by virtue of being surrounded by devils.

That was a feeling Miles understood quite well.

And through it all, *everyone* seemed to have forgotten about the unchained Metal God that had started this circus, a Metal God that Miles was certain was very much unaccounted for.

"Inspector Parker?" the receptionist finally called out from her desk on the other side of the room. She had been warily watching him the entire time he had been waiting, and her voice sounded visibly relieved. "Archon Elgin will see you now."

Miles took a deep breath and readied himself to receive his ticket to some desolate hell where he'd never be heard from again.

The Archon of Hope, Jeb Elgin, was sitting with his hands folded in front of his face, his eyes burning holes in the phone to his left.

"Apologies for the delay." Elgin said gruffly, finally affording Miles a glance. "The pope had decided to call me and was... extremely unwilling to let me get to business. Sit down."

Miles sat... as the Archon stood, taking even paces towards the west wall, where a portrait of Virgil Landry, Elgin's predecessor had been hung. Miles didn't remember that portrait being there the first time he had visited, which suggested that Elgin had it put there.

"You might not know that I was the Regional Judge assigned here in the City of the Saints. My opinions and my location were no doubt a major reason why the Evangelical Society had me at the top of the short list for a seat on the Archon Council, which is no doubt why Pope August nominated me for the seat."

Miles actually *did* know that, though he *had* needed the reminder.

"I knew Virgil through my father, who were both public defenders when they were younger. I wound up forging a casual and professional relationship with the man myself. Even though I strenuously disagreed with damn near everything that he considered and championed, I'd like to think that he valued my input."

Miles figured Archon Landry probably did. He took the words of damn near everyone into account, even from people that Miles would not have guessed he'd even give the time of day to.

"But even though we could not have had more different views on the world and the future, every time he spoke to me, he did so with respect and courtesy. Despite his position as an Archon, and that he was several decades my senior, he never once tried to shout me down or impose his station and experience on me.

"Compare that to the man I am supposedly obligated to, who spent the last thirty minutes making absurd demands, ridiculing me, talking down to me, and telling me repeatedly to 'know my place.' You tell me, Investigator. Which one should I give more reverence towards?"

Miles knew how he should answer that question, but dared not presume what was going on in the head of Archon Jeb Elgin.

And Elgin didn't expect him to. "You don't have to answer that."

The Archon took his seat again. "The Pope has gone just short of accusing you of sedition, and wants you terminated. He doesn't want to officially charge you, and wants me to get rid of you quietly, and I suspect I know why. Because *he* doesn't want to have to present his evidence. So, I need you to tell me the truth as to what the hell *actually* happened in the 'Depths of the Freelands', as he so calls it."

Every part of Miles's weary mind was screaming at him that this was a trap, trying to bait him into revealing what he saw. If so, they'd be disappointed to learn just how little it was, and how much of his conclusions were drawn from inference.

With a couple deep breaths, Miles said, "In regard to the Pope, I can't say much. I got the notice that he was coming to the trading site mere hours before he actually arrived. He then went down into 'the Depths' to meditate on what he had found."

"He claimed he desired to go alone to meditate, and that you and Captain Drake followed him down, and the latter attacked him under your instruction. He claimed, 'it was but by the Grace of God that he survived.' At which point he fled the ruins and was eventually found by a Republic patrol."

Miles tilted his head in confusion. How would Pope

August have known they both went into the depths? "Interesting. Because, yes, as evening turned to dusk, and the pontiff had shown no sign of returning from the depths, Captain Drake and I *did* eventually follow him down to try and find him. The difference is… we never did. We encountered a machine monstrosity patrolling those lowest levels, and even found another exit to the outside world at the bottom, but never once encountered Pope August. Upon reaching that lower exit, Captain Drake discovered a Freelander settlement on fire, and called on any of his men that wanted to join a 'little insurrection' against the Pope."

"And that was when all hell broke loose above," Elgin said, leaning back in his chair thoughtfully. "The survivors of that skirmish said that damn near half the regiment turned on the other, and it was a mad scramble to escape the chaos for what few survivors made it out."

"I never really got the chance to question any of them about what happened above," Miles admitted, pivoting into the cover story that Miles and the survivors concocted since Archon Elgin willfully walked right into it. "As far as I could tell, the fighting force broke almost evenly, and the support staff were in the crossfire. Seemed it was more important to get as many people to safety as possible and by the time that was done, no one was really in any state to give a clear picture of what happened."

Elgin nodded and ran his right hand through his beard. "As unbelievable as it may sound, that makes more sense than the story Pope August tried to spin. From what I had been able to gather, Captain Jordan Drake is one of the more accomplished and seasoned officers in the Republican Army, and I know you had military experience yourself. If the two of you wanted him dead, he would be.

"So, either he truly *does* have the 'Protection of God,' or he's lying through his teeth, and while I may be a man of tremendous faith, I am not one to believe in such fairy tale nonsense. Speaking of fairy tales, did you happen to see any evidence of the unchained Metal God that started this entire escapade?"

Thank *God,* someone who hadn't forgotten. "No. The only sign of any Metal God that I found was the ruins of one in the depths, one that I have reason to believe had already been deceased. If 'William Sterner' as he calls himself, truly found an unchained Metal God in one of the digs he had been doing, it is still at large."

Elgin grumbled, "No sign of Sterner either, I take it."

"No sir," Miles confirmed. "In the lower exit, there were signs of old Transcendent vehicles being used to leave the site. I suspect he, and anyone he might have been with, had used them to escape the initial army's strike on the compound."

"Wonderful," the archon said in exasperation, "A Cascadian terrorist, potentially with one of the greatest menaces of the archaic times, running around God knows where. And here we are instead, having to deal with a hysterical pontiff and his grudge with you. That man truly *hates* you, doesn't he?"

Miles shrugged, "So it seems."

"Any idea why? Outside of you always seeming to be the one that gets tapped to investigate him?"

"Maybe that's all it needs to be. People in power don't like to be questioned. And I've had dealings with him four times now."

Elgin had to think about that. "Four? You had this time... the Purge... the Papal Murder... oh yeah. You were *also* the guy that the council tapped to vet him for his ascendence to the holy seat, weren't you? I suppose that makes sense why he would see you as a stubborn little tick that needs to be burned out."

The archon sighed heavily as he slumped forward. "I don't particularly want to do this, but I'm going to put you on paid leave for the next two weeks. If only to get this fool Pope of ours on task to this goddamn war he wants to thrust us all in."

Miles supposed he should feel betrayed by this, but honestly, it was better than he expected. It didn't seem like he needed to send any "final business" to Archon Paul Anders, which was good. He didn't really like Anders very much and didn't terribly trust him with the sensitive findings that Miles had collected.

"That's fine, Archon," Miles said acceptingly.

"I'd still recommend you finish your report as promptly as possible. If you can get it done by next Wednesday so that we can enter it into our war deliberations, that would be preferable. Otherwise, we'll go with the notes I've compiled here."

"Yes, sir."

"And don't go too far, either." Elgin continued, "By all accounts, you're one of the best investigators in the entire Republic, and I see no reason to doubt that assessment. I want you back on the search for Sterner and whatever ancient weapons he may or may not have, and every day that he's on the loose is a day that he could be leaving this country or worse causing more havoc in this one. I'll certainly get someone else on this for the interim, but the *instant* that Pope August's attention is elsewhere, I'm going to have you back in the field, understand?"

"Yes, sir."

Archon Elgin nodded and leaned back one more time. "Dismissed."

Miles left the Archon's office honestly more concerned than relieved. The political dynamics that he had been expecting were completely off, and he wasn't entirely certain why they were so skewed.

It was *possible* that the disdain from Archon Elgin towards the Pope wasn't being staged. Jeb Elgin was a bluntly straightforward person. While many of his views could be considered brutally conservative, they *were* earnestly held beliefs. He truly felt that Holy American Republic society was not ready for the significant changes that the more progressive sect of the church and its allies in the public square were trying to push.

That was a far cry from Pope August, who Miles had quickly determined was a power seeker with distressingly few earnest beliefs; a man willing to say whatever he had to, to whoever he needed to, just to get one rung higher up the hierarchy. That he found purchase with conservative hardliners was more that they were more willing to overlook such flaws in their desire to find allies willing to resist change.

August was also *not* a particularly detail oriented person. In fact, if Miles was less charitable, he'd say the Pope was in fact rather foolish in *many* ways. It was entirely within the realm of the plausible that Pope August would have blindly just picked the name at the top of Evangelical Society's list without even bothering to vet the man to see if he would be a blindly loyal ally.

But even if all of that was true, Miles knew enough about the power plays and the nature of people to know that even the most earnest people will accept a *lot* of underhanded schemes, foolish actions, and empty words if it advanced their agenda. Archon Elgin could mean every single word he was saying, and still be faithfully in line with that "fool Pope" when it came time to pick a side.

No, Miles was not even going to *consider* that Elgin could be a potential ally any time soon. Which was unfortunate because he didn't have many, and of the few he could consider friends, most of them were dead.

Miles was so lost in his thoughts that he didn't even process that he had left the Halls of the Enlightened until he was in the outer courtyard heading towards the exit. William, the *real* William Sterner, would meet Miles here for lunch frequently before he had been coldly executed for being "deviant."

A "crime" without an official charge. Publicly executed, and tossed aside by the same damn Pope that was again trying to keep Miles from exposing the *true* crimes of the pontiff. And he only started seething *more* at the thought of a terrorist using William's good name as he kills God knows how many people and working with a fiend from antiquity with God knows what weapons at its disposal.

The family that had saved his life after disaster, pulling him out of the rickety boat that had been barely staying afloat in the waves after the storm that had flooded nearly the entire coast. Adopting him after his mother passed away, not even making him change his family name, to keep the honor of his birth family. Their two children, William and Katie, happily including him in their circle of friends even as other children in the area were wary of the dark-skinned boy.

It was those thoughts, and the stress of them, that ostensibly led him towards his next destination, the parking garage adjacent to the Halls. Climbing into his navy-blue Corsair, he felt the whirr of the motor take him onto the main highway south, and the six-hour drive towards the City of Hope.

The drive was always one that Miles found soothing, no matter how bad his mental state was. Especially as the height of summer rose, and the dark blue green of the grass and leaves of the trees really popped against the bright blue summer sky, with not even the scattered barn breaking into the natural landscape. To see such natural, casual beauty always helped Miles find a bit of ease, a perspective that no matter how rough his personal road could be, there was something out there that remained pure and unblemished.

Not that human civilization didn't have its charm and beauty. To the unenlightened there probably wasn't much difference between the City of the Saints and the City of Hope other than their respective size. While the City of Saints *was* larger, the lighter brick and mortar used in the City of Hope belied that it was in fact the *older* city. The *first* city, in fact, the refuge that the survivors of ancient wars and the environmental collapse that blanked half the world in ice and snow had taken to survive.

Some buildings, like the City Hall in the center, still

stood with much of the original brick used to build it almost five hundred years ago, pieces only reluctantly replaced when there really wasn't any other choice.

Parts of the city still imposed laws from that time, where motorized vehicles were prohibited, like the Historical Corridor on the south side leading towards the Gulf. *That* was a bit bothersome, because Miles's destination required a significant detour that could have otherwise gone straight through that district.

But at least the less traveled roadway meant it was easier to see if he was being followed. Which he wasn't.

Instead, he had to follow the south beltline around the city, then finally out towards the countryside, where the roads switched from brick to gravel. He reached the divot that marked the left turn he needed towards the Sterner house, his Corsair jarring roughly as the wheels bottomed out. It always made him wince. The lower sitting automobile he drove really wasn't designed for this type of road.

The Sterner house really didn't look terribly different from any other farmhouse in the area from the outside. It was a pale yellow rather than the conventional white, but that was hardly something even the neighbors besmirched them for. Even the residents of the home weren't terribly out of place. Plenty of retirees from the City's Industry District moved out into some of the old farmhouses after their workdays were done.

But what *was* different was that it was where Miles could still call home no matter how old he got.

Mary Sterner had already rushed out of the front door and down the deck before Miles could even get out of his car. He hadn't even taken two steps forward before she met him with a warm hug around his waist and her head bumping against his ribs.

She had been a bible teacher when he was growing up, one of the few jobs she had been allowed to hold once she married. Even at the time, he had thought it was a waste of her mind. His birth mother had run her own restaurant and had ruled that roost with a fist of iron, though he didn't remember many details about that anymore.

"Welcome home, sweetie."

"Good to be back, mom."

Miles still remembered the first time he had called her that. Five years after his rescue, and four after he had been officially adopted. She had cried after that, not because she had been so moved, but that she had been worried that she was replacing his birth mother. It had taken quite a bit of effort from all three kids to talk her down from that.

"You *could* have given us some warning you were coming; you know. Traveling down from the capital isn't exactly a short trip."

"I know," Miles admitted. "Spur of the moment thing."

Mary frowned. "Oh dear. What happened? That bad?"

"We'll talk about it when we're not in the open air, okay? I'll be around for the next couple of days if you'll have me."

"Always, Miles. For as long as you like."

She finally stepped away from Miles, wringing her hands nervously, "I don't like any of this, Miles. Every time you've come back home, its like you've made a new enemy, or you're getting closer to something that might get you killed. We've already lost William, we haven't heard from Katie in *years*... you're pretty much all Bobby and I have left."

Shortly after Katie had left for Cascadia, her brother had been killed in "The Purge" and Katie had stopped writing to her family. It was something that ate at her parents, and occasionally bothered him, to this day. An act of needless and senseless violence that had torn an entire family into pieces.

Miles remained as determined as ever to give his adopted parents the closure they needed.

He jerked his thumb towards a red and white barn about a hundred yards from the farmhouse. Much like the house, there was not much peculiar about it from the outside...

if you ignored the automobiles in various states of repair lining the west exterior wall.

"Dad in the garage?"

Mary clicked her tongue and put her hands on her hips. "As always. Since you're heading that way, see if you can get his attention long enough to let him know dinner will be in about an hour."

Miles laughed as he stepped away with a wave. "I will."

He had to unbutton his suit jacket as he walked toward the barn. It was *considerably* warmer along the Gulf than it was inland, and he never seemed to learn that lesson.

The barn, as far as Miles could tell, had originally been for breeding animals, one of many attempts earlier generations had salvaged the various feed animals that would have otherwise gone extinct during the calamities of the past. Nowadays, that was handled by a more centralized location inland about an hour from the City of the Saints, and left these old barns for different purposes.

Like as a garage for old engineers who just don't know how to quit.

Bobby Sterner had retired from his machining job five years ago, but you wouldn't know it from how he was up to his waist in the guts of a fifteen-year-old Beville tractor, one of many machines he was no doubt repairing for any number of neighbors. Judging from the six vehicles in the barn, business was good.

Despite the father's gearhead nature, neither of his boys had terribly much interest of affinity in machinery. It was Katie out of all of them had had really been drawn into it. And despite knowing that she'd *never* be allowed to practice the craft, Bobby had encouraged her. It was why they and William had appealed to the Republic so hard to let her continue to learn in Cascadia as she came of age.

Bobby's right hand rose out from the curved hood of the tractor and pointed to the right. "Just leave the keys on the first open hook. I'll figure it out. Leave your contact information with my wife."

Miles smirked. "Well, I would, dad, but my Corsair is running just fine."

Bobby startled, his head banging on the hood as the older man yelped then hissed. He quickly pulled himself out of the tractor, wiped his hands clean, and shook his son's hand.

"Damn it, kid, warn your father more properly next time," Bobby said, his free hand rubbing the back of his head.

Miles examined the tractor in question and was rather astonished that he recognized it. "Wow, Old Man Tucker still using that thing? This thing was ancient when *I* was a kid."

Bobby nodded, and said tiredly, "Yeah... damn near every month someone else is wrong with it. *This* time it's the gear box, but the bolts of the gear casing are all stripped, so it's been fun working that thing open."

The older man then frowned and said, "Lemme guess. Got something new for 'The Box'."

Miles nodded and reached into his suit jacked to pull out a stack of four folded sheets of paper. "Yeah. As always..."

"Yeah, yeah, I know," Bobby said, taking the stack carefully, and crossing the garage towards the tool rack in the northwest corner. "Don't look at any of it. Just follow the instructions on the top page if anything happens to you."

Miles genuinely didn't believe he was in any immediate danger of losing his life, mostly because of that black steel box that Bobby pulled out from underneath a trap door, unlocking it with a copper-colored key that Bobby always kept on him, putting the stack on the top of an already thick stack of paper, then locking the box and putting it back under the trap door.

That box was a compilation of most of the notes that Miles had pieced together of his investigations into Pope August, and if the pontiff had *any* inkling of what was in that box, Miles would *already* be dead.

Among many other notes and files and observations

was a single report, believed to have been unfinished. Pope August no doubt was certain that he had been able to shut the case down before Miles could reach a conclusion as to the murders of Pope Joseph V and Archon Virgil Landry.

In truth, the only thing August had done was stop the case before Miles could formally submit his report. Miles had already collected the vital evidence he had needed to determine and accuse the murderer.

Thanks to his uncanny ability to "rewind" a crime scene, Miles had quickly determined that the initial theory of a sharpshooter killing both men through a window in the Pope's chambers could not have been true, and the fire that broke out in the Pope's study had broken out in an attempt to cover up the evidence. Their bodies had been moved after the fact, with the window in question shattered and bullets fired into them *after* they had been killed.

But the most damning evidence was nothing more than a security ledger that had initially been overlooked, a log of everyone who had entered and left the Pope's private residence within the Papal Palace.

And on that day, at that time, there were only two people that were in the residence roughly at the time of the murders. One of them was Archon Landry.

The other was Cardinal Richard August, who claimed that he had arrived just in time to see the aftermath and report it to the Republican Police on site.

"Son?" Bobby asked, shattering Miles's trip down memory lane. "You okay?"

He smiled, nodded, and replied, "Yes. Just almost forgot Mom wanted you to know dinner was going to be in an hour. I'm guessing you haven't been getting in lately until its gone cold?"

Bobby chucked at that. "Well, you may not be a Sterner by blood, but you know..."

"If we're not working, we're working."

Bobby poked Miles in the chest, "And that's true

whether you're a strapping young buck, or a withered old man."

"You're not *that* old, dad."

He waved off his son's half-compliment, "Anyway, might as well do what your mother wants this one time. Come on, kid. You must be hungry coming all this way."

The older man strode towards the exit to the barn, humming to himself, flipping his hand in Miles's direction, beckoning him to follow.

Miles *hated* that he had roped his adopted parents into deep and dangerous criminal intrigue, but they were the only people in the whole country that he trusted implicitly. They were the only ones Miles could trust this information with until he had the opportunity to finally bring Pope August II to justice.

Other works by Thomas Knapp

The Broken Prophecy

The Sixth Prophet

The Tower of Kartage

Dire Water

Fire Fox

The Daynish Campaign

The Great Underground Empire

The Isle of Donne

For more information, visit http://
www.tkocreations.com